55,115-116, 210 ~2/3
2/6

WillowTree Press, L. L. C.

PERFECT TRUST

A Rowan Gant Investigation

M. R. Sellars

E.M.A. Mysteries
Paperbacks

This book is a work of fiction. Names, characters, places, and incidents either are the product of the author's imagination or are used fictitiously. Any resemblance to actual events or locales or persons, living or dead, is entirely coincidental.

PERFECT TRUST: A Rowan Gant Investigation
A WillowTree Press Book

PRINTING HISTORY
WillowTree Press First Edition / July 2002

All Rights Reserved
Copyright © 2002 by M. R. Sellars

Paraphrased Excerpts from *Everyday Magic: Spells and Rituals for Modern Living* on page 115 Copyright © 1998, Dorothy Morrison, Used With Permission

This book may not be reproduced in whole or in part, by mimeograph or any other means, without permission. For information contact WillowTree Press on the World Wide Web, http://www.willowtreepress.com

ISBN: 0-9678221-9-X

Cover design by Johnathan Minton
Text Layout by K. J. Epps
Edited by K. J. Epps

Printed on 20% Post-Consumer Recycled Acid Free Paper
Printed With Soy Based Ink

PRINTED IN CANADA
by
Westcan Printing Group
Winnipeg Manitoba

Books By M. R. Sellars

Praise for the Rowan Gant Investigations:

"Hooray for M.R. Sellars, the master of Pagan fiction! HARM NONE is a tale so real, so complex, and so terrifying, that it won't just keep you on the edge of your seat until the very last word - it's guaranteed to leave you breathless and begging for more."
— Dorothy Morrison
Author of *Everyday Magic* and *The Craft*

"HARM NONE is a superbly suspenseful thriller... highly recommended."
— Midwest Book Review

"...Sellars is a wonderful surprise all around...A good murder mystery has mystery, it has action, it has its dark sides, it has plot twists, and it has entertainment value. You can find all of that in this book."
— Boudica
The Wiccan - Pagan Times

"Fans of *Hamilton* and *Lackey* will want to religiously follow the exploits of Mr. Rowan Gant."
— Harriet Klausner
Literary Reviewer

"HARM NONE is a gripping, carefully plotted mystery that will keep pages turning right to the end."
— P.J. Nunn
Senior Mystery Reviewer,
The Charlotte Austin Review

"HARM NONE is one of the most remarkable books I've read this year. I bow to M.R. Sellars' superior story telling ability!"
— Elizabeth Henze
Murder on the Internet Express

"Fans of Mercedes Lackey's defunct *Diana Tregarde* Mysteries rejoice— a new witch is in town! Wonderful characterization from a first-person view, chilling suspense, and a baffling mystery make this first Rowan Gant mystery top-notch."
— Melanie C. Duncan,
The BookDragon Review

"Curl up one weekend with this book. You, too, will find yourself falling victim to Sellars' dangerously realistic descriptive style."
— Woody NaDobhar
Whispering Willow Pagan Newspaper

ACKNOWLEDGEMENTS

There are so many people who have come into and gone out of my life over the years that I've lost count, and each of them is in some part responsible for what happens between the pages of my novels. It is literally impossible for me to thank each and every one of them here individually, but there are some who stand out in the crowd, and I feel it a moral imperative that they be mentioned—

Dorothy Morrison, my own personal Goddess and friend extraordinaire. How I survived as long as I did without you in my life, I will NEVER understand. You, my dear, are the REAL Pro.

Officer Scott Ruddle, SLPD. Best-Bud, confidant, and real life "copper"— the true inspiration behind Benjamin Storm.

Trish and A.J. for their friendship through it all.

Ravenspirit and Chell for their friendship and a place to crash.

Randall and Angel; and everyone from Mystic Moon Coven. You are all part of my family.

J.D.— Thanks for finding me when I was lost.

Aislinn Awatake Firehawk for helping me breathe credible life into Helen Storm.

My good friends from C.A.S.T., H.S.A., S.I.P.A., and S.P.I.R.A.L.

Patrick— Thanks for all the cigars.

My parents for making the written word so fascinating to me.

Roxanne, Sharon, and Celeste, for reading, re-reading, and then reading some more.

"Chunkee" for not only reading and re-reading, but for arguing with me when I was being stubborn— and for being a brother as much as a friend.

Johnathan Minton for putting up with my endless changes of mind whenever he sets about the creation of a truly magnificent piece of cover art for me.

My daughter for making each and every day an adventure.

My wife Kat, who spent countless hours, both late and early, editing and then arguing her points when I was being too stubborn to listen. She has somehow put up with me throughout it all and for some unknown reason actually still loves me.

Chris, Evelyn, and all the wonderful folks at Westcan PG up in the Great White North.

Finally, and not the least of all, everyone who takes the time to pick up one of my novels, read it, and then recommend it to a friend.

Author's Note

While the City of St. Louis and its various notable landmarks are certainly real, many names have been changed and liberties taken with some of the details in this book. They are fabrications. They are pieces of fiction within fiction to create an illusion of reality to be enjoyed.

In short, I made them up because it helped me make the story more entertaining.

Note also that this book is a first person narrative. You are seeing this story through the eyes of Rowan Gant. The words you are reading are his thoughts. I know of no one who thinks and speaks in perfect, unblemished English, therefore some grammatical anomalies have been retained (under protest from editors) in order to support the illusion of reality.

For Chris, Jo-Jo, Eliot, Kat,
everyone on the hill that stormy afternoon,
the ladies at the Highway K canoe rental,
both sets of ambulance crews,
the Doctors and Nurses at
Ellington Hospital,
the entire staff of Three Rivers Medical
Center in Poplar Bluff,
and most especially
Dr. James W. Gieselmann.

You all know why…

Bide the Wiccan laws we must,
In perfect love and PERFECT TRUST.

Couplet One
The Wiccan Rede
Lady Gwen Thompson
Original Printing- "Green Egg #69"
Circa 1975

Late February
Old Chain of Rocks Bridge
St. Louis, Missouri

PROLOGUE

Eldon Andrew Porter was trying desperately to make sense of his current situation.

He knew that he shouldn't be unsteadily perched here on this cold steel girder high above the icy waters of the Mississippi river. He knew that he shouldn't be forced to finish by hand a job meant for, and started by, a hangman's noose. And, he knew he was short on time.

What he didn't know was just how this peril had come to pass.

One other thing he knew for certain was that this very simply was NOT how it was supposed to happen. Still, he couldn't focus on exactly what had gone wrong.

Once again, he mulled through the last few events leading up to this particular moment in time.

He had lured the Warlock to the bridge.

He had applied the razors of the *Malleus Maleficarum*, a mere formality as such, because by the Warlock's own public actions and admissions he was quite obviously guilty of the sin of WitchCraft.

He had applied the test of 'pricking' in order to be certain of the accused one's guilt. Of course, the Warlock had tried to deceive him in this test by screaming out in pain when the ice pick pierced his flesh, but he knew this to be a ruse. A trick used by the impenitent sorcerer in order to avoid his due punishment.

He had not been fooled.

With the Warlock's guilt proven, Eldon had then set forth the judgment as decreed by Almighty God and the Holy Church.

He had proceeded with the sentence by placing the noose about the man's neck and pronouncing his punishment as death by hanging.

And, finally, he had executed that sentence by throwing the Warlock over the side of the bridge.

That should have been it. End of story. But something had gone quite terribly wrong.

It was hard to think, his head ached so miserably. He vaguely remembered that for some reason he had pitched over the railing himself. Somewhere within that ghostly memory he also recalled feeling a jarring impact against the steel girder that stopped his fall. Then, everything had faded to black.

The top of his head burned like fire whenever he touched it. There was a tortured spot on his scalp that seemed devoid of hair. It was wet and sticky and that wetness clung to his hand when he pulled it away. He assumed it must be blood.

The raucous clamor of loud music blaring from the Warlock's vehicle on the bridge above blended hesitantly with the muted sounds of the icy river. The cacophony was disconcerting, and when combined with the pain, it made it just that much harder for Eldon to concentrate.

What could have gone wrong?

He rewound the sketchy memories and thought through the scenario yet again.

He had lifted the Warlock upward, pronouncing the punishment as he did so. Then, straining against the man's weight, he had pushed his arms outward to thrust the condemned over the railing and into the foggy night.

It was then that his head suddenly began stinging.

His scalp had felt as if it was on fire and he was instantly doubled forward against the railing himself. Gasping, he was deprived of the breath that had been forced from his lungs by the sudden crush against the blue and green steel barrier. The rest of it was a blur, and a split second later he had blacked out.

But he hadn't had any of those episodes for such a long time. Not since prison. Could it possibly be happening again? It had been years since he had blacked out, hadn't it?

Or had it only been months? He couldn't remember for certain.

Could he have simply fainted and fallen over the side?

No, there was something different. There was the burning in his scalp. His episodes had never been preceded by pain, ever. This felt like someone had physically ripped the hair from his head.

But how could the Warlock have done that?

His hands were bound.

He had tied the Warlock's hands, hadn't he?

Surely he had done so.

The sudden rush of recent events flooded in to answer the question. The Warlock had been clawing at Eldon's hand as he endeavored to choke the life from him.

His hands were free.

Had he been in such a rush that he had merely forgotten to bind the hands of the condemned?

No, he could not have been that careless. He refused to believe it. He would not have forgotten to do so simple and necessary a task before hanging one accused of the heresy of WitchCraft.

Somehow the Warlock had tricked him. He had conjured a glamour that made him believe he had completed the necessary tasks when in fact he had not.

This was wrong. He should be immune to the conjurings of the demonic, for he was righteous in his path. This was disturbing and bore the need for inner reflection and judgment upon one's self.

But not right now.

Not at this particular moment.

There was a more pressing judgment at hand.

There was also the question of why the hangman's noose had not done its job.

Eldon relinquished his single-handed grip around the man's throat for an ever so brief moment and quickly felt for the nylon rope.

But it wasn't there.

The Warlock coughed and gasped, quickly sucking in the air he had been denied.

Through the darkness and fog Eldon could just make out the rope stretched taut from the railing above, thinly scribing a tight line in the night to finally disappear behind the man's outstretched arm. He had thought perhaps the rope had merely twisted beneath the man's shoulder during the struggle, but now he knew this was not the case. The noose was cinched tight about the Warlock's arm instead of his neck where it should have been. A triple twist of the rope serpentined around the man's appendage and trailed through his tightly clenched fist.

The Warlock had managed to slip out of the noose and save himself.

But he would not avoid his final judgment. Eldon would see to that.

It wouldn't be long now, he thought, as he compressed his pale hand tighter about the man's throat. Just a few more moments and then the sentence would be carried out.

The Warlock would be dead.

He was sure he could feel his victim's windpipe starting to give way against the pressure of his long fingers. As his bony digits spasmed slightly from the force he was trying to exert he stretched them quickly, fighting to keep his grip secure.

Warlock.

Witch.

Sinner.

Heretic.

Different words but all the same. This one— the Warlock Rowan Gant— was himself evil incarnate. A minion of Satan set forth on this earth to do the bidding of the Dark Lord. Surreptitiously spreading the vileness of sin and debauchery among the lambs of almighty God under the false guise of goodness and light.

Eldon could not allow it to go on. He could not allow those who worshipped the devil to remain among the righteous. Why no one could understand this was a fact he couldn't fathom. Why no one realized what was happening by allowing these appalling sinners to cast shadows upon the earth, frightened him.

But, it didn't matter.

He understood what needed to be done. He hadn't at first. Not for the longest time. He had been just like everyone else, but then came prison and it had been a hidden blessing. It was prison where he had learned of his true purpose in life. It was there he had learned he was a part of God's righteous army. It had taken that incarceration for him to discover he was chosen by God himself to eradicate the infestation of heresy.

There would be others to help him, of course, of that he was sure. He needed only to find these brothers and sisters, and then together they would show everyone the true might of God.

The Warlock was struggling. Not as much as he had at first, but he was still fighting. The movement had all but stopped earlier, but when he had released his grip to check for the rope, even for that brief moment, the Warlock had gained a breath.

Now, something pressed upward from beneath his arm, cold and hard against the flesh of his wrist.

Puzzling.

It must be the Warlock clawing at his hand again.

But this was different.

It didn't feel like the hand that had fought to pry against his fingers before.

It was cold.

Hard.

Metallic.

A sharp, chemical odor blended with the moist air to tease Eldon's nostrils. He knew that smell. Its pungent edge was painfully familiar to him.

Gun cleaning solvent.

He released his grip and rotated his arm quickly away just as the explosion pierced his ears and the muzzle of the handgun erupted with bright orange flame.

He just didn't rotate it quickly enough.

Harried voices barked commands with life and death urgency through the cold night air. The tinny bursts of police radios punctuated the sounds coming from the scene above, all mixed with the frenzied pace of the music. The activity sounded rushed but methodical.

Intent.

Focused on the rescue of the Warlock, Rowan Gant.

A strong voice filled with authority, but edged with what sounded like fear, parted all sound to make room for itself. "Goddammit, somebody shut that fucking music off!"

After a moment, the frenetic instruments fell quiet, bringing what seemed an almost silence to the landscape, even though the voices and activity continued on unimpeded.

Fog was still clinging in a moist, grey shroud to anything and everything in its path, and most especially, to anyone. He felt its clammy insistence as it pervaded his clothing, sending tendrils of cold dampness inward to chill him all the way past the bone and directly to the soul. Through his mist-soaked clothes the cold metal of the girders pressed against him, leeching the warmth mercilessly from his body.

The sharp sting in his scalp, which had earlier occupied the foremost position in his list of unwanted sensations, had now taken a back seat to the fiery burn in his left arm. The bullet, expelled at high velocity and point blank range, had ripped into the soft flesh of his wrist and fragmented in a diagonal trajectory along several inches of his forearm. He wasn't entirely sure, but judging from the amount of movement still left in the appendage, the wound involved only muscle and no bone.

True, he hadn't rotated his arm away quite fast enough to avoid the handgun altogether, but it could certainly have been worse.

Far worse.

As the projectile had executed its damage upon his arm, he had pitched to the side, absenting himself from the precarious balance that once kept him planted on the supporting steel girder. With that tenuous stability gone, he had begun to fall.

To him, how he managed to keep from plunging into the ice-choked Mississippi river was nothing short of a miracle. As he howled in agony, his torso had slipped quickly through the open space between the girders, moving heavily downward beside the Warlock. At almost the same instant his knees slipped from the latticed girder in the exact opposite direction, landing his waist along its edge with a sound thud. Then, he had continued his rotation forward much like an out-of-control gymnast on the uneven parallel bars. He fought for a grip with his uninjured hand and through what, in his mind, could only have been divine intervention by God himself, entwined his fingers in the lattice on the underside of the steel beam. With the forward motion impeded, he came to a stop, folded dangerously over the support.

He hung there for a long moment, a mere foot away from

the suspended Warlock. He fully expected another shot to ring out and bring an end to him. But surely, Eldon thought, God would not save him from the icy plunge that would certainly have spelled death, only to allow the Warlock to execute his demise?

He had remained still as he could, gritting his teeth against the pain while waiting for any movement from the condemned Witch.

None came.

No, he would not die at the hand of Satan. There was a much grander plan at work, and his time had not yet come. There was still far too much for him to do on this earth.

Even as the ringing in his ears began to subside, he heard the sirens in the distance, punching sharp holes in the still clamoring music from above— and they were growing closer with every heartbeat.

The Warlock might well be dead. Perhaps the pull of the trigger had been done with his last breath. Or perhaps he was simply unconscious. Whichever it was, there was no time to check now. The authorities would be arriving soon, and God had seen to it that he had survived thus far. He knew that escape was his only recourse at this point, and that it would be entirely up to him. God would help him, but only if he helped himself.

And now, here he was, hiding in the dead space between the diagonal lattice of supporting girders and the deck of the bridge, intently listening to the activity above. He could feel a cramp forming along the muscles of his back as he used his shoulders to hold himself in place. His free hand was occupied with keeping pressure on the pulsing wound in his left forearm. He would need to make a tourniquet soon, that much was certain because he was going to be here for a while.

The cold and the pain were already taking their toll. He wanted desperately to sleep, but knew that he couldn't. He had to stay alert. He had to remain free.

He was positioned out of sight behind a diagonal upright support and beneath the deck of the bridge itself. If he kept himself still and quiet, he should be virtually undetectable. The detectives would most certainly piece together the visible evidence, and if so, they would assume he had met his end in the icy, muddy waters below. The assumption would be logical, as it had very nearly been fact. Eldon prayed that they would draw this conclusion.

Through a small gap between the girders he could make out the form of the Warlock, still suspended by the rope only a few feet away. A second rope had already been thrown down and it was obvious from the sounds of metal tinkling against metal that someone was being lowered at this very moment.

The commanding voice that had earlier demanded the music be quelled spoke again, thickly layered with concern. "Can you tell if he's alive?"

"Not yet," a much closer voice called back. "Another couple of feet or so… Slowly… Okay… A little more… A little more… Okay… Hold it. Right there."

Glimpses of someone outfitted in a climbing harness shone through the gap. Eldon pressed himself further into the shadows and held fast against the surge of pain in his arm.

No movement.

No noise.

He listened intently for the verdict, hoping against all hopes that his mission had been carried out to its conclusion. Praying that by the grace of almighty God the Warlock was dead.

His prayer went unanswered.

"He's still alive!" The nearby voice called upward with momentous relief, and then focused itself on the suspended figure. "Can you hear me Mister Gant?"

The Warlock lived.

He had failed.

He closed his eyes and waited in silence. All that he could do now is make certain he escaped.

More than a dozen hours passed before the scene was finally clear and he could safely extricate himself from his hiding place. Weak with cold, pain, and surely blood loss, even with the makeshift tourniquet bound tightly just above his elbow, he made his way cautiously across the steel beams.

He was deeply chilled and felt clammy with the remnants of a cold sweat. His trousers were still damp and beginning to stink. Hours ago his bladder had finally given up and he had been forced to urinate on himself while still in his hiding place. He felt degraded by the act but there had been no other choice.

The fog had long dissipated and he could see the ice-packed river far below. A swift wave of vertigo touched him and he held fast to the latticed girder. Several minutes later the wave of fear passed, replaced by his dire need to escape, and he continued his shaky climb.

Carefully, he pulled himself up and back over the railing to finally collapse on the concrete deck of the bridge.

He lay there for several minutes, breathing deeply, and feeling the warmth of the sun's rays soaking into his chilled body. He simply wanted to relax and rest after the constant strain of keeping motionless and stable on the cold steel beam for what had seemed a lifetime.

But rest was not an option.

At the beginning of the long night he had made a promise to God. During the prolonged police search, each time the swath of a powerful flashlight came close, or the echo of footsteps on the bridge stopped immediately above his hiding place, he had reiterated that promise in full. If he made it through— if he remained free and survived his wounds— he had promised he would not fail again.

Ten Months Later
December
St. Louis, Missouri

Heather Burke only half awoke, remaining submerged in a state of semi-conscious anguish. Among the heightened sensations to immediately register were a dry throat and a headache like no other she could remember in her thirty-three years. Rapidly following, and skirting the edges of the pain in complete disharmony, blind terror paralyzed her body. Her muscles were tensed, aching, and she felt clammy with cold sweat. Her heart was racing as she sucked in a breath with a startled gasp.

Holding tight to that frantic gulp of air she listened, waiting for the source of her terror to make itself known. She heard nothing but the beating of her own heart. Still, she refused to expel the breath until she could hold it no longer. When that moment finally came, the only new sound to be added to the silence was that of her timid whimper.

She continued to listen while fighting to keep her breathing quiet and shallow. She desperately wanted to suck in the cool air as fast as she could, but something was out there. Something fearful in the darkness and she didn't want it to find her.

Her mind raced through a thick fog as she tried to center on just exactly what it was that she feared so much. Each passing thought bringing her closer to the surface of consciousness. Her muscles began to relax as the wakefulness blossomed from half to full, though the thick fog remained, as did the fear.

Heather's head was throbbing in agonizing pulses. This was a mother of a migraine, she thought. No, she decided after a moment, not just a mother, this was the great matriarch of the entire clan— the very one that spawned all the others— and it had apparently elected to go into labor inside her skull.

Slowly, bracing herself against the unknown terror, she opened one eye. It seemed as though it took forever before she stopped squinting and allowed herself to see. As her blurry vision adjusted she took note of the gradient blue-black shadows slicing angular paths through the room.

Nothing moved.

Nothing leapt at her from the darkness.

Nothing.

She relaxed a little more.

Letting her eye roam she scanned the room. Her eyeball hurt as she moved it and she realized quickly both of them were sore and itching. They felt gritty and allergic, like something foreign had invaded their sanctity. She blinked hard, but the feeling remained.

At least what she saw in the room was familiar, shrouded by darkness though it was. There was the TV in the corner with a cheap plastic, tabletop Christmas tree sitting on top of it. The second hand papa-san chair was sitting catty-cornered from her— a basket of wrinkled, 'to-be-folded-someday' clothing occupying it as usual. Everything looked just like it normally did whenever she was sprawled out on the couch in sofa-spud mode.

And, there was still nothing there that shouldn't be.

Yes, this was definitely her apartment. That was comforting, but something still wasn't right about it all. Although it was continuing to dull, she just couldn't fully shake the feeling of terror deep down in the pit of her stomach.

She moved to sit up and pain lanced through the center of her head from back to front. She eased herself back down and lay perfectly still, not wanting to further aggravate the troll with the jackhammer that was excavating inside her brain.

This was not good at all. It was even a bit unnerving, because along with the pain there was an increasingly desperate feeling of disorientation, as if the fog of sleep had given way, only to be replaced by another obscuring mist in wakefulness.

Between staccato bursts of agony, Heather took mental inventory, searching to put her finger on a reason for the headache. It felt a little like a hangover, but not exactly, and she didn't remember doing any drinking last night. In fact, she didn't remember much of anything at all from last night. She remembered leaving work, driving home, and then... Then? She didn't know. She concentrated for a minute but gave up almost immediately when she realized that it only served to make the pain worse.

Her tongue felt thick. She swallowed hard and the dryness in her throat formed a lump that hesitated for a moment before painfully making its way downward.

It was dark, so maybe it was still last night, or tonight, or whatever. Hopefully it wasn't already tomorrow night. No, it couldn't be. Could it? It hurt too much to think about it so she gave up again.

"Oh man," she muttered. "This sucks big time."

She waited for a momentary lull in the migraine and thought about it again. She was at home, that much was for certain, but she couldn't quite remember how she had arrived here or even when. She wasn't even sure if she could really remember the last thing she remembered. Now, wasn't that a kick?

So, she was at home, on her couch, and it was dark. Not much to go on. But at least she was at HER home, and she hadn't gotten drunk and gone home with some sleazy bar asshole. Or had she? Had she gotten trashed and brought him here? God! She hoped not! If only she could remember.

Without thinking she lifted her arm to check her watch and regretted it instantly. A new ache added itself to the growing list, this one taking the form of a burning soreness in the vicinity of her ribcage. It seemed isolated to her left side, for the moment at least.

Opening both eyes this time she struggled to focus on the face of her wristwatch. Fumbling with her free hand, she finally managed to press the button to illuminate the digital timepiece, although she was fairly certain that said button had always been on the opposite side from where she eventually found it. Centered in the eerie blue glow she watched as the liquid crystal flickered from something that looked like the number 9: followed by the letter Ɛ, to suddenly become the word Lɪ:Ɛ.

The jumble of LCD segments made little sense to Heather's clouded mind and she blinked several times, trying unsuccessfully to get a clearer picture. The digits still read Lɪ:Ɛ .

"Lie?" she muttered aloud, her voice hoarse and thick. "What the? Awww, screw it."

The fear had finally become a faded shadow of what it had been a few minutes before, and she told herself that it must have simply been a nightmare. She gritted her teeth and pushed upward once again, until she was in a sitting position. Swinging first one leg, then the other, over the edge of the cushions she let her feet touch the floor, then she leaned forward. Elbows on her knees she cradled her head in her hands and massaged her temples.

The big question in her mind now was whether or not a nightmare could make you forget.

After something just short of forever, she stood and almost immediately fell. With a grimace she kicked off her heels, absently wondering why she hadn't bothered to do so earlier. Of course, she couldn't remember much of anything else, she thought, so why should she be surprised?

Heather stumbled through her apartment toward the bathroom on a single-minded quest for aspirin. If she could make the pain go away then maybe she could concentrate. Surely she would be able to remember how she got here. People don't just lose entire chunks of time out of their lives, except maybe in those alien abduction movies.

"Yeah, right," she almost laughed at herself as she spoke aloud. "Get real, Heather. You weren't abducted by aliens."

Her fingers found the light switch automatically and flicked it on. She squinted and turned her head away as the sudden flood of luminance assaulted her. She groaned audibly and wondered why her entire body seemed to ache. Flu, maybe? That could be it, she thought. Flu, fever, and the whole nine yards. Yeah, maybe that was the explanation.

Still squinting she looked up and reached for the medicine chest over the sink. Through slit eyes she caught a glimpse of herself in the mirror and gasped.

Her shag of blonde hair was an absolute mess, but that wasn't what startled her most. Bright crimson smears streaked across her mouth and her face looked splotchy, uneven. It was as if someone had haphazardly wiped away heavy makeup. Reddish-purple bruises stood out against the pale skin of her neck, almost as if they were glowing.

It was at this very moment that the source of her earlier fear called out from secret places within hidden memories.

The parking lot.

The pain in her side like an electric shock.

The medicinal bitterness on the back of her tongue.

The darkness.

The feeling of helplessness as rough hands groped her without apology.

A deep feeling of violation bludgeoned her now. She backed away from the mirror as the earlier terror returned full force. Hot tears were already streaming along her cheeks, and she soon found herself pressed against the tiled wall. She allowed herself to slide down to the floor and hugged her knees against her chest even though it hurt like hell.

Heather Burke sat on the cold floor and sobbed for a solid hour before finally summoning the courage to drive herself to the hospital.

"Did you already do a rape kit?" Detective Charlene McLaughlin asked before taking a cautious slug of her hot drink.

She was still working on a Chai Latté from the stop 'n grab she had hit on the way here, and was already regretting it. She knew better than to be adventurous and try something new this morning. She should have just stuck with her regular large coffee— two creams, four sugars. That way she would have known exactly what to expect. Charlee hated surprises, and what was in her cup this morning was definitely of the unexpected category.

Everyone called her Charlee. Some even called her 'Chuck', but only if they knew her very well. Even fewer people actually called her Charlene. Petite, and sporting an ash blonde pageboy coif, she could almost always be found wearing jeans and running shoes. Given her tomboyish appearance and tough demeanor, the moniker just seemed to fit.

Before her recent transfer to the sex crimes unit, she had been assigned to City Homicide. Among that close knit group of cops there had actually been a running bet that she didn't even own a dress or skirt. She'd made a deal and split the pool with an office worker by showing up one day wearing a nicely tailored skirt and jacket ensemble. She'd been totally uncomfortable the entire day, and vowed to never again wear pantyhose for as long as she lived, but it had been worth the looks on their faces— the hundred bucks cash was just icing on the cake. She never did tell them that she'd had to borrow the outfit from a friend.

This morning, she was dressed in her usual. A well-worn leather bomber jacket fit over her torso, hanging just loose enough to hide the nine-millimeter Beretta riding in a shoulder rig beneath her left arm.

"The nurse is finishing up with her now," the doctor nodded as they walked. "We called it in as soon as she arrived."

Christmas Muzak was filtering softly in from overhead to mix with the ambient sounds of the ER. It wasn't doing much to lift Charlee's spirits though. She had been on edge with an itchy, nervous kind of energy for over a week now. She'd had the feeling before and she knew what was coming.

She'd been fully expecting this call ever since that second case file hit her desk, and she'd been dreading it all the while.

"Good, good," Charlee nodded as she took another swig of the Latté. Yeah, this stuff was definitely an unpleasant surprise. "Get anything?"

"Unfortunately, not much."

"Did she wait?"

The doctor had traveled this road before and immediately understood the meaning behind the question. "No, not long. She said it had only been an hour or so since she regained consciousness. She had enough wits about her not to shower or clean up, so there's certainly evidence of the rape. We did collect semen, and that will be on its way to the lab shortly."

"So she was unconscious? I'm already not liking the sound of this, Doc. You get pictures?"

"The regular routine, yes," he returned. "But she wasn't really abused. It seems almost like a date rape."

"This may sound crass, but what I wouldn't give for a simple date rape. She say whether she can ID the guy?"

"She can't remember anything other than that she thinks she was attacked in the parking lot of her apartment complex."

"She THINKS she was attacked?"

"She appears to be suffering from anterograde amnesia. Possibly drug induced."

"Yeah, that fits." Charlee nodded as she spoke, her mood darkening even more as the conversation progressed. "Blood test?"

"Of course. We'll screen for Benzodiazepines. Rophynol, GHB, etcetera."

They came to a stop outside the door of the treatment room.

"How about hickeys? She have any of those?"

"Actually, yes, there are a few large hematoma on her neck," he answered with a hint of surprise.

"I was afraid of that. Okay, let me see if I can bat a thousand here," she continued. "This woman is in her early to mid-thirties, petite, and blonde— Am I right?"

"Of course, but don't try to tell me that you are psychic, Detective," the doctor returned. "We gave all of that information when we called it in."

"Yeah, well that information is exactly why I'm here instead of a uniform."

The significance behind Charlee's comment was in no way lost on the doctor. He acknowledged it with a simple nod and a query of his own, "Serial rapist?"

"You didn't hear that from me. Not yet, anyway, but let's just say I've got two case files just like it on my desk right now. In my book, three makes it a pattern."

"I see," he nodded thoughtfully and motioned to the door. "Well, she's in here. If you need anything else you can have the nurse page me."

"Hey, doc," she addressed him as he turned to go.

"Yes, Detective?"

"You going past a restroom or a sink?"

"Most likely, why?"

Charlee held out the almost full cup of Chai Latté to him. "Do me a favor and dump this crap, will'ya?"

CHAPTER 1

Overwhelming violation saturated my very being. I hated the feeling, but I clung to it like a piece of flotsam in a raging flood because very simply, it was all I had.

Waking up in a cold sweat seemed to be the norm for me as of late. When it had first started, it had only been once every few days, maybe twice at most. Now, it was rare for a week to pass without it happening three, or even four times. Recently, I'd even had an incident where it had occurred twice in one night. The lack of a decent night's rest was taking a measurable toll and I was definitely feeling the effects.

More often than not I spent my waking hours on autopilot, fueled by bitter coffee and an almost constant, insatiable desire for a cigarette. Considering that I'd quit smoking— well, except for an occasional cigar— somewhat over a year ago, I found the craving more than a bit unusual. Thus far, I'd managed to keep it in check with nicotine gum, but I wasn't sure how long that would last. The need was beginning to achieve absolutely ridiculous proportions.

Of course, one could easily imagine that after surviving a run-in with a crazed serial killer, nightmares would be expected. The problem was that I'm not exactly sure you could call these events nightmares; this is not to mention the fact that they hadn't even begun until several months after the fact. On top of that, the episodes weren't about my brush with death at all. At least, I don't think they were.

I couldn't really be certain to tell the truth.

The bald facts were that I would wake up in a cold sweat with my heart pounding in a furious attempt to escape the confines of my chest. My mind would be a jumble of nothingness and I would be incapable of pinning down a single thought. That, in and of itself, brought on sudden panic. I had always been very cognizant of my dreams and night terrors, remembering them in vivid detail. It went way beyond troubling for me to suddenly be devoid of that clarity.

And then there was this inexplicable feeling of violation.

To make matters worse, I wasn't always waking up in my bed. Sometimes I would find myself sprawled on the living room floor. Other times, it might be the kitchen. One time, I had even awakened lying next to my truck on the cold concrete of my garage. Rest assured, this is definitely not a place where you want to be half-naked in the middle of winter.

I think perhaps that is the one time that frightened me most. Upon gathering my wits I had even felt the hood of the truck to see if it was warm. It wasn't, but that didn't really mean much since I had no clue how long I'd been lying there. For all I knew, it could have had plenty of time to cool down. Of course, as cold as I was, I wasn't suffering from hypothermia so I must not have been lying on the concrete for too long. The only thing that finally quelled my panic somewhat was the fact that the fuel gauge hadn't appeared to have budged. So, most likely I hadn't been driving in my sleep, but if I had, then at least I hadn't gone far. Still, the not knowing was a threatening cloud that hung over me ever since.

One constant that I was able to grasp, in addition to the sensation of debasement, was that no matter where I awoke it was always with a very particular pain. It was always localized, though not always in the same place. Sometimes it would be in my side, sometimes my back. Another time it had been on my shoulder. Wherever it occurred though, it was always the same savage burning sensation. Then, it would always fade away within a handful of minutes and there would be no visible evidence with which to identify its cause.

The fear and panic brought on by all these constants usually took far longer to subside.

So far, I'd managed to keep these incidents to myself while I tried to figure out just what they were all about. However, the increased frequency was making them much harder to keep a secret. Unfortunately, my wife was bound to find out soon, and she wouldn't be happy about it. She knew as well as I that when these kinds of things started happening to a Witch— especially me— something beyond terrible was about to make itself known in spades.

And, as usual, I was going to be right in the middle of it.

As neighborhood diners go, 'Charlie's Eats' at the corner of Seventh and Chouteau was just about as boilerplate as you could get. Housed in the renovated and whitewashed cinder block remnants of a long-closed gasoline station, 'Chuck's', as it was affectionately labeled by the regular patrons, was busy twenty-four/seven. Being located well within the St. Louis city limits and not terribly far from Police Headquarters, it was also a regular hangout for cops. Time of day was never even a factor. Whether it was an officer— or officers— coming off duty, going on duty, or just taking a meal break, the greasy spoon never seemed to be at a lack for a uniform at the counter or occupying a booth. The small parking lot even had a pair of spaces reserved just for city police cruisers.

I took a quick right from Seventh into the entrance of the lot, and then slowly cajoled my truck between the rear end of an old station wagon and a slightly canted utility pole. As I tucked my vehicle into the first available space, the sun had just begun to peek up over the jagged horizon that was East St. Louis, Illinois. Now filtering across the Mississippi river in a glittery band, it was momentarily bathing the city in that indefinable yellow-orange glow that immediately precedes the actual dawn of the day. The eerie kind of color that occurs only in nature, and then, fleetingly— a shade of the light spectrum that will never be found in a box of crayons, nor be captured in exactness by any artist, no matter how talented.

As it always does, the glow rose quickly in intensity to become a full-fledged sunrise, raising several visual octaves from the chalky orange to bright yellow-white. I gave a quick glance around the parking lot and spotted a tired looking Chevrolet van which I knew from first hand experience was nowhere near as tired as it appeared. Its owner was the reason I had made this early morning trek into the city from the outlying suburbs where I lived, and since I couldn't see him through the windshield it was a safe bet that he was already inside the diner.

I switched off the truck and levered the door open, tucking my keys into my pocket as I got out. A crisp breeze was blowing and the temperature was holding steady for the moment at a brisk forty-two degrees Fahrenheit. According to the radio the high for the day was expected to be somewhere around sixty-five. Considering that it had been in the mid-twenties on Thanksgiving Day with snow flurries, this was about par for the course. It was December in St. Louis and it was as unseasonably unpredictable as it could get.

I locked my vehicle, even though it was probably unnecessary considering that there were two police cruisers on the lot, not to mention that the person I was here to meet was a city Homicide Detective. Security around here wasn't much of an issue, but locking up was a habit, and a good one at that.

Even though for all intents and purposes I was a morning

person, I had been dragging a bit when I climbed out of bed on this particular day. I had been up late working on a piece of software for a client of my home-based consulting business. I couldn't complain, really. I got to work from home and set my own hours. No neckties, no suits, and I did fairly well pulling down a decent enough living for my wife and I. And, with her being an in-demand freelance photographer, we were actually living rather comfortably. Still, I'd pull a late night every now and then, and last night happened to be one of the 'thens'.

Of course, in this instance it had been by choice. With what had been happening to me lately I wasn't in any real hurry to go to bed. Don't get me wrong, sleep was definitely something I had a strong desire to embrace, but I preferred to wake up in the same place I started with it, sans the pain, panic, and profanation. These days that was a game of chance with the odds stacked in someone— or something— else's favor.

Coffee, bacon, eggs, sausage, toast, and a host of other 'breakfasty' smells enveloped me in a warm, olfactory hug as I tugged open the glass-fronted door and stepped inside the small diner. My ears were filled with the murmurs of ongoing conversations between patrons, liberally punctuated with throaty chuckles, clanging utensils, and barked food orders; all of which were underscored by the sizzle and pop of items on the hot griddle.

Directly in front of me was the Formica-sheathed counter complete with vinyl-capped stools bolted to the floor before it, and a busy grill behind. Around the perimeter were small booths, the cushioned seats of which were covered with the same obnoxious red vinyl as the stools. A clear Plexiglas enclosure occupied one end of the lunch counter and its shelves were piled with donuts on their way to being stale. A squat cash register took up residence at the opposite end.

Aged, but carefully lettered signs posted on the wall offered such things as 'bottomless cups of coffee', and 'Slingers' to go— a local indulgence involving among other things, hash browns, eggs, and chili. A sheet of paper was laminated to the back of the cash register with strips of once clear, now yellowed, packing tape. Judging from the fuzzy edges and lack of clarity, it was obviously a photocopy of a photocopy to the power of ten at least. But it was still readable and posted in plain sight it boasted, 'These Premises Protected by Smith and Wesson'.

It took only a quick survey of the scene to spot my friend in a booth at the back corner. Of course, it would have been hard to miss him, considering that he was most likely the tallest individual in the room, with the possible exception of the cook manning the grill. At the moment, however, he was certainly the only full-blooded Indian present. Shrugging off my jacket, I made my way toward him, my progress impeded for a short time as I did a quick box step in the narrow aisle with a young coffeepot-wielding waitress. With the dance, and a quick apology out of the way, I hooked around the end of the counter and traversed the scuffed tile floor to the corner booth.

"Heya, Kemosabe," Detective Benjamin Storm greeted me as I slid into the seat opposite him.

"Yo, Tonto," I returned before stifling a yawn.

"Long night? You're usually the early bird."

"Yeah," I nodded. "Picked up a new client so I had quite of a bit of customizing and data conversion to do for them."

I wasn't about to tell him that the project was something I could have easily done during regular business hours. He had a tendency to worry about me just as much as my wife, and if I told him what had been happening lately I would have both of them to deal with. Besides, something told me that it was all going to come to the surface soon enough.

"Decent cash?" he asked.

"Yeah, it's a pretty good account," I answered.

"Good deal."

"Coffee, sir?" The young woman who'd done the two-step

with me moments ago appeared stealthily at our table, a Pyrex globe of the black liquid in each hand. They were distinguished, as usual, only by the green or orange pour spout.

"Absolutely," I answered, instantly turning the heavy mug in front of me upright and sliding it toward her. "Regular, please."

She deftly filled the mug, pouring expertly from the side of the pot, then topped off Ben's in the same fashion. "You guys ready to order, or you want a few minutes?"

"I'm ready." Ben looked over at me questioningly. "How 'bout you, Row?"

"Uhmm," I muttered as I pulled a single page menu encased in well-worn laminate from behind the napkin holder and gave it a quick once over. "How about... A number three, over-easy, wheat, and a side of biscuits with sausage gravy."

"Ewwww, runny eggs? Don't you know you can get sick from those," she said as she wrinkled her nose.

"Wendy isn't exactly the most tactful person when it comes to her opinions," my friend expressed.

"Oh, shut up, Storm," she chastised Ben with a good-natured familiarity, which told me he was a regular here just as I'd suspected. Then, turning back to me she offered, "How about scrambled instead?"

"Would that make you feel better?" I quipped with a grin.

"Yes. Yes it would."

"Okay, scrambled is fine."

"You want cheese on those?"

"Sure."

"Cheddar, American, or Monterey Jack?"

"Hmmmm, how about cheddar?" I hesitantly offered.

"Good choice. Now, what about you, Storm? You want your usual?"

"Yeah." He nodded and flashed a quick grin her way.

"You're in a rut, Storm," she told him with a grin of her

own as she turned and headed back up the short aisle.

"Hey, Wendy," Ben called after her, a good-natured chuckle tingeing his words. "Tell Chuck I said don't be so friggin' stingy with the onions this time."

He had purposely spoken loud enough to be heard by virtually anyone in the diner, but most especially the fry-cook. His answer came as a grumble and a mock threatening wave of a spatula from the large man behind the grill. "Yeah, yeah, yeah, Storm. Yer always complainin' about somethin'."

The exchange was met with a few lighthearted chuckles from some of the other regulars in the diner, along with some additional friendly jibes. Chuck finally threw up his hands in a good-natured imitation of surrender, announcing in the process, "Hey, if youse don't like it, go eat somewheres else."

The restaurant settled quickly back into its morning routine, leaving our booth in a quiet wake.

"Okay," I finally said after taking a healthy swig of coffee and giving Ben a solemn look. "So what's up? It's been my experience that when you offer to buy me a meal something is going on, and it's usually not good."

"Hey," he feigned insult. "Did'ya ever think I might just wanna buy ya' breakfast and visit with ya'?"

"It crossed my mind, but then reality got in the way."

"Jeez, white-man."

"So, am I wrong?" I asked. "Is this just social?"

He sat mute, took a sip of his coffee, and then stared out the slightly fogged window next to us for a moment before turning back to me. "Well, no, but it's not necessarily a bad thing. Maybe."

"Okay." I shrugged. "So what is it, 'maybe'?"

He sent his large hand up to the back of his neck and gave it a quick massage as a mildly troubled expression panned across his features. After a moment he reached down into the seat next to him and brought his hand back up with what looked like an oversized index card in it.

"Porter, Eldon Andrew," my friend told me succinctly, tossing the name out as a raw fact for me to digest as he handed over the black and white mug shot.

I took the card and stared at the muddy grey tones of the picture as I leaned back in my seat, feeling a slight wince of pain in my shoulder in the process. The twinge might very well have been psychological, but the surgery to repair the joint and its associated musculature was still less than a year old. If I could believe the doctor, whom I had no reason to doubt, an occasional pain wouldn't necessarily be all that unusual for a while yet.

I suppose that when you consider all the facts, a minor pain should actually be welcome. I mean, first, a madman bent on ushering me across into the world of death rams an ice pick into my left shoulder.

Nearly up to the handle…

Twice…

Planting it firmly into bone on the second plunge I might add. And, if that weren't enough, I ended up plummeting off the side of a bridge, only to have the very same shoulder forcibly dislocated by the sudden stop at the end of the fall. Of course, I suppose I should be thankful that the rope held, or the sudden stop would have been farther down and more along the line of fatal. And finally, I proceeded to hang from the damaged joint while the crazed serial murderer attempted to finish the job he'd started. I was lucky to even be alive, much less to still have the arm intact and functioning.

Still, looking at the photo that was officially labeled Texas Department of Corrections brought that night back to the forefront of everything with painful clarity. A finger of acidic fear tickled the pit of my stomach, threatening to invoke nausea. I ignored it, and continued to stare at the picture.

The countenance depicted in the photograph was younger, and lacking the greasy shag of white hair that had framed it earlier this year. In fact, in the photo his head was shaved. His cheeks were fuller, and though the picture was black and white, one could tell from the grey scale tones that his face held a healthy color. The one I had faced ten months before had been almost devoid of such pigment, appearing pasty and ghostly white in pallor— the color of death. Even so, the eyes hadn't changed at all. Dark and sunken, almost hidden in their deeply shadowed sockets, they burned with a furious malevolence. Just as they had done when I stared into them months ago.

When last I had seen this face, it had been firmly attached to the ice pick wielding lunatic.

The self-proclaimed Witch hunter…

The modern day, self-appointed inquisitor with a singular purpose— to eradicate from the world those he perceived as heretics. Being a Witch, and a male one at that, I matched up easily with his set of criteria for those belonging on his hit list.

He had managed to kill six others before getting to me, two of them not even actual Pagans. Why he had not yet killed again, I was at a loss to explain.

If you asked the authorities why— even the cop sitting across from me now that I call my best friend— you would be told that it was because he was dead.

You would be told that I had shot him in self-defense, perhaps mortally though no one could be sure. And, even if the wound was not fatal it didn't matter, because he had then fallen to his certain death from the Old Chain of Rocks Bridge into the ice-laden Mississippi river.

I knew better.

Yes, I will admit that I had most definitely shot him. In the arm he was using to try to choke me to death as a matter of fact. And while there was plenty of solid evidence that I had not missed when I pulled the trigger, something told me that the wound wasn't nearly so grievous as others believed. That same something also told me that he did not in fact fall into the river that night, but instead, escaped.

How? I couldn't begin to tell you, but it was a feeling far in the back of my head. A sensation that begins as a slight itch that can't be quelled by any means, and then quickly grows into a fearful foreboding. The kind of mysterious intuition you just don't ignore— especially if you are a Witch.

I think I might have breathed an inner sigh of relief while I stared at the picture. I had fully expected Ben to produce a case file or crime scene photo from beneath the table that would somehow tie into my current unexplained somnambulistic excursions. On second thought, the sigh might not have been only one of relief, but of disappointment as well. I really did need to figure out what was going on, and the sooner the better.

"I've been carryin' that damn thing around for a week," my friend told me, gesturing toward the photo. "I wasn't sure if I should even show it to ya' or not."

I could sense the concern in his voice, and the careful way in which he was watching me was physically palpable. I looked up from the mug shot and noticed that his jaw held a grim set to it. This expression wasn't a hard one for him to achieve, what with his deeply chiseled features and dusky skin that visually announced his full-blooded Native American heritage. Even sitting, he was better than a full head taller than me. Standing, he measured six-foot-six and was built like an entire defensive line. The nine-millimeter tucked beneath his arm in a shoulder rig and the gold shield clipped to his belt made him appear just that much more formidable.

His hand went up to smooth back a shock of his coal black hair and lingered once again at his neck, a mannerism that told anyone who knew him that he had something on his mind.

"You worry too much," I said as I dropped my eyes back to the photo.

"Yeah, you keep sayin' that, but I know how you are," he returned.

He was correct. He did know how I was. Until recently, he knew most of the details— though certainly not all— of the nightmares I had experienced, both during and after the investigations surrounding two separate serial killers. Both of which had terrorized St. Louis in the span of less than one year. He had personally witnessed me involuntarily channeling the victims, and their horrific ends. He had even saved my life in both instances when I had recklessly taken on the killers myself.

He was fully aware of the emotional toll the investigations, and especially the supernatural elements of them, had taken on me. I had been affected on many levels. Because of this and his deep loyalty as a friend, he worried more about my mental health than I did. The fact that I had only become involved in the cases at his request played more than a small part in it as well.

"I'm not going to wig out on you, Ben," I returned in a fully serious tone. "I'm okay."

"Yeah, but all that *Twilight Zone* shit you go through..." he let his voice trail off.

"Really, Ben. I'm fine," I offered, and then changed back to the subject at hand. "How did you find out who he is? I thought the evidence was inconclusive and there were no identifiable fingerprints in his van. Besides, it's been almost a year now."

"Dumb fucking luck," he answered. "A coupl'a weeks ago County got a call from a distraught woman babblin' about somethin' she found in her basement. Turns out she was the owner of the house where this wingnut was doin' his thing."

"Oh yeah?"

"Yeah, no shit. Right outta the blue. The house was a piece of rental property she'd inherited. She lives outta state and it was hung up in probate for a while so she didn't even know he was livin' there. She thought it was vacant. Anyhow, the legal BS finally gets cleared up and then she gets around to comin' into town to get it fixed up for sale. Well when she starts cleanin' up, guess what she finds in the basement? The fuckin' 'holy torture chamber'. The shrine, the candles, all of it. Everything just like you described from that vision thing you had. Even found a copy of that book you talked about."

"The *Malleus Maleficarum*?" I offered, referencing the fifteenth century Witch hunting manual the killer had adopted as his manifesto.

"Yeah, that one." He nodded. "So, anyway, the copper that took the call gets a hinky feeling and calls Carl Deckert over at County Homicide. Deckert goes and has a look, then calls me."

Carl Deckert was a mutual friend who had also been assigned to the Major Case Squad during the investigation. He was intimately familiar with the case and I'm sure that when he'd seen the basement of that house it had set off more than one alarm.

"So, why didn't you call *me*?"

"For the same reason I've been packin' that damn mug shot around for a week," he explained. "I wasn't so sure it was somethin' you needed to see."

"You're being overprotective, Ben."

"So sue me. Hell, I'm still not so sure I should be showin' it to ya now." He sighed, and then added, "Why do ya think I'm doin' it here instead of droppin' by your place?"

"You don't want Felicity to know," I returned, knowing for certain that he was alluding to my wife.

"Exactly." He nodded. "I promised her I'd keep some distance between you and the cop shit."

"She's being overprotective too."

"He looks real pleasant," a feminine voice came from behind me, interrupting us before he could object further. I looked up to see that the waitress had reappeared at our table and was looking at the mug shot over my shoulder. "Number three, scrambled with cheddar," she continued un-fazed and slid a plate in front of me. "And a side of biscuits with sausage gravy."

"Thanks." I smiled at her while laying the card to the side; face down and out of sight. I suspect it was just a reflex on my part, as she didn't seem bothered by the photo at all. With the diner being a cop hangout she'd probably seen and heard more than her share of things like this— probably even worse.

"Kitchen sink omelet with chili and extra onions." She stressed the word extra as she planted a steaming plate before Ben with a wide grin. "Anything else I can get you two? More coffee?"

"We're good. Thanks, Wendy," Ben answered.

As was my habit, I took a moment to twist the cap off of the peppershaker and liberally blacken my scrambled eggs while Ben watched, and then I returned the condiment to its original state before offering it to him.

"Jeezus, Row. That stuff'll kill ya'," he told me as he accepted the glass shaker.

"And what's on your plate won't?" I countered. "So anyway," I continued, pointing at the photo with my fork. "That's him all right. It's an old picture, but it's him."

"Yeah, when we compared it to the sketch that was made from your description, there was pretty much no doubt. We found enough good prints in the house to get a match through AFIS and in no time we had his file from the TDC. Seems he was a guest of the Lone Star state for a few years. Once we had the file, everything fell into place. Blood type, all that jazz."

"What was he in prison for?"

"Aggravated assault and manslaughter," he stated matter-of-factly.

"So have you notified NCIC or put out an APB or whatever acronym it is that you law enforcement types like to do?"

"What for?" He shrugged.

"So you can be on the lookout for the guy, maybe?" I stated incredulously.

"Jeez, Row, you aren't gonna start that again are you? The asshole is dead."

"Did you ever find a body?" I demanded.

"No, but so what?" he asked, but he didn't wait for an answer. "He's suckin' mud on the bottom of the river."

"The body would have surfaced by now, Ben."

"Not necessarily, Row." He shook his head. "What goes down don't always come up. Trust me. Plus, the river flooded pretty good this spring. Maybe I AM wrong and he ain't suckin' mud at all. Maybe he ended up bein' fish food in the gulf or somethin'. At any rate, he's gone. Dead. Eighty-sixed."

"I'm telling you he isn't, Ben."

"How do ya know?"

"It's just a feeling, but I know I'm right."

"Like I've told you before, white man, this is just one feeling I can't get with you on. I think you've just got some left over heebee jeebees or somethin'."

"No, Ben," I spat back tersely. "It's more than that."

"Okay," he took on his own hard edge, "then where is he? Why hasn't he killed again? Hell, why hasn't he come after YOU again?"

I had to admit that I didn't have the answers to these questions. It was somewhat of an ongoing theme between Ben and me. Something would tickle the back of my brain and I would have some manner of instinctual feeling or precognitive episode. I would tell my friend, stressing the urgency of the vision and he would start asking questions. Then, like an idiot, I would sit there and say, "I don't know."

I had to give him credit though; he had come a long way. The first time I had helped him with an investigation he had been a complete and total skeptic. This last time around, he had been extremely open-minded and willing to chase down the avenues I pointed out with only my word as a catalyst.

The real truth was that I had even been a bit of a skeptic myself at first. Even though Magick is a very real part of my religious path, until recently, I'd never experienced it to anywhere near the extent that I had during my time helping with the murder investigations. That's the funny thing about faith. Believing in something is one thing. Having it sneak up and bat you over the head is something else entirely.

Suffice it to say, I was only now getting over the headache.

But, as accepting as he had become, on this particular point of contention between us, Ben was not about to budge. He was firmly convinced that the now identified Eldon Andrew Porter was dead, never to return.

This was one instance where I wished with every fiber of my being that he was correct, and that I was completely and unequivocally wrong. But that itch in the back of my head just wouldn't go away.

"Yeah, I thought so," he replied to my silence, then let out a sigh. "Look, Row, I'm not tryin' to be an ass here. And this is exactly what I was afraid was gonna happen. I know your intuition is pretty good. Hell, I've come to rely on all that hocus pocus stuff at times, but I really think you're wrong on this one. ID'n this whack-job was just a piece of blind luck, and it's nothin' but clerical shit now. It's just a name and face to stick in the case file. The CLOSED case file."

I didn't argue. Belaboring the point was going to cause nothing more than strife between us. Besides, I really and truly DID want him to be correct this time instead of me.

"Yeah." I nodded. "Okay."

"Here's somethin' else we found out about him that you might find interesting," Ben offered, as if giving me a consolation prize for losing the disagreement.

"What's that?"

"During his trial it seems there was a bit of a ruckus over his mental state," he explained. "Coupl'a expert witnesses rattlin' a bunch of psycho babble about him being highly suggestible and incapable of distinguishing right from wrong. But, as it was he had an overworked and under funded PD for an attorney. Just couldn't get the jury to go for the insanity defense."

"So you think he was insane?"

"Who knows?" He shrugged. "I think any asshole that goes around killin' people is insane, but then I also don't think they should get off Scot free because of it."

"I'm inclined to agree with you, but I'm not sure I follow."

"That's 'cause you haven't heard the really hinky part yet."

"And that is?"

"When they locked him up he ended up in a special kind of cell block. Somethin' called a 'God Pod'."

"God Pod?"

"Yeah, it's a cell block that's run by a prison ministry. Rehabilitation by gettin' religion."

"That's not entirely a bad thing, Ben," I said. "Faith can be an important part of a person's life."

"Yeah, but this is some pretty strict shit," he returned then scooped up a forkful of the dangerous looking omelet. "They pretty much brow-beat the inmates with the holy scripture."

"And you think that if he was insane to begin with…" I let my voice fade; leaving the end of the sentence unspoken as the thought of the penal system having created this monster suddenly overtook me.

Ben picked up where I left off, expressing his own thoughts aloud. "What I think is that if you got a mentally unstable fruitcake who's that open to suggestion, and you subject him to Bible study and prayer meetins' from sunup to sundown, seven days a week, somethin's bound to snap."

"Don't tell me," I shook my head in disbelief, "Evangelical, Old Testament."

"From what I understand, yeah. Why?"

"That would explain a slight discrepancy that bothered me."

"What's that?"

"Well, he embraced the *Malleus Maleficarum* along with a very old, very outdated, and no longer accepted Catholic ideal— that being the literal eradication of heretics. He even went so far as to dress as a priest," I explained. "But, in my encounter with him, he seemed to come at things from a far more fire and brimstone approach. The words he spoke were more than sectarian ceremony. He was, for all intents and purposes, preaching."

"That's one screwed up wingnut," Ben offered. "But it'd be a hell of a sermon."

"Exactly." I nodded.

"Guess it's a good thing he's history then," he stated before shoveling a portion of the formidable breakfast into his mouth.

The twinge that had lanced through my shoulder earlier now returned with a treble hook of barbs trailing in its wake. The pain deep in the joint burrowed its way up the side of my neck and joined with that unforgiving itch in the back of my brain.

Now I had two problems to worry about.

I didn't say a word.

CHAPTER 2

I was trying very hard to remember exactly what it was that I was doing here. For some unknown reason, I was at a complete loss. Truth was, I didn't even know how I had come to be anywhere other than my own warm bed, and it was more than just a little disconcerting. Still, it wasn't the first time I'd experienced this phenomena recently, though the sickening feel of personal defilement was conspicuously absent this time. This fact did nothing to quell the oncoming panic however, so I forced myself to remain calm and try to think it through.

Cognitive reasoning isn't exactly an easy task when you feel like a refugee from the amnesia ward. My thoughts felt jumbled but I was heartened that I actually had some of them for a change. Unfortunately, I don't really think that they all belonged to me. Every now and then I would grapple one of the memories as it tumbled through my numbed consciousness, and then inspect it closely. I was reasonably certain that such thoughts as 'which pair of shoes I should wear with my new dress', and 'setting up an appointment to have my nails done before the party' belonged to someone else entirely. It was also a safe bet that said someone was female. What I was doing with her memories I couldn't say, but they were fading out of existence as quickly as they came in.

There were however two things that kept circulating repeatedly around my muddled grey matter with sharp clarity. One was a large glowing yellow rectangle. The other was a particularly nasty, and relatively familiar, burning sensation on the side of my neck coupled with a feeling of utter helplessness and disorientation. I couldn't quite tell which of us should lay claim to this pair of thoughts. Until recently I'd thought of them purely as my own. Now, in retrospect I had to wonder. I suppose it's possible that they were being shared by both of us.

I shifted uncomfortably in my seat and continued to stare at the scene before me while pondering the greater meaning of luminescent geometric shapes and inexplicable pains. For the moment I resigned myself to the present situation in hopes some thought of lesser obscurity would finally provide an answer.

The tableau beyond the slightly fogged window strobed frantically with patches of red, blue and white like an insane outdoor disco. Strings of holiday lights entwined through evergreen hedgerows winked in and out of time with the brighter flashes in a futile attempt to find dominance over the darkness. I should have found the panorama saddening, but instead felt little emotion for it.

Flickering light bars mounted atop emergency vehicles were things to which I was growing far too accustomed. I reached this conclusion quickly with no resistance whatsoever from my rational self. It was undeniable. There was a time that when gathered in such an excessive number the flashing beacons would have reminded me of severe tragedy. At this particular moment however, they were simply an annoyance that my eyes were being forced to contend with.

Once upon a different time in my life a garish slash of yellow crime scene tape would have insinuated itself into my soul, bringing with it quick fear and deep sorrow. Now, an example of that thin plastic barrier was close by, slowly undulating on a cold winter breeze. In this instance it seemed simply a part of the everyday landscape— to me at least.

Even the squawking radios and idling engines that tainted the night with their continuous disharmony seemed nothing more than a normal slice of reality. They neither belonged nor didn't belong. They were very simply just there.

The bare truth was that nothing mattered to me now. Nothing but the rectangle of light pouring through the open door of the townhouse apartment, a haunting incandescent spill that was being easily absorbed by a thirsty sponge of darkness.

Regrettably, it looked like I was going to have to answer some serious questions before I got anywhere near that doorway. At least, that was the impression I was getting from the stern look molded onto Detective Benjamin Storm's features.

I hadn't seen Ben since meeting him for breakfast earlier in the month. It wasn't surprising really, what with the holidays barreling in upon us— Chanukah having already arrived, securing first place in a yearly contest, with Yule, Christmas, and Kwanzaa hot on its tail. Schedules were tight; being full of parties, relatives, and even in light of the season, work. I had hoped that the next time we saw one another it would be at a gathering of family and friends where we could share a drink and forget about the everyday rigors of the world.

Of course, this was *my* bizarre life, and something like that wasn't about to happen.

I guess I should have known I wouldn't be blessed with such normalcy considering the circumstances, and given that just over one year ago my very existence had veered off course to follow a far more tremulous path. On a sweltering

August night, an ability that would soon become my life's bane had exited thirty plus years of shadow to come fully into the light.

It was on that night that a perverted serial murderer had taken the life of one of my friends— a student I'd instructed in the ways of The Craft. Her final passage across the bridge into Summerland had cost me dearly.

I would never again be the same. In fact, I often wondered if I would ever again be sane.

It was during the investigation of her death— as well as the subsequent victims— when I discovered that a cigar is not necessarily always a cigar. I had learned that for me at least, a nightmare is quite possibly a harbinger of reality; that an intimate supernatural connection with the 'other side' was my talent as a Witch— and at the same time, my torment.

Just as unfortunate was the fact that the random visions and nightmares didn't always make much sense— like now— and were very often accompanied by a headache that would make a migraine seem like a welcome relief. Sometimes a sensation would even manifest as an unexplained pain localized in some other part of my body— once again, like now.

The only saving grace was that this didn't happen ALL the time. There were actually long stretches where I got to experience life as usual. But, it did happen frequently enough to keep me off balance and always wondering. I just never knew when or where.

Judging from the current circumstances, this was obviously one of the when's, and wherever I was at the moment was, well, one of the where's.

And once again, as I'd known for some time that I would be, I was smack in the middle of something I'd rather have no part of. Especially given the fact that I was parked in the chilly back seat of a St. Louis City Police Cruiser, wearing a pair of handcuffs, and staring out the window at my best friend's incredulous face.

As I said before, how I'd come to be here I wasn't entirely certain. The last thing I remembered for a fact was climbing into bed next to my wife, Felicity. From there, to my knowledge, I had gone to sleep.

The next thing I even begin to recall after that is chasing after the glowing yellow rectangle. Upon adding up the imagery with the circumstances and carrying the remainder, I had concluded that that luminous shape was none other than the doorway to the apartment in the near distance. It didn't help that said doorway was quite obviously the entrance to an active crime scene.

"Rowan?" Ben's voice came to me, initially muted by the tempered glass of the windows, only to have the last half of the sentence leap in volume as he jerked open the car door. "What the fuck?!"

From what I could tell, the woman's thoughts that had commandeered my synapses were pretty much gone, for now at least. At the moment, I was feeling relatively lucid, though there was still a definite fog hanging over me that kept threatening to obscure rational thought altogether. I hoped it would hold off long enough for me to figure out what was going on.

"Hey," I answered sheepishly.

"Jeezus H. Christ, white man," he continued. "What's going on? What are you doing here?"

"Honestly?"

"Hell yes, honestly, Rowan!" he barked. "This is a crime scene, not a shopping mall."

"I don't know." There it was. The omnipresent and wholly unsatisfactory answer to a serious question, but once again it was all I could conjure at the moment. "I was actually hoping that you could tell ME."

"No way man." He shook his head. "No way. You're gonna have to do better than that." With a thick frown pasted securely to his face, he huffed out a heavy sigh and stepped back, pulling the door open wider as he did so. "Come on, get out of there."

I rocked myself forward and scooted across the stiff upholstery of the cold bench seat, then twisted toward the opening. Impatiently, my friend took hold of my upper arm with one large hand and guided me out onto the curb, telling me to watch my head at just about the same instant the back of it impacted with the doorframe. I'm pretty sure he timed it that way on purpose, because it was more than plain that he wasn't at all happy with me right now.

As amazing as it seems, even in the middle of the night, if you happen upon a crime scene, you will find at least a handful of onlookers seeking a morbid thrill. At the moment, I was apparently the object of that thrill. If that weren't enough embarrassment for one sitting, we were being paid even more intense regard by a clutch of reporters and cameramen. Blue-white cones instantly glared outward from their powerful lights, making the two of us the centerpiece of the harsh setting.

"Don't turn around," Ben instructed me in a clipped voice, helping me forward with a rough hand as he stepped quickly in behind me.

We walked at an even pace, him guiding me with a hand planted firmly on my shoulder, weaving through cops and evidence technicians until we were positioned in the shadows behind a Crime Scene Unit van. Out of sight of the cameras and prying eyes of the reporters, we came to a halt and he told me to stand still.

I heard the clinking of metal, followed by a muted ratcheting noise and my left hand was suddenly free. I rolled my shoulder and felt it give a slight pop as I brought it back to its natural position. A moment later, the metal was no longer chafing my other wrist and I repeated the motion for my right shoulder as I turned around.

"Thanks," I said.

"Yeah, thank me later after I kick your ass," my friend told me. "Now what gives? What're you doing here?"

"I was serious, Ben," I answered with a shake of my head. "I don't know. I don't even know how I got here."

"That's easy," he told me while jerking his thumb over his shoulder. "Your goddamned truck is parked right over there in the middle of the fucking street."

"Who was murdered?" Unconsciously dismissing his statement, I blurted out the question and looked past him at the glowing doorway.

"Me first, Row." He shook his head vigorously. "Is there somethin' about this I should know? Is this some kind of *Twilight Zone* shit here? Are you havin' one of those visions or somethin' like that?"

"It might be, Ben. I don't know." I shook my head again as I gravitated ever so slightly toward the scene.

"Whoa, Kemosabe." He reached out and stopped my progress easily. "Just where do ya' think you're goin'?"

"I want to have a look at the scene, Ben," I answered automatically.

"What for?"

I didn't reply, because I simply didn't know the answer.

"Look, Row, this is a pretty routine investigation here, if you can call something like this routine. Truth is we don't even know if it's a murder or an accidental death yet. There're no weird symbols or any crap like that so I don't get what you're doing here." He made reference to the anomalous evidence that had prompted him to bring me into the two previous investigations. "Now, did you know someone who lived in this apartment or something?"

The shroud of disorientation was descending on me again, rendering my fleeting clarity a thing of the past. My scalp was starting to tighten and the back of my head held fast to a dull throb that was threatening to increase exponentially. I still had no clue what I was doing here, but the growing pressure in my skull told me that there was definitely a reason. I was just too mesmerized by the doorway to recognize what it was.

"Look, Rowan, you're actin' pretty weird. How 'bout I call Felicity and get her down here to pick you up."

"I'm fine," I told him, focusing past him and on the door. Something was compelling me to move toward that oblong patch of light.

"No, man, you're not fine," he told me. "It's two-thirty in the morning and you just showed up outta nowhere at a crime scene. Uninvited mind you. Then you ducked under the barrier tape and started walkin' across the yard like some kinda zombie, completely ignorin' the officers who told you to stop. You know, not every copper in St. Louis knows who you are. You're damn lucky you didn't get hurt. I mean, Jeezus… Hey… Hey… HEY Rowan! Are you listenin' to me?"

"What?" I asked in a distracted timbre. I'd only barely heard him talking and hadn't really registered the words. The only thing that mattered right now was the doorway.

"Have you been drinking?"

"No, of course I haven't been drinking." At least I didn't think I had.

"You don't smell toast or somethin' do you?" he asked in earnest.

"What?" I shook my head and stared at him briefly. "Toast?"

"I read somewhere that you smell toast when you're havin' a stroke," he offered.

His words came to me in a random sputter of sound as

my cognizance shifted in and out of phase with the rest of reality.

"That's it," Ben said, sounding as much concerned as annoyed this time. "I'm gettin' you to a hospital. There's definitely somethin' not right with you."

Inside my skull I heard a loud electric snap and felt a burning sting along the side of my neck. The nasty tingling sensation that had been at the back of my concerns had now burst into searing flame through my entire side. I tried to reach upward and found my body to be ignoring any instructions issued by my brain. I felt myself shaking violently and beginning to stiffen as my brain short-circuited into oblivious disorientation. My chest tightened and began to sharply spasm with the same intense pain that accompanies a nocturnal leg cramp.

My sight was taken over by a darkened tunnel of fading vision and in a flash the ground leapt upward to meet me. On impact, a sharp hammer blow of agony peened the side of my skull and spread rapidly outward into a migraine-like ache that settled in for the long haul.

As I lay crumpled onto the cold lawn I could just barely make out the distant sound of my friend's frantic voice yelling, "Somebody get an ambulance!"

The last thought I remember clearly was that I had a pair of red patent leather pumps that would go perfectly with my new dress.

I'm not sure which assault on my senses was the most disconcerting— the smell or the sound. I suppose it could have been either one, or even a combination of both.

On the one hand, there was no mistaking the antiseptic funk of a hospital emergency room. An odor that was the filtered medicinal smell of alcohol, gauze, and used tongue depressors in an olfactory ballet with the stench of sweat, fear, and blood, all underscored by death. It carried with it an easily recognizable signature that told you exactly where you were without even opening your eyes.

Then, on the other, there was the terse exchange going on between my wife and my best friend. A pair of hedged voices, both straining not to outwardly display an overabundance of the anger that they were quite obviously holding back. They were bickering somewhere just beyond the door of the treatment room where I was now lying flat on my back.

Whichever it was, it jarred me back from the semi-conscious ledge of introspection I'd been tip-toeing along since the doctor had finished poking, prodding, and interrogating me.

"I asked you not to get him involved any more, Ben," Felicity was stating flatly. "At least not for a while. He still hasn't recovered from what he went through the last time."

"That's what I've been tryin' to tell ya', Felicity," he appealed. "He just showed up outta the clear freakin' blue. I DIDN'T get him involved this time."

Their tones were hushed and muted by the obstruction, but if I listened closely, I could still make out what they were saying.

My mind had continued to replay the memories of recent events ever since I had come to in the ambulance. I had quickly pieced everything together, but I was still at a loss to explain why I had suddenly 'awakened' from what I could only explain as a trance, at a crime scene in progress. One thing I knew for certain was that my midnight wanderings were no longer going to be a secret, and that I was now starting down a road toward an explanation. I only hoped that I would survive the trip.

The earlier fog that had been ruthlessly attached to my brain had apparently lifted, though a dull ache still persisted in the back of my head. I knew from past experience that this wasn't a good sign at all.

It was obvious to me that I was somehow connected to this crime. Ben had already verified for me that the victim was in fact a woman, and that her name was Paige Lawson. This at least explained the rogue thoughts I'd experienced. But I hadn't recognized her name at all. I didn't know her and I seriously doubted that she knew me.

I remembered feeling a sharp stinging sensation on the side of my neck just before I blacked out. An active tingle still occupied the swath of flesh behind and below my left ear, so I slowly reached up and gingerly probed the area with my fingertips. There were no obvious welts or abrasions that I could feel, but the burning sensation continued. No big surprise.

"Well what was he doing there then?" I heard Felicity almost hiss.

"I don't know," Ben answered as forcefully as he could without raising his voice. "Hell, HE didn't even know."

I had been trying to ignore them while I concentrated, but I was failing miserably at blocking out their banter. Also, I was getting the impression that they were going to escalate if something didn't alter their current course. I concluded that I had best intervene.

"He's right," I spoke loudly, casting my words in the direction of the door. "It's not his fault, so will you two please quit arguing."

Silence instantly replaced the tempered squabble. After a moment Ben and Felicity came sheepishly through the door and positioned themselves next to the bed.

"Row…" my wife sighed as she brushed my disheveled hair back from my forehead, "shouldn't you be resting, then?"

Felicity gave the outward appearance of a fragile china doll standing next to Ben. Petite, with a milky complexion, her own hair was a pile of flaming auburn resting atop her head in a loose Gibson girl. Whenever she let it down, it was a rush of spiral curls reaching almost to her waist. Her green eyes held more than a hint of concern as she gazed back at me and her normally smooth face was wrinkled with mild anguish. A second generation Irish-American, her voice usually held only the barest hint of an accent, but could blossom fully into a thick brogue if she were tired, stressed, or had recently spent time with certain members of her family. Right now, it was obvious that the former two options were weighing in.

"I'm trying to," I answered. "But it's a bit noisy."

"Sorry, white man," Ben offered apologetically. "Didn't mean to keep you up."

"You weren't, actually," I replied. "The doctor told me I had to stay awake until the test results came back."

"So you wanna tell the red squaw here that I didn't call you in on this."

"What were you doing there then?" Felicity queried without waiting for me to fulfill Ben's request.

"Ben didn't have anything to do with me being there," I stated for his benefit, then addressed her query. "And I haven't quite figured that part out yet."

The last half of my sentence was joined by the swooshing sound of the door to the treatment room swinging open. A tired looking brunette woman dressed in blue hospital scrubs and a lab coat followed the door inward. In her hand she carried an oversized brown enveloped clearly marked with my name, and a handful of other scrawlings that only made sense to someone in the medical profession.

"How are you feeling Mister Gant?"

"Same, I guess." I answered.

"Good." She nodded as she crossed the room to the

opposite wall. "No new pains or tremors?"

"No. Just a bit of a headache."

After pulling a rectangular x-ray from the envelope, she deftly popped it into a pair of holding clips on a wall-mounted box and then switched on the backlight.

"How about your memory?" she queried as she stared at the black and white study of my skull. "Can you tell me what day this is?"

"Tuesday, December eighteenth," I answered, exasperated that I was being put through this line of questioning for yet a third time. "My middle name is Linden, I'm thirty-nine years old, I'm married…"

"All I wanted was the date, Mister Gant," she cut me off, sounding slightly distracted. "And by the way, it's past midnight, so it is actually Wednesday the nineteenth."

"Do I lose any points for that?"

"There doesn't seem to be anything out of the ordinary on your x-rays," she began, ignoring my jibe and giving the film a final once over. She then turned and crossed her arms over her chest as she leaned against the wall. "And your blood work is fine."

"So why don't you look pleased?" I asked.

"I'm a little concerned about the fact that you blacked out as well as the description of your earlier dementia provided by Detective Storm. These could be indicators of a mild ischemic stroke. What I'd like to do is get a head CT and keep you under observation for a few more hours."

"I really don't think that's necessary," I protested.

"Well, I do," she returned flatly. "And while I certainly cannot keep you here against your will, I strongly suggest that you have this test."

The door whooshed once again and a nurse urgently poked her head through the opening. "Doctor Morrison, we need you in trauma two."

"Why don't you discuss it with your wife, Mister Gant," the harried MD told me as she headed out after the nurse. "Someone will check back with you in a few minutes."

As the door swung shut behind her I knew better than to open my mouth. Felicity and Ben were looking at me with steeled expressions and it was immediately plain that they were on her side. Effectively it had become three against one. I never even stood a chance.

It was just past six-thirty in the morning. Felicity had headed out in search of coffee and I was all but imprisoned in a hospital room against my wishes. Ben had headed back to his crime scene as soon as he was convinced that I would stay put without drastic measures. He had even gone so far as to offer Felicity his handcuffs. Something told me she gave it serious consideration, even though she had made a half-hearted joke telling him that she just might be interested when I was feeling better.

I was hoping the doctor would get the results of her test back soon, or at least see fit to release me so that I would be able to head home, but so far it wasn't looking very promising. I had been trying to squeeze in a nap ever since she had Okayed it but all I'd really managed to do was doze in and out for the past forty-five minutes.

My head was resting deeply into a too soft pillow and I was settled uncomfortably on the inclined bed. I was just taking another run at getting some sleep when I heard the doctor's voice.

"How are you doing Mister Gant?"

I opened my eyes and found her standing at the end of the bed. She appeared just as tired as she had a few hours ago.

"As well as can be expected I suppose."

"Good," she answered succinctly as she jotted something on a clipboard, then without looking up, she added, "Interesting talent you have there. Is it legible or are you just doodling?"

"Excuse me?" I asked.

"The writing without looking." She gestured to the adjustable table that was positioned across the bed in front of me. "You were even doing it with your eyes closed when I walked in."

I tilted my head forward to gaze in the direction she indicated and watched in astonishment as my left hand, gripping a pencil, moved swiftly back and forth across a small notepad. Several pages had already been filled and flipped upward.

The fact that I was right-handed isn't even what bothered me most. It was the realization that I'd had no idea what my left hand was doing until it had been pointed out to me.

As I watched, my hand automatically flipped the newly filled page up and set the tip of the pencil against an empty sheet. I stared on as it continued of its own accord to scribe in smooth, clear, and wholly unfamiliar handwriting, repeating over and over the same line of text as it had on all the previous pages.

Dead I am. Dead I am. I do not like that dead I am.

CHAPTER 3

"So what are you doin' now?" Ben asked as he stared at the pad of paper. "Tryin' to be some kinda morbid Doctor Seuss?"

I'd expected that. I didn't necessarily like it, but it was bound to come out of someone sooner or later. The more I thought about it, the more I suspected it would end up being not one or the other, but both. Even I had no choice but to admit that the similarity between what I'd written and one of the most memorable lines from a beloved children's book was uncanny. Under wholly different circumstances it might even have been amusing.

But it was under these circumstances, not different ones, and the word 'dead' played a prominent role in the repetitious line of text. Couple that with the fact that the pad full of paraphrased prose came out of me, involuntarily, and I didn't find it amusing in the least.

"I'm being serious here, Ben," I returned dully.

"Okay, okay." He tossed the notepad onto his desk blotter and leaned back in his chair. Propping one ankle across his knee then clasping his hands behind his head he looked at me seriously. "I'm listenin'. What's the deal with this notepad?"

I had called my friend as soon as I'd been released from

the hospital. The doctor still had no definitive results back from the tests that had been run, but I was feeling fine so she'd relented and allowed me to leave. I knew full well that I hadn't had a stroke, but I wasn't about to try explaining what had caused my very pronounced symptoms. If I had, I'd probably still be talking to the staff psychiatrist as well as being taken on a tour of their lovely padded accommodations. I'd been down this road before.

You tend to get a small spectrum of reactions when you look at someone and say, 'I'm a Witch.' The three biggies go something like this: One, they look at you like you are crazy. Two, they try to introduce you to Jesus and save you from yourself; or, three, they run screaming in the opposite direction. In my case, being male, I also get the added, 'Don't you mean Warlock?' This usually prompts me to give the actual definition of the word Warlock, that being "oath breaker." The short explanation of the fact that male or female, a Witch is very simply a Witch is usually good for glazing over the eyes of the uninitiated in less than sixty seconds.

Though I don't make a secret of my religious path or even my mystical leanings, I've learned to avoid the subject in given situations. Sometimes it just doesn't pay to be honest— plain and simple.

When I'd made my call, I had found Ben behind his desk at City Homicide working on the situation that had gotten him out of bed only a handful of hours before. I'd suspected as much would be the case and hadn't even tried calling him at home. When I told him what I wanted to show him, he'd suggested that I go to my own home and get some rest. I doubt he'd really expected me to follow the suggestion, because he didn't seem at all surprised to see me coming through the glass-fronted double doors of his department just over thirty minutes later.

Felicity on the other hand, had been a tougher sell. Though her outward appearance may be that of fragile beauty, my wife was as headstrong as they came. I was fully aware that what came across on the surface as stereotypical Irish stubbornness and temper was truly born of intellect, will, and protective instinct. Still, igniting that temper was something better left undone unless you had a damned good reason. I just didn't feel I had a choice this time around, even if my reason was no more than some nonsensical words on a notepad and a bad feeling about them.

In the end, it took me all of fifteen minutes to convince her that if she didn't take me by City Police Headquarters on the way home, I would simply find a way to take myself. She had finally given in and at this particular moment, she was parked next to me in one of the stackable, molded-plastic chairs the detectives used for visitors. She wasn't happy with me in the least, but I was betting she would get over it. She always did.

I shifted in my own seat, itself a refugee from the stack of seventies era furniture, and succeeded only in moving the discomfort from one side of my body to the other.

"Did you happen to notice anything other than the similarity to Doctor Seuss?" I asked.

"You've got nice handwriting." Ben shrugged. "I especially like that little curly-q thing you do with bottoms of the I's."

"Exactly," I affirmed, ignoring his sardonic addition. "It IS nice handwriting. But it's not MY handwriting."

"Whaddaya mean? I thought you said you wrote it."

"I did, but not of my own volition."

"You wanna elaborate?"

I sighed. I'd been through this with him already when I'd called, but obviously either I hadn't made myself clear or he'd been ignoring me. I suspected it was the latter, but considering the altered states I'd been in recently, I couldn't be absolutely certain.

"It's called automatic writing, Ben," I explained. "It's a psychic event that occurs when a spirit or entity channels through someone on this plane of existence. The person doing the channeling simply acts as the conduit for the spirit who then communicates by writing."

"Okay," my friend said as he tilted his chair back forward and picked up the notepad once again, "so what you're saying is that this is one of those *Twilight Zone* things?"

"It has to be." I nodded. "I was completely unaware of the fact that I was writing any of that until it was pointed out to me. Also, I was writing with my left hand. I'm right-handed."

He picked up a large mug and took a swig, then set it back on the stained blotter. "So if I'm connecting all the dots here, you think maybe Paige Lawson is trying to communicate with you."

"That's my guess."

"Okay."

I was dumbfounded by the matter of fact tone in his voice and his apparent lack of interest. I know I had at least one false start before I managed to stutter, "What do you mean, 'okay'?"

"I mean, okay." He shook his head and shrugged. "I've seen some weirder shit than this since I've been hanging around with you, so I'm willing to believe what you're tellin' me here."

"So? Are you going to do anything about it?" I asked.

"What do you want me to do, Rowan?" he asked. "I've got a pad of paper here that has a little rhyme written on it about five jillion times."

"Well shouldn't you look into it? It's a message from a

dead woman."

"You don't know that for a fact, but for the sake of argument, okay, let's say that it IS Paige Lawson communicating with you. I can see where she's comin' from. I expect that if I was dead I wouldn't be all that happy about it either."

"What?" I couldn't believe what he was saying.

"Look, it's not like this is some kind of hot clue you're handing me here. It's a piece of paper that says someone ain't happy about bein' dead."

"But…"

"But nothing, Row," he cut me off before I could even form the objection, and then ran his hand up to smooth his hair. "Look, here's the real deal, between you and me. It's looking like this might not even be a murder. We're still waiting on the autopsy, but there were no signs of a struggle. No forced entry. The place wasn't trashed. She wasn't shot, stabbed, or beaten. The only thing out of place is a small welt on the side of her neck…"

"Which side?" I interrupted quickly.

"Left, I think. Why?"

"Because I had a burning sensation on my neck last night." I indicated the area with my hand. "It was on the left side too."

"Okay," he shrugged, "but if you'd let me finish what I was saying, you'd know that didn't kill her. It could be from a thousand different things so even though we haven't discounted it, it's prob'ly nothing. The preliminary report I got from the coroner says she has a blunt force trauma to the side of her head that could be consistent with the corner of the end table just inside her doorway. It looks like she probably just slipped, fell, an' clocked herself. Damn shame for a young, good lookin' woman like her, but it happens."

"But why was I there, Ben?" I implored. "What made

me show up at the scene like that?"

"You tell me," he stated with a frown. "Because I'll be honest, it's got me a little worried."

"You mean you think it might not have been just an accident?" I latched on to the glint of hope in his words.

"No," he shook his head vigorously and turned the glimmer to worthless pyrite. "I'm worried about YOU. I think what happened out on that bridge earlier this year has still got you fucked up."

"That's not it, Ben, and you know it."

"Felicity?" Ben appealed as he looked over at her.

"I have to agree with him, Row," she stated evenly. "You haven't been yourself lately at all."

"You've got to be kidding," I muttered incredulously. "You're on Ben's side with this? Come on, Felicity, last time I checked you were just as open minded about this kind of thing as me. You've seen the things that have happened. You've even experienced them first hand."

"Yes, I have," she agreed. "But I was never in as deep as you have been. This is different somehow. Ever since you got involved in that investigation last February, you've seemed disconnected. Ungrounded. You even admitted it then."

"Yes I did, but that was months ago. I'm well over that."

"No, you're not," she replied. "In some ways you're even worse than you were then. You've seemed almost out of control at times."

"Out of control how?"

"Like tonight," she asserted. "Disoriented. Not knowing who or where you are."

"But this was an isolated incident." I spoke the lie and didn't look back. I figured I'd be caught in it eventually, but I thought I'd at least have some time to prove I was on to something important. I definitely wasn't expecting my capture to be so immediate.

"Rowan, you've been sleepwalking for almost two months now," my wife offered the truth back to me without judgment or anger— just a recitation of cold fact. "And the night terrors came like clockwork before that. I know you thought you'd kept them hidden from me, but you didn't."

We were fortunate, for the sake of my ego anyway, that the homicide division was less than fully staffed at the moment. There was no one close by enough to overhear the embarrassing revelations that were put forth. I looked over at my friend's somber face as he nodded and stared at me from behind his desk.

"I've known for a while too, white man. Felicity called me. Why do you think she was so mad at me earlier when she thought I might have brought you in on this? I gotta admit though, I was pretty surprised to have you turn up at an active crime scene like that."

I sat mute. I wanted to be angry with them both, and in a sense, I was. I wanted to lash out at them for engaging in these clandestine discussions behind my back. I wanted to admonish them for their conspiring to betray me. But I was still rational enough to realize that I was dealing with my wife and my best friend, and that they were obviously worried about me. The growing conflagration that was my ire was quickly reduced to a smolder when I asked myself simply, what if the two of them were correct? What if I was in fact out of control? What if I was so completely disconnected and ungrounded that I was starting to channel anything and everything without discrimination. The prospect brought a completely new, and totally real fear into the fold.

"Listen, Row," Ben now had a business card in his hand and was fiddling with it aimlessly, "remember I told you my sister had moved into town?"

"Yeah," I answered absently as I contemplated what my situation might possibly have now become.

"Well, here's the deal," he continued. "She's a shrink— a good one. Hell, I've called her a couple of times for advice myself. She's even helped me with some of the shit I deal with on the job, and you know how I feel about shrinks." Ben paused and brought a hand up to massage his neck, then held the card out to me. "Anyway, Felicity and I have discussed it and we both think it might be a good idea for you to talk to her."

"So now I'm crazy," I said.

"No, Rowan, that's not what we're saying at all," Felicity implored.

"It's called Post Traumatic Stress Disorder, Row," my friend offered. "Not that I'm qualified to diagnose it, but if anyone's a prime candidate bubba, it's you."

He had a point. It was even a valid one. Still, a painful depression was starting to set in. I'd fought harder than I'd ever thought I could just to get Ben to accept the things I was telling him at times when I had no tangible proof of their validity. I'd managed to convince him, and others, and he had for a time accepted my word on an almost blind faith.

Now, I was right back where I started— maybe even a step or two to the negative— and it was very possible that this time I wasn't the one controlling the dice.

"Just what do you think she's going to do when I tell her I'm a Witch?" I tried to play the only card I had left.

"Not much, Kemosabe," my friend replied. "She's quite a bit more open than most folks. Besides, she already knows. I've told her about the two of you."

Felicity had taken the business card from Ben as I sat there in silence, mulling over exactly how much I despised being backed into a corner. I felt a small spark of defiance deep inside, but I was going down fast. I still desperately needed something to cling to— some kind of life preserver that would keep me afloat long enough to give me a fighting chance.

I allowed my stare to fall on the surface of the desk before me and the answer became instantly clear. Deliberately, I reached across and picked up the notepad, which had been the center of our earlier discussion. Slowly, I peeled off a pair of the pages and tossed them back on the blotter in front of Ben.

"Now, here's my deal," I submitted carefully. "I go talk to your sister, and you have the crime lab compare the handwriting on those papers with Paige Lawson's."

"Row…" He began shaking his head as a furrow formed across his brow.

"I'm not asking much, Ben." I held fast. "Just find out if it's her handwriting and let me know one way or the other. That's it."

"Okay." He finally nodded, but still kept a frown plastered to his face. "Okay, but I don't know what it's gonna get ya'."

"A place to start," was all I said.

"So, are you mad at me?" Felicity asked somberly as she guided her Jeep down an exit ramp and off the highway.

Our trip from police headquarters thus far had been made in almost total silence— not so much because either of us were angry, but because there was simply too much to think about. The extent of our conversation to this point had been my asking whether we should swing by to pick up my truck. In truth, I actually had no idea where I'd left it, plus all I really wanted to do right now was sleep. I wasn't disappointed in the least when she told me it had already been taken care of.

It was approaching mid-day and the sky was still heavily overcast with a flat-bottomed stratum of grey clouds. A misty rain had begun to fall at some point while I was still being held captive by the hospital, and it hadn't subsided yet. Winter's chill was sharp in the air, even with the official start of the season still a few days away. The temperature was staying a few steps ahead of the magical point where precipitation solidifies, effectively making the difference between the landscape being a 'winter wonderland' and 'wintry blah'. Depending on your tastes, it was the kind of day that either made you feel great to be alive, or depressed you into a mood that begged to be slept off like a bad drunk. With my lack of sleep acting as catalyst, I was being pushed in the direction of the depression with little resistance.

"Not really," I replied. "Although, I wish you'd said something about all this earlier. Then maybe I wouldn't have wasted so much energy trying to keep you from finding out."

"Why didn't you want me to know anyway?"

"It wasn't something you needed to worry about," I answered. "You have enough to do without taking on my problems."

"Row," she admonished, "we've had this talk before."

"Yeah," I admitted, "but you get a little overprotective at times."

"Aye, and just what is it you'd call what you're doing then?" A slight hint of her normally veiled Irish brogue seeped into the question, audibly announcing her fatigue.

"Being overprotective too," I returned. "But that's nothing new."

"And it's something new from me then?"

"No, I didn't say that."

We were only a few blocks from home when she gave a quick downshift and turned the Jeep into a parking lot of what appeared to have been a multi-tenant strip mall, but was now occupied by a single business. Hooking past a light standard she serpentined through the lot then pulled into a space before the entrance of Arch Color Labs. She shifted into neutral then set the parking brake before switching off the engine.

"What then?" she asked as she peered at me, her green eyes searching for a hidden answer. "Are you saying it's okay for you but not for me?"

"Like you said," I sighed. "We've had this talk before, and obviously we've never resolved it or we wouldn't be having it again now. We're both just too stubborn, I suppose."

"Aye," she agreed softly, "I suppose we are."

We regarded each other quietly for a moment, neither of us certain where to take the conversation next. I finally motioned at the storefront and broke the lull.

"This doesn't look much like our house."

"Sorry, I forgot to tell you." She shook her head. "I need to drop off a batch job for a client."

"You don't need to apologize." I shook my head as the realization overtook me. I hadn't really thought about how my escapades might have affected her, and this detour drove the point home. "You'd probably already have this done if it weren't for me throwing you off schedule."

"It's no problem," she returned.

"Maybe not," I echoed, "but I still feel bad about it."

"You do? Good, then my mission is accomplished," she told me with a sly grin.

"I just walked right into a waiting guilt trip didn't I?"

"Uh-huh." She nodded as she rummaged behind my seat and withdrew a heavy-gauge envelope. "You can wait here if you want. I'll only be a few minutes."

"You sure?" I asked. "I know how long your 'few minutes' can be sometimes."

"I'm sure. I just need to drop this off."

"Okay."

True to her word, Felicity was in and out in less than five minutes, but then spent another ten beneath the awning in front of the lobby chatting with a wiry young man. I couldn't blame her for the delay though, because he had followed her out the door, talking nonstop except for quick lulls to light a cigarette. He'd been through two already and was heading quickly toward finishing off a third.

It was almost amusing to watch my wife as she maintained a constant distance between herself and the rambling chain smoker. What wasn't amusing was the fact that every time he took a puff I had to stop myself from getting out of the vehicle and bumming one from him. It did, however, serve as a reminder as to just how much she despised smoking, and that helped steel my resolve to fight the craving.

She finally managed to get away and flashed him a smile and a quick wave as she climbed into the Jeep.

"Friend of yours?" I asked as she buckled herself in.

"Oh, that's just Harold. Nice enough guy but Gods! He smokes like a fiend."

"I noticed." I nodded, trying not to let on that I was within inches of joining him in the act.

"So how about you?" I asked, changing the subject swiftly in order to avoid thinking about cigarettes.

"How about me, what?" She furrowed her eyebrows as she shook her head in confusion. "I don't smoke."

"No, not that," I explained. "What we were talking about earlier. Are you mad at me?"

"Oh, that." She nodded as she cast a glance back over her shoulder then backed the Jeep out of the parking space. "I was," she answered, chewing at her lower lip, "but I'm getting over it."

"How long before you think you'll be completely over it?" I asked.

"Aye, that's going to depend on you."

My truck was parked nose first beyond the gated fence that hemmed in our back yard. Felicity pulled her vehicle up to the chain-link barrier and popped the stick into neutral.

We sat in silence for a long moment, simply listening to the world continuing about its business around us. The stereo sound of tires against wet pavement grew in the distance, achieved its peak as they made their way past us, and then faded into oblivion on the opposite side. The Jeep's engine idled softly in the background. The mechanical whirr of the windshield wipers kept time in a widely spaced rhythm, announcing the languid tempo just when you'd finally given up waiting for the next beat. In a half bare tree next to us a raven punctuated it all with an ellipsis of forlorn caws, leaving the moment to hang in the moist air, and then fell silent once again.

Even with the heater running, the damp chill was working its way into my bones. On top of that, I was still dying for a cigarette and didn't have any of the nicotine gum with me that had thus far been my only barrier between abstinence and re-kindling the habit.

"So you think maybe we should go inside?" I asked.

"I'd love to, but I have a shoot to do and I've already rescheduled it once," my wife told me. "I'd rather not lose the account."

"Supermodels?" I asked jokingly.

"Sure," she replied, her own tenor lightened somewhat. "Super new models of anodized cookware for a catalog. Want to come along?"

"I think I'll pass." I gave her a weak grin.

"I thought you might."

"Actually, I could really use some sleep."

"Aye, that makes the two of us," she returned. "But I'll have to wait."

"Sorry," I apologized for something I could do nothing about. "Since I don't have my keys, any chance you could unlock the house for me before you go?"

"Oh," she replied, "Ben said he'd have them put your keys in the mailbox."

"Good enough." I leaned over and gave her a kiss then unlatched my door.

"Row," Felicity called after me as I climbed out.

I turned back to see there was still a hint of concern in her eyes. Her hand was extended toward me and in it was the business card Ben had given her.

"Promise me you'll call for an appointment." She made the statement more as a gentle command than a request.

I'd almost escaped, for another few hours at least. I should have known better, though, as this was something she perceived as far too important to wait. I sighed heavily and nodded as I reached back in and took the card from her. I'd made a deal with Ben as well as her, and my own principles wouldn't allow me to back out.

"Promise," she softly demanded again.

"I promise," I told her.

I stood in the driveway and watched her back out, then followed with my eyes as she headed off down the street in the direction of Highway Forty. When she was no longer in sight I made my way along the flagstone walkway and then climbed the stairs to our front porch.

My keys had been exactly where Ben had said they would be. After retrieving them I had unlocked the door and tripped my way across the room as our English Setter and Australian Cattle Dog expressed their great relief that someone had finally come home after being gone, in their doggish perception of time, forever. I punched in my alarm code and followed with a second series of key presses. A canned female voice issued from the panel announcing that it had switched from the away mode to the stay at home setting. Basically, switching off the motion sensors but resetting and rearming the doors and windows.

I'd never really thought all that much about the household alarm system. It was something we had really only used whenever we were out of the house, and then only to protect 'stuff'. It had always been there for the express purpose of guarding our possessions. These days, however, it had served yet another purpose. Protecting us.

In the month following the incident on the Old Chain of Rocks Bridge, I'd had the system upgraded. Every window in the house had been equipped with sensors and cell technology had been added to avoid the alarm being disabled by simply cutting the phone lines. There were additional motion detectors and even secondary panels added to main rooms to allow for quick access to panic buttons. It all seemed so terribly paranoid to me at times, and Felicity had thought it to be overkill, but I wasn't going to take any chances. I knew that Eldon Andrew Porter was still out there no matter what anyone else believed.

My first order of business was to go in search of a piece of nicotine gum. I hadn't even tried to hide my withdrawal like symptoms from Felicity— not that I'd succeeded in hiding anything else anyway— so I didn't have to get it from any secret stash. However, I did have to remember where I'd last put it. Once I found the box and quelled the immediate crisis level desire for a cigarette, I set about finding anything I possibly could do in order to waste time.

After a round of behind the ear scratches for the boisterous canines I disabled the back door sensor long enough to let them out, then back in once they'd discovered that the weather was not what they'd expected. Our three felines, Emily, Dickens, and Salinger, were nowhere to be seen, so I simply filled their food bowls and moved on to something else.

There were a few dishes in the sink, left over from the night before, so I took my time washing, drying and putting them away. I could have simply loaded them into the dishwasher, but that wouldn't have taken near as long.

I thumbed through the mail that had occupied the box along with my keys, discarding several pieces of poorly targeted direct market advertising in the process. After extracting those items pertinent to my consulting business, I tossed the remainder into the basket next to the front door.

Before starting up the stairs to my office, I took a moment to listen to the messages on our personal answering machine. Two hang-ups and one quick hello from a friend who was inquiring about what to bring to the Yule ritual we'd planned for a few days hence. I started to jot a note down as a reminder to call him but found that the notepad, which normally lived by the phone, had apparently gone AWOL. A quick search through my pockets for a scrap to write on rewarded me with two things— the pad containing the repetitious morbid rhyme, and the business card of Doctor Helen Storm.

I rubbed my bearded chin absently with the back of my free hand while I stared at the simple calling card. I'd very consciously been putting this moment off, but I'd made a promise and there definitely wasn't anything pressing at the moment that should keep me from making the call. Nothing I hadn't purposely produced for that very reason, at least.

With a resigned sigh I snatched up the handset and

punched in the phone number from the upper right corner of the card. Even in my tired fog, my mind began calculating, and I latched on to the idea that it was probably going to be at least a week or two before she'd be able to get me in. That might very well give me enough time to prove I was correct about Paige Lawson, although even I wasn't entirely sure what it was I was correct about.

After six rings the phone was answered by a pre-recorded message announcing that I had reached Metro Counseling and that the offices were currently closed for lunch. I felt a wave of relief as the voice continued on, telling me that if this were an emergency I should call the doctor's exchange, otherwise I should leave a message and someone would get back to me as soon as possible.

Following the high-pitched tone at the end of the message I began to speak, "My name is Rowan Gant and I need to see about making an appointment with Doctor Storm. My number is…"

I was cut off by a burst of squelchy feedback, combined with the fumbling knocks of someone rushing to pick up the phone. A female voice barely overrode the squeal, telling me to hold on for a second. Various warbles and clicks followed, then fell quiet as the person at the other end managed to stifle the recorder.

"Sorry about that, Mister Gant," the woman's soothing voice apologized. "This is Helen Storm. Benjamin told me I should be expecting your call."

My earlier relief turned to instant surrender when she told me that she wanted to see me late tomorrow morning.

CHAPTER 4

D-E-A-D-I-A-M!
D-E-A-D-I-A-M!
What's that spell?
Dead I am!
Louder!
Dead I am!
One more time!
DEAD I AM!

I awoke in darkness.

I really wasn't all that surprised. Nightmares and darkness— they tend to go hand in hand. I'd grown relatively used to the cycle by now.

The bizarre Seuss-like chant was still echoing inside my head with a frighteningly excited edge to its morose verbiage. I laid completely still, letting the imagined sound fade to crisp silence, only to have the quiet replaced by a low, repetitive rumble. I slowly turned my head and found myself face to face with Dickens, one of our resident felines. He had his paws outstretched to touch me and was purring incessantly as he kneaded my shoulder.

At least I wasn't feeling violated for a change. And I wasn't at a loss for the how's, where's or why's of my situation for the most part. I knew exactly where I was—safely tucked in my bed, under a blanket more or less, with one arm hugging my pillow against the side of my head. The other had gone thoroughly numb from the uncomfortable angle it was crooked into beneath my body. I shifted the appendage and circulation instantly took hold full force. I winced as an astronomical number of pinpricks began traversing up and down its length.

In addition to knowing where I was at the moment, I also had a fair recollection of how I'd gotten here. These simple facts may seem obvious and mundane to virtually everyone else, but to me they were comforting revelations.

As to the why I was here, well that was obvious— it was the middle of the night and I was trying to sleep. Unfortunately, there was a perverted mantra running around inside my head that was insisting that I do otherwise.

I rolled to the side, upsetting Dickens in the process and sleepily scanned the face of the clock. The digital readout showed it to be almost a quarter past four. That simply meant four for all intents and purposes since my wife kept the timepiece set fifteen minutes fast to avoid being late. The self-imposed mind trick didn't work, but that's another story entirely.

My arm was beginning to regain its feeling and every moment that passed was bringing me closer to being fully awake. The echo reverberating inside my skull had been absent for a good number of minutes now, but the words themselves remained present and accounted for.

> D-E-A-D-I-A-M!
> D-E-A-D-I-A-M!
> What's that spell?
> Dead I am!
> Louder!
> Dead I am!

One more time!
DEAD I AM!

The seeming approbation of death imprinted itself upon my consciousness and looped like a snippet of a song that you simply can't get out of your head. If its intent was to keep me from sleeping, it was accomplishing its task with absolute precision.

Letting out a resigned sigh, I climbed out of the bed as quietly as I could. My eyes were fairly adjusted and I managed to pull on some clothes without much fuss, and then retrieved my glasses and Book of Shadows— a Witch's dream diary of sorts— from a drawer in the nightstand. I figured I'd best record the morbid ditty that was keeping me awake, because I was certain that anything this insistent meant something important.

I just didn't know what.

"How'ya feelin'?" The left field greeting issued from the handset immediately following my 'hello'. Ben's down to business approach to telephone conversations, sans the typical salutations, was as identifiable as his voice, so I wasn't at all phased by the abruptness.

"About as well as can be expected, I suppose," I returned, glancing at the clock in the corner of my computer screen. "Considering that I have an appointment with your sister in a couple of hours."

I'd been parked in my office for the better part of the morning trying to get some work done. So far I'd accomplished little more than going through the previous day's mail and moving a pile of paperwork from one side of my desk to the other. I had not exactly been what you could call productive.

I still needed to return a few phone calls and put together some proposals for clients, but I simply didn't have the motivation. I was feeling so overwhelmed by everything that it seemed useless to attempt anything more than simply existing.

"Cheer up, white man," he told me. "She's good at what she does. It's not like she's gonna bite or something."

"I know, Ben. I know."

We both fell speechless, him just the sound of someone breathing on the other end of the phone and me quietly introspective.

"Well, there's really no easy way to tell you this," my friend finally spoke, "but I've got some news you prob'ly don't wanna hear."

"The handwriting?" I asked.

"Yeah. It's not Paige Lawson's."

"Are they sure?"

"No doubt, Row," he replied. "They don't look anything alike."

"Damn," I muttered.

This latest revelation did nothing to help my overall sense of demoralization. I had been certain that Paige Lawson was trying to communicate with me. Now, I couldn't even be sure that it wasn't simply all in my head.

"Graphologist said the sample was most likely from a left-handed individual," he continued. "And probably female, although they get a little hinky about swearing to one gender or the other."

"I told you that much," I offered.

"Yeah, I know, but the samples are worlds apart and yours is still not from Paige Lawson. I really didn't even need the crime lab for this, but I had them verify it anyway. The buck-fifty analysis is this— The moderate left slant coupled with the narrow spacing denotes an independent and possibly introverted individual. The heavy pressure and ornate loops in the letters indicate a secretive personality. There's some more here about the margins, size, and stuff, but it all boils down to the same thing. It's still not Paige Lawson's handwriting."

"It still isn't mine either."

"Yeah, I know. I went ahead and had them compare yours from some of the forms I've had you fill out down here. There wasn't enough to get a good analytical read on you, but they were confident that you weren't the one pushing the pencil. I didn't tell them any different."

At first I was surprised at what he'd done, but Ben's actions made perfect sense. He had to rule out all of the possibilities and since I claimed the writing had come out of me, it was a logical move.

"On the bright side," he told me, "there's a note here saying that the little curly-q thing with the I's is pretty unique. For whatever that's worth."

"Not much, apparently."

"It would be easy to identify in another handwriting sample if we ran across it."

"And the odds of that are?" I asked rhetorically. "Besides, you've proven that it's not her, so it doesn't really matter."

"So maybe it's someone else."

"Do you really believe that?"

"Hey," he contended, "like I said, I've seen weirder shit than this. Especially outta you."

"Yes, but neither you nor Felicity seemed terribly convinced yesterday." I allowed the words to hang between us in a verbal challenge of his professed faith in my sanity.

"Look, Row, let's not go there. I wish I'd been able to give you something here, but..." He sighed. Without even seeing him I knew he was massaging his neck with a large hand. "It's just not there, man. Sorry."

"It's not your fault," I told him. I meant it even though I'm sure I didn't sound very convincing. "So what about Paige Lawson?"

"Whaddaya mean?"

"You said yesterday that you weren't even sure it was a homicide."

"Oh, that. Well, it's looking less and less like it. Waiting on the final results of the autopsy, but there's just nothing there at this point."

"How was she found anyway?"

"Row…"

"Can you humor me?" I appealed dully. "You just blew my theory apart. You could at least throw me a bone here."

He exhaled heavily at the other end. "Nothing spectacular really. Squad car drove by on regular patrol and noticed the door hanging open. When the copper came through about half an hour later it was still open so he stopped to check it out. Found her laying facedown just inside."

"And he didn't notice anything else?"

"Rowan, he's a cop. We may not be perfect but this is what we're trained to do."

"Yeah, I know," I responded, feeling mildly chastised. "I'm just really having a hard time with all of this."

"I know, man. I know."

For the second time during our conversation silence insinuated itself, bringing all conversation to a halt. I'm sure Ben was thinking that I was worse off than he'd originally imagined, but was tactfully keeping the observation to himself. I was simply reminding myself of the old bromide about not being insane as long as you had enough wits about you to wonder if you were.

"So anyway," my friend halted the swelling pause with a change of subject, "that Yule thing of yours is this Friday, right? What time were you wanting Allison and me over?"

He was correct. Yule was only two days away and as usual we had invited some non-pagan friends to our traditional gathering. This was the first year that any had accepted.

The switch in the focus of the conversation was awkward, much like any shift that occurs in a chat such as ours. Even with its abruptness, it gave me something tangible and far more pleasant to grasp. Finally there was something welcome and familiar among the discord.

"You're welcome any time," I answered. "The official ritual will be around six-thirty or seven. I've already spoken to the group and they are fine with the two of you joining in if you'd like."

"We don't hafta do anything weird do we?"

"You don't have to do anything at all," I returned. "But if you do anything 'weird' it's going to be of your own accord, because we don't have anything 'weird' planned. Just a simple Yule ritual."

"Well, you know what I mean."

"You know, I think I've told you this before, but for a Native American you sure have a bizarre view of alternative spirituality."

"It's a long story, Kemosabe," he confessed. "But at least I'm tryin'. So what happens after the ritual? Do we like commune with ghosts or somethin'?"

"No, wrong Sabbat. That would have been back in October for Samhain." I referred to the traditional holiday non-pagans call Halloween. A night when the veil between the worlds is at its thinnest and we honor those who have passed before us. "Actually, after the ritual we have a late dinner and wait for dawn."

"Why? Is she going to be late?"

I winced as he delivered the joke in an attempt to further lighten the mood. It wasn't terribly effective in its intent, but I still responded in kind. "Yeah, Ben. She's probably not going to arrive until morning."

"So, you want us to bring anything?" He returned a serious question, thankfully leaving the pun to die a quick death before the exchange could deteriorate further.

"We've pretty much got it covered," I said. "If there's something special you want to drink, you might want to bring it along, but other than that, just yourselves."

"So what are we eating?"

"Food."

"Yeah smartass, what kind of food?"

"It's a surprise, Ben."

"You're not gonna try ta' make me eat nothin' but vegetables or somethin' are you?"

"No, Ben." Even with my current mood I had to at least chuckle at the seriousness of his query. "There'll be meat on the table."

"Beef? Pork?"

"You'll find out Friday."

"It's not gonna be somethin' strange is it?" he pressed.

"You'll find out on Friday."

"Jeez, Kemosabe." He let out an exaggerated sigh. "Okay, be that way, but don't be surprised if I bring a sack of Whitey Burgers as backup."

"Felicity will kill you."

"So I'll leave 'em in the van, and sneak out if ya' try ta' feed me bean curd ala whatever."

"If you stink up the van with a bag of Whitey's, then Allison will kill you."

"Yeah, you got a point there…Well, I'll find someplace to stash 'em till I know if I need 'em."

"You won't need 'em. Trust me."

"Yeah, we'll see about that," he said. "So look, I gotta get back to work. You gonna be okay?"

"Yeah, Ben," I assured him. "I'll be fine. Disappointed,

but just fine."

"Okay. Tell Helen I said 'hey' and I'll call her later about Christmas Eve."

"Will do."

"Later."

"Bye."

When I hung up the phone, the distraction it had provided immediately dissipated, leaving me once again alone in my thoughts. Or not so alone perhaps, as a cheerfully taunting voice echoed deep inside, *'What's that spell? Dead I Am! LOUDER! DEAD I AM!'*

There's a bromide that basically says if you are insane, you think that you are sane, and therefore are unable to recognize your illness. Conversely, if you are in fact sane, you should be fully cognizant of the two states and therefore able to question said sanity.

I made it a point to ask myself this question aloud. Even though I answered no, I am not insane, the old adage wasn't terribly comforting.

The offices of Metro Counseling were located just on the outskirts of downtown Claymont, only a few miles from my home in Briarwood. Still, it took me longer to get there than it really should have due to my two aborted stops to purchase a pack of cigarettes. Earlier, I'd even considered lighting up a cigar from my humidor, but I'd been doing my best to avoid them of late. I knew if I had one in my hand I'd inhale it, and that was the last thing I needed to start doing.

The craving had increased disproportionately over the past twenty-four-hour period, and the nicotine gum simply wasn't doing its job. At the moment, I had two fresh pieces stuffed simultaneously into my cheek and was thinking very hard about adding a third.

Without warning, the pains of the urge were temporarily replaced by of all things, a woman. I had just swung into a parking space and was switching off the engine of my truck when I noticed her. She was petite. Dressed in a long skirt and boots. A leather jacket hugged her torso from the waist up, and her shoulder-length blonde hair was flying on a cold breeze. She was light complected and her face bore a tasteful amount of makeup.

After a moment, I caught myself literally ogling her as she walked across the parking lot from her car, and then disappeared through the glass doors at the entrance of the building.

I physically shuddered as I shook off the stare. Two thoughts pin-wheeled around inside my head taking turns at the forefront.

The first was, of course, that I hoped she hadn't noticed my rude gaze.

The second was a bit disturbing.

I was having serious trouble understanding just why I was trying to imagine what she would look like if she had long, red hair.

CHAPTER 5

"Terrible habit," Doctor Helen Storm said aloud, and then took a drag from a cigarette. "I really should quit, but I enjoy it too much."

I had arrived early for the appointment, as was my nature in all things involving a scheduled time. We had actually met at the door as I was on my way in and she was on her way out. She'd been hoping to grab a quick smoke break. To her credit, instead of having me wait, she had invited me to walk outside with her. We were now standing at the railing of an outdoor lounge that occupied an architecturally truncated corner of the seventh floor of the building. The air was chilly but it had calmed, and with the late morning sun to dull the bite, the crispness was for the most part pleasant.

"I know what you mean," I replied, mentally beating down the desire to bum one from her as I shifted a half step away from the enticing smoke.

"I'm sorry, this isn't bothering you is it?" she asked, noticing my obvious move.

"Yes and no," I shrugged. "I quit a couple of years ago, but for some reason I've been having some pretty horrendous cravings lately."

"I'm so sorry, Rowan. I should have asked before I invited you out here with me."

"Don't worry about it." I shook my head and waved her off before she could extinguish the cigarette. "I'm fine."

"You're sure?"

"Absolutely."

"So why do you think you've been craving cigarettes?"

"Dunno." I shrugged. "Stress I suppose. Aren't you supposed to be the one telling me why I'm all screwed up?"

Helen Storm regarded me with mysteriously dark eyes that were a mirror image of her brother's. She bore an unmistakable family resemblance to Ben, but with a far softer edge to her features. Her pretty face was framed by shiny black hair that fell across her shoulders and was interspersed with strands of grey. My friend had once told me that she was a handful of years older than him, but the streaks in her hair were the only telltale sign of that fact. The one physical attribute that came into severe contrast with her sibling was her size, she being almost a foot shorter than he.

"You don't think much of psychiatrists do you, Rowan?" she asked after a moment.

"It's not really that," I answered, somewhat embarrassed that I was broadcasting my distaste for the situation so clearly. I thought I'd be able to maintain at least some amount of control, but quite obviously I had not. "I'm just not entirely sure that I need one."

"You might not," she answered easily.

I paused, slightly taken aback. "Well, I have to admit, that's not exactly what I was expecting you to say."

"I got that impression."

"I'm sorry," I apologized for my challenge. "That was pretty rude of me wasn't it?"

"Not really." She shook her head and smiled. "You're simply voicing your anxiety."

"I suppose you've dealt with worse."

"Were I at liberty to do so, I could tell a few stories,"

she chuckled.

"So, I assume Ben has filled you in on some things?" I posed the question without accusation.

"Yes. Some." She nodded. "I won't lie to you. Benjamin and I have talked at length about your situation. I've even spoken with your wife."

"The conspiracy grows," I remarked flatly.

"That's one way to view it," she returned. "Or you could see it as some people who care very deeply for you and are trying to help."

"You're right. That comment was unfair."

"It's all a matter of perception."

"So it's okay for me to perceive that my wife and best friend have conspired against me? I thought that was considered paranoia."

"It is perfectly natural to feel a sense of betrayal when a loved one disagrees with you on something such as this," she explained. "But healthy individuals will reason it out and understand that they aren't being betrayed at all. It would only be paranoia if you took it to the extreme."

"So you don't think I've taken it to the extreme?"

"Seriously, no I don't." She took a drag from her cigarette and made it a point to exhale the smoke downwind before bringing her penetrating gaze back to my face. "To begin with, you're here and I don't see anyone escorting you. Secondly, you aren't angry. Maybe a bit apprehensive... Some confusion... Yes, I can sense some definite confusion... But I don't really detect any fear. If anything you are somewhat curious about what I think about everything I've been told. All in all, I'd have to say you are probably a perfectly rational human being."

"Don't you need to show me some ink blots or play some word association games with me before you can draw that conclusion?"

"I'll just trust my instincts," she chuckled. "It would appear that you have as many misconceptions about psychiatrists as the general public has about Witches."

"So Ben told you about that." I offered the words more as an observation than a question.

"Of course, not that he needed to," she explained. "You've made no secret of the fact and you've attracted more than your share of media coverage from your involvement with the Major Case Squad."

She was correct. I had been the hot topic earlier this year in both print and broadcast media. Among the headlines were such things as 'SELF PROCLAIMED WITCH AIDS POLICE IN MANHUNT' and 'POLICE SEEK HELP FROM PAGAN PRACTITIONER'. There was usually a picture of me to accompany the story, so my faith and way of life weren't exactly secret. The worst had to have been the moniker coined by a local TV station news team. Ben, FBI Special Agent Constance Mandalay, and myself had been dubbed the 'Ghoul Squad.' That one, along with a particularly gruesome video clip of the three of us at a crime scene had even made it into the national media pipeline.

"So that doesn't bother you?" I asked.

"Should it?" She raised an eyebrow and questioned me as much with her gaze as her words.

"No." I shook my head. "But it did take some time to convince Ben, so I assumed maybe you might be…" I let my voice trail off as I searched for the least offensive phrase.

"…Just as closed minded?" She offered the verbiage to me. "My brother is peculiar that way."

"I thought so," I agreed. "Especially for a Native American."

"Benjamin never truly embraced his heritage," she told me. "Only on the surface, culturally perhaps, though not completely in that respect either. And especially not deep down. Not at a spiritual level. I don't fault him for it; he has his reasons. But, I can certainly see where it would seem odd to you."

It was obvious by the way she spoke that there was a history there that I was completely oblivious to. She didn't offer any further details, and I didn't ask.

"I didn't mean to pry."

"You didn't." She shook her head and gave a slight shrug as she crushed out the remains of her cigarette. "With that said, however, what do you say we go inside and see if we can't figure out just exactly what has been keeping you off balance as of late."

The remainder of my time spent with Helen Storm was relaxing if nothing else. She was so easy to talk to that I actually felt calm and even partially grounded while we chatted in her comfortable office. My early apprehension had melted quickly away, only to return for wholly separate reasons when the session came to an end.

While we hadn't stumbled across any great revelations, or uncovered any 'ooga-booga's' as she called them, lurking in my psyche, Helen felt that we had actually made some amount of progress. I just didn't know exactly how much or of what type that progress was, and she didn't elect to tell me.

Still, though it was hard for me to believe that simply talking with her for an hour could have such an effect, I wasn't about to knock it. Without a doubt, I was actually looking forward to my next appointment with her.

"Jeezus fuck! I can't believe this is happening!" an extremely agitated Ben Storm exclaimed as he came through my front door.

I'd barely managed to pull the barrier open in response

to the repeated jangle of the doorbell that was coupled with an impatient knock. His six-foot-six frame was already in forward motion the moment I turned the knob.

"Well, hello to you too," I said as I quickly sidestepped out of his way.

I was gnawing my way through yet another piece of nicotine gum, and for the moment, wasn't feeling nearly as jittery as I had fifteen minutes before. I'd been home for several uneventful hours now, and was actually in the process of throwing together dinner when Ben first assaulted the front bell. Felicity and I had intended to spend the evening going over our plans for the upcoming Yule ritual. Unfortunately, the frenzied tone of my friend told me that was about to change.

He flatly ignored my jibe. "Is Felicity home?"

"Not yet, why?"

"Shit. Has she got her cell phone with her?"

"Probably. What's going on, Ben?"

"Well, we can't wait, so you better call her and tell her to meet us then. Make sure you tell her to not even come home first." He shot his hand up to rub his neck as he began to pace. "Jeezus she's gonna freakin' kill me for this."

"Why not? Meet us where? What are you talking about?"

He didn't seem to hear me, and instead of answering simply muttered, "Dammit, white man, you are just too fucking spooky."

"BEN!" I exclaimed, raising my voice to capture his attention. "Would you mind telling me what you're going on about?"

He stopped and looked at me with a deadly serious gaze, then shook his head. "You know your little foray into the world of sick poetry?"

"What about it?"

"Well the handwriting might not have belonged to Paige Lawson, but it sure as shit belonged to Debbie Schaeffer."

"Debbie Schaeffer? Why does that name sound so familiar?"

"Because she was all over the news. She's the college cheerleader that went missing about two months ago."

D-E-A-D-I-A-M!
D-E-A-D-I-A-M!
What's that spell?
Dead I am!
Louder!
Dead I am!
One more time!
DEAD I AM!

The words rang inside my skull with painful clarity, and the exuberance of the morbid cheer now sharply obvious. Ben didn't need to say anything more for me to know that Debbie Schaeffer was no longer a missing persons case. Her legacy now belonged to homicide, and the Greater St. Louis Major Case Squad.

"Where should I tell her to meet us?" I asked quietly as I turned toward the phone.

It was going to be a very long night, in more ways than one.

CHAPTER 6

My wife's cell phone was either off or out of range, and based on the way her schedule often runs, I wasn't exactly certain when she would be home. Ben seemed almost in a panic, edged with a sense of urgency that he'd thus far left a mystery. He made it clear that he wasn't at all interested in waiting for her to call back and he insisted upon us leaving immediately. Knowing him like I did, I elected not to press for any further explanation until his adrenalin level started to drop off. As much as I hated to, I had done the only thing I could and left a quick message on Felicity's voice mail telling her to meet us at his house.

My keyed up friend was already navigating his van out of the subdivision before I could get fully into my seatbelt. The sun had fallen past the horizon almost an hour before, and the light of the waxing crescent moon was diffused into a weak halo by thin, wispy clouds that fell across it like a shroud of frost.

For some unknown reason, Ben cranked the van into a quick right turn onto a side street that was positioned diagonally across from our driveway. Considering where we were headed I thought it odd since it wasn't exactly the shortest route to the highway. Out beyond the windshield, darkness overwhelmed a no-man's land of unlit asphalt that stretched at regular intervals between the streetlamps. I caught only a brief glimpse of motion as a vehicle came barreling toward us from one of the puddles of blackness.

The van lurched left, then almost instantly to the right, narrowly missing a parked Thunderbird, and tossing me against my door just as I was about to snap the buckle of the shoulder harness into place. Judging from the blotches of primer decorating the otherwise darkly hued T-Bird we wouldn't have been its first scrape by far.

I hadn't remembered noticing the vehicle in our subdivision before, but there was something terribly familiar about it, although I couldn't put my finger on exactly what. Still, it was the kind of aggravating feeling that makes one say, 'Whoa, déjà vu.' The thought went as quickly as it came, however, since any further concentration on the subject was unceremoniously truncated by the sound of my friend's voice.

"Asshole!" Ben exclaimed the epithet as we narrowly avoided slamming into the oncoming news van. "Learn to fucking drive!"

I straightened in my seat and returned to the task at hand, quickly coupling the safety belt before my friend's legendary driving could send me tumbling again.

"So have you calmed down a bit?" I asked.

"Whaddaya mean?"

"I mean have you calmed down yet?" I repeated. "You just came through my front door like a runaway train and so far you've been a little short on explanations."

"I told you," he offered. "That handwriting sample matched up to Debbie Schaeffer."

"Correct me if I'm wrong," I started, "but if I'm understanding this turn of events correctly, Debbie Schaeffer has been murdered, right?"

"Yeah."

"Which by definition would make her dead already, right?"

"Oh, yeah, she's definitely dead. No two ways about that."

"Okay, then. So, I hate to sound cold," I remarked, "but what's the rush?"

"Simple," Ben returned. "Because of a chucklehead with a big mouth there's about to be a goddamned media circus bustin' out all over this thing."

"That's to be expected," I shrugged, not seeing the correlation. "It was news then, it'll be news now."

"Yeah, well did ya' happen to notice the logo on the side of the van that just tried to kill us? Whichever asshole leaked it also knew about the handwriting sample and decided to toss your name into the mix. The circus is headin' for YOUR friggin' front yard. Shit, I just barely managed to beat 'em there."

"So that's why you didn't want Felicity to go by the house."

"Exactly. I just hope she gets the message and doesn't blow it off." He let out a heavy sigh before continuing. "Look, it's bad enough that you're gettin' dragged into something like this again, especially now. I just want to at least make sure you don't get caught up in the hype this time."

"I don't see how you are going to keep that from happening, Ben."

"By doin' exactly what I'm doin'. Getting' you the hell outta there."

"Maybe that will work tonight, but what about tomorrow? And the next day? And the next?" I asked.

"There might not be a tomorrow, or a next day. My plan is to keep you as far away from this as possible," he told me.

"They'll just camp outside my door."

"Already on it. The coppers in Briarwood know what's up and they're gonna take care of it."

"Then why didn't they just take care of it now?"

"They are. We just gotta give 'em some time to do it."

"I don't think this is going to work, Ben."

"Well, we're gonna MAKE it work," he shot back.

"Think about it, Ben," I appealed. "You just said yourself that I'm being dragged into this. The damage has already been done. I think at this point it's out of your control."

"Not entirely."

"Wouldn't it be easier if I just made a statement to the press telling them I'm not involved in this investigation?" I offered.

"No reason for them to believe you," he answered. "Especially once they find out you're lyin'."

It took a moment for the balance of his comment to sink in. When it finally did, I almost stuttered my next question. "Just a second ago you said you were keeping me as far from this as possible. Did I miss something here?"

"I know how you are."

"What's that supposed to mean?"

"It means, number one, less than forty-eight hours ago you just showed up at a crime scene right out of the blue, so something tells me you just might do it again." He paused as he hooked the van through a quick right turn and down the ramp onto the highway. "And number two, you handed me a piece of paper with Debbie Schaeffer's handwriting on it that you say you wrote yourself. So, whether I like it or not, you're already connected to this through some of that weird ass *Twilight Zone* shit.

"Believe me, this is a decision that I did NOT want to make," he continued, "but the way I got it figured, I have two choices. Either I keep you as isolated as possible and not even let you know what is going on; or, I go ahead and bring you in on it right from the git'go and try to keep your involvement to a minimum.

"Considerin' what you've already done, and what I've seen you do in the past, I doubt the first choice has any chance of working, period. That leaves me with nothin' but option number two. So, I figure if I can exert some control over the contact you have with this case, then maybe you won't go off into la-la land on me."

"That's a pretty big maybe," I told him. "I don't exactly have control over it myself."

"That's why I want Felicity to meet us," he explained. "I want her there with you every goddamned second."

"She might not have that much control over it either." I shook my head at the comment. "You know, she's not going to be happy about this."

"Whaddaya mean 'not happy'?" he returned. "She's gonna be freakin' mad as hell. I just hope she leaves me some hair."

"I wouldn't count on it," I told him. "So what are you going to do? Sneak me in and out of my back door?"

"If I have to."

"You know, they'll get to me eventually."

"As long as that eventually is after it's all over and they've got no reason to put the spotlight on you, then I'm okay with it."

"I don't think we'll be that lucky," I sighed, "but I do appreciate the effort."

"Not a prob, Kemosabe."

Having dispensed with my confusion over the immediacy of the situation, I moved on to the next point that needed clarification for me. "So how did you make this connection to begin with?"

"Don't you watch the news, white man? Old dude out pickin' up aluminum cans stumbled across a body wrapped up in a plastic drop cloth this morning," he explained. "What was left of a body anyway— she'd been there for a while. M.E. says a couple of months probably.

"She was stuffed back up in the brush. Kinda isolated section out off of Three Sixty-Seven on the way to the Clark Bridge. Best guess is that's why she didn't get found until now."

Disgusting visions of a corpse left unattended for the better part of two months flitted through my head. Having never witnessed such a thing before in real life, the mental picture was an imagining based on remembrances of Hollywood special effects. The image was more than enough to turn my stomach, and I was afraid that the real thing might be far worse than anything I could conjure in my head.

I blinked back the imagining and willed away the sudden churning in my gut. "If she'd been out there that long, how'd you identify her so quickly?"

"We had our suspicions based on size, clothing, all that," he explained, "but positive ID came this afternoon from matching dental records. They were already on hand at the coroner's office from a check on another Jane Doe so there was no waiting."

"Okay, but all this still doesn't answer my first question. How did you make the connection with the handwriting?"

"Once this case went from a missing person to a homicide, and got turned over to the MCS, the investigation went in an entirely different direction.

"The real deal is that most of the time the victim knows the killer. It's standard procedure to look for anything in the personal effects that could give us a handle on who might've done it. So, we spent part of the afternoon back at her parents' house going over everything in her bedroom. The minute I looked in her notebooks and saw that curly-q thing on her I's, I knew. I had the graphologist in the crime lab verify it, but I knew."

"Did you find anything else worthwhile?" I asked solemnly.

"Not really. We got a couple of leads to run down but I don't think they'll go anywhere."

"So if you're pulling me in on this, why are we going to your house instead of the morgue or a crime scene or something?"

"Because right now I just want to keep you out of the spotlight while I figure out what to do," Ben answered. "Not to mention getting Felicity on board before I go any further with this."

"Have you figured out how you're going to do that yet?"

"I thought I might start with begging her not to kill me."

"What happened to the promise you made me, then?" Felicity asked in a carefully measured cadence that audibly displayed the weakening foundation of her composure. Her outrage was more than palpable; it was literally filling the room, and at the moment she was ground zero to what I'm certain was soon to be a catastrophic explosion of anger.

The three of us were seated around a small dining table that occupied one wall of Ben's kitchen at the rear of his house. Felicity was directly across from Ben, and I had taken up residence next to her.

My friend had at least been farsighted enough to send his wife and young son out to a local pizza parlor before Felicity had arrived. He had expected the worst, and it was looking very much like he was going to get it.

What had been a guarded smile on my wife's lips when she first walked in had morphed instantaneously into a thin-lipped frown the moment Ben outlined the reason for her being here. That frown had grown thinner and more severe with every word that came out of his mouth. The current set of her jaw was visible evidence of her tightly clenched teeth.

"I'm sorry, Felicity." He shook his head.

"You're sorry?" she spat incredulously. "You're SORRY? Is that the best you can come up with?"

"Whaddaya want me to say?" He held his hands out, palms upward as he shrugged surrender.

"Aye, for starters I want you to tell me this is all some sort of sick joke, then," she hissed.

"I wish I could, but…" He allowed his voice to trail off without completing the sentence.

"Then why don't you tell me you aren't really dragging him into another murder investigation."

"You might have noticed that he's not exactly kicking and screaming here."

"Are you two going to spend the whole night talking about me like I'm not even sitting here?" I interjected with a perturbed edge to my voice.

"Aye, you stay out of this," my wife commanded as she flashed an angry glance my way.

"Why would I stay out of it?" I shot back. "I'm the one that's being talked about here."

She ignored me and turned back to Ben. "You know how he is. But you're still bringing him into this even after everything that's happened."

"Well, if ya want the truth, he pretty much brought himself into it."

"He's right." I nodded assent.

"And how would that be?"

"Well you were there when he handed me that writing

sample," he answered.

"So?" she shot back. "You didn't have to take it."

"I didn't see YOU do anything to discourage it," he returned.

"Go n-ithe an cat thú is go n-ithe an diabhal an cat!" Felicity snarled.

"Excuse me?" Ben's face was washed over with abject confusion as he cast his questioning glance from me to my wife and then back again. "What the hell was that?"

"It's Gaelic. She just said something on the order of 'may the cat eat you, and may the cat be eaten by the devil'," I told him, having heard the Celtic epithet from her before.

"Do what?"

"It's an old traditional Irish curse," I responded coolly. "One that she's particularly fond of using when she's really, really angry."

"Fuckin' great," he huffed. "Now I got a 'curse' on me?"

"Not exactly, it's just…" I started to answer.

"Aye, I told you to stay out of it now," she ordered as she once again shot her glare my way.

"And I told you, I don't think so," I returned with my own stern look. "I'm not some little kid who can't make decisions for himself you know."

"Aye, I wouldn't be so sure about that. Look what you've done to yourself so far."

"You know as well as I do that I haven't got any control over this."

"Damn your eyes, but you do!" she snapped. "You didn't have to run off chasing a maniac in the middle of the night!"

"That's not what I'm talking about."

"But it's what I AM talking about, then! If I let Ben drag you into this you'll just do it again."

"That's what I'm tryin' to tell ya, Felicity," Ben interjected. "I'm not gonna let it go that far."

"Like you think you can stop it, then?" she chided.

"Why not? You think I can't?" he shook his head. "Look, Felicity, I wish it wasn't this…"

"Don't you 'look Felicity' me!" She cut him off. "We had an agreement!"

"I know," he pleaded. "But…"

"But what?!" she demanded. "It wasn't convenient for you, then?"

"No, it's…"

"Aye, what then? Your career is suddenly more important than your best friend's sanity?"

"Now dammit, you know better than that."

"I'm not so sure I do."

"Oh come on, Felicity…" I tried to wedge myself back into the dispute.

"No, Rowan." Ben held up his hand and sharply cut me off. "Stay out of it. This is between me and her."

"Excuse me?!" I rejoined. "Hello? What the hell has gotten into you two? You're arguing about ME here, so I think I have a right to voice my opinion."

He didn't seem to hear me. With each word, their voices had grown louder and even more strained. Ben's heretofore-defensive posture was starting to lean farther and farther toward the offensive. I could tell by the look on his face that there was next to nothing holding him back. My wife's hammering staccato of interruptions were taking a toll on his patience as the escalation of tempers progressed.

"So just what the hell are you trying to say here, Felicity?" Ben demanded.

"And what is it you think I'm sayin'?" she spat.

I desperately wanted to defuse the situation, but I had no real clue how I was going to do it. My temper was flaring just as much as theirs were, and that wasn't going to do any good. Thus far, every time I opened my mouth I only seemed to stoke the fire under them, and that blaze was starting to grow rapidly. In a very short time they'd reached a level where I wasn't entirely sure that they even acknowledged my presence in the room any longer.

It had now become plain to see that the issue was one that was most definitely between the two of them. It was also clear that it had festered for several months, and recent events were simply bringing it to a head.

"Goddammit, don't you think I have enough guilt over what happened on that bridge?"

"Well perhaps you should think about this all a bit harder then!"

The sharpness in their voices had intensified several-fold. I had no choice but to resign myself to the fact that we wouldn't get anywhere until this was played out to conclusion. Since they had drawn a bead on one another, for all intents and purposes ignoring me, I could only watch.

"What? You think I haven't?!"

"You're askin' to bring him into another investigation aren't you?!"

As angry as I was at being treated like a fifth wheel, I fought to stifle it. "Fine," I finally muttered. "Go ahead and kill each other. Give me a call when you're finished."

With that, I pushed my chair back from the table, placing some small, symbolic amount of distance between them and me. Hard as it was to stay out of it, I made a half-hearted attempt to distract myself by leafing through a cookbook that had been holding down a sheaf of papers on one corner of the table. However, just as I was afraid it would, the growing conflagration won out over recipes for such things as Beef Wellington and Broccoli-Onion-Cheese Casserole. Like a horrific train wreck that you just can't stop staring at, I again returned my attention to the duel between my best friend and my soul mate.

"Felicity, will you…"

"Will I what?! Stand by quietly and let you get my husband killed?!"

"Come on," he shot back. "You know that's not going to happen!"

"Aye, do I?!" She widened her eyes and shook her head. "Just what have we been discussing for the past several months then?"

"I know what we've been discussing, and YOU know I'm not going to let anything happen to him."

"Aye, just like you didn't let anything happen to him the last time?!"

"Dammit, you know I already blame myself for that!"

"As well you should!"

"Screw you!"

"Aye, like I'd give you the pleasure!"

A brief lull insinuated itself into the argument, brought on I can only assume, by the intensely personal level of the attacks. But, though it slipped suddenly in like the eye of a hurricane, its tenure was far shorter.

"Felicity, come on," he pleaded, making an attempt at reasoning with her. "Rowan is my best friend."

She wasn't having any of it. "You've an odd way of showin' it."

"Listen, do you really think…"

"What I really think is that you've lost your mind!"

"You know as well as I do…"

"What?! What do I know as well as you do?!"

"I'm tryin' to tell you…"

"Come on, then! Tell me! What is it?!"

Her relentless attacks finally brought the roiling argument beyond the red zone it had consistently occupied.

What had started as a simmer, then progressed into a rapid boil, now erupted like steam from a burst pipe.

"JEEZUS FUCKING CHRIST, Felicity! Will you just shut up for a minute and let me finish?!" Ben shouted in exasperation.

At that moment, for lack of a better description, my wife 'pulled her face off.' Her tight frown and locked jaw opened wide into a fanged maw as her own anger exploded outward.

"FINISH WHAT?! FINISH KILLING MY HUSBAND?!" she screamed as she physically rose from her chair. "DAMMIT, BEN, YOU PROMISED ME YOU WOULDN'T DO THIS!"

"SO I BROKE THE FUCKIN' PROMISE! DEAL WITH IT!" he returned in the same demonstrative tone, rising from his seat as well.

Even with the table between them, he towered over my petite wife. They locked spiteful gazes with one another and a tense silence slid smoothly in, as if to underscore their words.

A period of time that felt to be the greater portion of a quarter hour, but that in reality was surely less than one minute, oozed by as I watched them. Even with the quiet permeating the room, I didn't know if the conflict was fully over. I wasn't entirely sure that it would be to my advantage to make another try at interjecting my opinion, or if it would even be heard if I did.

Unfortunately, it wasn't by my own choice that I interrupted the terse mood that was now blanketing the scene. In fact, I didn't even realize I had done so until Ben and Felicity turned their stares away from one another and sighted them in on me.

The first sound I noticed came as a thin, rapid scratching that held an even and almost hypnotic rhythm.

The second sound came as the first abruptly ended, then was replaced by a rustling of paper— like the sound of a page being flipped.

The third sound announced its presence as a recurrence of the first, matching rhythm perfectly with the point where it had suddenly ended.

I didn't want to look. I already knew what I was going to see, but I also knew that I had little choice in the matter. I followed their gazes down to the tabletop and joined them in watching as my left hand methodically defaced the pages of the comb-bound cookbook— scribbling quickly and evenly across the paper of its own accord.

With a little concentration, focusing on the fluid scribbling and ignoring of the preprinted words that made up the recipes, one could make out the repetitious couplets.

> Hey, hey, hey, whaddaya say!
> Don't ya know I'm dead today!
> Hey everyone, I'm here to say!
> I'm dead today! I'm dead today!
> Gotta let Rowan come out and play!
> Gotta let him do it 'cause I'm dead today!

I looked back up as Ben huffed out a haggard breath and turned his gaze back to Felicity. My hand continued to move, though it now seemed to be slowing and had begun to falter at the end of each line. An effect, I assume, of the fact that I was now fully aware of its activity.

In a calm voice my friend finally asked, "You wanna keep arguin' about this or you wanna help me."

My wife kept her eyes locked with mine and let out her own sigh. "It looks like I don't really have a choice."

CHAPTER 7

The hands of the clock were firmly pressed up against midnight when we arrived at the St. Louis City Morgue. Situated on Clark Avenue, it was flanked by Police Headquarters on one side, an on-ramp to Highway Forty on the other, and across the street from the rear entrance of City Hall. All in all, the structure was less than obtrusive in appearance— simple brick and mortar construction with nothing that would make it stand out, architecturally at least— against the rest of the buildings in the area. In reality, there would be nothing outwardly distinctive about it at all if it weren't for the small, black-on-white, block lettered sign above the main entrance that stated simply, MEDICAL EXAMINER.

Even though it was clearly marked, it was easily possible for someone to drive past the building on an almost daily basis and not even realize just exactly what it was. It looked like nothing more than just another office building, and even the sign above the door didn't truly betray the fact that inside was the final stop for those departed from this world under suspicious circumstances. In fact, it was more than likely that the majority of the civilian population of St. Louis didn't even know that this was more that just a business office, it was the City Morgue.

But, unlike the majority, I knew.

I'd been here more than once, and each time when I had taken my leave, I'd been completely devoid of any desire to ever return. Still, it seemed that I always came back whether I truly wanted to or not. Even worse, it was sometimes at my own behest.

Like right now.

It had taken a good while to talk Ben and Felicity into allowing me to come here and view the remains of Debbie Schaeffer. Neither of them was particularly keen on the concept, least of all my wife, so she had taken the most convincing by far. If that weren't bad enough, my friend was absolutely no help. I had been completely on my own in accomplishing the task.

I suppose in some ways it was understandable. For one thing, Ben was already treading on thin ice with her, and both their tempers were only now beginning to cool as it was. Add to that the fact that my coming into direct contact with the young woman's remains didn't exactly fit with his concept of keeping me as far removed from the investigation as possible, and there you had it. The combination was easily more than enough to make him unwilling to help me plead my case.

Considering the fragility of the current truce between Felicity and he, I can't say that I blamed him.

Not much, anyway.

I might have simply given up, gone ahead without her, and then suffered the consequences later if it hadn't been for one simple fact— I needed Ben in order to get into the morgue, and his tenuous agreement with the idea was contingent upon her being present to keep an 'ethereal eye' on me just in case I started to slip.

At one point, in a failed attempt to change his mind, I had made the mistake of again mentioning the fact that Felicity may not be able to do anything about it whether she was there or not. For that remark I promptly ended up working double time not only to win over my wife, but to re-convince my friend as well.

When all was said and done, it was already half past eleven when we climbed into Ben's van and made the trek downtown. The intensity of my own stress level finally decreased a fraction as soon as we were under way. Unfortunately, the quiet ride also allowed for earlier forgotten nuisances to return full force.

I was completely out of nicotine gum, and my inexplicable desire for a cigarette was now reaching unnatural proportions. What was worse, I still had no idea why the cravings had come upon me. I hadn't even been this bad when I was actually addicted to them. It was becoming increasingly harder for me to keep the outward manifestations at bay. At the moment I was only slightly to one side of irritable and I was traveling directly toward it at high speed.

The impending collision wasn't going to be good at all.

"You aren't planning on doin' any of that hocus pocus stuff where you become 'one with the corpse' are you?" Ben asked me as he levered the gearshift into park and switched off the van's ignition.

"That's not something I actually 'plan,' Ben," I answered with an impatient edge to my voice. "It just has a tendency to happen."

"It might not if you kept yourself grounded," my wife expressed.

"I do."

"Yeah, right." Her voice held more than a hint of sarcasm.

"Don't even go there."

Felicity paused for a moment, obviously taken aback by the sudden bite of my words. "Excuse me?"

"Forget it," I answered, shaking my head. "Just forget it."

Emotionally, I was poised to bite her head off. Logically, I knew she was correct and that I had no valid reason to do so. But, that bit of reality didn't make the urge any easier to quell.

I simply couldn't afford to take it any further. If I let the comment bait me, it would only serve to re-kindle the argument we'd just barely settled less than thirty minutes ago. With all of us on edge as we were, such an altercation could turn ugly fast.

Given my current state, *very* ugly, *very* fast.

"Look," Ben interjected. "I've had enough arguin' for one night. Now, the last time we were here I seem to remember you havin' to come outside to get away from all the ooga-booga's or whatever you see in there."

"Lost souls," I offered flatly.

"Fine. Lost souls, ooga-booga's, whatever, it's all the same to me 'cause I can't see 'em. I just wanna know if all that is gonna send you over the edge or somethin' like last time."

"They weren't the real problem last time," I explained, fighting to keep the annoyance out of my voice. "It was the fact that I was channeling the actual death of a victim that…"

"Don't split hairs with me, Row," he interrupted. "I need to know whether to take you in there or start the fuckin' van and get outta here right now."

"We already talked about this back at the house, Ben," I rebutted harshly.

"Yeah, well B.F.D. Is it gonna be a problem or not?"

I gave up and told him what he wanted to hear. "They won't be a problem."

Apparently, he was a little short on trust at the moment.

"Is he yankin' my chain?" He directed his question to Felicity.

"If we take some precautions, I think it will be okay."

"You THINK it'll be okay?"

"Aye, what do you want? I don't do this every day then." A mild spark of anger flashed in her voice. She was tired; we all were. Her own irritability was showing just as Ben's was, and I'm certain my uncharacteristic moodiness wasn't helping in the least. As I had suspected it would, the night was getting longer by the moment.

"Okay, okay," Ben shot back defensively. "I'm not exactly an expert on this *Twilight Zone* crap myself y'know."

"Are we going to sit here and fog up the windows or are we going to go in?" I asked impatiently.

"When I'm ready," Ben returned. "Why don't you tell me again just what it is that you're expecting to find out?"

"We've already discussed this."

"Yeah, and we're discussin' it again."

Truth was, I didn't really have a good answer for the question. All I knew was that someone was communicating with me from the other side, and all indicators pointed to that someone being Debbie Schaeffer. Coming here was the only way I knew to 'complete the call,' so to speak.

"I don't know." I gave him the only answer I could. "A clue or something. You know, it's not like this is the first time we've ever done this."

"Yeah, I know," he affirmed, "but in the times I've seen you do this I've also seen it go south. Way south. You've almost died on me twice. Three's a charm, white man."

"Think positive," I grumbled.

"I am thinking positive. I'm positive I ain't willin' to trade your life for a handful of flaky clues in a murder investigation."

"Look," I sighed, desperate to at least get out of the confines of the van. "It took me half the night to convince you two that we should come down here, so can we just dispense with this never ending 'committee meeting'?"

"I just wanna make sure we're doin' the right thing here," my friend expressed. "'Cause somethin' in my gut tells me I should put some distance between you and this place and not look back. I tend to trust my gut."

"That's just you being overprotective, AGAIN," I spat.

"There's no such thing as being overprotective when dyin' is one of the possibilities."

"Well, that's why you wanted Felicity here, right?"

"Don't be dragging me into this, then," my wife declared. "I want to hear you rationalize this too."

I hadn't been backed completely into a corner, yet, but it was getting very close. I'd had my fill of the ping-pong oration I'd had to repeatedly deliver just to get this far. I was exhausted. I was ready to kill for a cigarette. Moreover, I was getting very tired of being treated like a child. My resolve was set in concrete, and I wasn't about to let them make me turn back now.

I knew that exploding wasn't going to get me anywhere, even though it was what my knee jerk impulse was telling me to do. I drew in a deep breath and held it for a moment before exhaling heavily. In my head I'd made a connection that they apparently had not. Thus far, I'd managed to hold it back as my one trump card and it appeared that now would be a good time to toss it onto the table.

"Look," I verbally threatened, "we can either do it this way, right now, or we can just wait until I go out sleepwalking again and see where that takes us."

"What's that got to do with it?" My wife shook her head slightly as confusion contorted her brow.

"Yeah, white man," Ben added, "you wanna expand on

that?"

"Debbie Schaeffer went missing two months ago, right?"

"Yeah, so?" he returned.

"So, I started sleepwalking two months ago. You do the math."

My friend puffed out his cheeks and expelled a deep breath as he sent one large hand up to massage the back of his neck.

"Shit. I just can't win with you," was all he said.

Luck seemed to be on our side for a change, as Ben knew the security guard on duty for this shift, so there were no prying questions or even odd looks. The two simply exchanged pleasantries, including what I'm certain was a tired joke about cadavers escaping, and then we were in. The watchman seemed perfectly content to return to the game of solitaire that was burning itself into the screen on the computer at the reception desk.

The dim lighting at this time of night lent an eerie feel to the corridors of the City Morgue. Pale shadows tempted your mind into playing sadistic tricks on your eyes, seeing movement where there was nothing to move.

Seeing light where there was dark.

Seeing dark where there was light.

In reality, some of those sadistic tricks weren't tricks at all, but anomalies within the veil between the worlds.

If they chose to listen, even those with closed minds could hear the tortured cries of spirits in transition— some in acceptance of their fate, some in utter disbelief, but, all with one thing in common. Each of them was trapped between the worlds of life and death, never making it fully to the other side.

Unfortunately for me, I didn't have the luxury of that simple choice. A relentless cacophony echoed from the walls to assault me even before we passed through the door. It was much like walking into a crowded party; only this party was one where most of the guests are screaming and sobbing with pain. It took almost everything I had to put up a mental shield and block them out. Even then they remained, a static-plagued radio, tuned between stations and set at low volume, interrupted every now and again with a burst of angry noise.

A brief glance told me that Felicity was feeling a similar buzz inside her own head.

Earlier this year I had actually spent the night in this place when the worst snowstorm in a decade had brought Saint Louis to all but a complete standstill. Ben and I had been trapped here with the Chief Medical Examiner and a severely charred corpse whose spirit staunchly refused to move on. My ethereal dealing with that victim was yet another piece of the puzzle that made up the current fractured state of my psyche. I can say without a doubt that to date, that had been the longest night of my life.

In the back we were met by the night morgue attendant. Ben simply flashed his badge and told him that we needed to view the remains of Debbie Schaefer. The pallid young man never even uttered a word, and simply handed a clipboard to my friend so he could sign us in. That completed, he mutely led us into the cold storage area, flipping on the overhead lights as we entered.

The right wall of the tiled room was lined with rectangular stainless steel doors. Each of them was a gateway to an individual compartment where a corpse would spend its stay with the Medical Examiner. On the opposite wall there were two large sinks, each equipped with a table capable of holding a body. Here were also such things as examination gloves, and implements I wasn't the least bit interested in knowing the purpose of.

At the back of the room was another set of doors which led, as I was told later, to the garage which was accessible from the back of the building. This was where recovered bodies were brought in, and would begin their journey through the various stages of the postmortem process.

The attendant took us to a wheeled table positioned near the individual storage compartments. On it was a rubberized body bag, an identification tag affixed to the heavy-duty zipper pull. The faint malodor of decay had been noticeable ever since we entered the back area of the building. Upon entry into the cold room the intensity of the strange funk began to increase several fold. Now, as our proximity to the remains was within a matter of feet, the foulness was thick in the atmosphere.

"That's great, thanks," Ben told the attendant who was just starting to pull on a pair of latex gloves. "We can handle it from here."

The young man stopped in the middle of sheathing his hands. Frozen in place like a statue he simply stared at Ben as if waiting for him to say that he was only kidding.

"Really." My friend nodded and coughed, wrinkling his nose at the smell. "We'll call you when we're finished."

I was right there with my friend, and I'm sure Felicity wasn't far behind. My stomach was already starting to churn and it was all I could do to keep from screwing up my face in disgust.

Giving a slight shrug the attendant pointed toward the sinks and displaying perceptible effort, muttered, "Gloves."

With the one syllable utterance out of the way, he left us

alone in the chilled room.

"That was bizarre," Felicity commented quietly after the young man disappeared out the door.

"If ya' ask me, all of 'em that work here are fuckin' nut cases," Ben asserted as he stepped across the room and began pulling a pair of oversized latex gloves onto his hands. With a nod, he indicated for us to do the same then turned his attention directly on my wife. "You said there were some precautions we need to take for this?"

"Do you think he's going to come back anytime soon?" She cocked her head toward the door.

For some wholly bizarre and unknown reason I took great notice of the way her hair almost shimmered in the light when she tossed her head. The perfection of her auburn mane as it cascaded down her back in a fiery plume of loosely spiraling curls. The way it softly brushed against the ivory skin of her neck when she tilted her head to the side.

"You mean mister personality? Not likely," he answered.

"It would be best if he doesn't," she continued. "Because what I need to do might look a bit strange to someone who doesn't understand."

"What, like he's not strange enough on his own?" Ben asked rhetorically.

"Aye, but that's beside the point."

I watched her closely— observing the way the layered cut of her hair framed her face and accented her dainty features. I was amazed that I had never noticed it in such intense detail before.

"So how strange are you gonna get?"

"Not terribly. I just need to cast a spell."

"Cast a spell? I thought you guys didn't do shit like that."

"No," Felicity explained, "we DO cast spells, just not the way most people think we do."

"So you're not gonna whip out some bat wings and crap like that, right?"

"Just some salt, Ben."

She used the back of her hand to brush a tousle of her feathery coif back from the side of her face, and I was entranced as she let it linger there.

"Salt?" he queried with a shake of his head.

"Salt."

"Where are you gonna get salt?"

Felicity rummaged about in one of the many pockets of her photo vest and when she withdrew her hand she was holding some individual condiment packets of the substance. "Not exactly sea salt, but it'll do."

I felt a rush of excitement course through my body and my skin literally prickled with the energy of overwhelming desire. I wanted to simply reach out and touch her.

"You always carry that stuff around with you?"

"Pretty much."

"What, so you can do shit like this?"

"No, not really. I just happen to like salt and you don't always get any when you order at a busy drive-thru."

I was beginning to have trouble containing the intense burst of longing for the woman in front of me. I couldn't turn my gaze away, and if I continued to stare I was certain to embarrass myself.

"Yo, Rowan!" My friend's urgent and concern-tinged voice slapped me hard in the face, breaking the trance. I felt his hand on my shoulder as he started to shake me lightly. "You alright? You aren't goin' all *Twilight Zone* are you?"

"Wh-wh-what? No… No, I'm okay," I managed to stammer as I blinked.

I had no idea what had just happened. I did know that I wasn't about to tell the two of them that I had been standing there having some sort of uncontrolled psychosexual fantasy about my wife's hair. That was odd enough in and of itself, but considering where we were and what we were supposed to be doing, I was certain they would have me committed immediately. I wouldn't blame them if they did.

I was, to say the least, more than a little disturbed by the incident, but I tried not to let it show. I made a mental note to mention it to Helen Storm during my next session with her. I was really beginning to wonder if my sanity had finally fled in a futile attempt to save itself.

"Aye, help me out here," Felicity demanded as she struggled to move the wheeled table out from the wall.

Ben stepped over to help her, and after a brief moment of struggling himself, located the parking brake and released it. The two of them moved the gurney out, and at my wife's direction centered it in the room before locking it down once again.

"What else ya need me to do?" Ben asked.

"I'm a bit disoriented," she returned as she looked around, trying to gain her bearings. "Which direction is east?"

"Shit, ummmmm," he muttered as he spun around as well, slowly motioning his arms in various directions while mumbling aloud to himself. "Clark runs east and west, building faces Clark. Highway would be there…

Headquarters…" he stopped and pointed at a wall, "this way."

"Okay." Felicity nodded as she directed her attention toward me and motioned for me to come over. "Rowan, you come stand here, then."

I did as I was instructed, still feeling somewhat wistful at the sight of her and that auburn mane.

"Ben, you stand on the other side here," she instructed.

"Alright." He moved into position. "What now?"

"Just be quiet and don't open that bag until I tell you to."

"This isn't gonna get all hinky is it?"

Felicity had already stepped behind him, facing toward the east and was tearing open the salt packets. "Just be quiet and do what I tell you to do."

"Yeah. Great," he answered flatly, then mumbled, "Jeezus I can't believe I'm doin' this."

Felicity carefully began sprinkling the salt along an arc as she walked slowly clockwise around us. She would stop only briefly at each of the quarters— south, west, and north— and give a slight nod of her head, silently acknowledging the elements. By the time she made her way back around to the east, she had emptied a half dozen of the small paper packets onto the floor in a rough circle, leaving only a small opening unsalted. Though it was not visibly perceptible, the energy of the purified barrier was something I could easily feel.

In a fluid motion my wife moved smoothly deosil— or clockwise— around us a second time. Holding her arms outstretched she moved silently until she was once again before the small opening where she started. After a slight pause she repeated the circuit twice more.

"What's she doin'?" Ben whispered the question to me from across the wheeled table.

"Cleansing the work area," I replied in my own hushed tone.

As Felicity came to rest at the end of the third revolution she brought her arms down, around, and back up in front of her as if gathering something unseen into a bundle. Then she forcefully pushed her palms outward, casting the invisible detritus she had gathered through the opening she had left just for this purpose. Immediately upon completing this task she sprinkled the remains of a salt packet on the floor at her feet, effectively closing the now purified circle.

"Is that it?" Ben voiced.

"Shhhh!" my wife warned as she remained at rest—arms at her sides, facing east with her back to us, and her head bowed.

He started to retort but halted before uttering a sound as I slowly shook my head and mouthed the word, "Don't." Instead he simply rolled his eyes and allowed his shoulders to fall slightly.

I could sense that Felicity had fallen into an easy rhythm with her breathing, taking deep lungfuls of air in through her nose and exhaling softly out through her mouth. In an almost symbiotic reaction, my own breathing slipped into time with hers.

After a short meditation, she slowly raised her arms from her sides, palms upward then allowed her chin to rise from her chest bringing her face upturned toward the ceiling.

"Lord and Lady spin about," she began in a quiet, singsong voice, "Watch over us this night throughout. In the dark ONE journeys long, in search of answers hidden strong. Please guide him through and guard his fate, for on this side, I shall wait.

"Please lead me through these passing hours, and grant to ME Your protective powers. For here and now are spirits still, kept at bay by MY own will. From head to toe, above and below, watch over him as west winds blow. From earth to air, sky to ground, keep Rowan safe and well and sound."

Chilled silence filled the room as her last words faded. Ben stood staring at me, mute, but questioning with his eyes. I'm not entirely sure what he had been expecting to happen in conjunction with this bit of SpellCraft, but he seemed almost disappointed. His face visibly betrayed his reaction to what must have been anticlimactic in a host of ways. The sort of letdown that comes from seeing real WitchCraft firsthand, but only after first being saturated with years of too many Hollywood special effects and inaccurate portrayals by the entertainment industry.

I couldn't place all of the blame in their laps, however. Even though they were only partially connected with my spiritual path, one could be certain that the bizarre psychic phenomena that seemed to plague me on a regular basis had helped to cloud his perceptions as well.

"Like I've told you before," I whispered in answer to his unasked question, "casting a spell for a Witch is pretty much just like praying is for a Christian."

Felicity had left her station at the eastern point of the circle and had now sidled up next to me. I felt her right palm press against my own and her fingers intertwine with mine in a vise-like grip. Immediately I felt the chaotic energy within my body connect with hers as she took firm hold of my ethereal self. She simply ignored my own earthly bond, fleeting and tenuous as it was, and forcibly grounded me through her own solid coupling with this plane of existence.

She looked into my eyes, silently daring me to even try letting go of her hand, and then glanced over to Ben with a look of extreme concentration furrowing into her brow.

"Aye," she said with a nod, "now you can open it."

CHAPTER 8

If nothing else, I was most definitely no longer fantasizing about my wife's hair.

The malodorous stench of decay spewed outward in a cloud of invisible, but uniquely vile smelling gases. They escaped the body bag in an instantly rising plume that marched lockstep directly behind the zipper pull as Ben tugged it open.

The noxious vapor forced the three of us to cough and twist our heads away as it pushed its way into our nostrils. I felt a column of bile searing upward in my throat, and I swallowed hard to force it back into the depths from which it came. My churning stomach did a somersault and twisted into a tight knot as it threatened to evacuate what little contents it held.

I shifted my watery-eyed glance between Ben and Felicity and saw that they were in no better shape than me. My wife was seriously green and Ben's head was cocked away with his eyes tightly shut. He had already seen this at least once, and he didn't appear to be particularly interested in a repeat viewing.

"Awww, Jeeeezzz…" my friend's voice trailed off as he mumbled.

Two months, fluctuating temperatures, and even some

of nature's children had been hard at work on the earthly remains of Debbie Schaeffer. What was left of her body was still clad in the tattered leavings of a pair of blue jeans and a sweatshirt that bore the partial logo of Oakwood College.

The clothing had already begun along the same journey of decomposition as the rest, and was heavily stained with the purge fluids that escape the confines of the flesh during decay. The fibers had already begun to break down in places, creating large holes in the garments. One side of the sweatshirt was particularly desiccated, revealing a substantial portion of her ribcage and even some remaining mold-covered flesh. One running shoe still hugged the remnants of her right foot, but the other was gone, leaving the left exposed and skeletonized within the disintegrating weave of a white cotton sock.

I suddenly remembered having once seen a cable television documentary about forensic pathology and a place in Tennessee nicknamed 'The Body Farm'. While a plot of land where decomposing human cadavers are studied wasn't exactly high on my list of things to recall, the sight before me triggered the forgotten memory and a handful of facts returned to the forefront of their own accord.

What came to me immediately was the recollection that there were basically five states the human body would go through post mortem— fresh/autolysis; bloating/putrefaction; wet decay/skin slippage and fluid purging; dry decay/partial mummification; and finally, skeletonization.

This young woman's remains represented at least four of these five stages, and were fully embroiled in continuing the process, held off only slightly by the gelid atmosphere of the cold room.

What came to me next was that these stages could be hindered or hastened by a variety of factors such as temperature, humidity, and even body type.

Debbie Schaeffer had been dumped in the woods, fully

clothed, and wrapped in plastic sheeting. To the best of the Medical Examiners determination, it had been sometime around the end of October or beginning of November. The temperatures had ranged from well below freezing, right up into the sixties and even seventies over the past two months. Rain had fallen. Sun had shone. Opportunistic predators from mammal to insect had come and gone. Mother nature had worked to reclaim what, in the end, rightfully belonged to her.

This young woman had literally become a self-contained forensic pathology specimen suitable for inclusion in a textbook. I had to consciously remind myself that she had once been whole and full of life, not the putrefied and skeletonized mass I had before me now. It wasn't easy.

"Jeeeezzz, white man," Ben sputtered, "you wanna do your thing so we can close this up. I'm about ready to spew."

His words rattled in my ears, and registered as little more than background noise.

I was already doing my thing.

A calm, like I had not felt in more than a year, fell over me. I had all but forgotten what it felt like to be fully and completely grounded. I squeezed Felicity's hand tight and basked in the vibrant flow of energy passing between us. Almost instantly I found myself wishing I could remain this way indefinitely.

Unconsciously, I drew in a deep breath and sputtered as I immediately regretted the action. After a quick shake of my head, I pulled myself back together and focused on the task that brought me here.

Slowly, I brought my free hand up and reached outward. I could feel a growing static electricity-like attraction flowing between Debbie Schaeffer's remains and myself. The ethereal magnetism took hold, and like the opposite poles of magnets, sucked my palm downward until it brushed against a tangled mass of blonde hair that had shrunk away from the skull.

Where am I?
Darkness underscored by a faint, high-pitched whine.
I scream... Or do I? I hear nothing.
What is happening to me?
An explosion of blinding light.
Blink.
Psychedelic spots before my eyes.
Staring into nothingness.
Darkness.
A second bright blast.
Blink.
My heart races.
The kaleidoscope goes on.
Darkness... Darkness...
Yet another sudden infusion of brightness.
More spots in the mix.
Darkness fading to a soft light.
A silhouette moving in the shadows.
Visceral fear.

My ethereal self jerks quickly back as the most recent experiences of Debbie Schaeffer's life— and perhaps death— assault me without apology. Her fear wraps its icy grip about my heart and begins to squeeze mercilessly. I have no idea what I am going to see, but I am certain it will be less than pleasant.

Felicity's grip on me remains steadfast; I don't think I could break free of her even if I wanted to. As I force myself back forward into the ethereal quest for answers, I feel a wholly familiar presence in the room. In the here and now— in the land of the living. But I could tell beyond a shadow of a doubt that it no longer belonged on this side of the bridge.

Phasing in and out of synchronization with time, the entity's feminine voice rings directly into my ear.

"Well, look who finally decided to show up. I've been waiting for you, you know, Rowan. What took you so long?"

Before I can respond, Debbie Schaeffer turns her attention elsewhere. She is apparently observing something that I myself cannot see. She continues her recitation off in the distance, speaking as much to herself as to me.

"What's he doing now? Oh man, is he kidding? Would you look at that, Rowan? Is he an idiot or what? I mean it's not like it's rocket science to pick out an outfit, you know. He's got to be color blind or something."

I have no idea what she is talking about.
I cannot see what she is seeing.
The volume of her voice fades from high to low, and then low to high as it moves about my head in an insane demonstration of stereophonic principles. The disconcerting pattern of her speech continues to shift in and out of time between planes of existence.

"Get a grip, will'ya? Those red shoes don't go with that skirt. The black ones you moron, the BLACK ones!" Her voice seems directed at someone unseen by me.
"I don't think he can hear me. Hell, I can't even hear me. What do you think, Rowan? Can he hear me?"

"Who?" I ask aloud. "Tell me WHO can't hear you."
"What's that?" Ben's voice shifts past me in a discordant echo.

Oh God, what is happening?
Where am I?
Absolute terror burns its way into my chest.

I can see only a silhouette in the dim light. I can't make out any features.

An explosion of brightness sears my eyes.

I'm blind.

I try to scream, but it catches in my throat and rests there for me to choke on.

I can feel the burn of tears welling in my eyes.

An angry voice exclaims, "Fuck! Not again! STOP IT! Your makeup is running!"

"I don't care. It serves you right you weirdo. Oh, no way. Are you blind? That lipstick is way too dark. Look at me you idiot." **Debbie Schaeffer's voice vibrates inside my head as she admonishes some unseen figure.**

She turns her attention back to me for a moment. "Can you believe this guy, Rowan?"

Before I can even begin to answer she is yelling at him again.

"Go ahead, make me look like a circus clown you dipshit!"

Her voice bounces around inside my skull, trying on my psyche for size. From one moment to the next, I am she and she is me. We are one and the same. We are neither and separate. We phase in and out of one another like playing cards shuffled into a deck.

She stands at my shoulder.

She faces me.

She steps into me.

She steps out of me.

She runs to the brink of a distant unseen abyss and casts deprecating observations into its depths.

The darkness enveloping me bleeds black, then suddenly shifts to blue grey.

Then blackness again.

She jumps in and out of my head as if trying to find the most comfortable spot to reside.

I try not to fight the process, but wonder if the pain is truly worth what I may eventually discover from her— if anything at all.

She settles in behind my eyes and the landscape becomes a muted haze. I am beginning to see the faint outlines of what she sees in vivid color.

Together, we watch with growing interest as the shadow moves about.

Who are you?
Why are you touching me?
No! Please, no?!
Oh God, please don't!

A violent thrust from nowhere purges Debbie Schaeffer from me. The suddenness of it all is even more painful than her careless entries and exits had been. The scene changes point of view and I see a young woman clad in a party dress. She is draped limply in a chair. Her face is a palette of colors, painted haphazardly on delicate features.

Visceral, primal thoughts race through my head.

Electrically charged sexual desire wells within me, coursing throughout my body with an animalistic passion.

The feeling is unnatural and foreign.

The intensity of the desire I am feeling frightens me, but I cannot back away from it.

In the real world I am disgusted by something dark that permeates the arousal.

In the real world I begin to feel physically sickened by the perversity that is woven within the shroud of lust.

Between the worlds I am engaged by it and craving

more.

> *Oh Jesus! She is just so gorgeous!*
> *She's so close! So close!*
> *Damn! She's almost perfect!*
> *Muted darkness.*
> *Explosive blinding light.*
> *Muted darkness.*
> *Explosive blinding light.*
> *Muted darkness.*
> *Jesus...So close.*
> *My desire is stiffening, and I can't wait any longer.*
> *I must fulfill the need.*
> *Quench the fire.*

On this side of reality I deny the urge to take myself in hand. In the darkness between, I am unable to resist.

> *"Dammit, Rowan! Don't let him do that to you!" Debbie's voice scrapes past my ears with anger charged static.*

> *Panting...*
> *Heart racing...*
> *Quickening...*
> *She's so close...*
> *She's the closest yet...*
> *If only she was really her...*
> *So close...*
> *Quickening...*
> *Faster...*

Again, Debbie's voice punches inward and wrestles me away, evicting the sudden perversion from its warm and comfortable place in my head. For all the disconcerting imagery she brings with her, I am thankful for the rescue. Her voice is frenzied and caustic— aimed at me, him, whomever. She slips into the three-piece suit of my Id, ego, and superego taking absolutely no care. The intensity of her emotion painfully strains the seams of the garment that is I.

"Look at me shithead. I must look like a two-year old who got into mommy's makeup. Are you blind or are you just stupid? How in the hell can that be getting you off?"

She slips out without warning and stands before me. I feel the hard sting of her palm against my cheek. "Don't you ever do that again! It's GROSS! You're supposed to be HELPING me, Rowan!"

Her voice calms, and she studies me carefully.

"Okay. That's better. So, now that you're back, you want to tell me what is up with this guy, Rowan?"

Again, she flits away before I can answer. I am left standing in the cold darkness.

I hear her distant tenor echo in the abyss.

"Hey, you! Perv boy! Are you listening to me?"

She returns as quickly as she left, making my stomach churn as she turns my neural pathways into an amusement park ride.

Her momentary occupation of my conscious ends as she is bludgeoned from behind and thrown forcibly into the cold.

My hand is warm and wet...
Panting.
Heart still racing.
I'm spent...for now.
I tug at my zipper.
She's so beautiful.

She's so very close.
If only she really was her.
Then...
Then she would be perfect.

I tap directly into the solid grounding Felicity is forcing upon me and fight to expand my 'self' outward. My growing consciousness forces the vile invader from within me. But it isn't enough. I'm outnumbered and each time I chase one of them away, another comes from behind to occupy the space. I struggle to follow the tennis match going on between the hemispheres of my brain.

For one brief instant, calm ensues and I find myself face to face with a petite blonde.

She strikes a pose then begins to dance about.

Hey, hey, hey, whaddaya say!
Rowan's here, now we can play!
Hey, hey, hey, whaddaya say!
Look at me, I'm dead today!
Take a good look, don't you turn away!
Just look at me, Rowan, I'm dead today!

She stops and glares at me with a serious frown.

So what are you gonna do about it?

"Rowan?" Ben's voice slides in behind the morose prose. "What are you seeing? Tell me what you're seeing."

Before I can open my mouth to answer, my 'self' is hijacked yet again.

"Oh yeah, that's a great dress, asshole— if I was going to some kind of retro masquerade prom, MAYBE.

Who the hell wears that much puke green taffeta? It makes me look like a bridesmaid from some kind of wedding from hell." She unleashes a verbal assault then whispers into my ear, "Can you believe this guy, Rowan? He's got the fashion sense of a rock."

> *I just can't even move.*
> *I'm just so tired.*
> *Don't know why.*
> *I'm so scared.*
> *What is he going to do to me?*

"But, you know, that dress is just plain ugly."

> *What is he doing back there?*
> *Oh God no, please…*
> *I'm sobbing inside.*

"Will you quit messing with my hair you freak?" She shifts her view and yells angrily into the darkness, "Can't you see that you're scaring me?
"Yeah, that's it. Come around here where we can see you."
She turns her attention to me with a quickly uttered instruction, "Watch close, Rowan, here he comes."

> *Blinding light.*

"Dammit! Did you see him, Rowan? Did you?"

I see nothing but darkness.

"All right you weirdo quit messing with my feet. Get up and turn around so Rowan can see you, fetish boy."

What is he doing now?
OUCH! That hurts!
What is he doing to my feet?
Why?
My heart rattles in my breast.
I can hardly breathe.
I'm so frightened.

"Look at that. The moron can't even tell left from right.

"Move so Rowan can see you. Yeah you, you fathead, Rowan needs to see you.

"Oh, this is good. Look at this, Rowan. Sequined pumps. SEA FOAM GREEN sequined pumps. And would you look at how high those heels are! Where the hell did he get those things? Now I ask you, do I look like I have Barbie feet?"

A sudden flicker of light.
Psychedelic spots again.

"I think he's got a wiring problem in that place. The lights kept doing that."

Another bright flicker.

Pain rakes through my grey matter like a cheap wine hangover as the sudden switch of personalities occurs again. The throb hammers in my temples as the trio of alternating psyches begin a knock-down, drag-out battle for possession of me.

Oh sweet Jesus, she's so beautiful.
She's so close.

So close...

> *"What are you doing?*
> *Please, no.*
> *PLEASE let me go?!"*
> *Please don't put that in my mouth.*
> *Please no!*
> *Somebody help me, PLEASE!*
> *Gagging.*
> *Bitter.*

"You shouldn't have given me that, you moron.
You already gave me too much to begin with.
You ever hear the word overdose?
Sheesh! What an idiot. Man, I just don't care anymore.
Just let me sleep."

Heavy breathing.
Struggle.

> *I feel so tired.*
> *My chest hurts.*
> *My heart is pounding so hard I can hear it.*
> *Breathe.*
> *I need to breathe.*

"Come on you jerk, I'm not that heavy."

Panting.
Excitement.
Arousal.

> *It hurts.*
> *Oh God, it hurts.*
> *Why is my heart racing?*

God it hurts.

**"Look, I may be a cheerleader,
but I don't bend like that.
Give me a break."**

Heavy breathing in the darkness.

Oh God, why can't I breathe?!

"Look at him, Rowan. LOOK AT HIM!"

*Hair just so.
Chin tilted up.
No, stay that way.
Yes.
Legs crossed.
The silky feel of her stockings
against the back of my hand.
Another rush of arousal.
Yes! Perfect!*

*POP!
Bright Light!
POP!
Bright Light!
POP!
I can't feel anything.
I can't even feel my heart anymore.*

"Talk to me, white man." My friend insinuates himself into the vision once again, only to become a fourth voice in the turmoil.

If only it was really her...
Really her...
Really her...

Darkness.
Fear gives way to warmth.
Warmth gives way to cold.
Cold gives way to nothingness.

"Oh, man, what are you taking
your pants off for you idiot?
You gonna jerk off some more?
Oh, no way.
You aren't going to are you?
Can't you see I'm already gone?
You're gonna be screwing a dead body you moron!
God, you're just sick.
Man, put 'em back
on, that's just disgusting.
You sick bastard."

So beautiful...
So close...
For now...
She'll do for now...

Look at me, Rowan, don't turn away.
Look at me, Rowan, I'm dead today.

So what are you gonna do about it?

CHAPTER 9

"If I'd been told it was anyone else, I never would have believed it."

The feminine voice issued from the doorway and was accompanied by the low whooshing sound of the door being forced quickly open. Sheathed in an authoritative tone the words glanced sharply from the tile walls, striking their targets from all sides. Those targets were, without a doubt, Ben, Felicity, and me.

The comment didn't exactly seem angry, but it wasn't altogether friendly either. It was more along the line of a mixture between disturbed chastising and a cold statement of fact. In any event, no matter what emotion could finally be pinned to the verbiage, the sentence cut through the atmosphere in the room on a determined course. The intent behind its mission was fulfilled as all three of us came instantly to attention, swinging our startled gazes toward the issuer of the remark.

Doctor Christine Sanders, Chief Medical Examiner for the City of St. Louis, didn't look at all pleased. Truth was, she looked like she would much rather be asleep. Considering both the hour and her rumpled appearance, she'd obviously been roused from bed. Her close crop of brunette hair, flocked with grey static, was tousled and her eyes were heavily lidded with a weary haze. She was hastily adorned in a pair of jeans, a baggy sweatshirt, and sneakers. Her parka-like coat hung across her slight frame, unzipped, with the hood carelessly thrown back.

"Hey, Doc," Ben offered sheepishly.

Under his breath, my friend muttered a quick trailer to his statement, "Damn, she got here quick." The barely audible addendum was spoken as if he wasn't at all surprised by her arrival.

"Just what the hell have you got against me, Storm?" she asked as she allowed the door to swing shut and ventured purposefully into the cold room. "Did I do something awful to you that I'm not aware of?"

"I dunno why you got called," Ben shook his head as he stepped toward her. "There was no reason to bother you over this."

It was obvious, to me at least, that he was playing dumb. The observation didn't escape the M.E.'s attention either.

"Excuse me?" she returned. "I should have been called before you ever came in here."

"I didn't wanna bother you."

"You didn't want to bother me," she offered the statement back to him incredulously. "What's wrong with you? You didn't think someone on my staff would call me anyway? You know better than that."

"What for?" he shrugged.

"Well, let's see." She rolled her gaze upward and gestured toward us. "For starters, three people show up in the middle of the night to view a body from an active homicide investigation."

"Yeah, so?"

"You know full well that this is outside normal procedure. If we didn't know her identity it would be one thing, but we know exactly who she is. I'm also betting that none of you are next of kin."

My friend continued to press his luck. "Yeah, so? Since when did viewin' remains become outside normal procedure?"

"Dammit, Storm! Will you quit it with the innocent act! You know exactly what I'm talking about. It's almost one A.M. for God's sake! This is a morgue not a quick shop!"

Felicity and I remained silent during the exchange. My wife still hadn't released her grip on my hand, and in fact, she was squeezing so tight that my fingers were beginning to go numb. I gave her a quick nudge and glanced down at the entwined extremities. She followed my gaze and immediately picked up the queue.

Itchy pinpricks assaulted my digits as blood flowed once again unfettered into my hand. Far worse, however, was the sudden feeling of isolation and detachment that washed over me as we separated. I had known that I was having trouble staying grounded— even if I hesitated to admit it— but the depth of this sensation drove firmly home the severity of my problem. It had been so long since I'd felt so truly centered and at ease that the feeling had been almost like a drug. I wanted it back, I wanted more, and I wanted it now.

Being instantly without the warm comfort it brought had ushered in its own brand of fear to fill the void. I had to consciously tell myself not to reach for Felicity's hand like a frightened child.

"Okay, so we aren't exactly keepin' banker's hours," Ben rebutted. "But we're just havin' a look. No biggie."

"If that is the case, Storm," Doctor Sanders contended, "then why did you send the diener out of the room?"

Ben shook his head at the mention of the morgue attendant. "I figured he had better things to do than stand around and watch us look at a dead body."

"That's a large part of his job to begin with and you know it. Are you sure it wasn't so he wouldn't see what you were doing with that dead body?" she shot back.

"We weren't doin' anything with it." He went on the defensive. "Just what are you implyin'?"

"I'm not implying anything, Storm," she declared. "Johnathan tells me he heard some kind of chanting back here after he left you three."

"That would have been me," Felicity chimed in.

"Stay out of this, Felicity," Ben ordered over his shoulder.

"I'm sorry," the doctor directed her gaze toward my wife, "I know we've met, but I don't recall your name."

"O'Brien. Felicity O'Brien."

"Right. Well, Ms. O'Brien, since Detective Storm seems to be stuck talking in circles right now, would you like to explain what is going on here?"

"Listen, Doc," Ben took another step forward and insinuated himself physically between the M.E. and us, "let's leave them out of this. If you've got a problem, take it up with me."

"I tried that already and it didn't get me very far, now did it?"

The tension was rapidly building between the two of them, and my friend's heretofore uncooperativeness was at its root. He was now making a bid for control over the situation, but I wasn't entirely sure he was going to win out. As was his nature, he was using his physical stature as an intimidation tactic; or trying to at least. Doctor Sanders appeared totally unfazed.

"So what are you gonna do about it, Rowan?" Debbie Schaeffer whispers softly into my ear.

The sudden return of the disembodied voice took me by surprise. I had been fully under the impression that any link with the other side had been completely severed the moment the Medical Examiner had interrupted us. Obviously, I was wrong.

"Look," Ben told the M.E., "I'm sorry. Let's just work this out, okay?"

She met his challenge with one of her own. "If you really want to work this out you can start by telling me what is going on here."

Ben's hand shot up to smooth back his hair and came to rest on his neck as his fingers began to work at a knot of tension. "It's not as bad as it looks, okay?" he appealed.

"Just tell me what's going on and I'll decide that for myself."

"Just let them have their little tiff," Debbie Schaeffer whispers into my ear again. "I've got something to show you."

I feel the touch of icy fingers against my palm, followed by them intertwining with my own. The frigid grasp of death encircles my hand and I feel its frost creep upward along my arm.

I looked down at my hand the moment the sensation took hold. There was nothing to see, but the chilled feeling was definitely there.

"Look, Doc, you've seen the stuff that Rowan does, right?" My friend was starting into his explanation.

"I've been witness to one or two of Mister Gant's episodes, yes," Doctor Sanders answered. "Is that what this is all about?"

"Come on, Rowan. You need to look at this." Debbie Schaeffer is pulling me by the hand.

"Yeah, pretty much," Ben affirmed.

"Is there a particular reason it needed to be done in the middle of the night?"

I glanced over to Felicity and saw that her attention was focused fully upon the exchange between Ben and Doctor Sanders. Consciously, I wanted to tell her what was happening. The recent revelation I'd reached regarding my own ability to ground and center once again brought forth the acid tang of fear on the back of my tongue. I knew that no matter how much I verbally denied it, my current state left me open and vulnerable. It wouldn't take very much at all to get me into deep trouble— potentially fatal deep trouble. My mouth opened as I started to voice the concern, but before any sound escaped I felt my hand squeezed and heard a rush echo inside my skull.

"Shhhhhh! Don't tell anyone. Just come with me and look. You need to see this."

I closed my mouth and looked over the tableau again. My friend had his back to us and his large frame was positioned such that he was almost completely blocking the slight Medical Examiner from my view. I could only assume that I was just as obscured from her sight.

I could feel something tugging at my hand and when I looked, my arm was actually moving. I tried to stop its progress, but the spirit of Debbie Schaeffer was fully in charge and her strength came from sources beyond this level of existence. I was no match for her. I closed my eyes and desperately fought to achieve a solid ground. It was the only way I could think of to regain control over my own body.

"Come on, Rowan. They aren't watching. You REALLY, REALLY need to see this. Trust me."

"It was a judgment call," Ben told the M.E. "Maybe it wasn't the best one I've made, but those are the breaks."

"You're pretty good for that aren't you?"

"Come on, Doc. There's no need to make this personal."

"Then what about the chanting Johnathan heard?" she fired off another question. "What was that all about? I don't recall chanting being a part of Mister Gant's episodes."

"I think maybe he misinterpreted what he heard."

"What did he hear then?"

"Felicity here said a prayer, that's all."

"COME ON, ROWAN! Don't you trust me?"

I started to appeal to my wife for help, only to find the words caught painfully in my throat. Instinctively I reached for her with my free hand, but grasped nothing more than a handful of gelid air. I opened my eyes and became suddenly aware that I was no longer standing next to her. Without any realization whatsoever I had moved several steps away, and now found myself positioned in front of the wall bearing the cold storage drawers. Directly before me a rectangle of stainless steel was annotated with a case number and the name, Lawson, Paige.

"Go on, open it. You REALLY, REALLY, REALLY need to see this, Rowan!"

I stood dumbfounded for a moment. The pit of my stomach was churning in a way vastly different from what had been brought on by the stench of decay. The acrid boil that was happening down there now was one of pure, unadulterated fear. I had felt such things before, and with even greater intensity, but what was most disturbing about this instance was that this fear was my own— no one else's.

I watched on helplessly as my hand moved of another's volition, guided by an invisible, though firm, icy grip. As my fingers drew closer to the handle of the drawer I fought to cry out for help. Still, my voice caught raspily in my throat, and I managed nothing more than a weak gurgle that went unheard.

"I said SHHHHHHHH!" Debbie Schaeffer *admonishes me. "Trust me."*

"A prayer," Doctor Sanders stated flatly, her tone betraying her lack of belief in what she'd just been told.

"Open it, Rowan. Open it."

My hand moved in a jerking parody of a mechanical appendage as it was forced to grasp the handle, and then tug the latch open. The drawer slid smoothly outward on the heavy-duty rollers with a mild roar of friction.

I was face to face with the pallid remains of Paige Lawson and still my hand moved, guided by an invisible, but wholly distinguishable force. My arm literally vibrated as I struggled against Debbie Schaeffer's ethereal control. My palm hovered mere inches above the chilled corpse of the young woman.

"Touch her, Rowan. You REALLY, REALLY, REALLY need to see this!"

"Is there a particular..." Doctor Sanders started to continue her interrogation only to be interrupted by the sound of the opening drawer. "MISTER GANT! JUST WHAT DO YOU THINK YOU ARE DOING?!"

The sharpness of the Medical Examiner's demand shattered the delicate pane of the trance like a baseball hitting a plate glass window. Unfortunately, it was too late.

Debbie Schaeffer's ghostly form drove my hand downward, bringing the clammy skin of my palm against Paige Lawson's cold flesh.

Colors flashed in a riot of sparks, blooming to absolute saturation then bleaching to dull shades of grey. Electricity coursed through my body on a never ending quest to jangle every nerve, seeking out and destroying anything in its path. Light flickered before my eyes, and then drained away in a chaotic whirlpool of luminescence, bleeding red then black.

A rapid burn ripped its way along the side of my neck.

Blinding pain erupted inward from the side of my skull and wrapped around to repeat the assault.

My chest tightened and spasmed as I felt the wind chased from my lungs.

My own words mixed with those of Doctor Sanders as the catch in my throat opened wide to release the escaping air in the form of a tortured scream, "HELP ME!"

CHAPTER 10

I had never really paid that much attention to acoustic ceiling tiles. Actually, I had never really had a reason to do so. At this particular moment in my life, however, the random pattern of decorative holes punched into their dull surfaces was occupying my full and undivided attention. I quickly discovered that if you stare at them long enough, the randomness of the indentations would become less and less chaotic. With little more than a spoonful of imagination mixed in, the dots became easy to connect and rallied themselves into complex pictures, complete with highlight and shadow.

In my mind's eye, I was just applying the final touches to a particularly intricate portrait when reality elected to position itself between my canvas and me. My carefully constructed image of a striking young woman with long, flowing hair exploded into a shower of bright red sparks that hesitated for a moment, then fell slowly earthward, systematically burning themselves out along the way like the dying bursts of holiday fireworks.

It really didn't matter that the fantasy had been disturbed, because the image was replaced in kind with a face of equal— if not superior— beauty, wrinkled with a mixture of anger and concern though it was.

"How's your head, then?" Felicity asked as she peered

down at me.

With the artistic trance broken, I set about focusing my attentions on the question I'd just been asked. I took a quick mental assessment and discovered that my head was still throbbing somewhat. However, there was another sensation that overshadowed the mild pain in a big way— I wanted a cigarette, and I wanted it yesterday.

"Hurts a bit," I croaked trying without success to ignore the craving.

"Aye, you kept mumbling something about that while you were out," she said. "That, and cigarettes."

The proverbial cat was now on the loose. "How long?"

"Were you out? A few minutes," she replied. "Barely long enough for us to bring you up here, really."

From the looks of everything around me, "up here" was apparently one of the offices on the main floor of the City Morgue.

"Great," I mumbled. "Did I do anything besides complain about my head and cigarettes?"

"You mean other than go off chasing after answers on your own?" She submitted the query with measured terseness born of her underlying anger with me, and the words themselves explained why.

"Whoa, before you unleash that wrath on me, it wasn't exactly my choice," I protested. "Debbie Schaeffer was apparently on a mission."

"What do you mean?"

"She insisted on my touching Paige Lawson," I said. "She kept saying there was something she needed to show me that I really, really needed to see."

"And that was?"

I shrugged. "Beats me. I don't remember much of anything after pulling the drawer open, and I did that under duress."

"So why didn't you say something before going off on your own?"

"Believe me, I tried."

"Aye," she nodded as the pieces fell into place for her, "now do you understand why I've been so worried about you?"

"Yeah." I nodded. "The experience was definitely a wake up call."

"How ya feelin'?" Ben's voice overtook the momentary silence as he followed the opening door into the room. He seemed tense, almost reserved, and businesslike.

"Okay, I guess," I answered as Felicity moved back and allowed me to sit up. "Rattled."

"So, who's the bad guy?"

"What?"

"All the hocus-pocus you did." He waved his hand around in the air. "Did you figure out who the bad guy is?"

"Well, no, not exactly."

"Wunnerful. Clues? Leads? Anything?"

"Maybe, I'm not exactly sure. I saw..." I realized suddenly that I didn't really remember what I had seen. "I think..."

He didn't allow me to flounder for long. "You good enough to travel?"

"I suppose, but shouldn't we..."

"No but's, no shouldn't we anything's, white man." He shook his head. "We need to leave. We can get some coffee down the road and talk about it there."

"But, I'm not sure I'm finished here." I wasn't lying. The memory of what I'd experienced downstairs was flitting around inside my head, just out of reach. "There might be something else."

"Look, you got no idea what it took for me to convince the Doc that there wasn't somethin' really hinky goin' on down there tonight. I wouldn't count on gettin' anywhere near those remains in the near future if I was you."

"I can talk to her…"

He cut me off again. "Leave it alone, Row. If I was to visit a proctologist right now he'd have two assholes to choose from, if you get my meanin'. We gotta go. Now. That's it. End of discussion."

"Doctor Sanders?" I let the remainder of the question hang, unspoken.

"She was just a warm up, my friend, and she wasn't the only one who got dragged outta bed tonight." He shook his head. "I just now got off the phone with my boss."

"Oh, man, Ben… I'm sorry. I didn't think…"

"Save it," he returned. "Let's just get the fuck outta here while I still have a badge."

We walked in relative silence down the corridor and past the reception desk. The guard who had earlier been pushing cards around the computer screen in a hot game of solitaire was now just outside the glassed-in front of the building. He pulled open the outer door and held it for us as we exited through the small foyer.

"Rough one?" he asked as the three of us came through the doorway. He seemed totally oblivious to what had been transpiring within the deeper recesses of the morgue.

"Yeah, Joe." Ben nodded. "But, they're never a cakewalk."

"Yeah. Damn shame. Sucks." He nodded in return as he took a deep drag on the cigarette he held between his fingers, and then let out a cloud of smoke. "Well, good luck finding the asshole that did it."

"Thanks, Joe."

The nicotine-laden cloud hung in the air and gently wrapped itself around me. The pungent smell was more than I could take. The stress of everything I'd experienced over the past hour combined with the guilt I was feeling at having gotten Ben into hot water became an irresistible catalyst. The omnipresent and still unexplained craving instantly expanded beyond management to become a dire need.

"Excuse me," the words left my mouth before I even realized what I was saying, "but do you think I could bum one of those from you?"

"Sure," the guard answered with a quick grin of smoker camaraderie, then warned, "they're menthol."

"Perfect." I nodded my head as I pulled a cigarette from the pack he held out to me.

I hadn't even realized that the craving had been for more than the nicotine, but the moment he had mentioned menthol, the need within me leaped another octave.

"Rowan!" Felicity admonished as she suddenly realized what I was doing.

She was too late. I'd already tucked the filter end between my lips and was touching fire to the other with the guard's proffered lighter.

Deeply inhaling I felt the volume of smoke surge into my lungs, cool and hot all at once. An immediate nicotine rush expanded just behind my eyes and flooded outward to every nerve in my body. Menthol giddiness warmed me from head to toe, then became an icy tingle across my scalp and down my spine. I closed my eyes with a deep feeling of satisfaction as I started to reluctantly let the precious smoke go.

What should have come out as a simple exhale sputtered, then burst forth as a barking cough. I bent forward and brought my free hand to cover my mouth as I violently hacked for a moment, then wheezed air in once again.

"You okay?" Joe asked.

"Yeah," I answered as I took another deep drag on the cigarette and expelled the smoke, this time without incident. "I'm much better now."

"Jeez, white man," Ben exclaimed, waving with annoyance at the dense scud of smoke hanging around us. "Give it a rest will'ya? You've hot boxed damn near half a pack already."

He was correct. In fact, I was working on number ten at this very moment, and the ravenous craving had only now begun to smooth around the edges. Upon leaving the parking lot of the City Morgue, I had done no less than demand that he pull into the first open gas station we came upon. There followed a few tense moments of opposition from both Felicity and him, however, I won out. I celebrated my victory by purchasing an entire carton of menthol-tipped 100's and a disposable lighter.

I'd had no choice but to give in to Ben's refusal to allow me to smoke in his van, and therefore ended up quickly huffing a pair of the butts before climbing back into the vehicle for the short trip back around the block to our originally intended destination.

We were now parked in an out of the way back corner booth at 'Chuck's'. Not that where we sat really mattered, as we were the only patrons at the moment. The three of us were taking turns administering doses of sugar and creamer to coffee that was an hour or so beyond its expiration. Promises of a fresh pot were already reaching our ears as the coffee maker behind the counter audibly spewed hot liquid into a stained Pyrex globe.

"Aye, slow down," Felicity chimed in. "It's bad enough you've started up with those nasty things again. You don't have to chain-smoke as well."

"Maybe you should talk to Helen about this too, Row," Ben offered. "She's probably got some psychobabble to help you out with quitting."

"Yeah, maybe so," I agreed if for no other reason than to hopefully get them to quit harping on me. I didn't bother to point out that she was a smoker herself. "I'll mention it."

Still, though I was embracing the practice for the moment, I was as disturbed as they were that I'd started up again. It had been almost two years since I'd quit, and it hadn't been easy. I'd told myself that the occasional cigar was as far as I was going to venture into this realm ever again, and I'd stuck to it— until now. It was true that I'd been under some very severe stress, but I couldn't see blaming it all on that. Something else was amiss. Some other factor was definitely at work here.

"Were either Debbie Schaeffer or Paige Lawson smokers by any chance?" I asked as the thought rolled in from the back of my brain.

Ben thought about it for a moment, and then shook his head. "Don't think so. I can check into it, but I don't recall either of them havin' cigarettes in their personal effects. Why?"

"Are you thinking that you're channeling impulses from one of them?" Felicity queried.

"Maybe." I shrugged. "Even when I went through withdrawals from quitting I didn't crave nicotine this intensely. There's got to be something more to it."

"Well, I'll check," Ben told me. "I'm almost positive it's a no on Schaffer, but I can't be completely sure about Lawson. But like I said, I don't remember any cigarettes with her stuff either."

"Maybe it's someone else entirely," I speculated.

"What?" Ben furrowed his brow. "Like another murder

victim?"

"Maybe."

"Well it would have to be another case entirely."

"Why do you say that?"

"Because we've already had our quota on serial killers this century."

I shrugged as I shook my head. "Just speculating."

"Well speculate something else," he instructed.

I stubbed the remaining couple of inches of the cigarette out in the small glass ashtray and its smoldering carcass joined the other half dozen yellow-brown stained filters. I felt a need to immediately light another, but resisted, and hoped I'd had enough of a fix to hold me— for a while at least.

"So," my friend directed us back onto the original topic we'd set out to discuss, "why don't you tell me what I just got my ass chewed for?"

"I'm not exactly sure," I returned.

"That's NOT what I wanna hear, Rowan."

"I know, Ben, but that's what I was trying to tell you back at the morgue. It's all a jumble. I don't really remember anything coherent."

He brought his hand up and massaged his neck, then sighed. "Let me cut you a little slice of reality here. We all know that I'm not exactly one for goin' strictly by the book, so I already walk a thin enough line as it is. Well, tonight just turned that thin line into a fuckin' tightrope, so you're gonna have to give me somethin'. Anything."

"What if you just start with anything that you can remember," Felicity ventured. "Maybe we can piece it together."

"Well…" I thought hard for a moment, trying to pick out something of consequence and settling for whatever I could grasp. "A lot of darkness, and a cheerleader with an attitude for starters."

"Whaddaya mean 'attitude'?" Ben asked.

"Exactly that." I shrugged. "She seemed really cocky... And demanding. She kept bouncing around, and she was kind of hard to keep track of."

"What makes you say she was cocky though?" he pressed.

"Well, she kept calling some guy a moron, I remember that. I seem to recall her referring to him as an idiot too."

"Who?"

"I don't know. If I had to guess, I'd say it was the guy that killed her."

"No shit. So you saw the guy?"

"No." I shook my head. "I don't really remember seeing anyone other than her..." I thought hard for a moment. "Although there was this shadowy movement here and there and I heard a male voice."

"What did he say?"

"He was angry. Something about her crying and her makeup running."

"What do you think that's all about?" Felicity asked.

"Search me." I didn't know what to say. "I told you I didn't remember anything that made any sense. I suppose it might not have been the guy that killed her at all. Maybe it was some kind of latent memory. Argument with a boyfriend or something?"

"Maybe her boyfriend is the killer," she offered.

"We've beaten that horse." Ben shook his head vigorously then took a sip of his coffee. "Boyfriend's clean."

"Ex-boyfriend?" I posed.

"There isn't one. You gotta understand," my friend explained, "this girl was like right out of a fifties TV show. A regular Stepford kid. Honor roll, cheerleader, never been in trouble, been dating the same guy since high school."

"That sure isn't the impression she gave me when she

was bouncing in and out of my head," I told him.

"What can I tell ya'?" he shrugged.

"It doesn't really matter." I was shaking my head now. "Because you're right, the boyfriend idea is the wrong track anyway. If it had been her boyfriend, then we'd be talking about a crime of passion, right?"

"Not definitely, but most likely. Why?"

"Well if it was a crime of passion then it would be an isolated incident. There wouldn't have been any reason for her to insist on me touching Paige Lawson. Unless, of course, there's a connection there that we're missing."

"We haven't had a reason to look for one. Lawson is an accidental death… So wait a minute, are you tellin' me Debbie Schaeffer's ghost had somethin' to do with that whole stunt?"

"Exactly." I nodded affirmation.

"So, she like what, talked you into it or something?"

"No, she actually physically dragged me over there and forced me to do it."

"She did what?" He stared back at me incredulously.

"I know it sounds bizarre, Ben."

"Yeah, well I've come to the conclusion that you're whole freakin' life is just one really long episode of the *Twilight Zone,* Kemosabe."

"Just since I got involved with murder investigations. Before that I was pretty normal."

"Says you," he grinned, his tone softening.

"Look who's talking," I returned the jibe. "Anyway, I wasn't in control of my actions when I went after Paige Lawson's remains. That was Debbie Schaeffer all the way. That's the one thing I can remember clear as daylight."

"See now, I just figured you were seizin' an opportunity, and THAT just pissed me off."

"Yeah, I kind of had the impression you weren't real happy with me."

"Yeah, well I was pissed when I turned around and saw you standin' there holding on to Lawson and screamin' your damn fool head off. And after what she'd just walked in on, the Doc wasn't sure WHAT to think. It didn't really help matters any."

"Like she said, we probably should have called her before going down there."

"Yeah, well we all know about hindsight now don't we?"

"Can we get back on the subject, then?" Felicity interjected.

"Yeah, let's," Ben agreed. "So you're sayin' that there's some connection between Schaeffer and Lawson."

"There must be." I nodded, and then took a sip of my own coffee before setting the cup down and pushing it away. One taste was all it took to convince me to wait for the fresh pot. "Why else would she have wanted me to touch the body?"

"But everything on Lawson points to accidental death," he objected. "So maybe the connection isn't that they were killed by the same person."

"Yeah, I suppose."

"You aren't being much help, Row."

"Hey," I shook my head, "I'm doing the best I can. I told you I'm pretty fuzzy on all this."

"Maybe Paige Lawson knew Debbie Schaeffer somehow, and the killer is a mutual friend or acquaintance," Felicity said.

"Paige Lawson was a marketing VP for an HMO. What's she gonna have in common with a college cheerleader?"

"You have a better idea, then?" she raised an eyebrow.

"No," he returned flatly. "Maybe they did know each other. If we can't find a direct connection, then we can make a list and see if any names match up as mutual acquaintances. I know Lawson had one of those electronic organizers in her briefcase. I think Schaeffer had something too."

"Do you remember anything else?" my wife pressed.

"Nothing important. Just something about Barbie in a Prom dress."

"Do what?" Ben looked as confused as ever. Since I was no clearer on what I'd just said than he was, I couldn't blame him.

"Yeah, it was green and she didn't like her shoes, or something like that."

"Who didn't like whose shoes?"

"Barbie. Debbie. I don't know, both of 'em maybe."

"You are talking about the toy fashion doll, right?"

"Yeah, I think so."

"Rowan," Felicity asked. "Are you absolutely certain you're okay?"

I slid number eleven from the pack and lit it up almost unconsciously. "I've been wondering that myself."

CHAPTER 11

"Are you coming to bed or not?" Felicity called to me from the hallway. "We've a long day, then. In case you didn't remember, Yule is day after tomorrow."

"You mean, Yule IS tomorrow," I called back while in the process of exhaling a plume of smoke through the crack where I was holding the storm door just slightly open. Pushing it a bit wider, I dropped the cigarette into a sand-filled can we kept on the porch for our smoking friends. "It's pushing five A.M., so it's already today."

We'd all finally decided that we were far too exhausted to continue the discussion, and since we weren't getting anywhere to begin with, it wasn't a hard call. The caffeine was all we were running on and I think we'd even started becoming immune to its effects in short order. Our bout of speculation was terminated with the idea that a bit of sleep might bring some more of what I'd seen to the surface. While I agreed with the idea in theory, I most definitely wasn't looking forward to the possibility of yet another Technicolor nightmare.

Upon returning to Ben's house, we had bid him goodnight and I had apologized once again for getting him into trouble with his superiors. His response had simply been for me not to worry, they'd get over it. I hoped he was correct.

"Aye, don't remind me," she called back with a resigned sigh. "We've far too much to do and we'll need rest if we're to get everything done before Friday, and still be able to tend the fire through."

Like zombies, Felicity and I had piled into her Jeep and then made the trek down Highway Forty, and home. By the time we pulled into the driveway, the minute hand was already well into its climb toward the top of the coming hour. Fortunately for us, true to what Ben had told me earlier in the evening, Briarwood's finest had seen to discouraging the media from camping on our lawn. How they'd done it without infringing upon the constitutional freedom of the press, I had no idea— I wasn't entirely sure I wanted to know either. I was just happy not to have to deal with them right now.

I pushed the front door shut and twisted the deadbolt until it gave a dull thunk. "Yeah," I returned as I punched in the code to engage the alarm system. "Not to mention that if you don't get some rest everyone is going to think you just got off the boat."

"What's that, then?"

"The accent. It's gotten pretty thick over the past few hours. Kind of obvious that you're exhausted."

"Aye, I don't have an accent," she replied, calling out from the bedroom now. "YOU do."

"Uh-huh. Whatever." I chuckled. "Are you done in here?"

"Aye. Did you let the dogs out?"

"Yeah, they've been out already. And yes, the back is all locked up."

"Did you check the answering machine, then? I noticed it blinking when we came in."

"So, why didn't YOU check it then."

"Because I wanted to go to bed."

"Uh-huh," I harrumphed. "Me too. I'll check it in the

morning."

"Aye, I thought you said that it WAS morning."

"How about, I'll check it later then?"

"Aye, I suppose. And, Rowan?"

"Yeah?"

"Brush your teeth and gargle," she instructed sleepily, her voice fading along a deepening arc. "Sure'n I'm not sleepin' next to an ashtray, then."

Disorientation gave way to longing.

There was only one thing that I cared about.

Her.

She was here.

But was it really her?

No.

She was close, but it wasn't really her.

Her hair spiraled softly across her shoulders, streaked with highlights from the sun's rays filtering through the mini-blinds.

She sat motionless, legs crossed, lounging seductively in the chair.

Looking at me with lust in her eyes.

Yes, the blinds worked. They were artistic.

But something still wasn't quite right.

Perhaps it was the sun.

Perhaps a bit less yellow.

Yes, that would help.

And maybe tweak the blinds just a bit more.

Yes, perfect.

Well almost.

It would only be perfect when she was really there.

She moaned softly.

Need to hurry.
She whimpered.
Yes, must hurry before she moves.
She slid downward, falling to the side, then off the chair; coming to rest as a tangled mess on the floor.
She was no longer perfect.

> *A flash of light.*
> *Fear.*
> *Pain.*
> *Loneliness.*

Lust.
Animal passion.
Needful desire.

> *Putrefaction sets in within twenty-four to forty eight hours.*
> *Purge fluids escape through*
> *the bodily orifices as*
> *the organs begin to decompose and*
> *breakdown of the vascular system occurs.*

Almost perfect.
If she'll just stay in one place a bit longer this time.
If only she was her…
Then…
Then she would be perfect.
Absolutely perfect.

> *Death settles in,*
> *warming itself briefly on the fading embers*
> *of a passing life.*
> *I'm cold.*
> *So very cold.*

Why me?

Darkness.
A mocking chant in the distance.

> *Listen everybody; I've got a story to tell,*
> *I'm lying here dead, and he just says, "Oh well."*
> *I called on Rowan; they said he was the best.*
> *They told me, "Go see Rowan," and forget about the rest.*
> *I called on Rowan, because I was afraid,*
> *But all he seems to want, is to get himself laid.*
> *Dead I am, yes, dead today,*
> *Will Rowan find my killer?*
> *Hell no! Not this way.*

I awoke more exhausted than I'd been when I'd crawled into bed next to Felicity. According to the clock almost seven hours had passed, but considering how I was feeling it might just as well have been seven minutes. I remained perfectly still, watching until the numerals on the face of the digital timepiece incremented forward enough times to make it officially noon. Of course, since my wife had a penchant for setting clocks a bit fast to avoid being late, it was more like quarter till.

A small voice rattled about between my ears— singing a song, or reciting a poem, I wasn't entirely sure. I couldn't actually make out the words, and the echo was so faint that I had no choice but to conclude that I was imagining things.

Still, something about it seemed intimately familiar.

My head was throbbing with a dull ache. Not enough to be debilitating, but more than enough to get my attention. All in all, annoying, and something that I hoped would disappear in the very near future.

After a moment, I started to sit up on the side of the bed and found myself bound in a wild tangle of sheets. When I finally managed to extricate myself, I wearily twisted my fists in my eyes to force the sleep away. I threw a slack-jawed glance over my shoulder and saw that the bed linens were in a chaotic jumble. One of us must have done some serious tossing and turning, and I presumed that I was the guilty party.

Taking in a deep breath, I started to let out a sigh, but was greeted instead by a grating cough. My throat was dry and felt a bit raw. Following the bout of hacking and sputtering, I wheezed in a deep breath and felt it rattle in my chest.

My hand automatically reached for the nightstand and pawed about, coming up empty. At first I really didn't even know what I was looking for, then it dawned on me.

Cigarettes.

I stared quietly at the floor and picked through the mild twinges in the back of my skull. Reality was setting in and I summoned a bit of concentration, then sent it on a quest for memories of the previous night. A quick inventory told me there didn't appear to be anything new to add to the nonsensical list.

The one good thing— or bad, depending upon your take— that came to mind was that I hadn't had any nightmares. At least, I didn't think I had.

Something still didn't feel right, though, and I definitely wasn't catching on to what it was.

"Good morning," Felicity greeted the back of my head from the doorway. "Or should I say, afternoon, then? Finally decided to join the rest of the world?" Her voice still held a Celtic lilt, and that told me that she must not have slept any better than I had.

"Uh-huh," I grunted, then forced out a scratchy query while thrusting a finger over my shoulder. "Is that clock right?"

"Aye," she returned as she ventured further into the room and made her way around the end of the bed. "Right as it ever is."

"Damn," I muttered, "I sure don't feel like I got seven hours of sleep."

"Aye," she laughed, "as it was I only got four myself. What makes you think you'd be gettin' any more than me, then?"

Now I was even more befuddled. "We went to bed around five A.M., right?"

"Aye."

I didn't say anything else. The comment seemed self-explanatory to me.

"Well?" I finally said.

"Well, what?" she answered as she tugged the bed linens off into a pile on the floor.

"Well, noon minus five," I offered through my haze. "Comes out to around seven. In my head anyway."

"Aye, it does," she replied as she hooked an arm around my neck and slid into my lap. Her hair was still slightly damp from her shower and she smelled faintly of roses. The sweet scent tickled my nose as she leaned in to kiss my cheek, then whisper, "And, I told you then that we should be spending it sleeping."

I was just about to ask her to explain what she meant when the various pieces of the equation started to fall into place. What had been unidentified variables up until now became known quantities. When the values were added up, the undeniable final product was obviously a prolonged and intense sexual encounter.

Unfortunately, it was one to which I was completely oblivious. Fortunately, I had enough wits about me to know better than to say so, at least until I figured out why.

"Oh, yeah, that," I lied for effect.

"I'm loving you a whole bunch right now," my wife whispered softly.

"Yeah, me too," I said while searching my memory for the slightest inkling of the recent passion, and finding none. "Me too."

Behind my quiet façade, confusion opened the door and invited fear to come on in and make itself at home.

It did.

CHAPTER 12

"I really appreciate you working me into your schedule like this," I told Helen Storm as we both sidled up to the balcony railing of the outdoor smoking lounge. "I know you're very busy."

Felicity hadn't objected in the least when I begged off from helping clean the house in order to attend a hastily scheduled visit with Doctor Storm. Had it been for any other reason, I doubt I would have gotten as far as the front door. I still hadn't told my wife about my amnesia regarding our intimacy, and I wasn't sure if I would. I wasn't even positive that I was going to tell Helen about it, even though it was the catalyst for the sudden appointment. Quite a bit was going to depend upon what conclusions were reached over the next hour.

"It was no problem, Rowan," she answered.

"Well, I felt bad about calling you on such short notice."

"Don't. That is what I am here for."

"Even so," I expressed, "I hate coming off as some sort of needy flake."

"You didn't. Really, Rowan, it was a light day for me anyway, and it was quite obvious that something was troubling you."

I suspected that there had been more to rearranging her

schedule than she let on. "I still appreciate it."

"I know you do, so stop beating yourself up about it. Truth is, I can't really say that I was surprised to hear from you," she expressed gently. "Benjamin called me early this morning."

"So, is he really that worried about me?"

"Yes he is, but please don't get the impression that he is checking up on you or trying to interfere in your life. He was actually calling me about getting together on Christmas Eve. I could tell he had something else on his mind, though, so I pried it out of him."

"That's not always an advisable task with Ben."

"No," she mused. "Not even for a friend who is as close to him as you are. But, being the older sister who's acted as his confidant for more years than she'd care to acknowledge, I can get away with it."

"I see." I nodded. "So, what did he tell you?"

"Not much in the way of details really. Just that you had experienced one of your psychic episodes last night, and that you weren't displaying your usual clarity in that regard."

"That's an understatement."

"He alluded that it was something very out of character for you," she agreed with a nod.

"I'm not usually this befuddled, no."

"That is what worries him most, I believe; your wife as well. They are concerned that this confusion might interfere with your judgment, and possibly your safety."

I knew exactly what she meant, and offered the unspoken evidence. "Just like it did when I chased Eldon Porter out onto that bridge. Yeah, we've been down that road."

"Then you know that they are merely expressing concern for a loved one. You."

"I know." I nodded. "I know. But it still doesn't make things any easier to deal with. Sometimes it just makes me feel… Like…"

I struggled to find any word or phrase that could accurately describe my feelings, but none were forthcoming.

"Diminished?" Helen offered.

"Yes. Exactly. Like they feel as though I'm incapable of making my own decisions."

"So, what about those decisions?"

"What do you mean?"

"With everything we've discussed so far," she explained, "it all seems to come back to Eldon Porter and the decisions you made then."

"It was a bad situation," I said.

"From what little both you and Benjamin have told me it sounds like it was a royally fucked up situation."

I was momentarily taken aback by the single spoken vulgarity coming from Helen Storm. Her soothing demeanor and calm voice made the expletive stand out even more against the backdrop of her words— effectively framing it and making it the succinct and perfect description of the situation. But, it was perfect only as she said it. Had the same statement been made by anyone else, it would have simply been an observation punctuated by profanity.

I already liked her, but the stark humanness of the expression ingratiated her to me even more.

"Yes," I agreed. "Yes it was."

"What about the decisions you made during that case?"

"Depends on who you ask. Ben thinks I was lacking in my judgment, that's for sure. And, Felicity has it in for Ben and me both where that is concerned."

"I'm not asking them," she submitted. "I am asking you."

"I don't know." I shrugged and took a hit from my cigarette before crushing it out. I stripped the butt, then discarded the filter and paper in a nearby trash receptacle before continuing. "I did what I thought I needed to do. In retrospect, I suppose chasing after a serial killer in the middle of the night, alone, probably wasn't the brightest thing I've ever done."

"Why do you think you felt you had to do it?"

"I didn't want him to get away." I gave her a statement of fact as I saw it.

"Are you certain?"

I wasn't sure where she was headed with this, but I was afraid I was soon going to find out.

"Fairly certain," I answered. "You think I might have had another reason?"

"I'm merely curious," she returned. "Could you not have simply called the police and notified them? Surely they were better equipped to handle the situation than you."

"Do you think I was grandstanding?" I asked her. "Attention seeking?"

"I didn't say that." She shook her head. "But in answer to your question, no, I don't. I am simply asking why you didn't call the police instead of going after him yourself."

"I didn't think there was enough time."

"Are you certain? The Briarwood police station isn't that far from your house is it?"

"Done some research, have you?" I queried.

"A little," she said.

"Well, I did tell Felicity to call Ben and have him call me on my cell phone."

"But you still chased after him on your own."

"Okay. Right now, given my current state, I might be a bit denser than I normally am, but I can see that you have a different idea about this. Would you like to share?"

"No," she shook her head again. "Not really."

"Excuse me?"

"What I think isn't the point, Rowan. What IS the point

is what your motivation for that decision actually was. Only you know what that motivation was, and my telling you my theory won't help, whether I am correct or not. You have to reach the conclusion on your own."

"So I'm paying you so that I can reach my own conclusions?"

"No," she smiled. "You are paying me to help you navigate unfamiliar terrain in order to work toward those conclusions. Just consider me a docent for your psyche."

I let out a quiet chuckle. "So you're basically an expensive tour guide."

"Something like that, but I'm not allowed to accept tips."

"You know, you really aren't what I expected from a shrink."

"I should hope not," she laughed musically.

The mood lightened for a moment as we stood there. Helen waited patiently for me to continue, without prompting, and allowed me to observe where she had taken us. Something in me wanted to rush along to the next exhibit buried deeper within my mind, seeking out the answer that would make everything right; the panacea that would return normalcy to my life. But, I knew deep down that no such cure existed. So did she.

Still, she wasn't about to budge, and remained steadfast in her silence. I obviously hadn't seen everything I was meant to see here.

"I know I wasn't very grounded at the time I made that decision," I finally said with a sigh. "And I really haven't been ever since. That certainly has become a problem for me now."

"Hence your lack of focus?"

"There's another understatement," I confessed. "I'm just this side of legally blind, I think."

"I doubt you are as bad as that," she said.

"I don't know. I feel like I'm trapped on the inside looking out, and it's midnight with a new moon, clouds, and a power outage," I contended.

"That could be an important milestone."

"What? Like I'm a prisoner of my own failings?"

"No, nothing so self-depreciating."

"Okay, I give. How about a hint?"

"What happens when you place a piece of black paper behind a pane of glass, Rowan?" she asked.

"You end up with a somewhat crude mirror," I answered with a shrug.

"Perhaps the darkness you see is doing just that for you, but instead, you are looking too hard for something else beyond that veil."

"So, you think I should just accept what I see?"

"I think you should take advantage of the opportunity to peer into your own reflection."

"Now, that really scares me," I returned. "I'm afraid that is where the REAL darkness is."

"We all have darkness within us, Rowan," she replied. "And when you encounter it, sometimes you just have to light your own way."

"I'm not so sure I've got enough of a candle to do that," I sighed.

"Of course you do. You must simply find it first."

"I think I'm running out of places to look, Helen."

"Don't worry," she grinned. "I guarantee that it will be in the last place you look."

I couldn't help but return a grin of my own in response to the cliché adage. Apparently, I'd seen enough and when she spoke again, we continued smoothly into a seemingly new subject.

"Something Benjamin didn't tell me was that you'd started smoking again."

I looked down at the freshly burning cigarette in my hand, and noticed that it was tucked between my two middle fingers. I didn't even remember lighting it. It felt completely natural but looked foreign positioned in the middle of my hand as it was, so I moved it up beneath my index finger.

Now that it looked normal to me, it felt extremely out of place.

I elected to ignore the sensation and took a puff.

"Yeah. Last night," I acknowledged. "I've been fighting the craving for a while, but falling off the wagon was kind of sudden."

"Stress can do that," she offered. "We subconsciously return to places or habits that once gave us comfort. I certainly hope my smoking in front of you yesterday had nothing to do with it."

"No, it didn't," I reassured her. "Nothing for you to worry about there."

"Do you remember when you first started smoking?"

"You mean before last night?"

"Yes."

"Oh," I did a quick mental calculation, "sixteen, seventeen years ago."

"And when did you quit?"

"Almost two years ago, except for a cigar now and then."

"Do you remember why you originally started?"

"I don't know." I shrugged. "Something to do, I guess."

"That is fairly thin reasoning, Rowan," she said.

"Yes, it is." I nodded.

"Had something particularly stressful happened to you around the time you started?"

"I don't think so." I shrugged again. "I don't really recall."

We both stood in silence for a long moment, alternately

inhaling and exhaling clouds of smoke that dissipated on the cool breeze. The sky was an expanse of slate grey that stretched from horizon to horizon, even and unblemished. The temperature was hovering in the upper forties after having threatened to push fully into the low fifties earlier in the day. It actually looked far colder than it really was, even with the breeze factored in.

"Rowan," she finally began after flicking the ashes from her own smoke and gazing thoughtfully out at the skyline. "I realize we've only recently met but you truly do not strike me as the kind of person who is deliberately contrary. Am I correct in this assumption?"

I mulled over the comment, reading between the lines and deciphering the base meaning of her words.

"I'd like to think that I'm not a jackass, if that's what you mean," I answered.

"Touché," she replied. "So much for tact."

"Please," I told her, "feel free to be tactful. It makes me feel appreciated. Anyway, you were saying?"

"My point was simply this: Why don't you tell me why it is you think you started smoking again," she instructed. "Because, I'm going to go out on a limb here and say that you don't believe it is because of stress."

"Am I that transparent?"

"Not really." She shook her head and smiled. "I just have better sight than most."

I gave the query some thought. Ben had already told her about some of the things he'd witnessed me do, and I'd spoken at length with her about it myself during our first session. I had nothing to lose by being honest.

"I think that I am physically manifesting the habit of a dead person."

"Whom?" She asked the question without even blinking.

"A young woman named Debbie Schaeffer, or maybe another named Paige Lawson," I told her. "Maybe even both. I don't know."

"Are you certain either of them were smokers?"

"I'm not actually sure. Ben is checking on it though."

"Debbie Schaeffer is the murdered cheerleader whose case Benjamin is assigned to, correct?"

"That's the one."

"And Paige Lawson is?"

"Another case Ben is,... Was,... Is working," I explained. "I'm not sure if it is still an open investigation or if they finally wrote it off as an accidental death. Something tells me it wasn't an accident though."

"What makes you think that?"

"I don't know." I shook my head. "Something just doesn't feel right about it. I assumed Ben had told you about that particular incident."

"By incident do you mean something involving you?"

"Exactly."

"Ahhh, just a moment," she nodded, "would this be the case where you recently showed up uninvited at the crime scene extremely disoriented and then passed out?"

"That would be the one."

"Mmhmm, mmhmm." She nodded again. "I do remember Benjamin telling me about that. I believe it is what triggered him calling me about you."

"Yeah, I think you're right. Although I've recently been informed that he and Felicity had been discussing my mental state for some time now."

"I believe you are correct," she agreed. "So what about this incident with Ms. Lawson. It seems to be weighing on you somewhat."

"Well, the big problem for me is that I have no memory of going there... To the crime scene... Not until I snapped out of whatever trance I was in, anyway. And, by then I just found myself handcuffed and sitting in the back of a squad car."

"PTSD can manifest in various ways, Rowan. Selective amnesia isn't beyond the realm of possibility for someone who has been subjected to emotional and physical trauma of the severity you faced."

"But, I had sex with my wife last night…"

I simply blurted out the comment, appending it to the conversation whether it appeared to fit or not. The resulting silence lasted for enough heartbeats to tell me that I'd even managed to stun Helen with the seemingly misplaced announcement.

I don't know that I consciously realized what I was saying until the words were out there for us both to hear, and by then it was too late. I could still make no real sense of it all, but pieces were falling into place to form a fuzzy image. The very subject that had been my impetus for this unscheduled visit was now revealed. In the process a subdued feeling was re-awakened, and the unnamed fear that had earlier made itself comfortable within me stood up and engaged in a formal introduction.

"Okay," Helen finally answered, scrutinizing my face with her eyes. "Has there been a problem with intimacy between the two of you?"

It took a moment to dawn on me that I'd only spoken aloud the first half of the thought that kept replaying in my head. "No, I'm sorry, you don't understand…" I sputtered. "What I mean is I had sex with my wife last night but I don't remember it."

"At all?"

"No. Not at all."

"Are you certain that this happened?"

"Oh yeah." I nodded. "No doubt in my mind. I got the message loud and clear from Felicity when we got up."

"I see," she posed thoughtfully. "Did you tell her you had no recollection of it?"

"No." I shook my head. "Not yet. I'm already walking a thin line with her as it is. If I tell her something like that, she'll have me committed."

"I seriously doubt that," she said with a shake of her head. "You know, this is very likely all part of the same post trauma stress."

"I don't know, Helen. Do you remember me telling you about the sleepwalking I've been doing over the past few months?" I asked, the viscid fear now running rampant through my veins and forcing the words out of my mouth as a confession.

"Of course."

"And how I don't remember any of it?"

"Here again, that is not unusual in cases of somnambulism, Rowan," she offered. "And these nocturnal episodes are most likely due to the stress."

"But, I'm afraid that maybe all of it is tied together somehow. The sleepwalking, the blackouts, even Paige Lawson…"

"I agree with you," she nodded. "Like I said, these things could be manifestations of PTSD."

"I wish it were that simple," I told her. "But, I'm terribly afraid that there's a different connection."

"And that would be?"

"I'm starting to wonder if maybe I'm the one who killed Paige Lawson."

CHAPTER 13

"You don't truly believe that now do you, Rowan?" Helen asked me after yet another considerably long and uncomfortable pause.

"To be honest, I don't know what to believe anymore," I answered her. "And that is starting to really scare me."

I was amazed at how calmly I spoke considering the rampant terror that was now racing around inside me. The sudden revelation that I, myself, could be the person responsible for Paige Lawson's death was almost more than I could bear to imagine. But, it was a fact I felt I had to face head on. The simple truths were that Debbie Schaeffer's spirit was very intent on my contact with the corpse; I had arrived at the crime scene in a demented state; And, I couldn't remember anything at all about going there.

Who was to say that I hadn't already been there a few short hours before?

"I honestly believe that you are leading yourself down the wrong path," Doctor Storm said with a look of deep concentration creasing her forehead. "You should look carefully at the facts which are before you, and refrain from wild conjecture."

"I am," I answered.

"No, Rowan," she replied sternly. "You are not."

"What am I missing then?"

"Evidence, for one; motive, for another. Think about it. Did you even know this Paige Lawson?"

"No." I shook my head and inhaled deeply from the cigarette in my hand. "Never heard of her before that night."

"Then what motive could you have possibly had for killing her?"

"Insane people don't always have easily discernible motives," I replied.

"True. But, you are not insane."

"I'm not so sure about that."

"I am."

"Well, at least that's one of us."

"And since I am the one with the degree in Psychology, let us assume that I am also the one who is correct on this point. All right?" She cocked her head to the side and flashed a quick smile when she spoke.

"Okay," I couldn't help but return the smile. Simply listening to her speak was quickly dulling the edge on the blade of fear that had been ripping through my gut.

"From what you have said, the crime scene was apparently devoid of any evidence of foul play— least of all, evidence of your participation in such an act."

"Maybe I was careful," I objected. "I've been involved in enough murder investigations to know what to avoid."

"While sleepwalking? I don't think so, Rowan." She shook her head. "For the sake of argument, let us forget for a moment that this is an incredibly rare occurrence. There ARE actually a few cases— a very few mind you— involving acts of violence committed by sleepwalkers, but this one simply does not fit the pattern."

"How's that?"

"The tragedies like this that have occurred during episodes of nocturnal automatism have been driven by emotion. Responses to stimuli the sleepwalker experienced during waking hours. Stress and emotional upset, and while there may be a triggering incident, in most cases the stimulus has been in place over a long period."

"Well," I said, "stress is apparently what brought me here to begin with, right?"

"Yes, but let me finish," she urged. "The crimes committed by sleepwalkers are commonly very brutal and born out of passion. For instance, there was a man who repeatedly stabbed his mother-in-law with a hunting knife; another bludgeoned his mother-in-law to death with a tire iron. Still another repeatedly stabbed, and then drowned his wife.

"There is a definite pattern established here with this type of crime. The attacker knows his or her victim intimately and the evidence left behind is abundant. There is no conscious, calculated attempt to cover it up, so to speak."

"There's a first time for everything," I continued my protest, though more as a devil's advocate than anything else because I desperately wanted to believe her. "Maybe I'm an isolated case."

She shrugged. "I suppose that is always a possibility, but I don't believe it for a minute. Neither should you."

"Trust me. I don't want to."

"Then don't, because you did not kill that woman."

There was a brief lull as I pondered her comments. I wanted to believe what she said was true, and in reality she had made some very strong arguments. Still, I was at a loss to explain my presence at that crime scene and it had become like a terrible itch that I couldn't reach, no matter how hard I tried.

By some convoluted reasoning it seemed almost logical that I might have murdered someone. The only thing that kept me from going over the edge was the fact that the reasoning was just exactly that— convoluted.

"I wonder if this whole idea crossed Ben's mind at all?" I speculated aloud.

"Possibly," Helen allowed. "Quite probably, in fact. But, you can be certain he dismissed it fairly quickly."

"Why do you say that?"

"If Benjamin had any inkling that you were responsible for the murder, you would be under the microscope at this very moment." She made the matter-of-fact statement as she stared out at the muted sky, then turned back to face me. "Had he any evidence to support such an idea, you would already have been arrested."

"Do you think so? I mean, we've been friends a long time. You don't think he'd hold back a bit?"

"Not if he had any evidence, most definitely. Not even if he had an intuition that you had committed a murder. As his friend you must certainly know that the only loyalty he holds in higher stead than to his friends and family, is the loyalty to his job. No, Rowan. If he thought you did it, you would be in custody. Friend or not."

"Yeah," I agreed quietly. "Ben Storm, supercop."

"It is a large part of who he is," she explained. "We all draw our identities from different sources. For Benjamin, it is his work. He is at his most comfortable as he is defined by his job. In a way, you could say that it is his destiny."

"Which would make mine to be what? The flaky, new-age sidekick?" I mused.

"Your life isn't defined by his, Rowan. It is defined by you and your choices."

"Maybe, but it seems that my choices over the past couple of years have put me smack in the middle of his world."

"Yes, they have," she conceded. "But in doing so you have been instrumental in bringing down two serial killers. Is that such a bad thing?"

"At what cost to me, though?" I said. "I've got no idea which end is up anymore."

"I will admit that the cost to you on an emotional level has been substantial," she replied. "But that cost is not a permanent deficit. That is why you are here talking with me."

"You really think I'm going to come out of this okay?"

"Of course you are, Rowan. You are far stronger than you give yourself credit."

"I wish I'd never gotten involved in that first case to begin with," I sighed heavily.

"No you don't," she rebutted. "Be honest with yourself. If you were in that same situation again, you would make exactly the same decision you did then."

"Yeah, probably," I admitted. "So I guess that makes me a bit of a masochist."

"It makes you exactly what your name purports you to be. A person of strength; a protector."

Had it been anyone else, I believe I would have been taken aback by the explanation. There aren't many people who know the inherent meaning of the name Rowan right off the top of their heads, and those who do are usually pagan. It seems we pagans have a penchant for knowing the significance behind our appellations. For some reason, however, it came as no surprise to me that Helen Storm would know this, and I took great comfort in it.

Thick silence cloaked us once again as she allowed me to continue mulling over her well thought out rebuttal to my hasty revelation. The fear had not yet vacated the premises but it had at least settled into dormancy for the time being.

"Just as long as I don't have to wear tights," I finally said.

"I'm sorry? I don't understand."

"If I'm going to be Ben's sidekick," I detailed. "I simply don't have the legs for wearing tights."

What had been an emergency hour of psychotherapy had turned into almost two hours of deeply thoughtful banter. I was feeling better than I had when I arrived, but I was by no means out of the woods. While I no longer harbored any serious suspicions about being guilty of murder, I couldn't shake the sense that I was somehow involved more deeply than it appeared on the surface. Whether directly or indirectly, I just knew there was something about Paige Lawson's death that connected solidly with me. I also had no doubt whatsoever that she was the victim of more than a random accident. I just had no way to prove it, yet.

Here and there, office doors were open as I strode down the corridor toward the elevators, repeatedly turning the plague of thoughts over in my head— inspecting each, moving on to the next, and starting the cycle anew when I reached the last one. To my left, the happy, synthesized chords of *Mannheim Steamroller's* rendition of 'Deck the Halls' issued from a doorway; to my right, the angst-ridden voice of *Ozzie Osbourne* was '*going off the rails on a crazy train.*' The two songs met in the middle, intertwined, separated, and then competed for my attention, neither of them ever actually winning the contest. Although, I did have to admit that the helpless anguish being described by the heavy metal lyrics on my right came closest to describing my mood.

When I reached the end of the hallway I punched the recessed call button and waited before the polished metal doors of the elevator. Eventually an electromechanical ding announced the arrival of the car and the doors slid open with a slight rumble to reveal the empty interior. A heavily syncopated version of 'God Rest Ye Merry Gentlemen' filtered outward from an overhead speaker to join the struggle begun by the other two songs. I stepped in and double tapped the button labeled with an L.

The even mechanical rumble began again as the two halves of the door began their journeys toward the middle. They would have met had it not been for a feminine hand thrusting quickly between them and engaging the safety. The split doors immediately reversed direction and slid back into their pockets as a harried, young blonde, balancing a stack of files in one arm, rushed through the opening.

"Sorry," she apologized as she shifted the healthy stack of folders into both arms. "It's just, sometimes this elevator takes forever."

"That's okay," I told her. "Which floor?"

"Three please. Thank you."

I leaned forward and punched the button for the third floor. "No problem."

The young woman remained standing immediately before the doors, obviously in a hurry. She was petite and dressed tastefully in a wool skirt and blazer. Her carefully manicured nails were lacquered a fashionable shade, and her pale skin was brushed with only the barest necessity of makeup needed to enhance her natural beauty.

My heart hesitated for a beat as I stepped back and caught a glimpse of her profile. Just twenty-four hours ago, I had sat voyeuristically in my truck and watched her as she made her way into the building, all the while fantasizing about what she would look like if she had red hair.

The recognition sparked a moment of internal embarrassment, even though I knew full well that she had no idea the incident had ever occurred. Unfortunately, the fleeting chagrin was the least of my worries, as the imaginings of her with an auburn mane suddenly returned, encroaching upon my mind even more powerfully than before.

I clenched my teeth and struggled to keep my breathing even as the thoughts once again assaulted me, this time bringing with them far more lurid imaginings. Dizziness flooded into my skull and induced a nauseating tickle at the back of my throat as darkly perverse desires welled within me. The fantasy no longer entailed a simple change in hair color; it had become a private reel of soft-core pornography directed by someone unseen, but most definitely felt.

The lights in the elevator seemed to flicker and dim as the sliding doors touched in the middle and the car began its downward journey. She didn't seem to notice the visual effect so I assumed that it was happening inside my head, not exactly the reassurance I wished for. I could feel myself slipping out of reality, losing control to the director of this lurid fantasy.

She allowed the stack of files to spill onto the floor of the elevator, turning toward me as she did so. Her hair had darkened to a deep red and cascaded across her shoulders and down her back. An intense light of desire burned in her eyes as she looked at me and smiled. Wordlessly she shrugged off her blazer and allowed it to fall to the floor, then began to slowly unbutton her blouse as she moved toward me.

I forced myself to seek any type of grounding that I could, no matter how thin or tenuous. I needed something to cling to if I were going to escape this unwanted ethereal bond. I stared directly ahead, fighting to breathe evenly, and willed the vision to evaporate. A flicker of colors insinuated themselves, flashing the scene from negative to positive, and back again. The young woman was standing in front of the doors, her back to me, still blonde.

I made the mistake of sighing in relief and my concentration shattered. The here and now slipped through my fingers like a greased rope.

She was half nude now and as I watched she seductively

allowed her skirt to drop and stepped out of it. Standing before me she was clad in nothing but a garter belt, stockings and heels. Her makeup had gone from subtle to extreme; her lips glossed with a garish slash of blood red. She pressed her body into mine without a word. I could feel her hot breath on my neck as she undulated against me.

Again I reached for reality, denying those things I thought I was seeing and experiencing. I could feel my back pressed against the wall in the corner of the elevator. I wasn't certain if the sensation was just another part of the cheesy skin-flick scenario being forced upon me, or if it was the real thing. I banked on it being the latter, and folded myself into it as I shut my eyes.

The sickening voice I'd heard echoing within my brain the night before suddenly returned. I squeezed my eyes shut even tighter and swallowed hard, fighting to ignore its existence, only to fail miserably in my attempt.

Oh god, she's so close to perfect!
Her skin...
Her neck...
She could be her!

I desperately wanted to scream. I had no idea how much longer the elevator ride was going to last, but it had already been an eternity. I was afraid I wasn't going to make it.

Look at her...
Oh sweet Jesus, so close...
The black gown...
She'd look so great in the black gown...
She'll be almost perfect...
Almost her...

Almost...

I opened my eyes to check the car's downward progress and sucked in a startled breath. My arm was extended and my hand less than a pair of inches from the young woman's shoulder. I was starting to tremble and I snatched my arm back quickly, grasping my wrist with my other hand and hugging it tight against my body.

The dark thoughts were now threatening to infect other portions of my anatomy and I held my breath, fighting to force them away. I concentrated on anything mundane I could grasp— anything that could replace the rampant sexual energies that were building within me.

A dizzying rush in my ears drowned out almost everything except my own frenzied heartbeat. I scarcely noticed as a muffled electromechanical bong sounded overhead, insinuating itself seamlessly into the barely audible, syncopated Muzak. There was a slight jerk and the doors split, opening wide upon a brightly lit hallway.

The young woman turned quickly to me and flashed a warm smile, "Merry Christmas."

She was gone through the opening before I could reply, not that I was able to do so. For reasons unknown, as quickly as it had begun the disharmonious reverberation in my ears was instantly gone, replaced by the muted sound of the elevator doors sliding shut and a synthesized melody that closely resembled 'Angels We Have Heard On High.'

I let out a heavy sigh as the red-tinted darkness pooled lower in my body, finally flowing outward to leave me feeling physically weakened and emotionally spent. I literally stumbled away from the wall of the car, grateful no one else was there to witness my condition. I had just begun to regain my composure when the doors again fractured down the center and opened onto the lobby.

In a fit of panic, I wondered if I should rush back upstairs to Helen Storm's office and tell her what had just happened, but I was halfway afraid I would encounter the young woman again on the way back up. If I did, I wasn't entirely sure I could control the urges that had almost overtaken me moments before. I thought about it hard, not moving from the corner of the car and stared into space at nothing in particular.

My immediate reaction was to seek the psychological relevance of the episode in order to understand it, obtain another dose of reassurance that I wasn't well on my way to criminally insane. But, something in the back of my head kept telling me that psychoanalysis wasn't going to reveal an answer to this one. This was something more— something completely out of the pail— for the mundane world at least.

I gave up on weighing the options when I realized the elevator doors had slid shut once again.

I absently punched the recessed 'door open' button on the panel and exited the confines of the lift, then quickly crossed the tiled lobby, hooked past a symmetrically decorated Christmas tree, and pushed onward out through the glass doors.

A cool breeze caressed my face and forced me to calm a bit more. I stopped for a moment on the sidewalk and turned away from the wind as I lit a cigarette, then inhaled the smoke deep into my lungs. As I exhaled, I was certain that I heard a familiar voice in the distance, but not the dark one as before. This one had plagued me for several days now, beginning as unfamiliar scratchings on a page before finally coming into its own. As usual, it was filled with a peculiar mix of desperation and mockery at the same time.

Gimme a D!
Gimme an E!

Gimme an A!
Gimme another D!
What's that spell?
DEAD! DEAD! DEAD!
DEAD, Rowan.
I'm dead for God's sake; so quit feeling sorry for yourself.
Do something about it.

My decision was made for me. My gut told me there was something more than just my addled psyche at work here, and that I was going to have to figure it out on my own. As frightened by the prospect as I now was, I had no choice but to follow its lead.

CHAPTER 14

When I exited the parking lot of the medical building, my head was telling me to turn left toward home. After all, Felicity would be expecting me and there were things that needed to get done before the gathering tomorrow evening.

My gut, on the other hand, asserted its newly assigned leadership and pre-empted the turn with a pair of rights before finally making that left, and I was soon motoring north on the Innerbelt. Thirty minutes later I awoke from an absent minded daze as I found myself pulling off onto the shoulder of an isolated section of Highway Three Sixty-Seven, not far from the Clark Bridge and Alton, Illinois.

I sat for several minutes, engine running while I pondered the autopilot that had brought me here. I had traveled this road more times than I could remember, and had even pulled off along the side to watch the eagles that would winter in the area. However, it wasn't yet the season for eagle watching, not to mention it was a bit late in the day for the activity. Besides, the prime spot for it was farther down the stretch of asphalt anyway. This particular spot on the roadside had attracted me for a far more sinister reason, and though I'd never stopped here before, I had arrived at this exact location with only my subconscious as a guide.

I sat staring through the passenger side window, peering

past my own reflection in the glass and allowed my eyes to adjust to the cold shadows. In what little was left of the fading light I could just barely make out a twisted ribbon of yellow and black crime scene tape stretched between spindly tree trunks in the distance.

I finally switched off the headlights and cast a quick glance at the radio before twisting the key to kill the engine. The digital clock on its face showed it to be almost five PM. With tomorrow being winter Solstice, the shortest day of the year, official sunset was rapidly approaching. In fact, it was less than an hour away. However, considering the thick blanket of grey clouds that was acting as a barrier to the sun's rays, dusk had been abbreviated, and for all intents and purposes nightfall was already upon us. The miniscule amount of illumination still available would be completely gone in a matter of heartbeats.

I felt more than a little queasy about being here. I wanted to believe that I was simply following my instincts by coming to the spot where Debbie Schaeffer's remains had been found. Still, I couldn't help but wonder if I was being guided by a tortured soul who had recently discovered she held a measure of control over me, even in this world. Realistically, she was probably pulling the strings and was the one directly responsible for bringing me to this place. What was left for me to come to terms with was whether or not I was capable of handling what she wanted to show me without outside help. The events of the previous night screamed, "No." My clouded judgment shouted back a resounding, "I don't know." Debbie Schaeffer's haunting voice just kept echoing in the back of my skull, "I'm dead, Rowan. Do something about it."

I continued to sit there, staring out the window while the grey shadows faded to inky black as if condensed into a single minute of time-lapse video. Taking a deep breath, I weighed my options and considered what was being presented. I was in no way naïve enough to believe that I was going to stumble across some enlightening bit of physical evidence that would break the case wide open. That was the sort of thing that always happened in dime store mystery novels, but almost never in real life. Trained crime scene investigators had already been over this area with eyes sharper than mine so the odds of my finding anything more than a pile of dead leaves were beyond astronomical.

Unless, perhaps, that piece of evidence was simply invisible to the unaware— latent, hidden from the view of those not able to see beyond this plane of existence. Still, it would need to be tangible for it to mean anything, and such a thing was far from likely.

Besides, something about that just didn't feel right either.

No, evidence was not why I was here. Not by a long shot.

I was here for the connection— for the proximity to ground zero. I was here for the express purpose of reliving someone else's nightmare— as if I didn't have enough of my own already. Deep down, I was beginning to resent the fact that these visions were being imposed on me against my will. I'd already had more than enough of them to last me a lifetime, but there seemed no end to the horrifying pictures that begged my attention. It was no wonder I felt like I was going mad.

I engaged in a few more moments of restless indecision before finally surrendering to the idea that I was already here so I might as well get out and take a look. I'd wasted enough time to deprive myself of any natural lighting so I rummaged about beneath the seat and eventually extracted a flashlight before climbing out of the cab and starting down the shallow embankment.

I wasn't entirely sure if it was just the darkness, or the place, or even if the temperature had actually dropped, but it felt far colder than it had just an hour or so before. I stopped for a moment to zip my jacket, shrugging it closer and turning up the collar to fend off the slight breeze. Standing there on the side of the small hill I looked to my left and saw the muted glow of the lights from the Clark Bridge just peeking over the barren treetops. Exhaling a frosty breath, I watched the foggy luminescence disappear from view as I ventured the last few steps down the grade and into the stand of trees.

My feet crunched noisily through the dry layer of leaves and with each step kicked up the damper stratum beneath, filling the air with the sharp, "composty" odor of decay. The flashlight wasn't the most powerful in the world, but I'd expected better performance than I was getting. The batteries were apparently just this side of dead, so the faint yellow beam quickly dissipated less than two yards ahead, making my progress slow and unsteady.

To my back, commuters were making their way home from jobs on this side of the river, and an occasional car would rush by; the beams of its headlights cutting a swath through the trees well above my head and totally useless for illuminating my path. They did, however, create oblique shadows that would quickly arc through a semicircular pattern as the vehicle approached, then flitter to obscurity when it passed. I'm sure it was nothing more than my anxiety fueled imagination, but some of the gloomy artifacts seemed to possess lives of their own— and they didn't look friendly.

I carefully picked my way through the scrub, tripping twice on the same fallen log, and only narrowly regaining my balance before almost being pitched to the ground. Leaning against a tree for support, I decided to stop once again in order to get my bearings. The crime scene tape had looked to be some thirty or so yards from the roadside. In my estimation, I had probably managed to cover half that distance so far.

With each step, the world had seemed to close off behind me, leaving me isolated in the darkness. Even the swish of randomly passing vehicles had faded so far into the background that the only sound left for me to hear was my labored breathing and pounding heart. As I stood in place, wheezing in the cold air, my body screamed for a dose of nicotine. I reached my hand inside my jacket at the impulse, but then thought better of the idea before fully withdrawing the pack of cigarettes. Shoving it back into my breast pocket I panned the dying flashlight across the landscape in search of a trail or break in the undergrowth.

A flicker of bright yellow lashed quickly through the weak beam as the wind swelled, and then fell off in a rolling wave. I had apparently made it further than I'd suspected. I cocked my head to the side and listened carefully as a static-laden hum began inside my head. In my ears there came a faint whisper.

Dead I am. Dead I am. I do not like that dead I am.

"I know you are." I found myself answering the voice aloud. "Trust me, I know."

Aiming myself in the direction of the yellow flicker, I stiff armed my way through a close huddle of saplings and pushed closer. Hollowness began to invade the pit of my stomach as I inched forward, mixing with the ingredients of the night to spin itself into a thin thread of fear. I continued listening intently to the breeze, waiting for the voice that only I could hear.

"Talk to me, Debbie," I muttered under my breath. "Tell me your story."

The thread of foreboding began to embroider itself up my spine, bringing a chill that made me physically shiver and hug my coat tighter. I rubbed my palm against the day's growth of scratchy whiskers on my cheeks then tugged thoughtfully at my beard as I let out a nervous laugh. If I wanted proof that I was insane, then this was it. I was out here in the dark with a dying flashlight, completely and totally ungrounded and unprotected. What's more, I was actively inviting the spirit of a murdered woman to pop into my head when I knew for a fact that doing so was no less than inviting disaster. Yeah, I thought, I'm definitely pushing the envelope with this one.

Silence still permeated the night, leaving me with the rattle of my breathing and thump of my adrenalin affected heart as the only audible companions. The burst of rational thought should have driven me to immediately turn and flee, but rationality wasn't my strong suit right now. I pressed forward and the droning hum began again.

"Dead, Rowan. Dead. That's what I am. Do something about it."

The voice whispered past me again, working its way around my head as it bounced between mono and stereo separation.

"That's exactly what I'm trying to do, Debbie," I answered her out loud yet again. "Talk to me. Tell me what you saw."

I could feel an energetic presence swirling unseen before me and I halted. Icy tendrils of death slapped outward from it and I felt them slice effortlessly through my body, making me gasp with each strike. I knew then that I'd gone that one step farther than I should, and needed to turn tail and run. Unfortunately, the message was being diverted upon leaving my brain and it never made it to my legs. I stood frozen in place, unable to move.

"You've done this before, Rowan," I told myself in a not quite calm voice. "This is nothing new."

My subconscious immediately objected, telling me in no uncertain terms that while I'd done this before, I had done it when I was capable of grounding and centering.

I didn't have time to argue with myself. I took in a deep breath through my nose and slowly exhaled through my mouth, trying desperately to relax and achieve a focal point. I could feel the hair on my arms rise as a field of static touched me. I became instantly aware that there was no time for the Wicca 101 exercises in which I was about to engage; I needed to be grounded now, and that simply wasn't happening.

I steeled myself against an invasion that I feared could very well bring about an end to what small scrap of lucidity I still retained.

Dead I am! Dead I am! I do not like that dead I am!
Dead I am! Dead I am! I do not like that dead I am!

Debbie's disembodied voice began shifting in phases about me. Pitches rose and lowered as the chant doubled and echoed; increasing in speed with each revolution as if winding itself up to deliver a blow directly into my soul.

Dead I am! Dead I Am! DeadIAm! DeadIAm!
DEADIAM! DEADIAM! DEADIAM! DEADIAM! DEADIAM!
DEADIAM! DEADIAM! DEADIAM! DEADIAM! DEADIAM!

The mantra blended quickly as the words joined, becoming multi-syllabic noises that made my head vibrate with its bass staccato. The cadence continued to increase toward a roar of white noise and I felt as if my head was positioned between the jaws of an ever-tightening vise.

A shrill scream pierced the darkness without warning

and my own voice joined it in absolute disharmony. I started quickly, physically tensing while my heart climbed into my throat in search of refuge. When I jumped, I involuntarily released my grip on the near useless flashlight and it spiraled to the ground in slow motion, landing with a muted thud.

As if on a sudden gust of wind, the twirl of ethereal energy exploded outward, rushing through me, around me, past me, only to dissipate into nothingness.

The sound of a car whooshing past back up on the blacktop instantly faded in, and was followed by a repeat of the shrill scream. After a beat, a third warbling scream announced itself, now identifiable as the electronic peal of the cell phone in my jacket pocket.

I allowed myself to breathe and thrust my shaking hand into my pocket, then withdrew the chirruping device and stabbed the answer call button.

"Hello?"

"Rowan?" Ben Storm's voice greeted me quizzically.

"Yeah, Ben," I answered; hoping the tremble in my voice wasn't noticeable. "What's up?"

"You sound like you're out of breath white man," the earpiece buzzed with his voice.

"It's a long story," I answered, not sure what exactly to say.

"You okay?"

"Yeah, I'm fine," I told him, then repeated, "What's up?"

"Well, I called the house and Felicity told me you'd gone to see Helen today."

"Yeah, she got me in this afternoon."

"Uh-huh," he grunted. "Well, I just talked to 'er and she said you'd left her office over an hour ago."

"Checking up on me?" I retorted, somewhat perturbed.

The leaves crunched as I shuffled about, then knelt

down to retrieve the flashlight.

"Actually, no," he remarked, "but I get the feelin' maybe I should be."

I turned in place and could see in the distance the silhouette of my truck up on the shoulder. Aiming what little glow was coming from the flashlight toward the ground at my feet I began working my way toward the vehicle.

My friend was correct. Somebody needed to be checking up on me if I was going to make a habit of being this reckless. Truth was, his unexpected call had probably saved my sanity, if not my life.

"Yeah." I softened. "You probably should."

The rustle of the fallen foliage was loud and I was certain he could hear it.

"Row, where the hell are you? Ya' sound like you're rakin' leaves or somethin'."

"Somewhere I shouldn't be," I told him, electing not to try hiding the truth.

"Where, Row?" he asked again, sternly this time.

"A little wooded grove out off of Three Sixty-Seven," I answered.

I could hear him sigh heavily at the other end. "Jeezus, Rowan. What the hell are you trying to do? Make Felicity hate me? She's gonna have your ass for this ya'know?"

"It's not my fault," I volunteered the thin excuse.

"You tellin' me Debbie Schaeffer made you do it this time too?" he queried.

"Kind of," I returned. "Something like that anyway."

"Yeah, whatever. Look, I want you to get yer ass outta there right now," he instructed.

"I'm working on it."

"Don't lie to me, Rowan."

"I'm not."

Silence filled the earpiece for a moment while I picked

my way through the last of the underbrush and started back up the embankment.

"Shit," my friend exclaimed softly. "I shouldn't even ask, 'cause it'll just encourage you…" He sighed as he fell into a thoughtful silence, then finally spoke again. "Well did'ja figure anything out?"

"Unfortunately, no."

"Man… I just don't know what to do with you… Jeez…" His voice trailed off.

"If it's any consolation," I offered, "you called me just in time to keep me from doing something really incredibly stupid."

"Like what you were doin' now isn't really incredibly stupid?" he shot back.

"No," I agreed. "It's stupid all right. But what I was about to do was even more stupid."

"Great," he muttered.

I scrambled my way to the top of the hill and sat down on the bumper of my truck for a moment in order to rest. I flicked off the flashlight and set it aside, then reached into my pocket and withdrew a cigarette.

"So," I asked after lighting the butt and taking a deep drag. "Why were you calling me in the first place?"

"Just wanted to let you know we looked into a connection between Lawson and Schaeffer."

"And?"

"Nothing there, Row," he told me. "No connection, no common friends, activities, or anything. Nada."

"Are you certain?"

"Certain as we can be with what we've got. The whole Lawson thing is a dead end white-man. She's got nothing to do with Debbie Schaeffer."

"So I guess you're closing the books on her then?" I asked, dejection filling my voice.

"Well, yes and no."

"What do you mean, 'yes, and no'? Which is it?"

I could literally feel his hesitation over the phone. "Man… I shouldn't even tell you…"

"Come on, Ben. You can't leave me hanging like that."

"Shit," he muttered the expletive. "Okay, but you gotta promise me you'll stay outta this and let us handle it."

"Fine. I promise."

"Yeah, right," he returned, not believing me for a minute, then he huffed out a breath before continuing anyway. "Okay, listen, it looks like you might've been right about Lawson's death not being an accident. Well, not entirely an accident, anyway."

"Go on." I was intrigued, even a little elated. Vindication appeared to be on the horizon, and it was something I sorely needed.

"Remember I mentioned she had a welt on her neck?" He didn't wait for me to answer. "Well, the M.E. says it's consistent with the type of mark that could be left by a high-powered stun gun."

"I thought those things weren't supposed to leave marks?"

"Depends," he explained. "Not always, but there are a lot of factors; trust me, they can definitely leave a serious welt. I speak from experience."

My hand lifted automatically to my neck and I focused on the memory of the burning sensation I'd felt. The jangle and buzz that had taken over every nerve in my body; the disorientation and paralysis that had driven me to fall helpless on the ground while at that crime scene. A piece of the puzzle locked securely in with another. I could only imagine the picture that was going to be formed, but at least now I had a start.

"So it's a murder case now?"

"Kinda," he acknowledged without enthusiasm. "We figure what prob'ly happened was that some asshole waited in the bushes and assaulted her on her way in the door. Most likely a doper or somethin' lookin' to score some quick cash. Jammed 'er with the stun gun, she fell and cracked her head on the table; shithead sees the blood, panics and runs without even lifting anything."

"You think that's it?"

"Wouldn't be the first time."

"But it could be more, right?" I asked.

"No." In my mind's eye I could see him shaking his head. "I really don't think so. There's nothing else there."

I thought about it silently for a moment. Logically, Ben was correct, but I wasn't subscribing to logical theories these days. There was something else there, and I wasn't going to give up until I found it. With what he'd told me, I had a start; now I just needed to build on it. I could tell from my friend's tone that he was already regretting that he'd told me anything, so I was just going to have to chase this lead on my own.

"So what about the whole smoking thing," I asked, changing the subject as much to hide my intentions as to let him off the hook.

"Yeah, yeah, I looked into it. Far as we can tell they were both clean. Neither of 'em smoked."

"Guess it's someone else then," I submitted.

"There is no one else, Rowan," he answered. "Listen, you still out there in the woods?"

"No. I'm at my truck."

"Good," he returned flatly. "Then go home."

He ended the call with that abrupt command, an almost angry click following the last words. I wasn't exactly making people happy.

I'd scarcely managed to climb into the cab of my truck and get myself belted in before the cell phone pealed for attention a second time. I gave the face a quick look before answering and the caller ID display registered my home number. I can't say that it was unexpected, but I can say that I was dreading it.

It was dead on six PM when I pulled into the driveway, fully chastised via phone. Felicity was waiting for me when I walked through the front door and she was armed and ready for round two.

If looks could kill...

It took the better part of the next day for me to finally redeem myself with my wife. I hadn't tried to hide anything from her, and while that helped my case to a small extent, she was still far from pleased.

I had a tendency to forget that even though Felicity wasn't prone to the same type or frequency of bizarre visions as myself, she was a Witch nonetheless, and very in tune with her surroundings. At this particular stage of the game, I had to accept that she was actually far more in tune than me, whether I liked it or not.

While she was unsure of the details— until she forced me to fill her in, that is— she had been perfectly aware that I was up to something. She had even experienced some sensations of my own fear because of the deep bond between us. Once she became privy to the particulars behind that fear, however, her initial concern folded quickly into anger.

Fortunately, since she had been a direct witness to what had happened at the morgue the evening prior, she was willing to believe that I wasn't necessarily the one in control of the situation. While that tempered the anger, it served to return her concern to the forefront.

Still, when everything was said and done, it was noon before she decided that she was speaking to me again.

CHAPTER 15

"Hello?" I had managed to snatch up the telephone receiver just as the fourth ring was dying away, and only a split second ahead of the answering machine.

My greeting was met with nothing more than dead air, although there was a distinct hollowness to it, which lead me to believe that there was almost certainly someone on the other end. After a moment, I repeated the salutation.

"Hello? Anyone there?"

My query was answered by what I thought might possibly have been a shallow breath, though I couldn't be sure. The sound was promptly followed by a soft click in the earpiece as the calling party hung up.

I dropped the handset back into the cradle and scanned the caller ID box next to it. The LCD display read, UNAVAILABLE. Whoever it was either lived in an area without the CLID service, or more likely, they'd keyed in the code to disable it.

"Who was on the phone?" Felicity asked, as she zipped quickly through the living room and hooked past me on her way upstairs with an empty box that had earlier contained the holiday decorations that now tastefully adorned strategic locations throughout the house.

We'd both managed to grab a fairly substantial amount

of sleep, and her brogue had melted back into a slightly perceptible Celtic lilt, minus the clipped affectations that had permeated her speech before. Of course, the extra time we'd spent resting was directly responsible for us now rushing about in a frenzy to get everything done before our guests arrived.

"Don't know," I called after her. "They hung up and the caller ID says unavailable."

"That's weird," she said as she came back down the stairs, quickly sidestepping to avoid a cat on its way up. "There were three hang-ups on the answering machine when I checked it yesterday, and another two this morning."

"There were a couple on there the other morning when you dropped me off here too. Did you check the ID box?"

"Uh-hmm," she acknowledged with a nod, as she shot past me in the opposite direction this time. "All unavailable except one, and it was a data error. What about the other ones?"

"Same. Unavailable."

"Hmmm," she remarked. "Wonder what that's all about."

"Well, the hang-ups on there yesterday might have been the media from the night before," I speculated as I followed her into the kitchen.

"Here." She pushed a cutting board holding a large knob of ginger across the island toward me. "Peel and slice. Goes in this bowl here."

"For the marinade?"

"Yeah. After you're through with that, mince three or four green onions and throw them in there too."

"How do you think ostrich is going to go over with this crew?"

"They probably won't even know it isn't beef unless we tell them."

"Well, I get to tell Ben."

"As long as I get to watch."

"You can run the camera," I offered jokingly.

"So, don't you think reporters would have left messages?" she asked after a moment.

"What? You mean the hang-ups? I don't know." I shrugged as I absently scraped the skin from the pungent ginger root. "Maybe. Maybe not. They probably didn't figure I'd return the calls, so they might have been trying to get lucky and catch me."

"It's probably nothing. Just some telemarketing outfit," she offered. "They always mask the caller ID."

"Maybe, but we hardly ever get any of those calls anymore. Not since we got on that no-call list."

"True, but even that doesn't eliminate all of them."

"Yeah, you're right," I agreed. "Just seems funny that we're getting so many all of a sudden."

"Well, it's the holiday season; whoever it is might not even be looking to sell us anything. They might be a charity begging donations."

"Yeah. That makes sense." I nodded. "Especially since September and all."

As if it had been listening to us all the while, the object of our discussion pealed once again.

"Don't commit to anything over twenty-five bucks," I half-joked as Felicity quickly wiped her hands with a dishtowel and stepped over to the wall phone.

"Hello?" she said, tucking the handset between her ear and shoulder.

I waited quietly for a moment, looking over at her and halfway expecting the call to be another hang-up.

"Oh, hi," she declared, instantly riddling that suspicion with holes. "Uh-huh... Yes... Uh-hmmm... Okay, that's fine. So, which paper are you using? Okay, that's good. Well, can't you adjust for it?"

This side of the conversation sounded extremely photographic so I turned my attention to the ginger and began thinly slicing the golden-yellow rhizome.

"Sure, that would be fine," my wife continued behind me. "Just dial in a bit of cyan for me if you would. Sure. That would be great. No, I don't need to see it; I trust your judgment. And, you've got the original print for comparison. No, really, I trust you. No problem. Thanks for calling. Yes. Sure. Uh-huh. Happy holidays to you too. Sure. I will, you too. Bye-bye." She hung up the phone and immediately exclaimed, "Sheesh!"

"Problems?" I asked, still focusing on the culinary task I'd been assigned.

"Oh, that was Harold over at Arch Labs," she told me as she stepped back over to the counter and rolled her eyes. "They're using a different lot of paper and the color was slightly off on that batch job I gave him a couple of days ago."

"So, isn't that something they can just correct for?"

"Exactly." She nodded vigorously as she began the task of cleaning the platter of fresh ostrich tenderloins and placing them into the bowl of marinade. "That's exactly what they are supposed to do. That's why I gave them an original print to compare to. There's no need to call me on something like that."

"I don't want to sound harsh, but is this Harold guy incompetent or something?"

"No, that's not it. He's very good at what he does, and he knew exactly what he needed to do," she answered with a sigh and a slight pause. "Actually, I'm afraid I might know why he called."

"That would be?" I tossed a handful of the ginger slices into the marinade and continued chopping.

"I hate to sound like I'm full of myself, but I think he's

got a crush on me."

"Hmmm…" I nodded. "That's not terribly surprising. I mean, look in a mirror, sweetheart. You're very easy to have a crush on."

"Still trying to score points are you?"

"If I can," I said. "I suspect I can use all of them I can get."

"Uh-hmmm," she returned. "Thought so."

"I meant what I said though."

"Thank you."

"So,…Is it working?" I asked.

"What?"

"The scoring points thing."

"Keep trying." She grinned. "I'll let you know."

"Oh, so that's how it works." I chuckled. "Do I get any hints on how I can get bonus points?"

"You want a hint? Okay. Think in terms of a full body massage."

"Long or short?"

"Long. Definitely very long. With warm oil, candlelight, and a nice bottle of wine."

"Could be fun. Anything else?"

"You could follow it up by drawing me a warm bath with lavender and chamomile, and then while I'm soaking you can do all the dishes that are going to get piled up from tonight's dinner."

"Ouch. Now it sounds like work. How about just the massage and bath part?"

"Nope." She shook her head. "Package deal."

"Okay, so how many points do I get for it?"

"I'll let you know afterwards."

"Ahhh, I see." I nodded with a grin, and then voiced a different thought, "So, anyway, back to the earlier subject, maybe our mystery caller is your secret admirer."

She shuffled a half step toward the phone and leaned forward, then stepped back. "Well, the ID shows Arch's number, so if it's him he didn't mask it that time. Besides, I don't think it's anything that serious. Only a bit of a crush, and I could be wrong about that."

"Oh well, it was just a theory," I returned, then feigned concern. "My, my, my, a secret admirer. Should I be worried?"

"What? Me with Harold?" She chuckled lightly. "I'm thinking maybe no."

"Whew!" I exaggerated a dramatic sigh of relief. "Had me concerned for a minute there."

"Of course," she mused aloud, "if you don't clean up your act and stop having all these little midnight encounters with the spirits of dead women…"

"Hey, you'll want to talk to THEM about that." I splayed my hands out in mock surrender. "I'm not entirely at fault there."

"Not entirely," she allowed, "but you do get some of the blame."

"Yeah, I do." I nodded. "I know I do."

"If it wasn't for the fact that they are all residing on a different plane, I'd be the one with something to worry about, I think."

"Never," I said. "Besides, I'm pretty sure they don't have crushes on me. They're all just looking for closure so they can move on."

"I know," she echoed. "I still get a bit… I don't know… Jealous, seems like too strong a word for it…"

"Yeah, I know," I said, stopping and looking over at her. "But you have absolutely nothing to worry about. You know that."

"Unless you keep taking chances," she stated matter-of-factly.

"I'm working on that."

Her hair was pulled back into a ponytail that fell neatly down the center of her back. A few fugitive strands of her spiraling tresses were brushed behind her ear; a dangling gold earring intertwined with them and lay softly against the pale skin of her neck. She was absently chewing at her lower lip as she concentrated on her task. The soft, indirect sunlight coming from the atrium at the back of the kitchen cast her in a beautiful glow. I caught myself staring as an entirely new set of thoughts overtook my brain.

"So, what are you planning to wear tonight?" I asked, not really knowing where the question had come from.

"What?" she echoed in a puzzled tone.

"Just wondering what you were going to wear." I shrugged, still following what seemed an unfamiliar path.

"What I've got on, I guess," she answered as she took a step back and gave herself a once over. "I'll probably change shirts. Why?"

"I don't know," I shook my head.

"Do you think I should wear something else?"

"I just… I don't know…" I was starting to feel a bit lost on this trail, but it appeared that a landmark might be directly ahead, so I gave in and continued deeper.

"What?" she pressed.

The landmark was there as promised, and it was even familiar. I should have been frightened by it, but since I was standing in my own kitchen with my wife and not an elevator with a stranger, I embraced it. Without a second thought I ventured, "What about your black dress?"

Felicity stopped what she was doing and shook her head slowly as she looked at me with an incredulous stare. "You think I should wear a dress?"

"Sure. Why not?"

"Well, we're going to be outside in the cold during a

good part of the evening for one thing."

"There's going to be a fire," I offered, a seductive vision continuing to coalesce.

"Okay, let's say I wear a dress." She canted her head to the side, and shot me a look that said she was just humoring me in order to see where this was headed. "Which black dress are you talking about? I have several."

"You know, that black dress," I rambled, simply following a curvaceous image in my head that seemed to be beckoning me further into a dangerous state of being. "Long… Slit up the side…"

"…Satin, backless, lace sleeves, lace panel in the bodice?" she offered a more detailed description. "You mean that one?"

The image was coming completely into focus. Her description blended itself with the ethereal and brought a rush of excitement coursing through my body. "Yeah, sure, that's the one."

"Well," she raised an eyebrow, "are you going to be wearing a tux?"

"I hadn't planned on it." I shook my head, answering her absently and directing my attention to the imagery dancing behind my eyes. "Why?"

"Rowan, that dress is a formal evening gown. Are you serious?"

"Sure."

The fantasy was rapidly heating up, speeding headlong toward becoming just as lurid as the episode I'd had in the elevator the day before. Although it was accompanied by a bit of an itch at the back of my brain, I didn't fight it. I can only assume it was that reason which allowed it to take over smoothly. No whirlpooling colors, no frantic heartbeats, and no fear; simply pure lust for a private showing of a wakeful dream that was about to become hardcore.

I must have been standing there with a ridiculous grin on my face, because the next thing I heard was my name spoken in a piercing tone of disbelief.

"Rowan!"

The insistence behind her tone told me that this wasn't the first time she'd called out. What followed immediately was an instant feeling of claustrophobia and isolation as ethereal shields formed a thick barrier around the both of us. My wife's response to her protective instinct, coupled with the sharpness of her voice, shattered my pornographic illusion and I stammered, "Umm... I don't know... I guess... I mean... Well, you really look good in it."

"Thank you, but I'm thinking maybe I'd be a bit overdressed for this particular gathering." Her voice was stern and she stared at me with a puzzled expression. "Not to mention that I'd freeze my tail off. Since when did you become so interested in my choice of clothing anyway?"

"Umm, I really don't know," I shrugged, all remnants of the image fading and leaving me to defend myself without its reward. "Uhh... Umm..."

"Row, are you okay? There was some pretty bizarre energy bouncing around in here."

"Ummm, yeah. I think so."

"Are you sure? I've never felt anything like that off of you before."

I really didn't think it would be a good idea to tell her the story about the young woman in the elevator at this moment in time. I'd managed to keep that one to myself and I figured it should stay that way for a while longer. Still, the fact that the sleepless dream had recurred made me think that there was even more to it than I'd suspected the day before. I still had no idea quite what that significance was, but it definitely begged deeper investigation. Even so, while it acted in some odd sense as yet another thin reassurance that I wasn't going completely nuts, it still incited a pang of fear in the pit of my stomach, and so I answered her as best I could. "Yeah. I'm fine."

"You could've fooled me." She shook her head.

"Sorry."

"That's okay, as long as you aren't actually expecting me to wear a dress tonight."

"No. Not really," I told her, then offered a weak explanation. "It just must have been that whole massage conversation. You got me all worked up."

"Uh-huh. All my fault." She wasn't convinced. "So, since we are on the subject, what are YOU going to wear?"

"The usual, I guess," I answered.

"The usual?"

"Yeah. Whatever you tell me to."

CHAPTER 16

"Be it known to all that no one is here but of their own free will," Felicity spoke aloud, raising her voice slightly in competition with a cold wind that sighed through the leafless trees surrounding our large back yard. "Those wishing to be in circle please join hands, left palm up, right palm down, and take a moment to ground and center."

We hadn't yet had any snow to speak of. A flurry or two here and there, but nothing that stuck around for any length of time. Now, with the temperature still above freezing it was looking very much like we were in for an "earth tone" Christmas a few days hence. Even so, the night was chilly enough that my shoulder was already starting to ache and we'd only been outside for fifteen minutes. I suppose there had been only just so much that could be done to repair the joint after my encounter with Eldon Porter, so I figured I'd better get used to it. Still, I was starting to regret not donning a heavier coat.

We were all positioned in a loose circle on our deck—Me, Felicity, Ben and his wife Allison, and a small group of pagan friends. We surrounded a portable, outdoor fireplace that had been stacked with carefully arranged kindling that consisted not only of dried sticks, but of pinecones and a remnant of the previous year's Yule log as well.

Felicity and I were actually solitary practitioners of The Craft and didn't belong to a particular coven. Truth was we rarely held ritual with anyone other than ourselves, and maybe a cat or two present; however, this was a special occasion. Of the eight generally accepted pagan holidays scattered about the wheel of the year, this was the final one before beginning the cycle anew. Though labeled as a minor Sabbat, Yule was without a doubt a holiday of immense importance, and a celebration that literally demanded the camaraderie of close friends. Ben and Allison were the closest friends we had, and those in attendance besides them fit the description perfectly as well, for they had become an integral part of our lives over the past year or so.

R.J., Cally, Randy and his wife Nancy, and a bubbly pair of identical twins named Jennifer and Shari— who had a proclivity toward finishing one another's sentences— were in some ways our adopted children. And, it wasn't necessarily because they were several years younger than us. The primary factor was really the horrific circumstances under which we'd met— a turn of events that had moved us to, for all intents and purposes, take them in. They had been the core group of a fledgling coven that had been formed and led by Ariel Tanner— an old friend and former student of mine back when I'd endeavored to instruct others in The Craft.

Ariel had met a gruesome end to her own young life at the hand of a sadistic serial killer, and through my connection with her I'd become deeply embroiled in the investigation. In the process, Felicity and I had befriended the leaderless young neophytes, and soon we had taken them under wing in order to provide some of the guidance that can come only from age and experience. It had been rewarding, though trying at times. Still, a strong bond was forged and they would forever be a part of our lives.

Eight of us formed the relaxed ellipse with Ben and

Allison standing quietly outside the group. Everyone had been in agreement, and we had made it clear to the couple that they were perfectly welcome to join us in the circle, but that they should feel no obligation to do so. While Ben was far less a skeptic than he'd been in the past, it was obvious that he felt somewhat uncomfortable with the idea of being a part of the ritual. However, the two of them were curious and since everyone else was fine with having an audience, they were content to watch from the sidelines as we proceeded through the simple rite.

"I don't suppose I need to ask if everyone is grounded, now do I?" Felicity asked on the heels of her own musical laugh. "This is feeling way too good."

Quiet chuckles and stifled laughs elicited from the small group. Being an eclectic, non-traditional group, we tended to practice in an informal, freeform fashion, and at times the steps of a given ritual would take on a mind of their own. She had drawn her proffered conclusion from the fact that energy had already begun to pass about the circle in a smooth, unrestricted flow, several steps ahead of being called for.

Even with my current state of being, I'd actually managed to achieve a solid ground in short order. It had taken serious concentration to do so; something I was still getting used to, but I'd done it. I'm sure that I had a bit of help from a particular redhead since she was latched tight to my hand, but none of that mattered to me right now. What was important was that I was fully grounded, and the combined energies of the group circling through felt absolutely wonderful.

"Well," my wife spoke again, "since this production doesn't seem to need a director, which one of you would you like to call the quarters this time?"

"We will," Jennifer and Shari both chimed in at once.

With no argument whatsoever, the two of them smoothly broke the ranks of the circle, opening ethereal doorways by which to properly exit as the rest of us shuffled around to close the ranks. Moving in opposite directions, they orbited us, passing one another at the easternmost point of our deck, and then continuing along the circuit until meeting once again in the east. There, they stopped, face-to-face, and joined hands in a miniature circle of their own.

"On this night…" Jennifer began.

"…Of darkness long," Shari continued.

"We join together…" Jennifer said.

"…Our circle strong," Shari completed.

"We raise our voice, above the rest…"

"…And make to you, this gentle request."

A short measure of silence fell in behind the quick chant, and we all waited.

"Watchtower of the east…" Jennifer finally said as they continued to trade off the lines.

"…Element of air…" Shari added seamlessly.

"…Guardian of the wind…"

"…Breath of life."

"We invite you," they spoke simultaneously this time, blending in a double-voiced harmony. "Join us this night and watch over us in our circle. Blessed be!"

"So mote it be!" the rest of us sang out in unison at the queue.

After a double beat of quiet, the two girls released hands and turned their backs to one another. Jennifer went into motion first, Shari remaining steadfast in place until her sister was on the opposite side of the circle, whereupon she set out in the opposite direction. They pranced, almost fairylike, as they made the circuit. It was obvious that they were enjoying the task at hand, and loved being in the spotlight. This time around they passed one another at the southernmost point of the group, again continuing about us until meeting once again in the south.

Repeating their earlier posture, they clasped hands.

R.J. canted toward me and I leaned in to hear him whisper, "They've been planning this for three weeks, ya'know."

I grinned at him as he stood there shaking his head.

"Guardians present…" Shari's voice met our ears.

"…We count now one," Jennifer followed.

"Demands of you…" Shari again.

"…We shall make none," Jennifer said.

"Now our quest, is but to ask…"

"…If in fire's glow, we may bask."

Again, a momentary lull followed their chant as we all anticipated what would come next.

"Watchtower of the south…" Shari said.

"…Element of fire…" Jennifer followed.

"…Guardian of flame…"

"…Bringer of warmth."

"…We invite you to…"

The twin's conjoined voices were unceremoniously interrupted by an evenly spaced staccato of piercing electronic beeps. An extremely brief interval of silence ensued, only to be followed by a second set of the annoying tones that increased in volume by at least half. A third set barely got off the ground as an abbreviated chirp. What was quickly followed was my friend's embarrassed sounding voice.

"Sorry about that. Thought I'd set it to vibrate," Ben apologized meekly as he scanned the face of his pager.

"Is it the sitter?" Allison asked, leaning closer to her husband to have a look at the device.

"No," Ben answered, then shot his glance my way. "But I'd better answer this. Row, ya' think maybe I can use your phone?"

"Help yourself." I nodded. "You know where it is. Feel free to use the one in the bedroom if you want."

"Ummm, I hope this doesn't offend anyone, but I'm kinda unfamiliar with this whole deal. Do I need to bow or genuflect or somethin' before I leave?"

The innocent seriousness of his question brought a round of chuckles to the group.

"No, nothing like that," I explained with a smile. "We aren't actually casting circle here at the moment, and besides, even if we were, you aren't actually IN circle with us. You can come and go as you please. Just come on back out after you're finished, it won't bother us, as long as you are quiet about it."

"Thanks," he told me as he started toward the door of the atrium. "Sorry I interrupted the deal here everyone…"

"Crap occurs." Randy made the simple statement with a grin.

"I think we'll survive," Felicity said. "It's not the first time."

"But, Detective Storm," the twins called after him simultaneously.

"Yeah?" he turned back, his hand already on the doorknob.

"Just don't let…" Jennifer said with a giggle.

"…It happen again." Shari finished, tittering as well.

"Man," I heard Ben laugh as he went through the door, shaking his head, "you two are a piece of work."

My shoulder was seriously starting to ache from the cold, and as Ben shut the door behind him, I felt the hair rise on the back of my neck and a dull throb begin at the base of my skull. The pain was apparently starting to expand, and I rolled my arm a bit to get comfortable.

"You okay, Rowan?" R.J. whispered to me.

"Yeah, I'm fine." I nodded as I answered. "Shoulder."

He shot me a grimace and nodded understanding at my one word explanation.

"All right, everyone," Felicity announced. "Are we

ready to move on?"

I thought for a second about excusing myself, but elected not to say anything. I decided to give it a few more minutes and see how things progressed. Worse case scenario, after the next tower was hailed I could go inside and down a handful of aspirin.

Everyone settled back in, and the twins completed their abruptly truncated hail of the southern watchtower before once again engaging in their opposing orbits around the circle.

"Watchtowers doubled..." said Jennifer as they joined at our west.

"...now stand in a pair," chimed Shari.

"Guardian of fire..."

"...and guardian of air,"

"We beckon you now, come join the rest..."

"...with ebb and with flow, as you do the best."

"Watchtower of the west," Jennifer's voice stepped in behind the lull.

"Element of water..." Shari continued.

"Guardian of ocean, sea, lake and stream..."

"Giver of life."

Their voices doubled together, "We invite you. Please join us this night and watch over us in our circle. Blessed be!"

"So mote it be!" we answered aloud.

Jennifer and Shari executed their dance for a fourth and final time, coming to rest in the north, and very close to their original positions in our circle.

"Thrice we've bid..." Shari began.

"...To watchtowers tall..." Jennifer completed.

"...And each have answered..."

"...Our humble call."

"Now at last, we come to four..."

"...The final tower, there are no more."

"Watchtower of the north..."

"Element of earth…"

"Guardian of the land…"

"Mother of all…"

And together they harmonized a last time, "We invite you. Please join us this night and watch over us in our circle. Blessed be!"

And as one, we all answered, "So mote it be!"

The girls rejoined our ranks as we spread out to accommodate them, and they stood almost dancing in place, excited grins plastered across their faces. As they clasped hands with the circle we could all instantly feel the intense level of energy they'd raised between themselves, and were now sharing with us. It was no wonder they couldn't seem to stand still.

A warm feeling coursed through my body, and though my shoulder was still bludgeoning me with discomfort, I decided I could bear it a while longer. Provided it didn't get any worse, that is.

"The wheel forever turns, spinning in harmony with nature; with the Lord and Lady; with the elements and all that is," Felicity said, picking up where Jennifer and Shari had ended. "It spirals through the seasons, bringing with it the balance of the cyclic birth, death, and rebirth of all.

"Winter solstice is both an end and a beginning. This longest night brings to a close our solar year, and with the dawn brings to us the hope and mystery of the next. It is a time when that which is spent is laid to rest, and that which is new and untouched bursts forth with wonder and promise.

"This is a time for new beginnings. This is a time we call Yule. It is a celebration of the cycle and the rebirth of the Sun God. In honor of this time, we celebrate with a pyre in its name."

The last sentence was my queue; I released hands and stepped forward into the center of the circle. Digging in my pocket, after a moment I withdrew a wooden match. Kneeling down, I struck it against the deck and shielded the flame from the wind with my cupped hand. I reached into the open fire pit and touched the small fire to a few strategic points. The dry kindling caught quickly, then I stood and stepped back into place with the rest of the circle.

The wood and pinecones crackled as the fire began to spread and consume them as fuel— an act of birth and death in and of itself. Flickering light cast outward to illuminate us in a yellow-orange glow.

Nancy knelt down and when she stood up again she stepped forward holding a medium-sized oak log, decorated with pine boughs. She carefully lowered it into the rapidly growing conflagration and allowed it to fall the last few inches, jumping back as a shower of embers plumed upward.

"The Yule log represents the cycle of birth, death, and rebirth." Felicity continued her recitation of the ritual. "Tonight, this pyre will light our way through the darkness; give us warmth to stave off the cold; and remind us of our good fortune past, present, and future as we welcome the rebirth of the Sun God. Blessed be!"

"So mote it be!" we answered her.

Felicity looked solemnly around the circle as a cloud of smoke billowed outward from the fire pit and lofted upward on the cold breeze. The sappy pine boughs had begun to burn now and their pungent odor was filling the air, riding on the back of the blue-white smoke.

"Well, let's make this thing safe so we can leave it alone for a while," she stated. "I don't know about the rest of you, but I'm ready to eat. It's going to be a very long night."

After we'd placed the lid on the portable fireplace and

closed the screens, we all started back inside for the feast. I had become so caught up in the ritual that it was my sole focus for several minutes. Until then I'd almost completely dismissed the fact that my shoulder was flaring up. I was suddenly reminded of it in no uncertain terms by a sharp twinge that drove inward, and then hung a quick right to shoot down my arm, ending with momentary numbness in my fingers. I decided then and there that I was going to need something to take it down a few notches if I was going to make it through the rest of the night.

Something else I'd forgotten was that Ben was already in the house making a phone call. He had apparently just finished as we all filtered into the living room and began hanging up our coats. I heard the door to our bedroom open as everyone was heading back into the kitchen and dining room to help get everything set out for dinner. I hung back a moment and waited.

"Hey, Tonto," I greeted my friend as he came around the corner and up the short hallway. "You missed all the fun."

"What? Oh, yeah, sorry 'bout that," he answered me thickly, a noticeable span of distance in his voice. He looked pale, which considering his dusky complexion was alarming in and of itself.

"Something wrong?" I queried, feeling the hairs on my neck snap to attention once again.

"No. Nothin'. No big deal." He shook his head.

I was unconvinced. "Are you sure?"

"Yeah, I'm sure." He shook his head a little too vigorously. "It was nothin'."

"Ben…"

He shot me a hard look and half whispered, "Not right now, Rowan. Drop it."

"Okay." I shrugged and held up a hand to let him know I got the message. "No problem."

I stood looking at him for a moment and could almost visibly see the wheels turning. Something was up, but for some unknown reason I was going to remain in the dark with regard to it. I didn't like this situation at all, because something deep down told me that whatever it was that Ben was laboring over, it definitely had something to do with me.

The earlier rampant fear that I had perhaps killed Paige Lawson myself now returned to the forefront with extreme prejudice. Everything Helen had said to convince me otherwise went instantly out the window, and I became my own prime suspect once again.

I couldn't take it.

"Am I a suspect?" I blurted.

"Do what?" Ben shook his head as if he'd misheard the question and stared back at me with a look of incredulity.

"You heard me, Ben," I rushed the words out before my brain could convince me to shut up. "Am I a suspect in Paige Lawson's death?"

"Hell no." He stared at me and screwed up his face in confusion. "Where the fuck'd'ya get that idea?"

"I don't know," I shook my head as I sighed. "I was there... All the stuff that's been happening... Now you've obviously got something bothering you— presumably because of that phone call— and you're keeping whatever it is from me..."

"Hey, white man," he said. "I don't even tell my wife everything about work, okay?"

"Yeah, maybe so, but I've got a feeling that whatever that phone call was about, my name got mentioned in there somewhere."

"Listen," he sent a hand up to massage his neck, and gestured at me with the other, "you'll just hafta trust me on this. That phone call is prob'ly gonna turn out to be nothin', but either way, I just can't discuss it with ya' right now."

"Probably going to turn out to be nothing," I repeated his words. "So, it does have something to do with me then?"

"I'm not going there."

"But if it has something to do with me…"

"Row, drop it."

"Ben…"

"Now, Row."

I wasn't going to get anywhere with him, that much was obvious. I was also breaking the cardinal rule of not pushing Ben Storm into a corner, and I knew better. I decided I'd better heed his advice.

"Yeah. Okay." I cocked my head in the direction of the dining room, changing the subject. "So, everyone's getting ready to eat."

"Great," he nodded. "I'm starving. You gonna tell me what we're having yet?"

"I think you'll like it."

"Okay, but what is it?"

"Food, Ben. Trust me, you'll like it."

"Well, if I don't, at least I'm covered."

"You didn't really bring a sack of belly-bombers did you?" I asked.

"No, but I got a coupl'a frozen pizzas out in the van. All I gotta do is borrow your oven and I'm good ta' go."

I shook my head and grinned at him, "I can't believe you did that."

"Hey, a man's gotta eat. By the way," he jerked a thumb over his shoulder toward the back of the house, "did you say your deal was over with out there?"

"We'll officially cast circle a bit later, but that's not for a while yet. So, except for tending the fire through the night, and clearing the towers later, yeah, it's done. Why?"

"So it's all clear for alcohol?"

"In moderation, yeah, sure."

"Good deal, 'cause I need a scotch like right now."

"Yeah, same here. Do me a favor and pour me one while you're at it," I said as I stepped past him. "I've just got to hit the restroom first."

"You sure? I thought you said alcohol wasn't allowed in the circle thing, and if you still gotta do that later..."

"I've got a while yet. Besides, in this case I don't think the God will mind if I relax a little bit."

"Okay. You're the Witch."

"Yeah. Don't remind me."

The hairs along the back of my neck were still on end by the time I returned to the dining room. Something very bad was waiting in the wings and I hated not knowing what it was.

CHAPTER 17

The sun was riding a southern arc in the cloudless sky, casting its brightness across the cityscape as I hooked my truck onto Clark avenue, and then a couple of blocks later found myself a parking space in front of City Police Headquarters. After easing between the diagonal lines, I levered the vehicle into park and paused a moment. Finally, I took off my sunglasses and tucked them between the headliner and passenger side visor, then switched off the engine.

December twenty-fourth had slid quietly in to follow our celebration of the winter's solstice; sneaking into the fold as always, no matter how prepared you may think yourself to be. Two entire days had passed now, each of them an almost indiscernible fraction of time longer in lighted hours than was the day before. The sun god had been reborn, but the new solar year had still brought with it the issues left unresolved during the previous turn of the wheel.

However, as if in honor of a secretly declared cease-fire, the forty-eight hours had passed with absolutely nothing out of the ordinary happening. No dreams, no visions, no sleepwalking. Not even the barest twinge of a waking nightmare. To Felicity, and those around me, this all appeared to be a display of my progress; an outward indication that my psyche was on the mend. I wished that I could agree with them, but I'd had a similar experience before, and the outcome had been less than pleasant.

To me, this period of supernormal silence was more frightening than anything that had occurred to date; very simply because I could feel the foreboding that they could not. Still, as I said, it was nothing horrific; nothing that was overtly driving me as had the events of recent past. This was merely an indefinable aggravation that would tickle and itch, doing all that it could to irritate me, asleep or awake. Each time I would think it had finally gone away, it would pop up in a different corner of my brain, tempting me with shaded emotions that hinted at a future it had no intention of actually revealing in advance.

The sense had been with me ever since Yule, bolstered in part by Ben's cryptic attitude following the secretive phone call. Deep down inside I knew this was a harbinger of things to come and that these fleeting days were merely the calm before the storm. What I feared the most however was that if this level of calm turned out to be directly proportionate to the intensity of the coming storm, then I could never be prepared for what I would have to face. I was truly afraid that in the grand scheme of things, everything up until now had been the equivalent of nothing more than a spring shower.

For a time, I made an almost hourly ritual of mutely begging the Lord and Lady to tell me that I was wrong. When it became obvious that my pleas were to be left unanswered, I gave up.

Truth be told, what I really needed to be doing right now was forgetting about it all and taking some time to relax. Whatever it was that was coming was still an unknown, and there was simply nothing I could do to stop it. Not at this stage of the game, anyway. I was just going to have to ride it out. On top of that, a new calendar year was almost upon us, and the more mundane tasks in my life would soon multiply.

January tended to be one of the busier months for my consulting business, for with a simple turn of the year, annual budgets magically refreshed and people started renewing support contracts and planning system changes. With that being only a week away, the lull in my day-to-day grind would be coming to an end. Once that happened, if I was still dealing with a plague of ethereal horrors, I was going to be a complete wreck— as if I wasn't one already.

For the moment, I had no place to be and nothing much to do. I really needed to take advantage of the situation. It would be a perfect day for some quiet meditation and grounding exercises, especially considering that I could have the whole house to myself with no distractions.

Today being Christmas Eve, Felicity— fully decked out as one of Santa's helpers— was visiting a local children's home with her nature photography club. And, I do mean she was fully decked out. In fact, I was actually finding it hard not to think about how she'd looked when she left the house. To the kids I'm sure she simply appeared to be a rather perky elf, but to your average red-blooded adult male… Well, let's just say she did the costume justice in ways Father Christmas hadn't originally imagined, if you know what I mean.

The visit was something that her group did every year at this time— handing out donated toys, clothing, and coats. Every holiday season the event managed to garner more and more press which in turn created more demand from various charitable organizations. Thankfully, the added press also brought more donations. So, as word got around, what had originally started a few years back as a small party for some underprivileged kids had now grown into a huge affair, encompassing not only the children's home, but visits to local hospitals and shelters as well. It was a good cause, and even though it was hard work, they loved every minute of it.

Considering this year's schedule, Felicity wouldn't be

back for the rest of the day, so I had plenty of time to just vegetate. In the end, I think it was that volatile combination of idleness and nervous energy that had finally set me in motion. She hadn't even been gone for two hours before I went in search of trouble.

And now, here I was, parked in front of City Police Headquarters and staring out my windshield in a semi-catatonic stupor. Considering my original intentions, though, this might very well be a good thing.

I had actually started out from the house with the plan of revisiting the wooded area on Three Sixty-Seven where Debbie Schaeffer's body had been found. Subconsciously, I suppose that like most, I found some comfort in the daylight. I really don't know why, because time of day really had no bearing on the unique curse of visionary abilities that had been terrorizing me for the past two years. Truth was, I had no idea what had any bearing on them, because they certainly weren't under my control. In any event, my automatic pilot had engaged almost as soon as I backed out of the driveway, and I was three quarters of the way here before it dawned on me that *here* wasn't where I'd planned to go.

Sitting there, I felt a shiver run up my spine and I forced back yet another soft-core image of my wife in her costume as my brain shuffled through the random thoughts it had kept waiting in the wings. Then, I frowned at the provocative cogitation.

Felicity and I had a perfectly healthy and even fairly imaginative sex life. While the male of the species supposedly has sexual thoughts every two minutes, I was really starting to wonder about myself. This constant fantasizing about her, while perfectly enjoyable in most respects, was becoming troublesome— especially considering recent events. I made a mental note to mention this constant obsession when my next appointment with Helen rolled around. This, of course, triggered remembrance of other mental notes I'd made and then promptly forgotten— such as the whole fantasy episode surrounding Felicity's hair when we were at the morgue. Then there was the episode in the elevator that I'd had when leaving her office, and I really should have called her about immediately. Of course, that one seemed driven by an outside force, though I wasn't even certain about that. It really didn't make much sense at all.

I suppose that if I was somehow becoming overly obsessed with sex, then the lurid thoughts could very well be my own. But, even that didn't seem correct to me. There really seemed to be an outside presence. I was almost certain that I could feel it. Moreover, it had something to do with Debbie Schaeffer and Paige Lawson.

Unfortunately, everything that happened at the morgue that night after I connected with Debbie Schaeffer was still an out of focus jumble. What little I'd been able to pick out here and there was completely nonsensical. Barbies in Prom dresses, makeup, a smart-mouthed cheerleader, flashing lights… Then there was Paige Lawson. Where did she fit into all of this?

If the outside presence that was forcing all of the lurid thoughts into my head was the one responsible for either of their deaths, then maybe the crime— or crimes— were motivated by sex. But, one was a kidnapping and the other appeared to be a robbery gone awry. Maybe Paige Lawson was just an anomaly; a piece of a totally different puzzle that I was trying too hard to make fit into a blurry and indistinct picture.

But then, every time I had one of these semi-pornographic fantasies, there was the thing with red hair. Both Debbie Schaeffer and Paige Lawson were blondes. So was the woman in the elevator. So, that almost had to come directly from me. I mean, I had to admit that I personally had a thing for red hair, so that could make it highly likely that it was just my own preference overlaying itself with the imagery.

Maybe?

It was starting to get very confusing again. I'd been mulling it all over so much that it was giving me a headache.

If Ben was correct, I was just chasing my tail anyway, and I needed to direct my energies toward something more productive. I finally gave up on my attempt at analysis and decided to leave it to Helen. After all, as she'd pointed out, she was the one with the degree in Psychology. Since all of the incidents seemed linked by sex, and that was apparently a driving force for me these days, maybe I'd remember to mention all of this at the next appointment.

After a moment I let out a purposeful sigh and muttered to no one but myself, "Yeah, right." Then, before getting out of the truck I made yet another mental note to start writing this stuff down.

I'd have to start doing that later though. Right now I just wanted to smoke another cigarette before going inside.

"Merry freakin' ho-ho-ho," Ben said as I dropped myself into one of the ancient molded-plastic seats next to his desk. "Wanna cuppa?"

"I don't know…" I shook my head, vivid recollections of the caustic liquid the Homicide division called coffee dancing on my tongue.

"Hey," he exclaimed, "it's Christmas Eve, Kemosabe. We actually washed the pot this mornin'."

"Yeah," I chuckled, "whether it needed it or not, right?"

"Exactly." He grinned.

An nth generation photocopy graced one corner of his desk blotter, and was positioned so that I could easily read it.

A blurred, but still recognizable pair of mug shots dominated the page, showing a rotund, bearded man in an instantly recognizable suit. The text beneath outlined a wrap sheet, stating that the individual was wanted for breaking and entering, cookie theft, and illegal dumping. It further went on to say that he was known by such aliases as Saint Nick, The Jolly Elf, Santa Claus, etcetera, and could often be found in the company of elves. Last seen fleeing in a late model sleigh pulled by eight reindeer. Approach with caution.

"Sounds like a real tough guy," I said, indicating the novelty on his desk.

"Yeah," he nodded and laughed. "The asshole dumped a whole pile of crap at my house last year and I ended up holdin' the bag for all the batteries. If I ever catch up with him I'm liable to kill 'im." Leaning back, he took a sip of his coffee and watched me carefully for a long moment. "So, what's up? Why aren't you with the little woman?"

"She's out doing that charity thing with her photography club."

"Yeah, I know. She was just on the news about forty-five minutes ago givin' an interview." He let out a low wolf whistle. "Nice outfit."

"Uh-huh," I grunted, not really needing the reminder.

"So, explain that one to me."

"What? Her costume?"

"Hell no, that was self-explanatory you lucky bastard," he said. "I'm talkin' about her doing the whole Santa Claus thing. How's that fit in with what you celebrated the other night?"

"It doesn't really," I told him. "Yule is a religious holiday, just like Christmas or Chanukah. Santa Claus, however, while associated with Christmas, isn't a religious figure. In his current incarnation he's actually an icon of commercialism created by a soft drink company."

"Yeah, I read that somewhere already, smartass," he grinned. "What I'm askin' is if you Witches celebrate Christmas too?"

"In the sense of it being a commercialized holiday, sure, many do. But it doesn't bear any religious significance for Pagans like it does for a lot of others."

"So you get like two holidays in one," he stated as much as asked.

"You could look at it that way, but Christmas is the generally accepted holiday by society as a whole. I doubt you'll find many employers who give Winter Solstice as a paid holiday."

"Yeah, I s'pose you're right," he nodded thoughtfully. "Anyway, the reason I asked is Allison and I wanted to invite you and the little woman over to the house tonight if you aren't doing anything."

"I thought you were having a family get together this evening."

"Yeah, Helen's comin' over, but that's about it. Besides, you two are like family anyway."

"Well, we aren't doing anything with our families until tomorrow," I conceded. "I'll have to check with Felicity, but I'm sure she'd love to come over. If you're sure we wouldn't be intruding."

"I wouldn't have invited ya' if you'd be intruding."

"Okay. I'll talk to her about it, but you can probably go ahead and just count us in."

"Good deal. I'll let Al know. So, now that we have that out of the way, let's get back to the original question. What gives, Row?" he asked again. "I know damn well you didn't come down here to explain the meanin' of Christmas to me. What're you doin' here?"

"Would you believe I just stopped in to say Happy Holidays?"

"I think I pretty much just said no to that."

"Yeah, didn't think so."

The telephone on his desk pierced the ensuing lull with a sickly trill, and he leaned forward and snatched up the receiver. "Homicide, Storm." Even as he spoke he kept his eyes on me expectantly. "Yeah… Uh-huh… Sure, I'm here. No problem. See you in a few."

He dropped the handset back into its base and leaned back once again, making the heavy-duty springs in his chair groan in protest.

"Do you need to leave?" I asked.

"Nope. Another copper is droppin' by for somethin'. Charlee McLaughlin, you probably remember her," he said.

"Sure," I nodded. "I remember Charlee."

Detective McLaughlin had been assigned to the Major Case Squad earlier this year when Eldon Porter had engaged in his one-man revival of the inquisition. I had gotten to know her when she had volunteered to work a secondary job guarding Felicity and me after it became obvious that I was one of Porter's targets.

"So, you gonna tell me what's up?" he pressed.

"I would if I knew, Ben."

"And that's s'posed to mean?"

"I don't know." I shrugged. "I didn't actually set out to come here. It's just where I ended up."

"Where'd you start out for?"

"You don't want to know."

"Jeez, Row." He shook his head. "What're you up to now?"

"I wish I knew," I answered him. "Something just doesn't feel right about everything that's been going on."

"Yeah, well, that's not exactly news white man."

"No, that's not what I mean." I shook my head vigorously. "Ever since Friday night…"

"Whoa." Ben held up a hand to stop me. "If this is about the phone call, I already told ya' I'm not goin' there."

"It's not about that," I stammered my objection. "Not really... Well, maybe... A little... But not entirely... I've just got a weird feeling. It's been way too quiet for the past couple of days."

"What? Like no disturbances in the *Twilight Zone*?" He followed up his comment with an abbreviated whistle of the old TV show's opening theme.

"Something like that."

"Yeah, so?" He shrugged. "In my book, quiet's good."

"But it's been TOO quiet."

"You sure you're not just lettin' your imagination run away on ya'?"

"I don't think so. Not this time."

"So, you got somethin' to work with?" he asked with more than just a hint of sincerity in his query this time. "One of those hinky visions? Some more morbid Seussian poetry? Anything?"

"No. Not at the moment. Like I said, it's been quiet. This is just a feeling."

"That doesn't really help me, Row."

"I know, Ben. It doesn't exactly help me either."

"Hey, Chief," a voice came from behind me.

"Yo, Chuck," Ben returned, looking past me. "How's Sex Crimes treatin' ya? Gettin' any?"

"More than you, would be my guess," Detective Charlee McLaughlin joked as she came into view. "And I'm being treated about as well as a sex crime can treat anyone I suppose." With that she turned her attention to me. "Hey, Rowan. I didn't know you were here. How're you doing?"

"I'm good, Charlee," I acknowledged. "You?"

"Can't complain."

"How's your daughter doing?" I asked, almost grateful

for the sudden distraction the chitchat provided.

"Great. She's planning to transfer up to Columbia after the spring semester."

"Terrific. Still planning to major in Journalism?"

"Yep. That's the plan."

"Good deal."

"So what brings you down here?" she asked, and then continued with a good-natured chuckle. "Storm dragging you into something else he can't figure out?"

"Hey now," Ben interjected with a grin, "I'm not the one that transferred out of Homicide to go slummin' in Vice."

"I just got tired of seein' your ugly face every morning, Storm," she told him.

"Yeah, yeah, yeah," he waved her off, "so what brings you up here?"

"Chasing a hunch, actually." She turned serious. "You got a minute?"

"Do you two need me to leave?" I asked.

Ben gave Detective McLaughlin a questioning look, and she shook her head.

"No, just don't repeat anything you hear."

"Of course not."

"Then grab some real estate," Ben said as he motioned to another of the seventies era plastic chairs that was positioned next to a desk behind her. "Whatcha' got?"

"Rumor is," she began as she slid the seat over and parked her small frame in it, "you've got a dead blonde with a stun gun welt on her neck."

"Yeah," my friend nodded acknowledgement. "Looks like a robbery-assault gone south. What about it?"

"Well, I assume you've been watching the news and have heard about the serial rapist?"

"Yeah. Kinda hard to miss. You workin' that one?"

"Yeah, I'm up to my ass in it. Anyway, we've been

playing some of the facts close to the vest." She looked him square in the face. "And, like I said, this is just a hunch... But the deal is, as of this past Thursday morning I've got eight very confused, very blonde, rape victims. All of 'em with stun gun welts, and testing positive for Roofies."

Detective Benjamin Storm's chair canted forward with a slow rumble; sliding smoothly along with the groan of the springs beneath until all motion finally halted. The inevitable stop was announced with a dull thunk, followed immediately by the proverbial pregnant pause. He shot me a quick glance then leveled his gaze on McLaughlin.

"Don't make me wait till tomorrow to open the present, Chuck," he said. "Tell me you got this asshole in lockup."

"Actually," she said, "I was kinda hoping for a stocking stuffer from you."

"Shit," Ben muttered. "You got anything at all?"

"Well, we've been lucky and gotten some of these right away. Seems he doesn't bother with condoms and he's a secretor, so we've got blood type and the whole DNA pedigree. But I don't have a warm body to hang the dog tags on."

"That's more than we've got. You chasin' any good leads?"

"Haven't got much. He's apparently got a kink about necks though."

"How's that?"

"Shithead sucks hickeys on these women the size of Rhode Island. Guys down in Sex Crimes are calling him 'The Rapist Lestat.'"

"Fuckin' lovely."

"Yeah, tell that to the victims."

"You got anything else? Any of 'em able to give you a description?"

"Nope," she sat back and shook her head, shifting in the

uncomfortable seat. "Not really. Like I said, Roofies. Outta the eight, five of them went to the hospital within the first forty-eight hours, and they all tested positive. We're guessing it would be the same on the other three, but they didn't come forward right away. Lab says they can probably pick up trace amounts in hair if we have to go that route.

"All of 'em pretty much remember gettin' zapped. Apparently he's got this stun gun jacked up pretty good, and it's kinda hard to forget getting hit with one of those. Anyhow, after that they're pretty sketchy until they wake up."

"How's he get to them? B and E?"

"Only on one." She shook her head. "So far he's grabbed three of them from parking lots at shopping malls, two when they were leaving their places of employment, one that was jogging, and another who was leaving a doctor's appointment. Now, here's the spooky part. He's keeping them for a while."

"Whaddaya mean keeping them?"

"I mean all of them are missing anywhere from twenty-four to forty-eight hours out of their lives."

"So he's gotta be takin' 'em somewhere," Ben mused.

"That's how we're looking at it."

"Is there any connection there?" Ben pressed. "Where are they waking up? Is he dumpin' 'em in the same general area?"

"Check this out," she said. "The asshole is taking these women home."

"You mean like home, home?"

"Yeah, as in takes them back to their respective domiciles and leaves 'em. Locks the door and everything. Even leaves the keys in the mailbox."

"No way."

"Yeah way. It's like he doesn't want 'em to get hurt or anything."

"Except by him."

"Well, yes and no. I'm not trying to diminish the crime here by any means, but we're not talking a typical rape scenario. There's no real physical abuse to speak of, other than the stun gun and the hickeys. Very non-violent statistically. We're guessing that's why he uses the Roofies on them."

"Bizzarro," Ben replied.

"Yeah, that's what I said," Charlee acknowledged with a knowing tilt of her head.

"Any patterns we can do somethin' with?"

"We've run it all. Common acquaintances, ex-husbands and boyfriends, the whole nine yards. What we've got is that they're all blonde, around five-four, five-five, good looking. Ages range from twenty-two to forty-one."

"Just City, or County too?"

"That's another squirrelly thing." She frowned. "Not only is he pulling from City and County, but one victim is in St. Charles, another is across the river in Godfrey, Illinois. If that's not bad enough for ya', I just got a call from the Sheriff's department out in Jefferson County. They're faxing us a report, but from what was said when we talked, it looks like they might be hosting victim nine."

"Fucker's all over the map."

"Yeah, and these are just the ones we know about," she said. "You know the stats on unreported rapes. Especially where Rophynol is in the picture."

"Yeah," Ben nodded and frowned. "So Paige Lawson might have been an attempted rape gone bad instead of a robbery-assault."

"Sounds like she fits the profile," Charlee agreed. "That's why I wanted to talk to you. I just heard the facts on Lawson an hour or so ago."

"Yeah. Not surprised. You've had a lot on your plate."

I was listening intently to the entire exchange, keeping

my mouth shut, and taking in the information. The jumble of puzzle pieces I'd been laboring over earlier was suddenly starting to make sense; for the first time in a very long while I had a feeling that a significant number of them actually belonged to the same picture.

"It might be a good idea for us to compare notes," Ben told her.

"Yeah, although I'm thinkin' I'll be helping you more than you'll be helping me."

"Yeah, maybe so, but you owe me one."

"How do you figure?"

"I lost twenty bucks on you when you showed up here in a skirt."

"Yeah, serves you right," she laughed. "Oh yeah, there were actually a couple of other things all the victims mentioned, although I don't think it will help your cause any since it didn't go very far."

"What's that?"

"Several of 'em mentioned having quite a bit of makeup smeared on their faces. Kinda like it had been wiped off, but not very well. And they all remembered bright, flashing lights— like blindingly bright I mean."

There's a funny thing about approaching storms and squall lines. Sometimes you can look out across the vast, empty plain of life and see them coming miles before they ever reach you. Then there are other times when there is so much clutter in the way that they are already battering you with gale forces while you are still trying to figure out if the sun just went behind a cloud or if you should seek immediate shelter.

This particular squall was on top of me before I even had a chance to look up.

The calm was definitely over.

CHAPTER 18

Dead I am! Dead I am!

The painfully familiar chant echoed in the back of my skull as a repressed memory from the night at the morgue revealed itself in halting disharmony. A ghastly feeling of disorientation began spreading outward from my brain in a frantic race to meet the abject panic that was vomiting upward from the pit of my stomach. They arrived simultaneously in the middle of my chest and proceeded to join forces in an attempt to bring my heart to a complete stop.

I heard myself gasp loudly as I sucked in a breath. Then, with no precursor, the memory became an explosion of light that burst directly in front of me. The sight stealing flash was accompanied by a muted pop, and then followed by an electronic whine. Everything before me was immediately washed out, leaving me temporarily blinded. As the flare faded, after images blurrily joined with a grey-toned reality that began repainting itself, only to be bleached out once again by a second bright strobe.

I started, and out of reflex raised my hand as I blinked and turned my head away from the source of the overbearing luminance. It didn't help. A third and fourth flash followed quickly on the heels of the first two, and it was still as if I was staring directly into them, wide-eyed and oblivious.

"Hey, Row," Ben's concerned voice met my ears. "You okay? What's wrong?"

"Debbie Schaeffer," I muttered, 'or at least that is what my brain told my vocal cords to do. What came out was an unintelligible burst of syllables as I tried to force the words past a catch in my throat.

With the anticipated fifth flash not yet forthcoming, I slowly lowered my hand and directed my squinting gaze toward my friend.

"What was that?" he questioned again.

"Debbie Schaeffer," I offered again, this time my voice winning out.

I could still see brightly colored spots dancing against a backdrop of rapidly fading after images, and it was making me a bit queasy. I blinked hard, trying to will them away. Fortunately, the blur was lessening at a quick pace and this page of reality was starting to come back into focus.

"What about her?"

"That's the connection between her and Paige Lawson," I explained, suddenly as sure of myself as I'd been in months. "This rapist."

"How do you figure?"

"The lights."

"This one of those *Twilight Zone* things or are you just guessing, Rowan?" He was interested but not yet convinced.

"At the morgue the other night," I continued. "When I made the connection with Debbie Schaeffer I kept seeing flashing lights."

"You didn't mention anything about flashin' lights then."

"I didn't remember them until now."

"Row…"

"I'm not just plucking this out of the air, Ben," I

snapped back at him. "You know as well as I do how this works sometimes. Besides, if I'm channeling the memories of someone who was drugged with Rophynol, then maybe I'm experiencing the effects of the drug as well."

"Okay, okay," he held up a hand to stave me off, "calm down. I wasn't tryin' to say you were makin' it up. I just wanna be sure we're not chasin' down a blind alley."

"Sorry," I apologized.

"S'alright," he said. "Now, do you remember anything else besides the flashin' lights?"

"Yes," I nodded vigorously, "a popping noise and a high-pitched whine."

"Popping and whining?" Charlee speculated aloud. "Wonder what that could be?"

"I know exactly what it is," I answered as I realized I'd heard the sound many times before. Living with a professional photographer, it was hard to avoid. "It's a photo strobe. He's taking pictures of them."

"There's a thought." She nodded as understanding overtook her. "It would certainly explain the bright lights, and it's not unheard of for a rapist to take an item from the victim. A keepsake that gives him a way to relive the act. That could also explain why he keeps them for a while."

"Exactly," I agreed. "And the smeared makeup too."

"Well," she volunteered, "I suppose pictures would be as good as anything else, but I don't think they're doing it for him anymore. The frequency of the attacks has been increasing."

"Whoa, hold on." Ben was shaking his head. "Back up for a minute you two. I've got a minor problem with this theory."

"What's that?" Charlee asked.

"Debbie Schaeffer," he stated. "I'm willing to accept Paige Lawson bein' an intended rape victim. If we apply a little creativity to the Coroner's report, then we can assume that what we have is this asshole jamming her with the stun gun. Zap! She falls and cracks her head on the corner of the table, then he freaks and runs at the sight of blood. I've got enough on the physical side to back that up, so, in my mind, that all fits.

"Now, Debbie Schaeffer, that's a different story altogether. We've got no physical evidence, and the way you've played this guy up, he apparently doesn't want these women harmed. Schaeffer was murdered and dumped in the woods."

"Are you certain she was murdered?" I asked.

He looked at me incredulously. "Well just what the hell would YOU call it?"

"Maybe her death was an accident too," I offered.

"Okay, what if it was?" he allowed. "Even if her death wasn't deliberate— which I'm not convinced of— it's still murder if it occurred during the commission of a felony. So, yes, that makes Lawson's death murder as well. But, what sets the two apart is the fact that Schaeffer's body was dumped in the woods. That indicates that whoever did it was trying to cover it up, and that doesn't seem to fit with this guy's established pattern of dropping the victims off at home."

"What if that pattern hadn't been established yet?" Detective McLaughlin interjected.

Ben gave her a thoughtful glance, then nodded. "Okay…Okay, that might fit. Keep talkin'. What's the date on the first case you've associated with this guy?"

"November. Day after Thanksgiving as a matter of fact," she said.

"Nothing earlier?"

"Not that's been reported."

"Well, Schaeffer went missing late October," he mused aloud. "That could fit."

"That puts a month between her disappearance and the first reported rape," I voiced my observation as I set my mind to the task of filling the blanks— and there were plenty of them, even taking into consideration my latest secular epiphany.

"Okay," Ben nodded. "That fills in that hole, but it still doesn't give us anything concrete. Not to mention we still don't have a suspect either."

"You're positive Debbie Schaeffer didn't have any ex-boyfriends?" I asked.

"None that her parents knew of, why?"

"Well, this is just speculation, so take it for what it's worth." I confessed the thoughts that had only now started to gel in the front of my brain. "But, if everything we've discussed here actually pans out, then that would make Debbie Schaeffer the first victim, right?"

"Yeah, go on."

"Well, what if she's the impetus for the entire string of rapes?"

"You mean," Ben looked at Detective McLaughlin, then back to me, "like he's trying to relive raping her through these other women?"

"Not exactly." I shook my head. "I was thinking more along the line that she was the actual object of his desire, and through whatever course of events transpired he accidentally killed her. So, by acting out his fantasy with the other women he is somehow bringing her back to life. In his mind anyway."

"Jeez, white man. Now you're startin' to sound like my sister."

I shrugged. "Maybe she's who we need to be talking to."

"Hello?" Helen Storm's voice issued from the phone.

We had regrouped in a conference room to allow for less distraction and more privacy. Ben had begun dialing her number almost as soon as the door was shut.

"Helen, it's Ben," my friend spoke quickly. "You're on speaker. I've got Detective McLaughlin and Rowan with me. You got a minute?"

"Since you already have me on speaker, I suppose it would be rude of me to say no, wouldn't it?"

"Gimme a break, Sis."

"Oh, I suppose I can let it go this time," she laughed musically. "What can I do for you, Benjamin?"

Detective McLaughlin gave me a grin then turned to Ben and mouthed "Benjamin?"

My friend fired back a wordless glance that said in no uncertain terms, "Don't even go there."

"First off, everything we discuss here is strictly on the QT, right?"

"Of course."

"Great. Then we've got a situation we'd like to run past you and get your professional opinion on."

"You understand that Forensic Psychology is not my area of expertise, correct?"

"I know, Helen," Ben said. "We aren't that far yet. We just wanna see if the theory will fly."

"All right. I will certainly do what I can to help then."

Ben proceeded to outline our recent discussion for her, up to and including my theory regarding Debbie Schaeffer. When he finally finished giving her the run down, there was a long pause at the other end.

"You still there, Helen?" Ben quizzed the phone.

"Yes, Benjamin," she answered. "I'm still here. Do you have any idea how Debbie Schaeffer died?"

"Nothing conclusive back from the Coroner's office, so,

no, not yet. Why?"

"It would certainly help to know if her death was in fact an accident or deliberate. Of course, I'm sure you realize that since this one fact is the lynch pin of your entire theory."

"Yeah, we know. We're just battin' things around right now," Ben said.

"All right then, let us assume that her death was accidental," she outlined. "Emotional transference is not uncommon, especially if an individual is incapable of retaining a firm grasp on the realities at hand. But, one does not necessarily need be psychotic or possessed of severely diminished faculties for this to occur either. A classic example is very simply that of the proverbial rebound relationship when a couple parts ways.

"However, as with any emotional upset, the severity can have a direct bearing on the outcome. If the individual directly affected— or even in part responsible for— the upset is already unbalanced, then this could certainly tip the scales in a dangerous direction."

"So what you're sayin' is we could be right?" Ben questioned.

"Perhaps." There was an almost audible shrug in her voice. "Can you tell me about the disposition of her remains? How was she when she was found?"

"Wrapped in a plastic drop cloth and dumped in the woods."

"Was she dumped, or was she placed?"

"I dunno. I guess she coulda been placed."

"You see, that is a factor as well. Was she clothed? Were there any personal items with her? How carefully was she wrapped in the plastic? Was this done haphazardly or was there reverence shown for her remains? Each of these things goes toward forming a picture of the person responsible."

"So, now you're sayin' we're probably wrong?"

"No, Benjamin, what I am saying is that there are several other factors which must be weighed in order to reach a truly viable conclusion. As it stands now, the best I can say is that your theory is a definite maybe."

"Okay," he huffed out a breath. "I guess that's better than a definite no. I appreciate the help, Sis. See you tonight at the house?"

"Of course. Is Rowan still there?"

"I'm here," I spoke up.

"Good. Would it be possible for me to speak with you for a moment?"

The tenor in her voice left no question that she wanted the conversation to be a private one. Ben picked up the receiver and handed it to me as the phone automatically disengaged the speaker, then motioned for Charlee to follow him out. I waited for the door to shut before pressing the handset to my ear.

"What's up?" I asked.

I had actually considered for a moment the mental laundry list of items I wanted to speak with Helen about, but quickly decided that this was neither the time nor the place.

"I simply wanted to see how you were doing," she returned.

"I'm fine."

"You are certain?"

"Well, I was until right now," I said. "Do I have a reason not to be?"

"Only you can answer that, Rowan. When you left after our last session you were still dealing with some very serious issues. I'm concerned that those issues may be what are compelling you to become so entrenched in this investigation."

"I think my compulsion is actually a bit more otherworldly," I offered, not entirely sure where she was headed.

Something didn't seem quite right but I couldn't pin it down. I wasn't sure if it was her words or maybe just the clinical way in which she presented them. All I could say for sure was that she didn't sound like the same Helen Storm who had just been speaking to us moments ago.

"While I do not doubt that fact in the least, I also do not want you to lose sight of the here and now. You should not allow your strength to become your vulnerability."

"How do you mean?"

"That remains to be seen, Rowan, and will be based solely on the decisions you make."

"Is there something that I'm missing here, Helen?" I had no idea what she was talking about. "Pardon me for saying so, but you don't sound quite like yourself."

"You are my patient and I am simply expressing my concern for your well being, Rowan."

"You're sure?"

"Yes, I am sure."

"Well, I'm not sure I'm understanding what you mean."

"You will," she stated without emotion. "Though it may sound cliché, simply bear in mind that one should sometimes follow the road less traveled."

"Okay." I paused for an awkward moment, not knowing what I should say. "So, anything else?"

"No. We will talk about it more during our next session."

"Okay," I said again, and physically shrugged out of reflex. "Did you need to speak with Ben?"

"No," she returned. "Just tell him that I am looking forward to this evening. Bye."

I barely managed to get my own parting words out before the line disconnected at her end, leaving me to feel thoroughly confused by the entire conversation.

"Everything okay?" Ben asked me once I'd rejoined him at his desk.

"Yeah, I think so. Where's Charlee?"

"She got called back down to Vice. You sure everything's okay?"

"Yeah, everything's fine. So, what happens now that my theory might be a non-theory?"

"Depends. We still don't have a suspect, whether your theory is right or not."

"But the connection with Paige Lawson could lead to something couldn't it?"

"Possible connection," he corrected me. "A very strong possibility, yeah, but we don't have a smoking gun."

"Maybe not, but there's definitely something there."

"I'm not sayin' there isn't."

"Good, because I know I'm right about this."

"You're just fuckin' dyin' to say it, aren't ya?"

"Say what?"

"I told you so."

"Yeah, maybe a little."

"Well, you might wanna wait until we've got more to go on. Who knows, we…"

For the second time in the past hour, the phone on his desk demanded attention, and brought our conversation to an unceremonious halt.

"Homicide, Storm," my friend answered the device with an annoyed clip in his voice, but then his tone quickly changed. "Oh, hey, what's up?"

I wasn't really paying much attention to his "uh-huhs" and "yeahs." I was concentrating instead on a blank spot on the wall across the room while still trying to figure out the strange conversation I'd just had with Helen Storm. It was when he stopped grunting into the phone that the silence prompted me to look up and find him staring at me.

"What's wrong?"

"I don't know if I'd call you wrong, but you sure as hell ain't right, Svengali."

"What are you talking about?"

"That was Chuck on the phone. Apparently the reason she got called back down to Vice was because one of the rape victims showed up to tell her somethin' she remembered."

He just continued to stare at me, then after a moment began to shake his head.

"What?"

"Apparently this woman remembers something about a Prom Dress."

"Can I say 'I told you so' now?"

"Shut up."

CHAPTER 19

"So are you going to talk to her?" I asked.

"Yeah," Ben nodded. "McLaughlin said we could meet in one of the interview rooms down there."

"Mind if I tag along?"

"I don't, but she might. I actually wouldn't mind having you where I can keep an eye on you, but you need to remember this woman was raped. She might not be all that keen on a couple of men descending on her all of a sudden."

What my friend said made perfect sense. What didn't make sense was the fact that I hadn't considered that fact from the very beginning. Normally, I was far more sensitive to the feelings of those around me, and the circumstances arising from a situation like this should have been painfully obvious. At this particular moment, however, I was oblivious.

My brain had pretty much been a jigsaw puzzle for the past two months, but instead of drawing closer to completion each day, entropy had been taking its toll. It even felt like some cosmic basket of kittens had been stealing pieces here and there when I wasn't looking. For once, the forces of nature seemed to be acting in my favor. The smothering cocoon that had been spun around me by those wanting to keep me safe was now giving way, whether they were ready for it to do so or not. Vindication was just around the corner and the very fact that it was so close imbued me with confidence.

Things were finally starting to come together, and I was determined that I would not be left out. I wasn't about to miss any chance I had of regaining my stability. I wanted my life back, and something told me that an important piece of it was in the possession of this victim.

"What about those one way mirror things?" I suggested.

"You've been watchin' too much T.V.," my friend told me as he gathered up his notebook and shrugged on his jacket. "Look, you can come downstairs with me. Short of kickin' you out or gettin' a restraining order, I doubt I can stop you from doin' that much. But, remember, this woman is a victim as well as a witness and you're not a cop, so if she doesn't want you in there, you're out. Got it?"

I nodded. "Of course."

We were already on the move, me at an almost jog to keep up with my friend's normal long-legged pace. He rummaged around in his pockets and withdrew a tin of breath mints, offering them to me after popping one in his own mouth.

"You need one, smokey," he said. "Trust me."

I took his advice, and then he snapped the lid shut and stuffed them back into his pocket.

"You gonna call Felicity and tell her you're down here?" he asked as he jerked open a stairwell door and motioned me through.

I took a quick glance at my watch. It was almost ten-thirty. The Santa Brigade, as they liked to call themselves, would be right in the middle of entertaining a group of kids at the moment. If everything were following the intended schedule, they would be heading out for the next stop in about an hour.

"She should have a bit of a break around eleven-thirty," I told him. "I'll probably call her then."

"Don't forget to check with her about tonight."

"Will do. So, if we're able to make it, what should we bring?"

"Just yourselves."

"You sure?"

"Yeah, it's not a big deal and we'll have plenty. Although, ya'know, if you happen to think about it, Allison wanted the recipe for that beef tenderloin you guys served the other night."

His request reminded me that we had completely forgotten to tell everyone what they had actually eaten for the Yule feast. I was sorry that Felicity wouldn't be here to see his reaction.

"Ummm, that wasn't beef," I said as we started down the stairs.

"Well, it sure didn't taste like pork," he said.

"That's because it wasn't pork either."

"It sure as hell wasn't chicken."

"Actually, it was Ostrich."

My friend slowed his pace, almost stopping as he gave me a long look, one eyebrow raised questioningly. "Ostrich. You mean like big-ass-stickin'-its-head-in-the-sand-bird? You mean, that kinda Ostrich?"

"Actually," I offered, "they don't really stick their heads in the sand, they just lay them along the ground."

"Ostrich?" he repeated, ignoring the bit of trivia.

"Yeah," I nodded as we rounded a landing and picked up the pace once again, "Ostrich."

"Jeez, white man."

"Didn't you like it?" I asked.

"I had seconds didn't I?"

"And thirds as I recall, so what's the problem?"

"I ate a fuckin' ostrich, that's the problem."

I hung back as Ben conferred with Detective McLaughlin at the doorway to the interview room, and then after a moment waved me over.

"Okay, this woman was raped about two weeks ago, and she's still pretty skittish. Right now, she's all right with you bein' here," he told me in a stern whisper. "But here's the rules— you're an observer. Let us handle it, and if you get some kinda hinky *Twilight Zone* thing goin' on, gimme some kinda sign so I can get you outta there."

"Like what?"

"I dunno, anything. Better yet, just don't go off into never-never land on me and we won't have to worry about it."

"I'll try," I said. "That's all I can do."

"Yeah, well try really hard. I don't need ta' be worryin' about you goin' off the deep end and spookin' a witness too."

Charlee pulled the door wide to allow entry and we were greeted with a thick haze of blue-white smoke that hung in languid ribbons on the already stale air. A thin shiver arced down my spine and I knew instantly that I was on the correct path.

"Ms. Hodges," Charlee said as she shut the door behind us, "this is Detective Storm and Mister Gant. Detective Storm is the officer I was telling you about. Gentlemen, this is Miranda Hodges."

The woman seated at the table in the small conference room fit the victim profile perfectly— early twenties, very petite, very blonde, and very pretty.

She was also very nervous.

There was a noticeable tremble in her hand as she brought a cigarette to her lips and inhaled deeply. A half empty pack of the indulgences was on the table in front of her along with a disposable lighter, and the ashtray was filled with better than a half-dozen butts. I stole a glance at my watch. They hadn't been in here for very long.

"Hi," she said in a meek voice, then stubbed out the remaining inch of the burning tobacco, only to immediately light another.

My own craving for nicotine re-awakened, and I wanted desperately to sit down and join her in the chain smoking frenzy, but decided that I'd better not. Ben shot me a glance and I nodded perceptibly. I'd been telling him all along that my return to smoking had to be due to the outside influence of a victim. I had simply thought that I was channeling the vice of a dead victim, not a living one. But, here was Miranda Hodges; cigarette in hand, and there was no denying the possible correlation. Maybe I was wrong, but doubted it. The timeline and the intensity fit.

I smiled inwardly for a moment. Score another one for me. If things kept falling into place this quickly, I just might get the gift of my sanity for Christmas.

"Good morning, Ms. Hodges," Ben greeted the young woman as we ventured into the room.

"Detective McLaughlin told me that you work with Homicide," Miranda ventured.

"That's right," he answered.

She looked past Ben and locked her eyes on mine. "Are you with Homicide too, Detective Gant?"

"Mister Gant is a consultant," Ben told her, answering before I could open my mouth and stressing the Mister. "He's helping us with another case and I thought his input might be valuable here. But if you're uncomfortable…" he allowed the comment to hang, unfinished.

"No," she shook her head. "No, it's fine. What kind of consultant?"

"Umm…"

"Latent memory analysis and dream interpretation," I

interjected, plucking something impressive sounding out of the air since Ben seemed at a momentary loss. I knew full well that I was stepping outside the boundaries that he'd set, but I wasn't going to miss this opportunity.

I'd been allowing everyone else to guide me for far too long. It was my turn to drive.

"Like a psychiatrist," she said.

"Not exactly," I told her with a shrug, and then nodded as I moved closer to the table. "But something similar I suppose."

"I'm not crazy," she immediately announced.

"No one thinks you're crazy, Ms. Hodges," Charlee told her.

I could feel Ben's stare burning a large hole in my back. I was going to be in deep trouble with him when this was all over, but I knew he wouldn't make a scene. Not in here, and not as long as things remained on an even keel anyway. Still, the only way I was going to redeem myself in the least was if I could make some progress, so I continued.

"Not at all," I echoed. "I'm just here to help you with your memory, but if you'd rather I leave, I'll certainly understand."

She sat quietly for a long stretch before finally answering, "I'm not so sure I want to remember."

"That's perfectly normal," I offered calmly, pressing my voice into a soothing monotone. "But eventually we always do. Perhaps not everything, but enough to fill in at least some of the blanks."

Her eyes were fixed with mine, and she gave me a shy smile before looking down at the table. She was outwardly displaying a tenuous amount of confidence in my presence here, and I accepted it for what it was worth. I fought back my own desire to rush headlong into a series of questions, and ushered it into the background. I couldn't afford to betray her trust, nor did I want to.

"I have plenty of those." She gave a nervous laugh. "Blanks I mean."

"Rophynol does that," Charlee told her. "That's one of the reasons it's called the Date Rape drug."

I continued to watch the young woman, not placing any demands on the situation, but keeping my attention focused directly on her. Engaging in a simple exercise, I allowed my breathing to grow more and more shallow as I drew air slowly in through my nose and let it escape from my mouth in a quiet stream.

"While it may seem painful at first, Miranda," I offered, keeping the measure of my voice even, "filling in those blanks can offer closure."

She turned her gaze back to me and brought her eyes to rest directly on mine once again. I continued to stare, unblinking as I spoke, "And with that closure can come peace of mind."

She was beginning to relax as I soothed her with my voice. I could feel a connection beginning to flow between us, and I prepared to press forward. Ben, however, immediately figured out what I was about to do. He had seen me enter into such a hypnotic state before, and he wasn't going to allow it this time around.

My friend cleared his throat with almost over-animated gusto and purposely gave me a nudge. The thin connection was immediately broken and Miranda Hodges, wearing a mildly bewildered expression as if she'd just awoke, shook her head and blinked.

"I want you to know I appreciate you talking to us," Ben offered, stepping forward and insinuating himself even more prominently into the scene.

"So, why are you interested in this, Detective Storm?" Miranda turned her attention to Ben as she took a hit from her cigarette. "Did... Did the sonofabitch that raped me kill someone too?"

"We don't know for sure," he told her. "But I'll be honest, yes, that is a possibility. That's why I wanted to talk to you."

Her reaction was instantaneous and not all that unexpected.

"Oh my God," she whimpered as she brought her hand up to her mouth. She rolled her eyes up to the ceiling and blinked hard before squeezing them tightly shut. She let out a low, nasal whine as she began trembling. Large tears proceeded to roll down her cheeks, and we all stood in awkward silence.

I personally erected a shabby wall of ethereal defense against the woman's burgeoning emotions as I felt a lump begin to rise in my throat. Empathy can be a very good thing, but it can also get in the way if you are too sensitive. That seemed to be a large part of my problem.

I managed to stave it off, thankful that the distress wasn't aimed directly at me, because I still wasn't all that well grounded. Right now, I needed to take things one at a time.

Charlee found a box of tissues and offered it to the young woman. She took them and sniffed loudly as she dabbed at the tears, and then looked up at us and weakly uttered, "I'm sorry."

"S'okay," Ben told her. "Can we get you anything? Maybe somethin' to drink? Coffee? Soda? Water?"

"A soda," she nodded. "A soda would be good."

"Particular kind?"

"Anything diet."

"How about you, Chuck?"

"Coffee's good. Two creams, four sugars."

"Okay, one diet soda and one coffee, two by four," Ben repeated. "Come on, Rowan, why don't you come with and give me a hand. We'll be right back."

"Just what the fuck was that?" Ben snarled at me as we entered the corridor and rounded the corner toward the vending machines.

I didn't answer and just kept walking.

"You were tryin' to do one of those hocus-pocus things weren't you?" he continued angrily.

I felt his large hand come down in a firm grip on my shoulder and with a quick jerk he twisted me around. "Goddammit, Rowan! Don't walk away from me when I'm talkin' to you!"

"Back off, Ben," I spat.

"Me back off?" he asked incredulously. "I talked to you about this before we went in there. You promised me you wouldn't do any of that shit."

"I didn't promise you anything," I shot back. "I said I'd try. That's it."

"You didn't try very fuckin' hard!"

The few people that were in the hallway were giving us wide berth as each of them selected the nearest escape route. Ben was seething, and the very sight of him like this tended to strike fear directly into the heart. He hadn't been willing to make a scene in front of Miranda Hodges, but apparently once the door to the interview room had closed we were center stage.

"Guess again! I've been trying 'very fucking hard' for a week now. Maybe it's your turn!"

My comment took him completely by surprise. He just stared at me dumbfounded with his jaw hanging open. Whatever biting comment he'd been prepared to hurl at me had instantly evaporated into nothingness. After a moment he spoke, this time with a little less fire in his voice. "What the hell is that supposed to mean?"

I sighed and consciously forced some of my own anger to drain away. "It means that it's time you started trusting me again."

"When haven't I trusted you?"

"For the past week, at least," I told him. "Ever since I walked in here with that notepad it has been like pulling teeth to get you to listen to me."

"Yeah, well, I thought I had reason for that."

"Fine. I'm willing to accept that. But start adding it up, Ben. How much more do I have to do to prove to you that I'm right? Do you really still have reason to keep shutting me out on this?"

"You mean besides the fact that you aren't a copper?"

"That's never stopped you before."

"I promised Felicity."

"And we saw how that ended up, didn't we?"

"Yeah, well that wasn't entirely my fault."

"I didn't say it was." I shook my head. "It was nobody's fault. But it's a moot point anyway. All the promises in the world aren't going to keep these nightmares out of my head."

"But if I keep you out of it, I can keep you safe."

"Not from the visions you can't." I shook my head.

"That's Felicity's part of the deal." He held up his hands in surrender. "I just handle what I can see."

"That's just it. It's not what you see that is doing the harm. It's what I see," I appealed. "And even she can't protect me from these things, Ben. You've both seen that."

"Jeezus, Rowan." He shook his head and rested one hand on his hip while sending the other up to smooth back his hair and begin massaging his neck. "Man, if I had a freakin' time machine…"

"You'd do what? Go back in time and never get me

involved in the Ariel Tanner case?"

"Somethin' like that."

"We'd still end up right where we are now, Ben." My voice softened as I spoke. "She was a friend of mine and I would have gotten involved anyway. You know that. If you hadn't shown up that night to ask me about the Pentacle at the crime scene, maybe someone else would have. Or I would have heard about it somewhere. Even I don't believe in pre-ordained destiny, but I know I was meant to do this. Otherwise, I wouldn't have these visions.

"You need to get over this guilt of yours. The real truth is that neither of us is responsible for this. I know you don't necessarily believe it, but there's something bigger at work here and it's what keeps dragging me into these things; not you— or even me for that matter. And like it or not, that's my problem, not yours."

"Yeah, tell that to my conscience."

"THAT is your problem, not mine," I told him with a grin.

He huffed out a heavy sigh. "Shit, white man, every time you get involved in an investigation we end up arguin' about somethin'."

"Been a bit worse this time around," I acknowledged. "Good thing we're friends."

"Yeah," he grunted, "so why the hell do we do this?"

"Probably because we're both strong-willed individuals who although we are seeking the same result, have diametrically opposed ways of going about achieving it."

"You HAVE been hangin' around my sister too much." He returned his own grin.

"So, have we cleared the air?" I asked after a moment.

"I'm still not exactly happy with you blindsiding me like that," he returned.

"Would it help if I apologized?" I asked.

"Right now? Not much. Later, probably."

"I can live with that," I allowed. "So, can we get back to the business at hand?"

He gave me a long, hard look, then rubbed his chin with the back of his hand before pointing a finger at me. "Can you do this without Felicity here?"

"Yeah, I should be okay."

"Don't try to snow me."

"I'm not," I answered with genuine sincerity. "We're not talking about channeling a spirit here, just a bit of interactive hypnosis. There shouldn't be a big problem."

"What if the stuff she remembers is graphic?"

"It probably will be," I conceded. "But she's alive and she obviously wasn't tortured or anything, so it should be okay."

"Nothing funky?"

"Well," I shrugged as I spoke, "depending on what I see, it could get a little spooky."

"Yeah, that's what I figured," he nodded. "Better let me fill McLaughlin in before you go all *Twilight Zone*."

"So you're going to let me try it my way?"

"I dunno yet," he said. "Lemme think about it."

CHAPTER 20

Detective Charlee McLaughlin came within inches of colliding with us as we entered through the squad room door on our way back to the interview room. There was an almost wild look contorting her face, and the level of energy she was exuding was physically palpable.

"Whoa!" Ben jumped back, juggling a pair of hot coffees. "Where's the fire?"

"Forget about Hodges," Charlee announced the matter-of-fact statement. "She's gone."

"Do what?" Ben exclaimed. "Whaddaya mean gone?"

"She left," she continued, obviously worked up about something. "You guys weren't gone for two minutes, and she bolted. Said she was sorry, but all she wanted to do is tell me she remembered something about a dress."

"It wasn't because of me was it?" I asked.

"I doubt it," she spoke in a rapid fire staccato, her voice building into a near frenzy. "She was still way too spooked when she showed up. I'm surprised she stayed as long as she did to be honest. But, anyway, that's not important."

"Not important? But…" Ben started to object.

"No, listen to me." Charlee shook her head vigorously and gestured. "I just now got off the phone with University Hospital. They've got a thirty-two year old blonde rape victim sitting in Emergency right now."

Ben stopped cold and looked at her. "You pretty sure it's our guy?"

"Can't be positive, but according to the Doc, her neck is bruised up and she can't remember where she's been since Saturday night."

Ben quickly looked around for a place to dispose of the drinks he was carrying. Finding none, he shoved the cups of coffee into the hands of a uniformed officer who was walking past, giving no explanation other than a muttered, "Here. Merry Christmas."

His attention remained focused on Charlee and I could almost feel the surge of adrenalin that kicked into him as he ramped up to her level. We were already hurrying through the Sex Crimes squad room as he spoke, "Get the CSU on the horn now. Tell them you need an evidence team at this woman's residence immediately if not sooner. We need to hit this before anyone can screw with the scene."

"Already done," she answered as we jogged.

"Did they tell ya' who's runnin it?"

"No."

"Call 'em back and tell 'em you want Murv. I don't care if they have to drag his ass outta the shower or what. We want the best on this and I'd almost swear that guy could lift a print off a fuckin' puddle of water if he had to."

"Got it."

"I'll go check in upstairs and let 'em know what's up, then we'll meet you out back. I'll drive."

"See you in ten," she told us as she peeled off toward her desk.

"Make it five," Ben called after her.

I had to break into a near run to keep up with my friend as he hooked around the desks and shouldered open the door leading to the stairs.

"Why are we in such a rush," I asked, following him through into the stairwell and lagging far behind as he took the stairs two at a time.

"Because I wanna get you together with the victim while everything's still fresh," he said.

"This is kind of an about face. I thought you were still a bit leery about all that."

"Oh, I am," he called down. "I'm just taking my turn."

"What?"

"My turn," he repeated, his voice starting to fade in the distances as it echoed from the concrete walls. "You said it was my turn to trust you for a change. Well, I'm gonna trust you to figure out who the sick asshole is that's doin' this."

He had already disappeared from view, and I could hear the creak of the door slowly closing behind him. Finally topping the first flight of stairs, I rounded the landing and started up the next set, only to halt dead in my tracks.

Seated on the top stair was a blonde in her early twenties, clad in a cheerleader's uniform. Her arms were crossed and she was leaning forward with them resting on her knees. The toes of her unnaturally white sneakers pointed slightly in toward one another, and she was staring at me quizzically.

After a brief interval of motionlessness, her mouth began to move. A short measure later, completely out of sync with her lips, words began glancing from the walls with a phase-shifted quality that I'd come to expect from the earthly manifestations of spirits.

I'm dead, She's dead.
D-E-A-D, dead.
She's dead, I'm dead.
D-E-A-D, dead.

Her head bobbed back and forth in time with the ditty as she spoke, making the lack of synchronization between the movement of her mouth and the words just that much more disconcerting. Her eyes remained locked with mine, unblinking, and I could do nothing more than return the stare.

The past two days of quiet had lulled me into a sense of complacency where such ethereal visits were concerned, and her sudden appearance here took me by surprise. I simply stood there, unsure of what to say.

She continued the piece of morose poetry, picking up the disharmonious pace as she went.

Rowan, Rowan, he's our man!
If he can't do it, nobody can!
She's dead, I'm dead, what to do?
Find the killer, we're counting on you!
Eeny, Meeny, Miney, Moe,
Catch the killer, don't let him go.
Eeny, Meeny, Miney, Moe,
Make him suffer, don't you know.

If he screams, well we don't care,
If he cries, then we'll be there.
We want him to hurt, and to be afraid.
We want him to die in this bed he's made.

Now go catch the killer,
We'll make him pay.
And pay, and pay,
And pay, and pay,
And pay, and pay, and pay, and pay, and pay...

The vengeance laced words continued to echo inside my head as they faded in concert with the rapidly dissolving image of Debbie Schaeffer. I felt a hard knot in my stomach and nausea gripped me. This wasn't good at all.

Debbie had literally taken over my body once before, and even though I was in better shape now than I had been that night, if I wasn't careful she could do it again. The last thing I needed was for her to use me to commit murder— even if the victim was a killer himself. There's no way in the world I'd ever be able to convince a jury that my physical body had been possessed by the spirit of a dead cheerleader with a taste for revenge. No, this was worse than not good. This was just plain bad.

I'm not sure how much time I spent standing there contemplating this threat, but it couldn't have been long. I started with a violent jerk as the door at the top of the landing bumped open with a heavy thud and Ben stuck his head through the opening.

"Hey, Rowan," my friend called down to me, "you comin' or what?"

The doors leading from the ambulance bay slid open before us to reveal something resembling an all-day-long progressive holiday celebration in halting swing. The on-again, off-again nature of the work here was managing to consistently interfere and prevent the festivities from ever making it to the status of a full-blown party.

As we entered, for the second time this week the antiseptic atmosphere of an emergency room assaulted me full force; but at least this time I wasn't a patient. The sweet smells of cookies and candies mingled with the savory aromas of cheese and cold-cut trays on the cool air. They were in turn undercut with the sharp fumes of isopropyl alcohol and other medicinal preparations. The entire mélange was bound together by the peculiar plastic odor of adhesive bandages.

Fortunately, it didn't appear to be too terribly busy at the moment— yet another calm before the storm considering that statistically, holidays bring out the worst in some. Still, even with the lull, the staff wasn't exactly twiddling their thumbs either. The nurse behind the desk was involved in paperwork, presumably from a recent admission. Others could be seen, here and there seeing to tasks or simply snatching a cookie from one of the many plates.

The young woman tending the desk had made an effort to offset the plainness of her scrubs, having adorned herself with a holiday bow in her hair and an electronic reindeer pin above her name badge. As we approached, The LED in the plastic novelty's nose was flashing wildly and the circuitry embedded within was belting out a medley of holiday tunes comprised entirely of a series of off-key electronic tones.

"Can I help you?" she asked cheerfully as she looked up, obviously noticing that no one in our trio appeared to require immediate medical attention.

"City Police," Charlee told her as she flashed her badge. "I'm Detective McLaughlin; this is Detective Storm and Mister Gant. I received a call from a Doctor Kennedy a little while ago."

"Yes," the nurse nodded, her smile fading. "The rape. He said to expect you. Treatment room four." She stood and leaned slightly across the counter, then motioned with one hand. "Down this corridor, left at the end, through the double doors and it will be about halfway down on the left."

"Thanks," McLaughlin told her.

We rounded the corner of the admitting desk, and headed down the corridor with Charlee in the lead. Ben reigned in his extra long stride and put a hand on my arm to hold me back as well, allowing us to fall a few paces behind her.

"I haven't had a chance to talk to Chuck about the hocus pocus stuff," he half whispered to me. "Not to mention that this victim is coming right off the incident and she hasn't had time to come to terms with it."

"I understand," I replied.

"Really, Row," he admonished, "don't go in there slingin' fairy dust or whatever right outta the box. We gotta feel out the situation first."

"Okay, Ben," I reiterated, "I've got it. I'm sorry about what I did back at the station and I won't do it here. Promise."

"Okay, I just gotta be sure," he told me as he rummaged in his pockets again.

"What? Do I need another breath mint?" I queried, noticing his preoccupation with the task.

"Probably," he huffed flatly. "You hot-boxed four cigarettes before we got here and it only took us ten minutes."

"Yeah, well, blame it on Miranda Hodges. Besides, I seem to recall seeing a *Fuente Chateau* clenched between your teeth, my friend."

"Yeah, but I was just chewin' on it. Actually, I wanted to give you somethin' else." He finally withdrew his fist from his pocket and held it out to me. "Here."

I extended my palm and he dropped a wad of small paper packets into it. "What's this?" I asked.

"Salt," he answered matter-of-factly. "I stole 'em outta the break room before we left."

"What do you want me to do with them?"

"Hey, you're the Witch, you tell me. Felicity seemed to think it was pretty important to have salt the other night. I'm just tryin' ta' help."

"She was doing something a bit different than what I'm about to do."

"It's all the same in my book," he returned. "Besides, I haven't seen Felicity go off the deep end yet, so maybe you oughta try it her way."

I was going to object again, but we were almost to the door of the treatment room and I really didn't have time to explain the difference between Magickal workings and psychic abilities to him.

Of course, the real truth was that in my case they were probably closer to one another than I wanted to believe. On top of that, he was most likely correct in his assessment. Given my current state, a little caution might very well go a long way. Especially since I now had an ethereal vigilante cheerleader threatening to use me as a weapon to exact her vengeance.

I almost had to laugh at that thought. The entire concept sounded like a bad fifties Sci-Fi/Horror movie— *I Was A Killer Teenage Zombie Cheerleader*, or something equally ridiculous. Unfortunately, I was playing the starring role in the production and it was all far too real.

I stuffed the handful of salt packets into my coat pocket and kept my mouth shut.

CHAPTER 21

Detective McLaughlin stepped back out of the treatment room, already shaking her head. Ben and I had waited outside so as not to overload the victim. With what she'd been through, she definitely didn't need us coming at her full force without some kind of warning.

"Unless he's breaking his pattern, this isn't our boy," she told us as the door shut behind her.

"You sure?" Ben asked.

"No welt from a stun gun that they can find, and the bruising on her neck is from hands." She motioned to her own neck with a gripping posture as an example. "Looks like she was choked. Turns out that after talking to her, she's in an ongoing abusive relationship with a boyfriend."

"Some friend," Ben muttered. "Someone needs to kick his ass."

"Tell me about it," she returned.

"What about the roofies?"

"They don't have the blood test back yet, but I'm betting it will be negative."

"Why's that?"

"Because here's the real kicker— This isn't the first time she's been in."

"The abuse?"

"Overdose." McLaughlin shook her head. "She's an addict. More tracks than a train station."

"Don't tell me." Ben shook his head. "Last time she scored was Saturday night."

Charlee laid one index finger against the side of her nose and simply pointed at him with the other.

"So what the hell did they call you for?"

"She's blonde,…"

"…And petite, and doctors aren't cops." Ben finished the diatribe for her while nodding his head, then slapped his open palm against the tiled wall and leaned into it. "Shit! Hodges bolts and now this is a dead end. We can't catch a fuckin' break!"

His voice echoed down the corridor directly behind the fading sound of his hand impacting the tile. He was still riding the adrenalin rush that had hyped him up less than half an hour ago, and the disappointment at this turn of events ravaged his features. His free hand went up to smooth back his hair and then fell to rest on his neck as he huffed out a disgusted sigh.

Benjamin Storm, supercop— protector of the innocent.

"I'm right there with you, Storm," McLaughlin told him, showing mild surprise at his outburst. "But you gotta stop taking it so personally."

"Yeah, well tell that to Debbie Schaeffer's parents," he said. "It's Christmas freakin' eve and what's left of their daughter is spendin' it in a body bag over on Clark Avenue. Merry fuckin' ho, ho, ho."

"You can't change that," I offered to my friend.

"No," he admitted, "I can't change it, but I can give 'em this asshole as a gift. At least that would be somethin'."

"We don't even know for sure if it's the same guy," Charlee said.

"Maybe not, but it's the best lead I've got at the moment."

"Then let's follow it," I interjected flatly.

"How?" he shot back.

"There are other victims," I offered. "We talk to them."

"Jeez, white man, it's freakin' Christmas eve!"

"Yes it is," I acknowledged. "But you are the one who wants to give Debbie Schaeffer's parents this guy as a gift. By my calculations you've only got about twelve shopping hours left."

"Yeah, well I'm thinkin' it's gonna be a disappointing holiday."

I looked over at Charlee. "You said there have been eight rapes reported so far?"

"Yeah," she nodded.

"You have all the victims numbers?"

"Yeah, I've got their numbers." She gave me a nod then looked at Ben. "It's worth a try, Storm."

"Maybe," he huffed, "but I'm not gonna hold my breath."

"Okay." I shot my glance between them. "Rule out Miranda Hodges and that leaves seven. At least one of them has got to be willing to talk to me."

McLaughlin cocked her head to the door of the treatment room. "Let me get someone down here to take care of this, and we'll start making calls."

"I guess I'd better call the crime scene guys and cancel," Ben added. "Did they end up getting' Murv?"

"Afraid so." McLaughlin nodded.

"Afraid so? That doesn't sound good."

"Yeah, they called him in off of a vacation day."

Ben puffed his cheeks out and let the breath go with a slow hiss. "Well, guess I'd better stop by the smoke shop on the way home. I'm gonna owe 'im some cigars for this one."

"Christmas eve. Remember?" I said.

"Crap. Well, guess it'll have to be Wednesday."

"Look at the bright side," I told him. "Maybe you can get them on sale."

Thirty minutes and five no-answers later, the woman in the treatment room was giving her statement, the CSU call had been cancelled, and a young woman named Heather Burke said yes.

"Sorry about the mess," the petite blonde apologized while shifting a basket of clothing from a chair and onto the floor beside it. "I wasn't really expecting company today."

"No problem," Charlee told her. "We really appreciate you talking to us. Especially with it being Christmas eve and all."

"I'm not going anywhere." She shrugged. "I don't have any family, and I'm taking a bit of a hiatus from the dating scene if you get my drift."

Heather Burke was a perfect example of the quintessential 'perky' blonde. Large, bright eyes peering out from a soft face framed by a feathery shag of yellow hair. Five foot four, slim, and blessed with what some would call 'eyeball measurements'— a textbook victim for this particular predator. Looking at her, I couldn't help but think she bore a close resemblance to my wife, except of course for the hair.

She was dressed in a pair of jeans and a T-Shirt that sported a faded but still readable iron-on transfer, which announced, 'Don't let the hair fool you, I belong to MENSA.'

"Nice shirt," I offered thinking to myself that she even had Felicity's headstrong attitude.

"You like it?" she asked rhetorically, looking down at the lettering then back at me. "Made it myself. It tends to stop the blonde jokes cold."

"I can imagine." I nodded.

"Have a seat." She motioned to us. "Can I get anyone anything? I've got coffee on. Soda? Water?"

We all declined the offer and she simply shrugged, then dropped herself onto the couch and crossed legs in something close to a relaxed lotus position. "I'm not sure what I'm going to be able to tell you," she began. "It's been three weeks and I haven't really remembered anything yet." She directed her attention to Charlee. "Other than what I originally told you, I mean."

"I understand," McLaughlin told her with a nod. "That's why Mister Gant is here with us. Like I said on the phone, we'd like to try some things to help jog your memory."

Heather wrinkled her face in concentration, lifting one eyebrow and cocking her head to the side as she muttered, "Gant... Gant... Now I remember..." She focused her gaze directly on me. "I thought I recognized the name. You're the Witch aren't you?"

From the corner of my eye I saw Ben shoot an almost startled glance at me. I suppose her recognition caught him by surprise, but I'd been expecting something like this all along. In recent days a file photo of me had been flashed across local TV screens as the media speculated about my involvement in the Debbie Schaeffer murder investigation. There had even been a few column inches devoted to me in the local paper, so someone had been bound to recognize my face, my name, or both. It was only a matter of time.

"I don't know about being THE Witch," I nodded with a slight smile, "but, yes, I'm him."

"How cool is that," she nodded back, then continued in a matter-of-fact tone, "So, that would mean that Detective Storm here is the same Detective Storm from Homicide who is investigating the case with the murdered cheerleader. And if that is so, it stands to reason that since you are here talking to me, you think that murder is somehow connected with this rapist."

Ben answered with a tentative note in his voice as he slowly nodded, "That's the going theory."

"Don't look so surprised," she told him.

"I know," he said, "you're a member of MENSA."

"Yeah, but it doesn't take a genius to put two and two together," she returned with a quick shake of her head. "I watch the news."

"If you don't mind my saying so, Ms. Burke," I dove back into the conversation to save my friend from the embarrassment of his misconceptions, "given that it has only been three weeks, you seem to be handling it very well."

"I have my moments," she half shrugged as she spoke. "You happened to catch me on a good day."

"Are you certain that you're up to talking about it?" Charlee chimed in.

"This is as good a time as any," she nodded. "The sooner I can put this behind me the sooner I can get on with my life. That's what they say, anyway."

"How do you feel about hypnosis?" I asked.

"Do you mean, am I willing to be hypnotized?"

I wasn't surprised by her directness. "Yes."

"Where would you like to do it?"

"I should warn you that if this works you will for all intents and purposes be re-living the incident."

"If it works will it help catch the prick who raped me?"

"I can't say for sure," I told her. "But it's a good possibility, depending upon what you remember, of course."

"Then I'll ask you again," she said, casting a confident gaze directly into my eyes. "Where do you want to do it?"

I turned slowly in place, first twisting my head to look over my shoulder, and then following with the rest of my body. I caught a glimpse of myself in a mirror and immediately noticed the puzzled expression that my brain had already told me I was wearing. Still, the sudden tickle that had sent me into this physical spiral didn't subside. If anything, it just grew worse— nagging and clawing at the back of my psyche, and sending a wave of gooseflesh across my scalp.

"Somethin' wrong?" Ben asked, staring at the befuddled mask that was my face.

Heather had excused herself to use the bathroom before we began, leaving the three of us alone in her living room, so at least she wasn't seeing this display. I had serious doubt that it would have done anything to bolster her confidence in what we were about to do.

"Are you okay, Rowan?" Charlee added her concerned voice to the mix.

"I don't know," I muttered at first, then reeled my wandering thoughts back in. "I mean, yes, I'm okay... That was just weird."

"What was weird?" McLaughlin queried.

"We're talkin' about Rowan here. Everything's weird with him," Ben interjected. "You know, 'don't adjust your television set, yadda yadda'. So, what's up, white man? You already goin' all *Twilight Zone* on us?"

"It felt like..." I began, then frowned, and shook my head. "Don't worry about it. It's probably just nerves."

"See what I mean?" Ben jibed.

"Are you positive, Rowan?" Charlee asked.

"You just haven't been around him enough yet, Chuck," Ben told her. "He does this kinda shit when he starts doin' the hocus pocus stuff."

"Really, Charlee," I said, "I'm fine. It's nothing."

Too bad I didn't believe that. I couldn't shake the

feeling that I was being watched, and the sensation was extremely disconcerting. My first instinct was to think that Debbie Schaeffer might be waiting in the ethereal wings for me to pinpoint a target for her. But, the more I dwelled on it, the more the presence felt nothing like her. It was familiar, yes, but not her. No matter how hard I tried I couldn't pin it down to an individual or even a place, and as I continued to think it, it just became worse.

A thin lance of pain stabbed through my bad shoulder and I winced inwardly. I was starting to feel jumpy and my hands began to clench and unclench with the nervous energy. I was still wearing my jacket so I shoved them into my pockets to hide the fidgeting from outside notice, and immediately felt the wad of salt packets Ben had given me.

"Are we ready?" Heather asked as she came back into the room.

"Row?" Ben raised an eyebrow at me.

"What? Oh, yeah." I was still contemplating the perceived invasion of my privacy, and hadn't even noticed her return. "One question though, Ms. Burke?"

"Yes?"

"This may sound odd, but would you mind terribly if I sprinkled a bit of salt around?"

"Purification and protection?" she nodded at me knowingly as she spoke.

"You're familiar with the ritual practices of The Craft?" It was my turn to be surprised, and ultimately chagrined.

She stretched the baggy T-shirt out with her hands to display the iron-on more prominently. "I read a lot, Mister Gant."

I had never been much for the poetic showmanship of

spell casting. While I certainly wasn't opposed to the process, I tended to get tongue-tied whenever I set about reciting a series of couplets. Stumbling over rhymes did little for the actual effectiveness of the spell, and in turn served only to destroy my concentration, which in reality was the true driving force behind SpellCraft.

By the time I would reach the end of the poem, I would have spent so much energy trying not to make a fool of myself that I usually forgot what it was that I set out to do in the first place. So, out of a sense of self-preservation, I usually opted for the silent approach. I would gather myself, steel my energies, and project them outward on the task to which I'd set my mind— all without uttering a sound. It worked well for me, so I never really saw a need to change it.

Something told me that this time, however, a word or two might be in order. Unfortunately, I was drawing a blank. I stood there silently for a moment with an open packet of salt poured into the palm of my hand, and feeling incredibly self-conscious. I heard Ben clear his throat and felt my heart skip a beat.

It was at that moment, just before I was sure to break out into a cold sweat, that a not so random thought crawled out of its hiding place and announced itself.

I had once attended a workshop on Magick and SpellCraft given by a noted Pagan author. After the lecture I had had the opportunity to discuss with her the method by which I practiced the art. While she found no fault with my methodology, she told me to always keep in mind that the Lord and Lady loved to be entertained, and that to them, poetry was a joy. Therefore, if one's intent was truly focused on the task, it didn't always matter what was said, but how one said it. I seized on that memory and began to mumble the first thing that entered my brain.

"Tis the night before Christmas, and this I do fear,

someone is watching, with intentions unclear. My back is wide open and there's a pain in my head, could you please watch out for me so I don't wind up dead."

It wasn't the most eloquent Spell imaginable, but I kept my voice low as I walked a small circle, sprinkling salt in my wake. I doubted that anyone could actually make out the words, but the cadence was probably crystal clear. For all they knew, I might very well have actually been reciting *'Twas the Night Before Christmas*. If that is what they thought, however, none of them voiced it, and for that I was grateful.

When I completed the circuit and looked up, Ben was staring at me with one eyebrow arched. He'd never before seen me take it upon myself to engage directly in the ritualistic trappings of The Craft, save for the recent Yule Circle he'd witnessed. This was something that was Felicity's forte, not mine, so I knew he was going to have some questions. They would simply have to wait.

"Go ahead and sit down," I told Heather as I turned, and then took a seat opposite her.

"You've done this before, right?" she asked.

I nodded in response. "Yes, several times. Why?"

"You seem a bit nervous."

"That's because I am."

"Why?"

"Honestly?"

"Of course."

"Because I'm not entirely certain I really want to see what you are about to show me."

"Oh," she said quietly.

"So, with that said, are you sure you want to go ahead with this?" I gave her one last chance to back out before we started down the path.

"You really think this asshole might have killed that cheerleader?"

"There's a strong possibility, yes," Ben interjected.

"Then let's see what I can remember."

"Okay, everyone quiet please," I announced to the room, then focused my gaze directly on Heather Burke.

As our eyes met, I willed a connection to form between us. My respirations evened out and slowed, and I felt a solid bond between the earth and myself. This was the strongest ground I'd accomplished on my own in some time, and I took a moment to revel in it. My confidence was steadily returning, and the light at the end of this long tunnel seemed to be growing brighter by the moment.

"How are you feeling?" I asked her in an unwavering monotone.

"Fine," she answered, her voice betraying the calm that had begun to permeate her being. "Very relaxed."

"Good." I held my voice to the baseline I'd set with my first words. "I want you to imagine nothing but a blank sheet of paper; white, clean and unblemished. Allow it to fill your field of vision. Let it grow and fill your mind until there is nothing else. Just pure white from top to bottom, side to side, corner to corner, above and below, before and behind."

Some people are like resistors in an electronic circuit, impeding the flow of energy. Others are like capacitors in the same circuit, grabbing that energy and hoarding it, unwilling to share. Still others are simply conductors of energy like the wires that complete the connections between the components in that circuit. Heather Burke was an excellent conductor.

I watched her face as I spoke, feeling the rhythmic ebb and flow of an ethereal plasma moving between us. Her eyes slowly took on a glassy quality, remaining locked with mine, unblinking. The trance met no resistance, and overtook her quietly and comfortably.

"When was she attacked?" I asked aloud, shifting the tenor and lowering the volume of my voice so as not to disturb the young woman in front of me.

I could hear Detective McLaughlin rustling about behind me, flipping through pages of a notebook. After a long moment she whispered, "The call came in to Sex Crimes on five, December."

"So probably some time on the fourth?"

"Just a second..." I heard some more rustling. "Make it the third. She was last seen leaving work that Monday evening, and was a no show for work on the next day."

"Okay," I answered, then shifted my attention back to the tranced woman across from me, and then tuned my voice back into a dull monotone. "Heather, can you hear me?"

"Yes," she returned softly.

"Good. I want you to let your mind drift now. Allow it to float free."

She giggled, and then whispered, "This is fun."

Through the connection between us, I could feel giddiness she was experiencing. I allowed it to flow freely, but maintained my earthly bond as a counterbalance to its almost overwhelming seductiveness. Moving with her, I struggled to keep a measure of distance between our ethereal selves, for to connect with her fully would draw me far too deeply into her experience.

"Good, Heather. You are doing wonderfully. Now, if for any reason you can no longer feel my presence next to you, I want you to come back to this place. Okay?"

"You aren't leaving are you?"

I could feel a tremor of fear roll through her voice and begin to well between us.

"Not if I can help it, but sometimes things happen that we cannot control. I just want you to be safe, so, if you lose me, just come back to this place and nothing can hurt you. Understand?"

"Yes."

I breathed a quick sigh of relief. The streak of anguish had come on far more quickly than I'd expected, and I hadn't been prepared for it. I now realized just how tenuous the connection between us was, and knew that I was going to have to effectively disengage some of the safeties I'd put in place for myself.

I didn't want to do it, but in my mind I could see no other way. On a plane beyond time and space where the two of us now stood, I took a step closer to her in order to tighten the bond. The hazy miasma of energy, visible only to me, thickened and intensified.

"We're going to allow ourselves to drift back now, Heather." My voice continued to speak in this reality, though it no longer needed to do so. "Back in time. Back a few weeks to the evening of December third. You've just left work. Tell me where you went."

"Home. I came home."

"All right," I answered, "what happened when you came home?"

"I parked my car and got out. It was dark. I dropped my keys and they went under the car. Dammit!"

"What, Heather? What's wrong?" I almost physically jumped at her exclamation.

"I just put a giant snag in my pantyhose trying to reach my keys."

"Okay," I soothed as I settled myself. "Forget about that, it's not important."

"Not important?" she returned with a hint of attitude. "Do you know how much a pair of pantyhose costs?"

I was losing control. She was drifting in her own direction and it was completely opposite of the way we needed to go. In the ethereal world I inched myself closer to her, struggling to tighten our bond but maintain enough distance so as to remain an observer only.

A familiar voice to my rear had a different idea, however. *"Salt, Rowan? Get real. It's only evil that can't cross a salt line. Now I ask you, do I look evil?"*

My otherworldly self spun quickly at the sound and came face to face with Debbie Schaeffer.

"Dead I am, dead I am," she chanted, our faces only a breath apart. *"I do not like that dead I am!"*

I steeled my defenses and like an underwater swimmer who was running out of breath aimed myself toward the surface. It was too late. I felt a dainty pair of hands slam open palmed into my chest and I stumbled backwards— backwards and directly into Heather Burke.

There was a burst of blinding light, searing deep into my brain, and I let out a silent scream.

When sight returned, all color had fled and I was left in a world of halftone greys.

When sensation and feeling returned I was devoid of warmth and chilled to the bone.

When clarity of thought returned I was in the middle of an identity crisis.

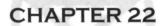

CHAPTER 22

I'm reaching for my keys, kneeling next to the car. A cold breeze whips across the parking lot and finds its way under my skirt. Guess I should have brought a coat, but it was sixty-four when I left for work this morning! This weather is just insane. December and it still can't make up its mind if it is going to be warm or cold. Should have paid more attention to the forecast I suppose. Well, it's not like I have that far to walk. If I can just get these damn keys!

Another gust angles around the car and sends a chill down my back. I'll check the weather channel when I get settled. If it is going to stay cold I guess maybe I'll wear slacks tomorrow... Or my tartan wool skirt, maybe. Wait a minute; did I pick it up at the cleaners? Hmmmm, I'll have to check. I can't remember.

I can smell the lingering exhaust and petroleum fumes from the vehicle. I cough as another gust of wind pushes the foul gases up into my face. I can feel the heat of the noisily cooling exhaust system as it seeps down toward the hand that is groping for the keys.

Where the hell are they?

I scoot around, balancing on the balls of my feet and stretching my arm beneath the vehicle at an awkward angle. It's too dark for me to see under the car, and I wonder if I have a flashlight in the glove box. Then I remember that I do, but the batteries are dead.

The wind dies for a moment and I hear something that sounds like footsteps. My heart thuds in my chest as I jump, startled, and lose my balance. My knee brushes against the rough asphalt and I literally feel the tear happen.

I look around and see nothing. I must have imagined the noise. Great! So now I'm hearing things. I take a moment to inspect my knee. Dammit! This was my last good pair of hose. Well, at least I'm not bleeding, but there's no saving the stockings. They're shot, and I'm not going back out to the store tonight. That settles it for sure. Slacks tomorrow.

I send my hand in search of the keys once more. I can get a better angle now because I don't have to worry about ruining my pantyhose anymore. My fingers touch something and I hear a jingle. I stretch my arm a bit further and slowly move my hand from side to side.

My fingers touch something cold and I hook them around the keys, then I pull them out. Standing up I lock the car door and close it. God, it's been a long day. I just want to get inside, kick off my shoes, look at the television for a while, and then go to bed. I look at my watch. Six forty-five. Traffic was horrible. But then, it always is around the holidays.

My heels make rapid, purposeful clicks against the surface of the parking lot. I hurry through the shadows and glance quickly around in the few small swaths of light. I'm still a bit jumpy. I don't know why, because the noise was all in my imagination. Wasn't it? I glance about once again and I twist the key ring in my hand, allowing the points of the keys to protrude between my fingers as I clench my fist.

It is way too dark out here. And with the parking lot on the backside of the building it is too isolated. I don't like it. Damn superintendent still hasn't done anything about the lights. Over half of them have been burned out for six months now. During the summer it wasn't that bad, but it gets dark earlier now. I'd better call and complain again tomorrow.

Hmmph, like it will do any good. It hasn't yet.

Oh well, just another hundred feet and I'll be inside. Out of the dark and into the warmth. This next part is the worst. All of the lights are burned out here. And then there's the overgrown evergreen bushes casting their own angry shapes into the dark void. I aim myself at the distant door and hasten my steps.

Dammit, Heather! Get a grip girl. You'll be inside soon. You're getting yourself worked up over nothing. This is a safe neighborhood. Chill out.

Seventy-five feet left to go. Why is my heart racing? I'm not usually this skittish. The clicking sound below me is coming faster now.

What was that?!

This time I KNOW there was a noise!

I stop dead in my tracks. The footsteps behind me make a soft thud, halting just enough out of time with my own to strike fear into the pit of my stomach. Stupid! Stupid, Heather! What the hell did you stop for?! If someone is coming after you what are you going to do? Just stand here and wait for him?

The footsteps behind me begin again and I glance over my shoulder to see a shadowy figure moving toward me.

Oh my God! This can't really be happening!

I begin to sprint without any thought. Instantly I know how those women in the horror flicks manage to run in high heels. They're just too scared to know better, that's all.

My shoes are click clacking rapidly against the pavement now; my heart is firmly entrenched in my throat, blocking all attempts to scream. Panic has stolen my breath.

I've never been this frightened before.

Fifty feet, I'm almost there. I can hear him back there, running, getting closer. He's not even trying to conceal himself any longer.

I can feel hot breath against my neck.

I can smell stale cigarette smoke and bad breath.

The sour reek of B.O.

Something hits me hard in the side and I stumble into the tendril-like branches of the evergreen. What little wind I have left is forced from my lungs and I struggle to disentangle myself.

He grabs me and I flail wildly. I fall into him and we both crash to the ground with me on top. He is clawing at me, trying to maintain his hold. I kick and twist away, slipping out of my blazer and crawl quickly as I try to stand. Scrabbling across the sidewalk I fight to regain my footing.

I open my mouth to scream but nothing more than a choked whimper comes out.

A hand wraps around my ankle and I kick hard with my other foot. I twist onto my back and kick again, aiming my heel for the ski mask staring back at me. I miss and my shoe goes flying.

I roll frantically and manage to pull away again, then drag myself upward. I start to run, but trip over my remaining shoe. The time it takes me to kick it off and begin to run again is all the time he needs.

My blouse has become untucked in the struggle and it is riding up as I try to regain my balance. Something cold presses hard against the bare skin at my waistline.

I hear a quick electric snap, like a light bulb blowing out.

My teeth clench hard and I freeze in place, every nerve scrambled into a tangled rats nest of jittery disorientation. I shudder for a moment and fall to the ground. There's a metallic tang in my mouth that is slowly replaced by the salty taste of my own blood from where I've bitten my tongue. Or at least I hope that is all it is.

Fear still grips me through the disorientation, but my voice is nowhere to be found. All I seem to be able to do is twitch.

I hear him moving nearby.

I see the shadow over me.

Once again I can smell the B.O. and stale cigarettes, as he looms closer.

I hear panting breaths and a hoarse, almost awestruck whisper intermixed, "Perfect...She's almost perfect."

I can feel the keys in my hand, their metal points still poking between my fingers, as my fist remains clenched. The shadow moves in closer and I summon everything I have to flail at it with the only weapon I have left. But my arm doesn't move.

I'm still twitching uncontrollably. He forces my mouth open and pours something onto my tongue. It's bitter and I gag.

As I sputter, the message I had earlier sent to my arm finds its way down a detour of nerves and the handful of keys slings upward in a flaccid arc, glancing harmlessly against my attacker.

Still, he yelps with surprise and rocks back away from me.

Hard points press against my flesh once again, and I hear the crackling hum. The last thing I feel is my back arch as electricity courses through me, and the lights dim quickly to black.

I really should have tried to break the connection the moment Debbie Schaeffer pushed me. But, in all honesty, I was far too shocked to even think, much less act.

Throughout the investigations I'd been involved in over the past two years, I had channeled some terribly horrific things. In doing so, I had been guided— and even led around by the nose to some extent— by the spirits of those I was trying to help. I had pretty much come to expect this kind of treatment from the other side.

However, this was the first time I could recall ever having been outright pushed around by, for lack of a better description, a vengeful ghost. It was a wholly new experience for me, and something I wasn't enjoying in the least. But then, I knew better than to do this without someone to back me up, so I had no one to blame but myself. And trust me, I was already pointing the finger.

As I had told Heather Burke before this all began, I wasn't entirely certain that I wanted to see what she had to show me. But now, I was no longer seeing it; I was living it. What was worse, I knew that the piece of her life I'd shared thus far was only a prologue to the horror show.

The only saving grace was the fact that on the physical plane, Heather was sitting right in front of me. Alive, uninjured, and for the most part, well— very well, in fact, for someone who had been through what she had. This meant that at least I wasn't running the risk of following her into death.

Of course, until now, she couldn't actually remember any of the events that had transpired in any detail. So, the real question was: Just how well was she going to be after this was all over?

Or, should I say: Just how well were WE going to be after this was all over?

I awake.

I don't know where I am.

My head hurts and so does my side.

I'm too afraid to move.

I try to move.

I can't.

It's like I'm just too tired to do anything.

I feel as though I am sitting.

But where?

My hair feels funny.

Like I'm wearing a stocking cap or something.

My scalp is hot and it itches, but I'm too tired to scratch it. I try to ignore it.

Where am I?

I try to remember.

Someone was chasing me, yeah.

Did he catch me? Did I get away?

I'm supposed to be afraid now, right? I think I am. I'm just so tired that I don't care.

I take the plunge and slowly open my eyes.

I think I'm staring at my lap.

The light is subdued, dimmed, and almost ethereal.

It's just a bit on the cold side.

I blink slowly and my eyes begin to adjust, then my lap comes into focus.

Hmmmph, interesting. I don't remember owning a red garter belt and red stockings.

The fog in my brain parts a bit more.

Well no wonder I'm cold, I'm half naked!

A rough hand comes out of nowhere and cups my chin. I would scream but I'm just too tired. Still, terror rips through me as my head is tilted back.

Tired or not, now I am definitely afraid.

I manage to whimper.

I smell B.O. and cigarettes.

Smoke rolls cloudlike in front of my face and I gag on it.

I hear a familiar voice; rough but filled with a bizarre reverence, "Almost perfect..."

My head is tilted even further back. My hair feels so very odd. My scalp feels tight and constricted, but the hair against my shoulders feels fluffy and teased.

Bizarre.

I must be tripping.

He must have drugged me.

I stare upward, afraid.

All I can make out is a shadow.

The voice comes again, "Almost her..."

I see a hand come toward my face. I try to shut my eyes, afraid that I am about to be struck. I feel his fingers on my eyelid and he pries my left eye open and holds it wide. I still cannot see him. I watch in horror as his other hand comes directly at my eyeball.

I whimper and try to struggle, but he holds tight.

My eye waters against the foreign object that has been inserted, and now he does the same to my right eye. My vision is so completely blurred now that I cannot even make out complete shapes. Only shadow and light.

I whimper again and feel a hot tear roll down my cheek.

"Stop crying!" the voice demands, the former reverent tone disappearing. "Why do all of you have to cry?!"

All of you?

I wonder about that.

I must not be the only one here.

Are they just as afraid as me?

The hand grabs my face once again and it feels as though it is crushing my jaw. He shakes my head, pressing his fingers and thumb hard into my cheeks.

"Stop crying dammit! You aren't HER! You don't have the right to cry! Stop it!"

I whimper and feel more tears begin to flow. I can't stop. I'm so afraid.

He releases his grip, and I see the shadow seem to turn. Then it suddenly spins back to me and I feel his palm slap me hard across my face.

My head is wrenched to the side and the hot sting on my cheek spreads outward. I just cry harder.

"Now look what you've done," he screams. "Now I have to fix your makeup!"

The shadow moves away but returns quickly. Something hard stabs into my side and my teeth chatter as I stiffen and vibrate with the electric shock.

The last thing I hear is the voice screaming, "YOU AREN'T HER!"

I was swimming toward the surface, laboring to break free of the current that had swept me so deeply into Heather Burke's recent past. The darkness around me was thinning; changing in hue from black, to indigo, to blue, then charcoal grey. I felt myself break through and the colors of the room bloomed around me.

I felt a wave of relief that was followed by a tsunami of disbelief. I knew that I should be staring directly into the eyes of a petite blonde who was positioned across from me.

Instead, I was staring directly into the eyes of a longhaired man who was sporting a greying goatee, and a blank expression. The problem was, I wasn't looking into a mirror.

"So what happens now?" Detective McLaughlin queried

Ben in a low voice.

I could tell she was whispering, but to me, her words rang out clear and strong through the void. I called out to the two of them to help me, but my plea fell on deaf ears.

If I could hear them so clearly, why couldn't they hear me?

I tried calling again, louder this time, but realized quickly that even I could not hear my own voice. I had no choice but to simply listen.

"Guess it all depends." I could sense the shrug in my friend's voice when he answered her.

"On what?"

"On what he sees."

"What do you mean?"

"I dunno. I've watched 'im do this maybe half a dozen times. Either he sits there starin' for a minute, then just snaps out of it, or he starts floppin' around and screamin' like a banshee."

"Why would he do that?"

"'Cause of what he sees."

"I don't understand," she sounded puzzled, "I thought he was going to hypnotize her."

"He did," Ben grunted. "Look at her."

"But shouldn't she be talking or something?"

"That's not exactly how he does it."

"How exactly does he do it then?"

"I dunno. Hocus pocus *Twilight Zone* shit. He's the Witch, not me."

"So, what's he see that would make him start screaming?"

"I don't really wanna know. Do you?"

I know I didn't.

I'm drifting in a semi-conscious haze.

I remember flashing lights.

Bright. Blinding.

Over and over.

Darkness.

Flash!

Darkness.

Flash!

And the sound of shuffling.

I remember being moved.

At least I think I do.

I'm no longer cold, but I'm terribly uncomfortable.

I feel as though I'm still seated, but my hip is aching and I can feel my own knuckles pressing hard against my cheek. My arm tingles as if it has gone to sleep.

My back is starting to hurt.

My hair still feels incredibly bizarre.

I start to move but then I remember.

I'm afraid to open my eyes.

I know he is close... I can hear him.

I can smell him.

I gag on the stench

I open one eye and find that the blur is no longer as bad as it had been earlier. Still, I can feel something in my eyes and they are sore. Itching.

I'm in different clothing now.

It looks like it might be a party dress. All I know is that it is shiny and red and frilly and there is a lot of it gathered around me. My right leg is draped over the arm of the chair. My left leg feels like it is being stretched and pulled out of its socket in the opposite direction. From the way that my feet feel, I guess that they are crammed into a pair of high heels that are about a half-size too small.

My side begins to cramp up and I whimper.

He doesn't hear me.

He is making far too much noise.

I can hear him panting.

I feel him close.

A shadow moves in front of me and in the dim light I can see that he is nude from the waist down.

His hand is pistoning back and forth at his crotch and I can hear him mutter, "So close... Almost perfect..."

A lit cigarette smokes in his free hand as the other pumps faster between his legs. I concentrate on the glowing coal, not wanting to witness his self-stimulation. I watch him raise the cigarette to take a puff and notice that it is positioned between his middle fingers.

Curious.

I've never seen anyone hold a cigarette like that before.

I try to follow his hand, but my head feels heavy, and I cannot move.

He moves closer, standing between my legs.

I want to scream.

He starts grunting as something warm and wet splatters me. I'm afraid I know what it is, and I feel sick.

The scream escapes as a gurgle.

My brain overloads on the fear and disgust.

I close my eyes and pray.

He keeps panting and muttering, "Oh sweet Jesus, she's so close... She's almost HER."

"Did you see that?" Charlee McLaughlin's voice echoes past me in a distorted roar.

"See what?" Ben's voice rumbles behind.

"They flinched."

"Yeah, so?"

"No, like both at the same time."

"Yeah?"

"Well does that mean something?"

"You're askin' the wrong guy, Chuck."

"It's been almost five solid minutes," her voice continued to echo out of phase. "Should we try to wake him up or something?"

In my mind I was screaming YES! Of course, they couldn't hear me. I couldn't even hear me.

"First time I ever saw him do this," Ben explained, "he said, whatever you do don't touch me, or you'll break the trance. Or somethin' like that, anyway. Just let it go. As long as he's not screamin' and they're both still breathin' he's fine."

No I'm not! I screamed at them again to no avail.

One thought crossed my mind. Dammit, Ben! As I remember, you didn't listen to me then— so why are you suddenly deciding to do as I asked now?

The sense of absolute violation transcends even the pain.

I know he's been inside me, I can feel it.

I'm still so weak, so tired, that I cannot move.

I just lay there in the cold and cry.

Hot tears stream from the corners of my eyes, rolling across my face and finally dripping into my ears.

I'm on my back.

It's dark and there's something covering me.

I can feel cold vinyl against my skin.

The stench of stale cigarette smoke fills my nostrils.

I'm still with him.

How long has it been?

I've lost all track of time.

I feel motion.

We are moving.

I can hear the roughness of the mistuned car engine.

The vibration rattles me.

My arm slides across my chest, making tiny jumps in time with the vibrations until finally, it falls, glances from the edge of the seat and lands in the floorboard; or more accurately, into the trash covering the floorboard.

I can hear him in the front seat.

He's humming.

He's humming a happy, satisfied tune. He's humming Merry Christmas, Baby.

I feel the vehicle turn— left I think.

I wonder if I can remember the turns. Isn't that what they do in spy movies? Count the seconds traveling straight, then the turns? Make a map in their heads?

Who am I trying to fool here?

I wonder where he is taking me?

My stomach wrenches itself into a knot as fear grips me.

He's probably taking me somewhere so he can kill me and dispose of my body!

I feel the car turn again, begin to accelerate, then the forlorn squeal of worn brakes reaches my ears.

The car lurches to a sudden halt, rocking hard on worn shocks. I bounce against the seatback like a rag doll, then roll forward. My body slides from the edge of the seat and crumples into the floorboard, face down.

I groan.

"Don't worry," I hear him say, "you're almost home."

Fear slices through me again. I wonder what he means by home? The bottom of a ditch? The river? A shallow grave somewhere?

My mind races.

I struggle to open my eyes and find my face buried in a pile of trash. As we pass beneath a streetlight I see that my pillow consists of fast food bags, empty cigarette cartons, and things best left unidentified.

We travel in darkness, then pass beneath another streetlamp. My roaming eye catches a glimpse of an envelope.

Darkness falls.

Again, for a fleeting instant, the glow of a streetlamp.

Mister something.

Darkness.

I count out the thrum of the tires in my head, keeping my eye focused on the spot where the envelope lay.

Three, two, one.

The light floods the interior for a split second.

Seventy-five...

Darkness, three, two, one...

Thirty-four...

Darkness, three, two, one...

No, thirty-four is the stamp.

Darkness, three, two, one...

Seventy-five again...

Darkness, three, two, one...

Thirty-four again. Was it the stamp again? I don't know...

Two, one...

Mister something again.

Concentrate!

Darkness, three, two, one...

Seventy-five thirty-four something...

I can feel the car slowing...

Darkness, three, two, one...

The car quickly arcs into a turn, and then bounces over a curb just as the streetlamp's glow fills the cabin.

The envelope shifts.

I shift.

I catch a final glimpse as a fast food bag falls in front of it.

Mister and Ash something...

Mister Ash?

Mister Ash what?

The darkness remains and I can feel that the car is moving very slowly now.

We stop.

His voice reaches my ears again. "It's okay honey. You're home now."

CHAPTER 23

Sudden calmness enveloped me, followed immediately by the screaming pain of a midnight leg cramp— only this leg cramp encompassed my entire body. I could feel myself double forward, then without warning propelling backward with explosive force.

And then, the cramp-like pain melted away, leaving behind the sickening, dull ache that usually accompanies a bad hangover. In the span of a heartbeat, I felt myself slowly sinking into a murky darkness that was deepening with each passing second.

For some unknown reason, I had been summarily expelled from Heather Burke's nightmare. Or it had reached its end. Or maybe I had been unceremoniously, but purposefully extracted? I wasn't sure. Whatever the case, I was grateful for the relief.

The psychic hangover was dissipating and as I continued to sink, I began to feel warm and comfortable. Had it not been for the sharp noise that suddenly stabbed its way through my eardrums, I think I could have simply gone to sleep.

I was once again swimming in an inky void, the atmosphere thick around me like water. I wanted to do nothing more than relax and allow the calmness of the dark to overtake me, but the echo in my ears told me that such comfort wasn't to be.

Stark awareness seeped in to replace the drowsy feeling and poked at my grey matter with an annoying finger. It started by reminding me that I was once again Rowan Linden Gant, and that I really needed to wake up.

The sharp noise shot into my left ear once again and rattled around inside my skull without remorse. It sounded for all the world like someone with a speech impediment saying 'yo-yo'. It took a moment for me to realize that the words were actually "Yo, Row."

A dim light in the distance seemed to beckon me and I aimed myself toward it. Again, darkness began bleeding away, leaving in its wake first indigo, then blue, then charcoal grey. In a psychedelic explosion, color bloomed before me and settled slowly into the proper hues of reality. As if I didn't have enough to deal with, the ethereal hangover returned, and followed me into this plane of existence. Something told me that aspirin wouldn't help.

Heather Burke was seated across from me, quietly sobbing, her face buried deeply into her hands. Her shoulders heaved and she sucked in a breath before advancing the level of her grief another octave up the scale.

I knew exactly how she felt.

Utter violation permeated me. I felt disgusted, sickened, and even in a way, filthy. I felt as though something had been taken from me. And worst of all, I still felt fear.

"You okay, Row?" Ben's voice came from behind as he rested a large hand on my shoulder.

"Yeah," I choked past a rising lump in my throat. "I'm okay, but we'd better get someone for Ms. Burke here to talk to. We've...She's got a lot to deal with."

"I'm not one hundred percent positive," I told Ben and Charlee, "but I think we might be looking for someone with the last name Ash, or Ash-something. It's also possible that his street number is seventy-five thirty-four."

We were all back in my friend's van, me riding shotgun this time. We were on our way to police headquarters after having finally reached someone to look after Heather Burke. I felt terrible just leaving her after dredging up the chemically repressed memories, but we had no choice. I'd obtained information that we needed to go over and decipher. I don't know why, but something told me that time was a commodity that we simply did not have in abundance.

Still, before we left I gave her my home number and told her to feel free to call me if she wanted to talk about anything at all. I wasn't exactly qualified to help her in a clinical sense, but for all intents and purposes we had shared the exact same experience. Sometimes that kind of understanding can be worth far more than the highest priced sheepskin.

"How'd you come up with that?" Detective McLaughlin asked.

"When he was taking her home he had her on the back seat of his car," I explained. "At some point when he hit the brakes suddenly, she rolled off into the floorboards. He's a bit of a slob so she ended up on top of a lot of trash, and it just happened that one of the things that was staring her in the face was an envelope."

"And she read the address from it?"

"Actually, she more or less tried to. How conscious the effort was, I can't be sure. It seemed like it was, but she was still under the influence of the drugs. She was at a severe disadvantage. At any rate it ended up as a latent memory that I was able to pick up. Unfortunately due to the darkness and shifting from the motion of the vehicle, she only made out a small part of it."

"Sheesh, Storm was right," she exclaimed. "You are spooky."

"You get used to him after a while, Chuck," Ben offered, then turned his attention to me. "Do you know for a fact that it was his name and address she was looking at?"

"No, not for a fact," I admitted.

"So the envelope coulda just been some trash that wasn't even his mail?"

"I suppose, but it's worth looking into, right?"

"Yeah, we'll check it out, but you gotta figure there's gonna be a hell of a lotta Ash's and Ash-whatever's in the phone book."

"Shouldn't the address help pin it down?" I submitted.

"Maybe," he answered, "if it really is the address. If it was on an envelope it could be a piece of a zip code or somethin'."

"Plus, we don't know if he actually lives in Saint Louis," Charlee added. "We know he gets around, so he could live outside of the metro area in another county, or even in Illinois."

"I thought I actually had something," I said in a dejected tone.

"You might," she returned. "But we can't chase it as if it were our only clue."

"Ya'know, eggs, basket, all that shit," Ben expressed. "So, what else did'ya come up with?"

"He's dressing them up and taking photographs of them."

"You already said that much before the mumbo-jumbo," Ben returned.

"I said he was taking pictures," I reminded him. "What I'm telling you now is that he is not just taking pictures, he's dressing them up in order to take the pictures."

"Like how?" McLaughlin asked.

"Well, I only remember a couple of the outfits, but one was lingerie. A garter belt and stockings is what I saw for certain. The other was a party dress or something of that sort."

"So this guy has a kink for prettying up his victims," Ben offered rhetorically.

"It's more than that." I shook my head. "He does something with their hair. I'm not sure what, but from the sensation I'm thinking he may put a wig on them."

"So the asshole really is playing 'dolls' then," he harrumphed.

"In a way, yes," I acknowledged. "He even put something in her eyes, and I'm betting they were tinted contact lenses. He's doing all this with a specific purpose in mind…"

"What? Is he trying to make the 'perfect woman'?" Charlee asked in a disgusted tone.

"No, it really feels like more than that. Helen would be more qualified to judge on this than I would, but he kept flip-flopping. Like a bipolar disorder stuck in overdrive. One minute it would be like he was worshipping her. He'd say things like 'She's almost perfect', then he would suddenly shift into an abusive mode and scream at her, saying things like 'You're not her'."

"Any idea who 'her' is?" Ben asked.

"No clue." I shook my head again. "I can't even tell you what she is supposed to look like. I never actually saw how he had Burke made up. Just bits and pieces of the outfits, although he mentioned something about makeup."

"You mentioned somethin' about that earlier, right Chuck?"

"Yeah. So far all the victims have had smeared makeup on their faces that they didn't put on," she answered, then offered thoughtfully, "You know, all of the victims have pretty much resembled one another. More than just their size and hair. I mean, not dead ringers or anything, but close enough that at a distance they could be mistaken for one another…"

"Especially if he did a makeover on 'em?" Ben added the question more as a comment.

"Exactly," I agreed. "They must fit the profile of the woman he is trying to re-create. Maybe it's a former girlfriend who dumped him, or even a wife who passed away."

"Yeah," Ben ran down his own list, "or a woman who works in his office, or at the deli down the street, or the star of his favorite TV show. Or a model out of a magazine, his sister, his mother…"

"Maybe the first few, but this is definitely sexual in nature. I'd rule out siblings or matriarchal figures."

"What rock you been hidin' under?" he retorted as he hooked the van through a light that was somewhere between yellow and red. "Ever hear of Oedipus? This guy's a whack job. This might be his way of doin' sis or mom, or both for that matter."

"I'd rather not think about that, Ben," I said.

"Yeah, well it comes with the territory. If it turns out to be a lead then we hafta look at the big picture, not just what we wanna see. Anyway, this is all fine and wonderful but it doesn't get us really any closer to who this asshole is."

"Sorry," I told him. "I'm just telling you what I saw."

"I'm not complainin'. I'm just tellin' it like it is. So, I don't suppose you saw the asshole's face."

"No, just shadows."

"So that's a dead end," Charlee chimed in from the back.

"Is there anything else?" Ben pressed.

I concentrated for a moment but drew a blank. I was still fighting off some severe emotional effects from the entire episode. On top of that, the nagging feeling that I was being watched had returned, and it was starting to occupy my mind to the exclusion of all else.

"Maybe... I don't know... It kept fading in and out, so I'm not sure I'm remembering everything."

"You mean like you were talkin' earlier about feelin' the effects of the roofies?"

"Yeah, I think so," I replied with a distracted note in my voice.

I was tilting my head down and to the side, trying to get a look in the side view mirror as we traveled. My concentration on the task must have completely taken over, because I suddenly felt something thump my arm and I jumped.

"Hey, Ground Control to Rowan. You wanna answer me?" Ben's voice flooded into my head.

"What?"

"What the hell are you doin'?"

"Are we being followed?" I answered his question with a question— something he absolutely hated.

"Do what?"

"I don't know, Ben," I shrugged. "I just got this weird feeling. Like I'm being watched. I had it back at Heather Burke's apartment too."

The color drained from my friend's face. This was only the second time I'd seen him go this pale and the first had been only a few days ago at the Yule celebration. He looked into the rear view mirror, then at both sides, dwelling long enough to get a good scan of the area behind us.

"Is this like one of those *Twilight Zone* things?" he finally asked.

"I think it might be," I acknowledged, disturbed by the way he was suddenly acting. "Why?"

"Do you know who it is that's watching you?" he

pressed.

"No. Do you?" I pressed back.

"What are you two talking about?" McLaughlin interjected.

"No. Why would I?" Ben shot back, ignoring Charlee altogether.

"You're lying, Ben," I told him. "I can tell."

"Hey," Charlee spoke up again, "is someone going to tell me what's going on?"

We had arrived at our destination, and Ben pulled the Chevy into a space, then cranked it into park and twisted the key off.

"Forget it," he commanded as he levered his groaning door open. A cool gust of wind made a beeline for the interior of the van and dropped the temperature a few degrees.

"Not this time, Ben," I returned. "Something's going on, and it involves me. I can tell."

"This isn't the time, Rowan," he answered sternly.

"Well then make it the time," I demanded.

"Rowan…"

"It's got something to do with the phone call the other night doesn't it?"

"Dammit, Rowan…"

"Tell me, Ben."

With an angry huff he yanked the door shut and turned to face me. "Goddammit, white man, haven't we argued enough today?"

"I'm not arguing," I returned. "I just want to know what's going on."

"Just trust me, Row. You don't need to be hearing this right now. I'll tell ya' when things settle down."

"It is about me, then," I retorted.

"Yeah, it's about you. Now leave it alone."

"Then tell me what it is!" I demanded again.

"I'm serious, Row."

"I am too!"

"Alright." His voice rose slightly as he struggled to contain what seemed to be as much fear as anger. "You wanna know what it is so damn bad, then I'll tell you. That call the other night was from Mandalay."

The name told me that the call couldn't have been good. Constance Mandalay was a mutual friend, but she was also a Special Agent attached to the FBI's Saint Louis field office.

"She was calling about a murder in southern Missouri," Ben continued. "It's been kept out of the news so far, but everything points to a single suspect, up to and including a partial set of fingerprints found at the scene."

"Me?" I asked, not fully grasping what he was telling me.

"Hell no, not you," he returned. "Eldon Andrew Porter. You were fuckin' right. The sonofabitch isn't dead."

CHAPTER 24

I was stunned, but not by what Ben had just revealed.

I wasn't at all surprised that Eldon Porter was still alive. I had, of course, been the one person who had believed that all along. What caught me completely and utterly unprepared was that Ben would keep this fact from me.

I sat for what seemed a lifetime, silently gathering my thoughts and staring back at my friend. He was correct with his earlier comment. We had already argued more than enough for one day, but at the moment, I couldn't help feeling as though I'd been grievously betrayed.

The silence was finally broken by Detective McLaughlin clearing her throat, and then unlatching the sliding door on the van. "I'll see you two inside," was all she said before climbing out and yanking the door shut on the rumbling slides.

"Are ya' happy now?" Ben said coldly as we continued to play stare-down with each other.

My jaw worked for a moment before I could get any words to come out. When they finally did, I had to force my voice to remain even and calm, although my query was thickly coated with an angry frost. "You've known this since Friday? Exactly when were you planning to tell me?"

"Suspected it since Friday," he corrected. "I didn't get a

verification from Constance until this morning just before you showed up."

"And?" I pushed hard. "You still didn't tell me."

"Yeah, and right now I'm starin' at why," he stated flatly.

"What? You don't think I have the right to be upset?"

"Sure. You got the right to be just as freakin' upset as you want." He nodded. "But you've got enough shit goin' on right now, so I thought it was for the best to keep it under wraps for now."

"That's insane!" I told him. "You know as well as anyone that I'm probably number one on his hit list. I could tell by the look on your face when I said I felt like someone was following me that this has got you scared too."

"Yeah, and I'm not the only one," he offered. "But it's taken care of."

"How so?"

"You've got a lot of people lookin' out for you, white man," he explained. "There was more than just one call made Friday night. The local coppers stepped up patrols in your neighborhood that night as a precaution, and Mandalay called Carl Deckert over at County. They're keeping an eye on you too."

"I haven't noticed anything."

"You aren't supposed to," he sighed. "You know, Mandalay is all over this too. She's even been keepin' an eye on you."

"You still should've told me," I spat. "Especially this morning."

"You were gonna find out tonight."

"Is that why you invited us over for Christmas Eve?"

"Actually, we were gonna invite you anyway. It just worked out that way and I figured it'd be easier to keep you at the house if I already had you two there."

"Keep us at the house?"

"Yeah, I'm movin' you in where I can keep an eye on you until we find this fuckhead and lock 'im up."

"I suppose you've talked to Felicity about this?"

"No. She didn't need the headache either. Besides, I'm guessin' she's gonna be just about as reasonable as you are right now."

"You should be so lucky," I chided.

"Yeah, I know," he grunted.

"Dammit, Ben," I muttered. "Felicity is running around the city unprotected right now."

"In public, with a group, and at one time or another a freakin' camera crew from every local TV station has been followin' them around. She's as safe as you are. We've got it under control, Rowan."

"I hope so."

"We do." He sat for a long moment, allowing the words of reassurance to hang in the air between us, before finally speaking again. "Now that you know, you might as well pack a bag before coming over tonight."

"You know Felicity won't go for this, Ben." I shook my head. "She didn't last time. She won't this time either."

"Yeah, well last time you almost got killed, so I'm not givin' you a choice."

"You can't do that," I returned.

"Ever hear of protective custody, Kemosabe?"

"You wouldn't…"

"Fuckin' try me."

"How's it going?" I was fighting to keep the mix of depression, anger, and fear out of my voice as I spoke into the telephone. "Everyone having fun as usual?"

It was early afternoon, but the 'Santa Brigade' was booked right up until five-thirty PM this year. I had managed to remember enough of the schedule to catch my wife on her cell phone in between stops. I could hear the upbeat chattering of the rest of the group in the background when she answered.

"Great," Felicity's voice came back to me over the handset. Her brogue was returning, and I could hear how tired she was. But, at the same time it was obvious that she was still running on excitement and a healthy dose of adrenalin. "Aye, so far I've had three marriage proposals— one from a twelve year old, mind you so you'd best watch out, then— Younger men do still find me attractive." She punctuated the comment with a giddy laugh.

"I'm not surprised. But, I've told you that before."

"Aye, I still like hearing it, then. Of course, I still attract the older men it seems. About thirty minutes ago we were at a nursing home and an elderly gentleman in a wheelchair grabbed my arse. Three times, now."

"And you're still calling him a gentleman?" I chuckled, the visual helping me to forget if only for a moment. "You didn't hurt him too much did you?"

"He was harmless," she laughed. "Besides, it was probably the biggest thrill he's had all year, then."

"Beats a nut log, I guess."

"Aye, he said something like that too, but with a much different connotation."

"So, elderly gentleman is short for Dirty Old Man?"

"Aye, filthy would be more like it," she giggled.

"Well, considering the way you looked when you left this morning, I guess I can't blame him."

"Liked the outfit, then?" her voice held an undertone of satisfaction.

"What do YOU think?"

"Hmmmmm," her voice lowered to a purr. "Maybe I'll leave it on when I get home, then... For a little while anyway if you know what I mean."

If we'd had this conversation a few hours earlier, I would probably be looking for a place to hide so I wouldn't embarrass myself. Unfortunately— or perhaps fortunately as the case may be— the recent revelation from Ben was severely dampening my heretofore-overactive libido.

"You might want to hold on to that thought, Lass," I told her. "Allison and Ben have invited us over to their house for dinner."

"Aye, that's nice," she said. "What did you tell them?"

"I said I'd have to ask you."

"You know," she lowered her voice to a whisper, "you didn't see what I put on underneath this costume."

She wasn't making this easy, even with the preoccupation that was permeating my brain. I had considered telling her the whole story, but immediately decided against it. There was no reason for both of us to worry over this. Not at this particular moment, anyway. People were depending on her and I needed to let that come first, for now.

I just kept telling myself that Ben was correct. As long as she was with her group and out in the public eye, she was safe.

"As much as I would like to unwrap that package— And believe me, I really, really do," I told her, "I think we should probably go to the dinner."

"Are you sure?" I could hear an audible pout in her voice. "Wouldn't we be intruding on their family time, then?"

"Ben says no," I replied, then added a generic weightiness to the invitation. "It seems pretty important to him that we be there."

"Why is that do you think?"

"Dunno," I said. "But I think it's important enough to

him that we should oblige."

"Aye, what I'm wearing underneath came from a catalog, then," she offered in a sexy murmur.

"Felicity…"

"And, I could wait for you under the Yule tree." She gave it one more try.

"Uh huh," I fended her off. "Tomorrow. I promise."

"Okay, then," she pouted into the phone again. "Are you going to make something to take? I'll be late, and…"

"Already taken care of," I cut her off. "He said don't bring anything, so I figure I'll just grab a bottle of wine out of the rack."

"Aye, sounds good," she acknowledged. "How about that eighty-six Zinfandel?"

"The Caswell we bought a case of?"

"Aye, that one."

"Okay."

She paused at the other end, and I could literally feel her checking me out on an otherworldly level. "Are you okay, Rowan?"

"I'm fine," I lied. "Why?"

"You sound distant. Like something is bothering you."

"I'm okay."

"You don't FEEL okay to me, then."

"I'm just disappointed that I'm going to miss out on your offer." At least that was only half a lie.

"Hmmmm," she purred again, accepting the explanation, "not missing out, just postponing."

"I like the sound of that better," I said.

"Aye, it will be worth the wait," she murmured. "Trust me."

"Did ya' tell her?" Ben asked as I walked out of the conference room.

"No," I shook my head, "I'll tell her later."

"Row,..."

"Hey," I held up my hands to stop his objection, "I convinced her that we should go to your house for dinner tonight. I can pack a few things for her before she gets home and we can both tell her when we get there."

"Isn't she gonna be pissed when she finds out that you ran a game on 'er?"

"And what I'm doing is different from what you planned to do, how?"

"Touché."

"In answer to your question, however, yes, she's going to be pissed," I told him. "You know that. But look at the bright side. Your way she would have just been mad at you. My way she'll be mad at both of us."

"Somehow I'm not all that comforted by that fact," he answered.

"You shouldn't be."

"I got a brand new bottle of sixteen year old *Bushmills* at the house. Think we should get her drunk first?"

"Neither of us can drink that much," I mused. "She'd win and then we'd really be in trouble."

"There are thirty-eight Ash's in the metro phone book," Detective McLaughlin told us. "Spelled A-S-H, right, Rowan?"

"That's what I saw, but it might not have been the whole name," I nodded with my answer.

"Exactly." She returned the nod. "Which is why we went right down the line on everything beginning with A-S-H.

Still, it was a big help to cut out the A-S-C-H's. All totaled there are three-hundred forty-nine Ash's or Ash-whatever's in the white pages."

"That's better than I was expectin'," Ben offered.

"Don't get excited yet." Charlee shook her head. "That's just the metro phone book. We're getting a printout from DMV right now, as well as a computer search on phone books from the surrounding counties. The number is gonna get bigger."

"Yeah, well happy holidays to you too," Ben told her sarcastically.

"Then you're gonna love this. I was talking to Ackman and he asked if we were certain that Ash is the surname." At the end of her sentence she turned a questioning gaze in my direction.

"Honestly, I can't be sure," I shook my head and returned a frown. "So, I'd have to say that it could be a first name."

"Well, that's going to add some more to the pile."

"What about the street number?" I asked.

"No hit so far," she returned. "Not against the names anyway. There's a handful of seventy-five thirty-fours in the metro area alone. Some businesses, some residential."

I seized on the information and posed a different question. "Are any of the commercial addresses Photographic Studios by any chance?"

"No such luck. It would really help if we had a street name, or even a zip code."

"Assuming the number isn't part of a zip code to begin with." Ben poured more water on the fire.

"Any way you look at that it puts him too far out of state," she replied. "If you plug numbers in before or after the seventy-five thirty-four you end up with zip codes in Pennsylvania, North Carolina, South Dakota, Texas, and

Oregon."

"Yeah, and he coulda moved here from one of those places," Ben remarked. "We should probably make some contacts just in case there's somethin' open that didn't make it into NCIC."

"Shouldn't you be trying to narrow the scope instead of expanding it?" I voiced.

"We'll start pickin' the dolphins out as soon as we're sure the net's full," he told me.

"Okay, so what do we do now?"

"We start looking at printouts and making phone calls," Charlee answered.

"That could take forever," I exclaimed.

She shrugged and shook her head. "Welcome to the fast-paced and exciting world of police work."

Ben clapped me on the shoulder. "Yeah, what she said. Who wants coffee?"

CHAPTER 25

I never wanted to see another telephone book or stack of green bar for as long as I lived.

According to the window at the back of the conference room, it was dark outside. We had been at it hard and heavy for a few hours now, and I had lost all track of time. Since, in Ben's words, I wasn't a 'duly authorized law enforcement officer', I wasn't allowed to make any of the actual calls. Instead, my presence had been utilized cross-referencing listings in various phone books against computer printouts and screens full of data on an ancient, out-of-focus monitor.

I was tired, I had a headache, my eyes were itching, and I wanted a cigarette; but, most of all, I was depressed. We didn't seem to have accomplished a thing. In fact, we were still perched firmly in the middle of square one, and someone else was redeeming a free turn card.

"Stick a fork in me, I'm done," Ben announced with a tired yawn as he sat back in his chair. He and Detective McLaughlin had been contacting other police departments within the range of possible zip codes. What I had been overhearing of their conversations had not sounded promising.

"Anything at all?" I asked aloud.

My elbows were resting on the table in front of me and I was holding my head tight between my hands, palms on either side of my face. My brain felt as if it was about to explode, and I couldn't be certain if it was from staring at all the shrunken print, something more sinister, or a combination of both. I had my eyes closed and was slowly massaging my temples, trying to will the pain away.

"Nada," my friend returned. "And that was the last one, so that's all we're gonna get tonight."

"What about all these numbers from the phone books?" I asked. "Shouldn't we start calling them?"

"And say what, Row?" he contended. "Hi, this is Detective Storm with the City Police Department and I'm just wondering, are you by any chance a crazed serial rapist?"

McLaughlin half snickered and began massaging her own temples. "Storm's right. We can't just start calling people arbitrarily without something more to go on. Besides, what if we did happen to call the right guy? Then he'd know we were getting close and he'd disappear."

"Yeah, remember the 'South Side Rapist'?" Ben added. "When things got hot and heavy around here Dennis Rabbitt took the whole 'go west young man' thing to heart. The last thing we need ta' do is call the guy and tell 'im that we're on to 'im."

"There's got to be something we can do," I appealed.

"There is," my friend answered. "Call it a night and come back at it fresh."

I opened my eyes as I twisted my arm around and looked at my watch. "But, it's only a little after five."

"Yeah, and it's freakin' Christmas Eve, Rowan," he said. "Remember? Santa Claus, reindeer, divine births of babies in mangers, goodwill towards men? You know, all that holiday stuff? We've done all we can do today."

"What about Debbie Schaffer's parents?" I pushed a button he had revealed earlier in the day.

My friend frowned at me, hard. The kind of thin-lipped

scowl that told me instantly that I shouldn't have ignored the sign next to the button that said, 'Caution: Do Not Press'.

"Like I said before," he snarled, "it's gonna be a real disappointin' holiday."

"Sorry, Ben," I apologized, "I shouldn't have gone there."

"Yeah, well now that you've been there, do me a favor and remember that."

"Okay, you two," McLaughlin spoke up. "I'm going to leave you to beat each other up by yourselves. I've got a husband and daughter waiting at home for me."

"Big plans?" Ben asked without looking up.

"Scott always makes the traditional Turducken for dinner and then we just relax and enjoy being a family."

"What the hell's a Turducken?"

"A turkey that's stuffed with a duck that's stuffed with a chicken. Oh, and there's sausage in there too."

Ben finally cast an eye over his shoulder with a look that said give me a break. "I was serious, Chuck."

"I'm serious too," she told him with a grin. "Scott's from Baton Rouge. It's a Cajun thing."

"No way."

"Yes way."

"I've had Turducken before, Ben," I interjected. "She's not kidding."

"Maybe you two should get together then."

"Why's that?" I asked.

"Well why stop there," he submitted. "Shove that damn thing into the bird you served the other night and you can have yourself one big Osturduckenrich."

The *Trans Siberian Orchestra* was filling the cab of my

truck with their particular brand of no holds barred holiday music when I merged onto Highway Forty. I had the volume set mid level so as not to drown out my cell phone if it was to ring. My headache was still with me, but thankfully it had settled to an almost ignorable dull thud somewhere in the vicinity of the right rear portion of my skull. Even so, had it not been for the two-fold reason of A) I liked the song and B) I liked the song enough that it was helping keep my mind off of things I'd rather not think about, I would have turned the radio off completely.

Unfortunately, there was still one thing that my mind insisted that it be allowed to dwell upon— I still couldn't shake the sensation of being watched. In fact, the feeling had just grown worse as the day wore on. I'd been able to keep it at bay for the most part since I was intensely occupied with the cross-referencing tasks. However, now that I was alone and somewhat relaxed, even the frantic rhythms of the music weren't enough to drive away that annoying itch at the base of my neck. I physically shivered, trying to shake off the feeling, and took another long glance in the rearview mirror.

There wasn't much to see. Just a wide span of blackness, marred here and there by a pair of headlights— nothing on my tail. No one was purposely following me that I could tell— not that I was any kind of expert on the subject. But the feeling was still there.

I punched the lighter in on the dash and fished a cigarette out of my breast pocket. This would be the third one since I'd walked out of Police Headquarters. I spit out a hollow cough and noticed tightness in my chest, then stuck the butt between my lips. I really needed to do something about this. Maybe now that I had connected the recurrence of the habit with one of the victims it would be easier for me to break it.

The lighter popped and I snatched it out of its

receptacle, touching the glowing end to the cigarette and taking a deep drag. After replacing the device I took another puff and tucked the smoldering roll of paper and tobacco between my fingers.

"You know that's really gross don't you?" a painfully familiar voice bled through the music.

I tried to ignore the presence. I'd seen enough for one day, and I simply wasn't sure I could take any more. I continued to stare straight out the windshield.

"I said, you know that's really gross don't you?!" the voice insisted.

I still pretended not to hear.

"Hey, I'm talking to you, Rowan!" Debbie Schaeffer demanded my attention again.

Without a word, I reached over to the controls on the radio and moved the volume up a few notches. Almost instantly the speakers went dead.

"I said I'm talking to you, Rowan!" she asserted.

"Well, I'm not talking to you," I muttered under my breath.

It didn't really matter. I didn't even have to speak for her to hear me. The simple fact that I acknowledged her with my thoughts was enough to set her in motion.

"And why not?"

"Hmmmm, let me see," I offered sarcastically, still speaking aloud. "Could it be maybe that I'm not terribly impressed with that little stunt you pulled this afternoon?"

As I finished the sentence, I glanced over at the passenger side. As I suspected, there she was, fully decked out in her cheerleading uniform, hair up in a ponytail, and her arms crossed over her chest.

"I helped you find out what you were after didn't I?" she stated more than asked. *"You just needed a little push in the right direction, that's all."*

All of the progress I'd made so far seemed to simply fly out the window. If anyone were to pull alongside it would probably look like I was talking to myself. I felt utterly insane sitting here having an argument with a ghost while traveling down the highway on Christmas Eve. Of course, what better night could one pick to be visited by a ghost?

"I think I liked it better when you just did the automatic writing," I told her. "You were a hell of a lot less annoying that way."

"You weren't paying enough attention," she spat. *"Besides, this is more fun."*

"Fun? Give me a break, will you. I'm doing the best that I can. I've got my own problems you know."

"What? Like I don't have problems?"

"In case YOU weren't paying attention, Debbie, the guy who tried to kill me last February is running around loose."

"Yeah, so? I'm already dead."

"So you've told me."

"Don't be so selfish, Rowan. You're supposed to be helping me. Paige is counting on you too."

"What?" I exclaimed aloud. "Me being selfish? What about you?"

Yes, it was official. I had to be insane. There was no other explanation.

"Yes, you being selfish. Here you are all worried about your problems when I'm dead. Dead I am, dead I am,..."

"...I do not like that dead I am, yeah Debbie, I get it," I expressed. "Can we move on to something else?"

"That's up to you, Rowan. If you'll just start paying attention."

"What's that supposed to mean?"

She didn't answer. I glanced over at the passenger seat and found an empty void. She was gone. Great, I thought to myself. Now she's going to give me riddles. I've never understood why spirits can't just say what they mean.

Although, I had to admit that this was a first. Most of the ethereal visits I'd experienced tended to take place during a heavily tranced state or even sleep. Clues were often complex strings of symbolic messages that required serious deciphering. Debbie seemed to be phasing back and forth between the planes at will, and was even carrying on conversations— cryptic yes, but conversations nonetheless. This was definitely one I needed to record in my Book of Shadows.

I jerked with a start as the music suddenly returned, blaring through the cab of the truck. I reached over and turned the volume down, then took a drag from my cigarette and propped my hand up on the steering wheel.

The center dividing line flashed by in my headlights, flickering in on-again/off-again reflective stripes. I continued to stare out the windshield, over the top of the steering wheel, and through the rippling column of smoke that was rising from my burning cigarette. Eventually, reflex drove me to bring my hand toward my face for yet another puff, and my vision was suddenly replaced by a Technicolor flash of memory.

A lit cigarette smokes in his free hand as the other pumps faster between his legs. I concentrate on the glowing coal, not wanting to witness his self-stimulation. I watch him raise the cigarette to take a puff and notice that it is positioned between his middle fingers.

Curious.

I've never seen anyone hold a cigarette like that before.

As the bloom of color faded, I jerked the wheel quickly to the left to avoid running off the road at the Hampton exit. When I'd settled the vehicle back into the lane, and swallowed my heart back down into my chest, I stole another glance at my hand. There, between my middle fingers rested the smoldering cigarette.

No wonder I was so screwed up. I'd been channeling the rapist all along.

I started to reach for my cell phone in order to call Ben, but stopped mid stretch. There was nothing he could do with the information at this point in time, so why bother him. Besides, I'd be home soon. I'd pick up Felicity and we'd head over to his house for dinner, so I could tell him in person.

I glanced at the clock on the dash and saw that it was now a quarter after six. It had taken longer to get myself together and get out of Police Headquarters than I'd expected. The last stop for the 'Santa Brigade' was merely a drop-off at a food bank less than a mile from our house, so Felicity was most likely already home.

My biggest concern at this point was going to be figuring out how to pack an overnight bag for the two of us without her asking why.

This was going to be a tough one.

It was six twenty-five when I turned my truck into the driveway of our Briarwood home. I urged the vehicle toward the garage at the back of the house, and discovered the gate that would normally bar the path was propped open. The motion from making the turn around the deck triggered the outdoor sentry and floodlights snapped on to light the landscape. Felicity's Jeep was already parked in the garage.

My suspicions about timing had been dead on, and I still had no idea how I was going to get the overnight bag past her. The only resolution I had come upon was to forget the bag altogether. One of us was going to have to come back to the house tomorrow anyway, that much was a foregone conclusion. For one thing, there was a house full of animals that needed to be taken care of.

I sat there thinking about it for a moment. We could easily set up extra food and water for the cats. The truth was, they would probably enjoy having the run of the place for a while. However, the dogs were going to require quite a bit more attention. Either they would have to go with us, or we would need to board them somewhere. Depending on how long this all took, that could get expensive.

This lead to yet another thought— there was the fact that we both worked out of the house. My office was here and so was Felicity's darkroom. Over the holidays it would be slow, so we'd be able to manage, but that lull was going to be over soon enough.

What if they weren't able to find Porter right away? What if he went on another killing spree in the process of coming after me? What if he targeted my friends in order to get to me?

I could feel myself shaking my head almost unconsciously. I had no idea how we were going to make this work, and I was starting to obsess about it.

I shifted the truck into park and switched off the engine, then took a deep breath. Just take things one step at a time, that's what I needed to do— just one step at a time.

I climbed out of the truck and made my way up the stairs and across the deck to the atrium door. The temperate day had folded itself into a chilly night, and I could see my breath in a frosty cloud. I shuffled through my keys then raised my free hand to the door handle, but I never got the key into the lock. The latch clicked and the door swung inward.

Under any other circumstances I wouldn't have thought anything of it. Felicity was home, and even though she tended to keep the doors locked, she sometimes forgot.

This time it was different.

Every hair on the back of my neck immediately rose to attention. The dull thud in the back of my head expanded to encompass my entire body. My ears began to ring, and every ethereal alarm I had was going off in sequence.

I pushed the door further inward and stepped through. A cold gust of wind followed behind me and rustled a stack of newspaper that was sitting in a nearby chair. The door into the house was hanging ajar, and the interior of the house was dark.

I carefully shut the outer door, beating back the desire to panic, then took the few steps across the atrium to the kitchen door and pushed it slowly open.

"Felicity?" I called out.

I waited in the darkness, but received no answer. I listened intently and could hear muffled whimpering and barking coming from the interior of the house. Acid began churning in the pit of my stomach as the panic began to break free and crawl up my spine like a thousand spiders.

"Felicity?" I called again, louder, as I hurried through the door and in my haste glanced against the corner of the island.

I let out a yelp and grabbed my side, then aimed myself for the dining room. "Felicity? Are you here? Answer me!"

The only sound to meet my ears was the fading echo of my own voice and the excited yelps of the dogs from somewhere deeper in the house.

The light was on in the living room and it cast an eerie glow into the dining room where I stood. Looking around, I could see my wife's purse on the side table, and her long coat draped across the back of the chair.

My racing heart slowed and I took a deep breath. She was here somewhere. Maybe she'd gone downstairs into her darkroom for something. Or maybe she was in the bedroom and couldn't hear me over the dogs, assuming that's where they were.

I crossed the room and flipped the light switch. Even with the wave of relief sweeping over me, the supernatural alarms were still raising a raucous clamor. Adrenalin was dripping into my bloodstream on full flow, and I was beginning to shake.

The fleeting moment of calm dissolved. Something was still very wrong. With the dogs raising that much ruckus, Felicity should have shut them down by now, or at least come to see what was going on.

I bolted through the house, stumbling over my own feet with the clumsiness brought on by unchecked anxiety. I was screaming my wife's name like a madman, flinging doors open as I went. The dogs immediately charged out of the bedroom and followed me on the rabid quest.

In less than two minutes I had covered the entire house— upstairs, downstairs, her darkroom, everywhere. I was panting hard, struggling to catch my breath when I returned to the dining room.

I stood staring at the scene that had escaped my attention in the darkness. Now that I was turned to face it, and the lights were on, my heart plummeted into the depths of abject despair.

The dining room table was canted askew as if it had been pushed or knocked out of place. A chair was overturned and laying on its side. Scattered across the disrupted tableau and onto the floor was the day's mail.

I began to shake even harder when my disbelieving stare came to rest on the center of the table. There, as if placed with the utmost reverence rested a book. Gold letters were embossed along the spine and across the cover, spelling out the ominous words: Holy Bible.

I dropped the phone four times before my unsteady hands managed to dial nine one-one.

CHAPTER 26

I was sitting on the floor staring straight ahead; the handset of the phone still clasped tight in my hand when the first uniformed police officers arrived on the scene. I was in so much pain I couldn't move. Emotional distress had transcended the boundaries of the physical and I literally ached with despair. I could feel a hole deepening in my chest and spreading outward in a bid to consume me.

I let it.

I didn't fight, didn't struggle. I just sat and let the cold darkness eat away at my soul. Right now, this pain was all I had to cling to. It was the only feeling I had left.

I had no idea what I'd told the emergency operator. All I knew is that I could hear his voice issuing faintly from the earpiece. He was asking me something it seemed, although it was just so much gibberish in my mind. Whatever I'd said to him, it had to have been barely coherent but ultimately grievous, as the two officers entered with extreme caution and weapons drawn.

I continued to sit, unmoving, watching as they came toward me. They were speaking but their words made no more sense than the nine one-one operator. It was obvious to me that until they'd fully assessed the situation, I was considered a possible threat.

I didn't care.

At this moment— this horrifically drawn out and extended instant in all of time and space— my life meant absolutely nothing to me. If Felicity was gone then I had no desire to continue.

A brief spark of a thought glowed in the forefront of my brain. All I had to do was move. Make a threatening gesture. Act as though I was about to train a weapon on the officers and it could all be done. They could end this hollow pain for me.

Fortunately for me, I couldn't make myself do it.

I just continued to sit and embrace the pain, letting it pool deeper and deeper until finally, I was immersed in it.

Sinking.

Drowning.

Then the unexpected took place. The pain began to fade. Warming slowly from cold agony to hot anger. From the moment I laid eyes on that Bible, my life had taken on a completely surreal property. Everything I'd ever seen, everything I'd ever accomplished, everything I'd ever set out to do, no longer mattered to me in the least. The standard by which I had lived my life seemed like a cruel joke.

I had raced immediately into the blind desire to end my life, and while that was a prospect I'd not yet ruled out, it would have to wait. I was now climbing out of the hole. A desire for vengeance was upon me and I was becoming driven.

I was going to find him, and now the rede was no longer an option. Harm none, my ass; I was going to send him to meet his God in person.

This wasn't the first time my home had been a crime scene. I could only hope that it was going to be the last. CSU technicians assigned to the Major Case Squad were going over every inch of the house, including the garage and Felicity's Jeep.

I could have stayed inside, but I simply couldn't bear to watch them at work. Not when I recognized so many of them from working the Porter case earlier this year, and especially not when I considered that everyone knew what Porter had done to his victims.

No, not when I could look into their eyes and know exactly what they were all thinking.

I wandered out of the house and found myself standing outside the perimeter, smoking yet another cigarette in what had become one unending chain. Yellow and black crime scene tape cordoned off my yard, and I'd ducked under it to get to the sidewalk. I didn't need the reminder so I turned my back to it.

I'd already given a statement, but I knew the drill. They'd want to talk to me again. There was even a chance that those who didn't know me might consider me a suspect.

I thought about that for a moment. I guess I'd better be prepared for it. It could very well present itself as an obstacle to my finding Porter and bringing about his end. Someone would set them straight, though, of that I was certain. I was, after all, up to my neck in the previous investigation, and it had been no secret that Porter had tried to kill me. It stood to reason that he would be trying to finish the job.

I gave brief notice to the fact that I was standing outside on Christmas Eve, coldly calculating and planning to kill someone. I knew this should disturb me greatly, but it didn't. It was a curious feeling, and it was keeping me warm.

A quick glance around told me that there were still a few of my neighbors ogling the scene. I didn't even waste time being angry about it. It wasn't worth my time.

I heard a loud screech in the distance and turned toward

the sound. Thirty yards up the street, Ben Storm's van screamed around the corner and accelerated through the puddles of luminance cast by the streetlamps. The magnetic bubble of an emergency light flickered wildly on the corner of his roof and he locked up the brakes, sliding to a diagonal halt in front of the house. He was out of the Chevy and running toward me before the engine stopped knocking.

"Rowan, are you okay?" He fired the question at me with genuine concern.

I stared back at him and didn't utter a word. I took another drag on my cigarette and tried to find a reason not to hit him as hard as I could. Not that I believed I could inflict any damage, but I felt willing to try.

Deep down inside I suppose I knew that this wasn't his fault, but right now I needed someone to blame. He had known Porter was alive and on the loose, but he'd kept it from me.

While I'd doubted Porter's demise right from that night on the Old Chain of Rocks Bridge, my friend hadn't believed me. No matter what I'd said, he hadn't been willing to give in to trust. And then, when I was finally proven correct, he'd hidden the fact from me. Whatever he claimed was his motivation for the secretiveness, at this moment it didn't wash. It was unacceptable.

I continued to stare into his eyes, feeling my own expressionless face harden to a blank mask.

"Rowan? Talk to me." His voice held a pleading tone.

I quietly lit another cigarette from the one I'd just finished, and then flicked the spent butt out into the street. I took a deep breath and shook my head.

"Where were they, Ben? Where the fuck were all those concerned people that were supposed to be watching after us when the sonofabitch came and took my wife?"

"Rowan…"

"Save it." My voice was cold and sharp. I could tell that each word was cutting him deeply and I didn't care. "You had a chance to stop this and you didn't."

"Row…"

"Go to hell, Ben," I cut him off again. "Just fucking go to hell."

I turned and walked away.

"Benjamin is terribly concerned about you, Rowan," Helen Storm spoke to me in a soothing voice.

She was direct, and wasted no words; still, her tone had the ability to lull one into the fold of her confidence. I was glad that she was here, even if I didn't show it.

I had been spiraling through the various emotional states one can experience at a time such as this. Disbelief, anger, fear, guilt… All of them rolled into a tense ball that I couldn't escape. At the moment I was experiencing some form of defiant hostility that had arrived directly on the heels of an uncontrolled fit of sobbing.

"What about you, Helen?" I asked dully, the words forming a weak challenge. "Are you concerned about me too?"

We were seated on my deck, both of us holding lit cigarettes and staring into the darkness. Well, I was staring into the darkness; she could have been staring at me for all I knew. I didn't bother to check. It was nearing ten PM. Crime Scene technicians were still finishing up around the interior of the house, but had finally vacated the garage, so this one spot had become my safe haven for the time being. Out of sight, out of mind— if only that really worked.

A biting wind rose and fell in a serpentine arc around the corner of the house and dragged its icy claws across my face. I ignored it. I could hear Helen shift and I glanced over as she pulled her heavy shawl tighter, but that was her only acknowledgement of the chill.

"Of course I am, Rowan," she said.

"Humph," I grunted. "There seems to be a lot of that going around lately."

"You do understand," she began, and then paused for a brief second. I could tell from her silence that she was gingerly picking the words she was about to use. "There is every indication that your wife has not been harmed."

"I don't feel her, Helen," I stated plainly. "If she were okay, I'd be able to feel her."

"I am not so certain of that. You have been dealing with a severe emotional trauma, Rowan," she offered. "I would be greatly surprised if you could feel anything at all in the sense to which you refer."

Helen was correct. I couldn't even feel her, and she was sitting right next to me. How could I expect to sense Felicity, wherever she was? The only thing I really felt was bitter hatred for Eldon Andrew Porter.

"So, did Ben bring you over here to make sure I didn't wig out?" I changed the subject.

"Benjamin asked me to come here with him because, as I said, he is very concerned about you."

"He thinks I blame him for this, doesn't he?"

"Yes, he does," she answered. "You all but told him that yourself when we arrived."

"I guess I do, in a way," I sighed. "But not completely. Not irrevocably."

"That is understandable, considering the circumstances. But be aware, Rowan, that he blames himself much more than you blame him. The judgment that my brother is exacting upon himself is a far higher price than you would ever dream of asking."

"Are you asking me to feel sorry for him?"

"Not at all," she confessed matter-of-factly. "I am simply showing you both sides of the coin."

"How clinical of you," I remarked with an underlying harshness in my voice. "Aren't you supposed to be coddling me and telling me everything will be okay?"

"If I was dealing with someone else in this situation, perhaps. But, not you, and not now."

"What? I don't deserve a little coddling? My wife has been kidnapped and is probably dead," I spat the comment almost angrily.

"What you deserve, and what you want are two vastly different things, Rowan. You know that," she answered. "Besides, I have a feeling that your particular talents will be necessary to find her, so the time for coddling will have to come later."

"You seem convinced that she's still alive."

"You should be too."

"I want to be." I closed my eyes and took in a deep breath. "Gods, I want to be. But, then at the same time, for her sake, I have to hope that she isn't. I saw what he did to his other victims, Helen."

"I understand that."

"Do you?" I asked. "Because when I say that I saw what he did, I mean I SAW what he did. I saw it, felt it, and experienced it."

"Yes, Rowan, I understand that far better than you know."

"Then you know why it's hard for me to believe that Felicity is still alive."

A healthy supply of anxious energy was crackling along every nerve in my body and I found myself fidgeting almost constantly. I was unable to maintain a grip on myself for more than a few minutes at a time. This latest period of calm reached the end of its somewhat protracted cycle, and I angrily leapt from the chair.

"What the hell are they doing in there?" I exclaimed as I began to pace. "Shouldn't they be out there looking for the sonofabitch?!"

"They are, Rowan," Helen told me calmly. "You know that."

"A few minutes," I muttered. "If I'd only been here a few minutes sooner."

"What would you have done had you been here?" she asked with a shake of her head.

"What would I have done?" I echoed the question back to her harshly. "I would have blown the sick bastard into next week."

"Would you have?" she asked simply.

"I have a gun and I know how to use it," I retorted. The words sounded sophomoric even as they tumbled out of my mouth.

"I do not doubt that, Rowan," she tactfully ignored the childish bravado of my comment, "but neither the implement nor the skill to use it are what I am questioning. What I am curious about is your innate ability to take a life."

"I shot him once," I offered.

"Yes, you did," she agreed. "But you shot him to wound, not to kill. Furthermore, you did so when your own life was literally hanging in the balance."

"I assume you have a point here?" I contended.

She didn't allow my adversarial posture to faze her. "My point is that when presented with the opportunity to kill this man, you did not. Furthermore, when you believed that there was some possibility that you may have been responsible for his death— however unintentional— emotionally, it brought you very close to the edge."

"I never really believed he was dead. I made no secret

of that," I told her. "Besides, this is different."

"Now it is," she nodded in agreement. "But what if you had been here? Would he not have set his sights on you instead of Felicity? At least, initially?"

"I think that's a given," I responded with a shrug.

"Then you would simply have been repeating history," she commented.

"So, maybe I realized I made a mistake out there on that bridge," I offered.

"Perhaps," she returned. "But I do not believe that, and I am inclined to think that you do not either. You are a man of firm conviction, Rowan. The rede by which you have lived your life is more a part of you than you wish to admit."

"Maybe it's time for me to wake up," I told her sadly. "Idealistic beliefs are for fools."

"That would be a terrible loss, Rowan," she offered. "Your ideals are a very large part of who you are. And, I know that you do not truly believe that idealists are fools."

Before I had a chance to formulate a retort, our conversation was interrupted by the sound of someone purposely clearing his throat. I looked over toward the door and saw Ben standing on the top step. The light cast at a downward angle across his face and his chiseled features were craggy with lines and shadows. He looked tired, and he looked very old. Helen was correct. He wasn't taking this much better than I was.

"Ben." I acknowledged his presence with a curt nod. I no longer wanted to hit him, but he wasn't at the top of my list for chatting with either.

"Listen, Row, I know you don't wanna talk to me, but this is important," he began, smoothing his hair back and bringing his hand to rest on his neck. He was thinking hard.

"I will leave you two alone," Helen offered, starting to stand.

"No, stay," I told her.

I needed her to be here. As much as I didn't want to admit it, everyone was correct. I was very close to the edge. Right now she was the only one standing between me and the sudden stop at the end.

"What is it?" I asked, trying to keep the bark out of my voice.

"It doesn't look like Porter has anything to do with this." He blurted out the words as if he could no longer contain them. "There's some shit that just doesn't add up."

"Excuse me?" I stared back at him like he'd grown an extra head. "What are you talking about? Of course he did this!"

"Hear me out, Rowan." He rushed the request out as quickly as he could, and moved down the steps toward me. "The only thing that really pointed to Porter to begin with was the Bible, and he didn't leave it…"

"How do you know that?" I demanded before he could continue.

"I made some calls," he explained. "Everyone in Felicity's charity group got one of those Bibles. They were gifts from the kids at the children's home they visited this afternoon."

"W-W-What?" I stammered.

"Yeah," he nodded as he spoke, "everyone I talked to said Felicity didn't have the heart not to accept it. She left it on the table, Row. Not Porter."

"Then where the hell is she?!" I snarled the demand.

"I don't know yet, white man," he returned. "But I'm gonna find her."

CHAPTER 27

Hope ignited from a miniscule spark and set flame to a tiny candle somewhere deep inside me. Its glow was so incredibly faint so as to be almost beyond notice, but it was there— flickering defiantly into the face of the shadowy fear that threatened to extinguish it.

"According to your monitoring service, the alarm was disabled with Felicity's code via the keypad in the kitchen at six-oh-seven PM," Ben told me.

"Then it had to have happened after she was in," I offered. "We have a duress code she would have used otherwise."

My friend nodded agreement. "Figured as much. There wasn't a trigger from the panic buttons either."

"He must have followed her in."

"Maybe, but I'm workin' a different angle. We've done a door to door. Nobody saw anything, but considerin' what day it is, no big surprise there."

"What about the people who were supposed to be watching the house?"

"That's a cluster." He shook his head. "Left hand didn't know what the right hand was doin'. Locals thought the Feebs were on, Feebs thought the locals were on, and… and well… There's just no way to sugar coat it, Row. Somebody fucked up and there hasn't been anyone watchin' since about three this afternoon."

I closed my eyes and shook my head. I wanted to explode, but logically I knew that doing so wouldn't help. Still, just how much longer I was going to stay on the side of rationality remained to be seen.

"That doesn't sound like Constance," I said.

"That's exactly why it's a cluster. Mandalay had to go back down to the scene in Cape, so she wasn't here." Ben's disdain for the FBI was almost legendary. Constance Mandalay was the only agent he trusted, and the events of this evening added just that much more evidence to his personal case file against the agency. "But let's not go there, 'cause it's not gonna get us anywhere. Front door was unlocked," he continued. "Did you do that?"

"No," I shook my head vigorously. "They've already asked me that."

"I'm just checkin'," he told me. "Since you two normally come in the back, that would mean Felicity had to have opened it since there was no sign of a forced entry."

"The mail," I offered.

"What?"

"The mail was on the dining room table," I explained. "She probably got the mail."

"Okay, what about the back?"

"Unlocked."

"What about the lights? Were any on?"

"I've been over this twice now!" I threw my hands up in exasperation. "What does it matter?"

"Calm down," Ben appealed. "I'm just tryin' to get a handle on this."

"Get a handle on what, Ben?! My wife is gone!"

"Listen to me for a minute," he ordered. "We're talkin' about Felicity here, she…"

"No shit!" I spat. "Did they give you your badge as a reward for recognizing the obvious?!"

His voice raised a notch. "Shut the fuck up and listen to me goddammit!"

"Benjamin!" Helen admonished, breaking her self-imposed silence.

"Stay out of it, Helen!" he barked.

"Why don't you quit screwing around and tell me something I don't already know!" I almost screamed at him.

Without warning he lashed out. I flinched, fully expecting his fist to connect with my jaw. In retrospect, I certainly would have deserved it if it had. Instead, I felt his large hand twist into the collar of my shirt at the back of my neck and I instantly felt myself being propelled forward. Less than a minute later I had been forced up the stairs, through the atrium, then the kitchen, and finally, into the dining room.

The Crime Scene Technicians had all but vacated the premises, and were finishing up in front of the house. Helen had followed after Ben, and the three of us now stood before the spectacle that had so thoroughly thrust me into despair.

"Look at the scene, Rowan!" he demanded. "Stop acting like an asshole for just one second and take a good look at it!"

The bright incandescence of the artificial lighting cast a stark picture before me as my eyes fought to adjust. Just as it had been earlier, the dining room table was canted at an angle, pushed a few degrees from its original position in the room. The chairs were in minor disarray from the movement, and as before, one was on its side. The mail we'd just discussed was spread out toward one end, with a trio of #10 envelopes, and a medium-sized box resting haphazardly on the floor below.

The Bible still stared back from dead center as if mocking me.

The only thing that had really changed was that a patina of graphite and lycopodium powders now enhanced the latent fingerprints throughout.

"Whaddaya see?" my friend asked, his voice stern but slightly calmer.

"I don't know," I shot back. "My dining room? A mess? What am I supposed to see?"

He let go of my collar and I immediately wheeled about to face him.

"Like I said," he thrust a finger at me, "we're talking about Felicity here. This is a woman who once tackled a mugger and sat on 'im until a squad car arrived. Now take another look. Does this room REALLY look like she put up a fight?"

I didn't need to look again. He was correct. In reality, the disruption was minor in comparison to what it could have been. My wife was not one who would go quietly into the night without first extracting her own pound of flesh. She would have fought. She would have kicked. She would have screamed like a banshee. No matter how big, or how strong her attacker, she would have wrecked the entire house trying to get away.

Ben could see the light dawning in my face, and he knew that I was beginning to understand where he was headed, so he pressed forward. "In your statement you said the dogs were shut up in the bedroom, right?"

"Yes," I nodded. "They were."

"How would they have gotten there?"

"Felicity would have had to put them there," I murmured.

"Why?" he kept going, forcing me to see what he had already surmised.

My voice fell almost to a whisper. "That's what we do if someone they aren't used to is in the house and they are being bothersome."

"Exactly," Ben nodded. "Whoever took Felicity is

someone she knows, Kemosabe. Someone she was comfortable enough to let into the house, but unfamiliar enough that she had to lock the dogs away. She wasn't afraid, so he was able to take her down so unexpectedly that she didn't even have a chance to fight."

I stared at him, dumbfounded by the realization that had overtaken my grey matter.

"You've gotta work with me on this, Row. We're gonna find her, but I've gotta have your help."

My mind was racing, applying a mental litmus test to a list of possible suspects I was compiling in my head. I couldn't imagine anyone that we knew wanting to harm her. I was disregarding names as fast as they popped into my head, and soon, I found myself placing the yardstick up against the same people over and over again.

"Rowan? Talk to me," Ben prodded.

"I... It just doesn't... I'm not..." I stammered. "I don't know, Ben. I just can't think of anyone we know who would do something like this."

"Enemies? Radical religious groups maybe? You two are pretty open about your religion," he suggested.

"You pretty much know who my enemies are," I shook my head. "And to my knowledge Felicity doesn't have any. And religious groups? I can't imagine any going this far."

"Try tellin' that to the dead doctors who were killed by the anti-abortion wackos," he harrumphed. "It takes all kinds, Row. Have you pissed off anyone that you know of?"

"I can't think of anyone off the top of my head."

"What about Felicity? She have any acquaintances you're not familiar with? Someone who might be a bit hinky?"

"Sure," I shrugged. "Business contacts, clients, members of her photography club."

"We're already checkin' out the folks she was with today," he nodded. "She have a rolodex or somethin' we can look at?"

I glanced around for her purse and found that it was no longer on the side table in the living room where I'd last seen it. "Her purse," I expressed. "It was on the table over there."

"It's already been bagged," Ben told me. "She have an address book in there?"

"Her PDA," I acknowledged. "She keeps everything in there. Contacts, appointments, everything."

"Okay, stay here," he told me, punctuating the command with a quick gesture of his hand as he headed for the front door. "I'll be right back."

Silence fell in behind him for a moment and I turned my head to see Helen looking studiously back at me.

"How are you holding up," she asked simply.

"As good as can be expected, I suppose."

She nodded slightly, and continued to watch me as she offered comment. "Benjamin can sometimes resemble a bull in a china shop with his methods."

"Yeah," I acknowledged, "I've seen him be gentler."

"It is only because he is frightened, Rowan. He fears for your wife's safety, and for your sanity. He considers you family, and you know his sense of duty."

I nodded. "I know."

She pursed her lips and her brow furrowed deeply. Pressing her palms together she held her hands up and rested her chin on her steepled fingertips. We stood quietly for a moment, and it became my turn to watch her.

"Rowan, your wife is going to be fine," she finally told me.

"Is this the coddling I was asking for?" I asked with a flat tone to my words.

"No. It is merely an observation."

"Do you know something that the rest of us don't?"

"I simply know what it is that I feel," she answered as

she canted her head to the side and blinked. "You of all people should understand that."

I allowed her words to comfort me, though the solace was brief. "Thanks, Helen. I hope you're right."

"This what you're talkin' about?" Ben interrupted as he entered and thrust a thin, silver case at me.

"Yes," I nodded as I took it from him and opened the cover to reveal the electronic device within.

I activated the PDA and withdrew the stylus from its recessed holder, then began systematically tapping it against the touch sensitive screen. "Here." I offered the device back to him. "This is her address book."

"You go through it," he told me. "See if anyone rings a bell. Someone she might have mentioned having a disagreement with. Anything like that."

I turned the small LCD display back toward myself and proceeded to page through the listings, one entry at a time. She had combined our home address book with her own, so various bits of data stood out as familiar while others did not. Before long, however, they all began to look like just so many letters and numbers jumbled together.

I stopped and removed my glasses, then rubbed my eyes.

"Somethin' wrong?" Ben queried.

"Not really," I answered as I slipped my glasses back on to my face. "It just seems like I've been staring at small print all day."

"Recognize anything?"

"Well, yeah," I said. "But nothing that leaps out at me as particularly suspicious."

"So, what are ya doin' now?" he asked as he nodded in the direction of the device.

"What do you mean?"

"I mean what are ya' doin'?" he reiterated, raising an

eyebrow. "You aren't even lookin' at the damn thing."

The sound of the stylus clacking against the touch sensitive plate reached my ears and I realized my hand was moving completely of its own accord. As I rotated my head and looked down at the PDA in my hand, the out of phase tones of a voice echoed quietly in the back of my head.

"There. Is this better?"

Unconsciously, I had switched the handheld computer into a notepad mode, and even traded it off to my right hand. My left was now rapidly scratching the stylus against the surface of the screen.

A quick glance at the LCD showed a digitized string of handwriting that repeatedly scrawled, DEAD I AM, DEAD I AM, DEAD I AM, DEAD I AM...

"Dammit!" I exclaimed as I immediately forced my hand to stop moving. "Leave me alone! Just leave me alone!"

"Whoa," Ben raised his voice to compete with mine. "What the hell?"

"Schaeffer!" I exclaimed, dropping the PDA and stylus onto the table, then shaking my hands as if trying to rid them of something disgusting. "She won't leave me alone!"

"What? Like she's here now?"

"Yes, dammit!" I was angry, and I spun in place looking for any indication of the girl's spirit around me. "Go away, Debbie! I can't help you right now!"

In my head I could hear her chanting at an ever-quickening pace, *"DEAD I AM, DEAD I AM, DEAD I AM, DEAD I AM, DEADIAM, DEADIAM, DEADIAM, DEADIAM, DEADIAMDEADIAMDEADIAMDEADIAMDEADIAM..."*

I seized on the welling anger within me and thrust it outward in a violent rush, attempting to sweep away anything ethereal in my path. The energy exploded outward, only to reach unanticipated limits, and return in force. A shockwave of pain backlashed through my head as the energy ricocheted around the room. I saw Helen turn her head then squint, which told me that she had felt it as well, a fact that for some reason, I didn't find all that surprising. Fortunately for her, she was only a spectator; I was the target.

A pinpoint of agony drilled into my skull directly between my eyes and sent me physically staggering backward. I felt my heel thump against something and I started to fall, then a tight grip latched on to my arm as someone guided me into a chair.

"Rowan? Rowan?" Ben's voice flowed thickly into my ears. "Are you okay? What's goin' on? Answer me."

I leaned forward in the seat, dropping my face into my hands and heaved hard against the pain. I'm sure that to him it looked like I was having a seizure.

"ROWAN?!" he demanded again.

I held up a hand as a signal to him as I grimaced through the onslaught of agony. I'd brought this upon myself. My own anger was bouncing around inside the ethereal barriers Felicity and I had placed around the house, and it now came back to me threefold. I was simply paying for my own lack of control.

While my presence within had acted as a doorway for Debbie Schaeffer to enter, it hadn't been terribly effective as an exit for the burst of energy. On top of that, I hadn't been the least bit grounded when it returned.

I mutely cursed myself for the stupidity of the action as the pain slowly began to subside. After a moment, misery faded into something resembling a severe sinus headache, and I sighed heavily.

I remained motionless as I opened my eyes and allowed them to focus on the object I'd tripped over.

There on the floor was a sealed cardboard box, roughly eight by ten, by maybe twelve inches tall. I stared at it as the image clarified, then slowly allowed my eyes to come to rest on the label. It was upside down from my point of view, but I could still read it without difficulty.

It was addressed to On The Edge Photography, attention Felicity O'Brien. What really caught my attention, however, was the return address: Arch Color Labs, thirty-seven fifty-four Ash Bend Avenue.

CHAPTER 28

There is an old adage that everyone has heard about snakes, nearness to them, and getting bit by same because of said proximity. The fangs of this particular serpent were to say the least, firmly embedded in my carotid artery and the venom was now reaching my brain.

Bits and pieces of information, snippets of conversations, and channeled vices began coalescing in my frontal lobes to form a mental picture that should have been crystal clear all along. How I'd managed to avoid putting this all together, I had no idea, but there was no stopping it now. Whatever mental block had been shielding the overtly obvious from my sight had now been obliterated, and it was all making sense.

"You've got to be kidding me," I muttered just loud enough to be heard.

"Do what?" Ben asked. "Rowan, what's going on? What the hell was that all about?"

"Harold," I said a bit louder. "It's Harold."

"Harold who?"

"Harold the sonofabitch that owns Arch Color Labs," I announced, ignoring the throb in my skull and looking up at my friend. "That's who."

"You're gonna have to elaborate, Row."

"This box," I explained as I pointed to the offending container. "It wasn't here when I left this morning."

"Yeah, so maybe it got delivered while you were with me and Chuck. You haven't been home all day ya'know."

"No. Wouldn't happen. Arch is less than a mile from here. He never ships orders to Felicity. She picks them up."

"Okay, so just playin' devil's advocate here— Are you sure she didn't?" he asked.

"She didn't have time. Not today. And before you ask, they're closed on weekends so it wasn't riding around in her Jeep for the past few days."

"Okay, good, we're maybe on to somethin' here. So what makes you think it's this Harold guy, and not an employee?"

"Because it's a one man operation. Besides, he smokes like a fiend and that's why he's been dressing them up."

"Whoa, back up," my friend said. "What are we talking about here?"

"All of it, Ben," I said in exasperation. "All of it. He's the one who killed Debbie Schaeffer and Paige Lawson. He's the one who's been raping all these women, and he's the one who took Felicity. Now can we go?"

"Whoa, slow down white man," he instructed. "I think maybe you're gettin' some stuff crossed up here."

"No, no I'm not." I shook my head; incredulous that he couldn't understand as clearly as I, then realized that he had no reason to. I'd told him next to nothing in the way of the facts as I saw them. I forced myself to stay in my seat and tried to explain how I'd reached my conclusion. "Okay, here it is. Did you by any chance notice the resemblance between Felicity and Heather Burke?"

"Heather Burke is a blue-eyed blonde, Row."

"I know," I rebutted. "I'm talking about her other physical attributes. Size, shape of face, skin tone. That's why he uses the wig and the tinted contacts. Try to imagine her with red hair."

"Okay." He nodded slightly after a thoughtful pause. "I guess maybe I can see that."

"Now, what about Miranda Hodges and Paige Lawson?" I urged.

"Yeah, they all kinda resemble one another, but don't you think you're pushin' it a bit?"

"No, I don't." I shook my head hard. I wanted to get moving but I knew it was never going to happen unless I could convince him I was correct. "He has been dressing them up to look like Felicity, and then taking pictures of them. He's been living out his fantasy about my wife through them."

"I dunno, Rowan."

"Fine," I snarled, "fine, just forget all that. The important thing is that he's the one that's got Felicity, and we need to stop him before he hurts her."

"I'm not doubting you," Ben held up a hand before I could object, "but we don't need to go off half-cocked and chasing our tails right now. Can you at least give me a motive?"

I heaved out an exasperated sigh. "Felicity just told me the other day that she thinks he has a crush on her."

"Just a crush, or something more serious?" he asked. "Like, has he been stalking her?"

"I don't know," I couldn't keep the urgency out of my voice, "but he has called here for no good reason, and I don't doubt what Felicity said."

"Okay, then let's check him out. You got a last name so we can get a home address?"

"He won't be at home," I told him confidently as I glanced down at the label on the box. I suddenly realized that in my haste I'd neglected to give him a piece of information that would have made my theory a bit easier to swallow.

"He'll have her at the lab where he can take pictures of her."

"Okay, we can start there. What's the address?"

"Thirty-seven fifty-four Ash Bend Avenue."

He was scribbling in his notebook as I recited the address. His pencil slowed and he looked up at me silently.

"It wasn't a name. It was an address."

"But…"

"Dyslexia," I said before he could finish. "I'll bet you anything that Heather Burke suffers from Dyslexia."

Ben killed the headlights on the van and eased it slowly into the parking lot of Arch Color Labs, allowing the high idle of the engine to propel us forward as he surveyed the building. It had taken us less than five minutes to make the trip, and my earlier overabundance of nervous energy was returning in full force. I reached for the door and popped the latch while the vehicle inched along at a pace that would make a tortoise ashamed.

"Dammit, Rowan!" Ben hissed as he quickly twisted a control on the dash to extinguish the dome light. "What the fuck are you doing? Close that door!"

"Well what are you doing?" I shot back between clenched teeth. "Felicity is in there and you're just screwing around out here!"

"Listen, I understand where you're at, believe me, but we can't just rush in there like the cavalry or somethin'."

"Dammit, Ben, he's got Felicity!"

"We don't know that for sure yet."

"I do!"

"Fine," he spat, "but we're doin' this MY way."

It was all I could do to contain myself. The earlier thud that had occupied my head was still there, and seemed to be acting as a pump for the visceral rage I was experiencing. With each thrum of pain, I could feel the anger course through me. It was rising fast, and it wasn't going to be long before it consumed me.

The van idled its way around a low retaining wall to reveal the opposite end of the 'L' shaped parking lot. There, in the shadows of the far back corner sat a car. The tall lamps positioned around the building poured their sodium vapor glow into the night and cut a small swath across the front quarter of the vehicle.

A vague memory of the night Ben had hurried me out of my house in advance of the descending media flitted through my mind. It was the Thunderbird that had been parked on the side street across from my driveway. I recognized the blotches of primer.

Ben brought the van to a halt next to the concrete retaining wall and switched off the engine. The silence that followed rang hollow in my ears, piercing directly into my soul.

Through the windows, the interior of the building appeared dark. The only sound inside the van was that of me, Ben, and Helen breathing. The coldness of the night began to seep in.

"What now?" I finally asked, my words riding out on a cloud of visible breath. "Are you waiting for an invitation?"

"Rowan, you wanna can it?" my friend ordered more than asked. "If you were anyone else I woulda kicked your ass by now."

"Well, what are we doing?" I demanded, though with a bit less harshness in my voice.

"WE aren't doing anything," he instructed as he unlatched his door. "You and Helen are going to sit right here while I check around back."

My friend carefully unfolded himself from his seat and

climbed out of the van. Before I had any chance to retort, he had quietly pressed the door shut and stalked off into the darkness. I watched on as he disappeared into the shadows.

"Benjamin is correct, Rowan," Helen told me in a quiet voice. "He knows what he is doing. Let him handle it."

"I know that, Helen," I answered, "but I'm having some trouble with the concept at the moment."

Her soothing voice and no-nonsense advice was a welcome salve on my wounded psyche, but I was desperately afraid that the prescription was too little, too late. Something that felt completely beyond my control had already been set in motion. What was most frightening to me was that I wasn't entirely sure I even wanted to try stopping it.

"That would be an understatement, Rowan, but as I have told you, it is a normal reaction to the situation," she returned. "Do you remember what I told you earlier today?"

I twisted in my seat so that I could see her. "You mean about not letting my strength become my vulnerability?"

"Yes."

"I'm sorry, Helen, but it still sounds like some kind of cryptic eastern philosophy type of advice to me. I'm just not getting it."

"Your innate strength, Rowan, is your need to protect."

"Okay."

"By allowing this rage to consume you, you are walking a very thin line between protecting someone you love and exacting vengeance. To do the latter would, in turn, make you vulnerable to a host of unspeakable things— including your own fears."

I pondered her words for a moment before I spoke. "Helen, did you know this was going to happen?"

"Not exactly." She shook her head. "I sensed that something was going to happen, but nothing specific."

"There's quite a bit more to you than you let on isn't

there?"

She simply smiled.

I turned back to face forward, then reached out and unlatched the glove compartment. I thrust my hand into the darkness and rummaged about carefully. I was banking on a recent memory, and when my fingers landed against the cold metal I knew the account was still open.

Ben always carried a backup weapon— an actual pearl handled, stainless, Smith & Wesson Model 649 'Bodyguard' thirty-eight special to be exact. The only reason I knew the specifics in such detail was that he'd sung the praises of the short-barreled revolver and its shrouded hammer to me more than once.

When I withdrew my hand from the compartment, Helen couldn't help but see the belt clip holster and handgun that now filled it. To her credit she didn't even gasp.

"I was under the impression that we'd just discussed this, Rowan," was all she said.

"We did, Helen," I sighed, as I withdrew the gun from the worn leather and checked to make certain it was loaded. Then I looked back over my shoulder at her. "And I appreciate everything you said. I really do. And, to be honest, you are probably correct. But, right now I need you to get out of the van."

"Why, Rowan?"

"Because I don't want you to get hurt."

"Tell me what you are going to do, Rowan."

"Tempered glass doesn't really break as easy as they make it look like in the movies," was all I said.

The anger had blossomed far beyond the most severe point I had been able to imagine. I was so consumed with it that I had gone beyond blind rage and moved completely into calculated hatred.

Helen did exactly what she should have done. She tried to stall me by refusing to get out of the vehicle. But I had ventured well to the other side of reason, and since I'd expected her to use this tactic, I was more than ready to call her bluff. I climbed across and into the drivers seat, and then adjusted it forward enough to reach the pedals.

She continued to calmly talk to me as I twisted the key and fired up the engine.

She never once lost her cool as I slowly backed the van across the lot in order to make enough room to build up speed.

She finally got out when it became obvious to her that I was going to go through with my plan whether she did so or not.

I was already standing on the brake and revving the engine until it was screaming when she exited through the sliding door. When I felt certain she was safely away, I let off the brake and the van bucked hard as it lurched forward.

From the corner of my eye I caught a glimpse of my friend racing around the side of the building as his van flew across the asphalt toward the front of the structure. I braced myself with my arms stiff against the steering wheel and glanced quickly down.

The speedometer read thirty-two miles per hour when the nose of the Chevy leaped over the curb and connected with the plate glass windows.

CHAPTER 29

The initial impact was utterly surreal.

Uncountable shards of glass showered the front of the van, sparkling in the glow of the exterior lights like a torrential downpour of semi-precious stones. The tortured scream of the over wound engine was joined by the multi-pitched peal of the shattering windows, and everything seemed to stop for the briefest instant. Languishing in an otherworldly vortex, devoid of the passage of time for only a tiny fraction of a second before rushing headlong into insane reality once again.

The jarring crash reverberated up my stiffly locked arms and rattled my entire body. I fought hard to hit the brakes, missing twice before finally connecting with the pedal, and raking my shin on the underside of the dash as I flopped around in the seat.

The vehicle bucked hard and plowed directly into the front desk, splintering the base and countertop as it pushed it from its mounting place on the floor. I pitched forward on the second impact and my face bounced against my hands at the top of the steering wheel. My breath was forced from my lungs, and I grunted hard as I was then lashed backward into the seat.

Intense quiet suddenly filled the passenger cabin of the vehicle. All motion had come to an end, and I was staring through the windshield at the dark interior of the front office area. I regained my breath and reached for my pocket where I'd stuffed the revolver before starting my run at the building. My fingers contacted the smooth surface of the weapon, and I tightly clutched my fist around it. Shouldering the door open, I climbed out of the vehicle and landed unsteadily on a pile of glass and former countertop.

The van's engine was idling roughly— sputtering and choking as it fought to remain alive. The sharp odor of photographic chemistries mixed with the stale water funk of engine coolant. A cloud of steam was rising steadily from the front of the Chevy and I could hear water dripping onto the floor. In the distance to my back, I could hear Ben screaming my name. In front of me, through an open doorway, I could hear the muted strains of Judy Garland singing *Have Yourself A Merry Little Christmas*.

My body was already starting to ache, and I could taste blood in my mouth. I ignored it and pressed forward. Just over a minute had passed since the van had first struck the windows; there was no longer any time to think, there was only time to act. Picking my way through the debris I stepped quickly through the doorway and into the dark corridor.

I could hear the muffled sound of someone frantically rushing about intermixing with the low tones of the music, and I followed it. I heard the dying sputter of the van behind me as it gave one final cough before shutting down. My footfalls were echoing through the darkness at their own frenetic pace, and Ben's voice was growing louder. He would be upon me soon.

I met the door at the end of the hall at almost a dead run. I simply assumed that it would be locked. Whether it was or not, I don't suppose I'll ever be sure. At any rate, the discount store special, pre-hung barrier gave way on the second strike. The luan-encased frame shattered at the handle, splintering loudly as the door swung inward on its hinges.

The pistol was stiff-armed in front of me in my right hand as I pushed through the opening and into the large, dimly lit room. My bad shoulder had been the battering ram for the door and it now burned with absolute agony. My ears were filled with a rush of noise and I realized that it was my own tortured scream as the pain blossomed outward.

The room was laid out like a studio. Light stands strategically placed with gel filters resting in holders. Reflective umbrellas perched at angles, pointing diagonally toward the ceiling in order to shower their bounced luminance back down onto the scene. Rolls of backdrop fabrics were suspended from a wheeled rack in a cascade; ready to be spooled out behind the subject.

In the center of it all was a chair, and in that chair sat my wife, clad in an ornate wedding gown and staring vacantly into space. A garish mask of makeup was painted onto her face, lending an almost plastic quality to her features.

"NO!" a distinct and vile male voice screamed from the shadows. "She's MINE!"

I'd heard the voice before. I'd even felt the ragged insanity of it inside my own head. I twisted toward the words, and my eyes came to rest on Harold. He was standing twenty feet away from Felicity, and twenty yards away from me, a camera in one hand and a cigarette protruding between the middle two fingers of the other. He stepped closer to the chair as if to protect a prized possession.

"Stay away from her!" I screamed at him, tracking his movement with the pistol in my outstretched hand.

I wanted him dead. I wanted him dead right now. But I had a huge problem and I knew it. He was far too close to her and I was a lousy shot.

"She's MINE and you can't have her!" he screamed back at me with crazed defiance in his eyes. "She doesn't want you! She wants ME!"

If I was in a movie, I knew I would have a suitably dramatic line to deliver. Somehow, reality just isn't quite like the movies. All I could muster was a hoarse scream of, "Get away from her you bastard!"

I heard heavy breathing and the shuffle of feet behind me, but didn't turn. I knew full well who it was.

"POLICE! Step away from her now!" my friend's voice ordered sternly.

"SHE'S MINE! CAN'T YOU SEE THAT?! SHE'S MINE!" Harold screamed once again.

Ben was moving slowly forward. On the periphery of my vision I saw the muzzle of his nine-millimeter move into view. The tip of the sidearm was followed by his arms, which were locked into a rock steady firing position, and then finally the rest of his body filled the corner of my eye as he came alongside me.

As I directed my attention forward, I could see my hand shaking— the polished surface of the revolver flickering in the dim light.

"I'm ordering you to step away NOW, sir!" Ben returned, keeping his attention fully focused on Harold. In a quieter, but no less demanding tone he issued a command to me. "Put the gun down before you get yourself killed, Rowan!"

"GO AWAY!" Harold demanded wildly. "GO AWAY, SHE'S MINE! SHE'S PERFECT AND SHE'S MINE!"

"Put the fucking gun DOWN, Rowan," Ben ordered me again.

Logically, I knew it was what needed to be done. In my mind, I knew this was over for me. Ben had control of the situation and he was the professional. The emotions that were driving me had no choice but to give wide berth to the reality of the situation. I knew that I couldn't pull the trigger and risk hitting Felicity. As much as I wanted this man dead, there was literally nothing I could do, so I started to lower the gun.

My arm didn't move.

"Rowan, Rowan, you're the guy! You found our killer, now don't be shy! We wanna make him suffer, don't you know. We wanna make him die, don't let him go!"

The angry cheer rang inside my skull, audible only to me and the cheering section that was chanting it. My hand continued to shake but never wavered from its target.

"Dammit, Rowan, we've got a problem here," Ben hissed. "I can't take this guy down if I've gotta worry about you shootin' me in the back!"

I could feel my finger tightening on the trigger, and as I watched, the cylinder of the revolver started to perceptibly rotate.

"STEP AWAY FROM HER!" Ben ordered Harold again, and then said to me, "Help me out here, white man. I don't think this asshole is real stable."

"I...Can't..." I managed to stammer before gritting my teeth.

It was taking every ounce of will I had to keep my finger from squeezing the trigger any tighter. The colors in the room were blooming in a kaleidoscope of contrasts, and my head felt like a hollow chamber. An urgent voice bounced from every corner, riddling my brain.

"Come on, Rowan! Do it! Make him die!"

My entire body was shaking now. Harold was staring at me as if he was completely unaware of the guns that were trained on him. I looked past him at my wife's slackened face and in the dim light saw a dark line running down her cheek. Even at this distance it was obviously a tear.

"Jeezus, Rowan, put the gun DOWN!" Ben ordered again.

I felt the control over my index finger slip and watched

in horror as the cylinder began turning again. It was less than a second away from rolling over and being struck by the hammer when I made my decision. If Debbie Schaeffer was exerting that much force on my finger, I had to hope that she was ignoring something else.

In a final bid I thrust every ounce of energy I had left into changing the target. With a scream I twisted hard to the side, bringing the weapon to bear on a blank wall just as the firing pin released. There was a loud roar and fire flashed from the muzzle in a bright burst. Dust flew as the projectile punched a hole in the sheetrock well away from any human targets. The gunshot echoed in my eardrums as the explosive sound bounced from the walls. My ears felt suddenly clogged and they began to ring with a painful stab deep inside. The recoil jerked my arm upward and its force allowed me to loosen my grip on the weapon. As my hand opened, it went flying and clattered across the concrete.

I detected motion from the corner of my eye and saw Ben rushing toward Harold, then slamming into him full force, and knocking him to the floor.

It was all over in the proverbial blink of an eye. Harold was screaming, "SHE'S MINE, SHE'S MINE..." repeatedly as Ben snapped a pair of handcuffs onto his wrists and patted him down. I scrambled across the floor, putting as much distance as possible between the discarded revolver and me before finally climbing to my feet and bolting for Felicity.

I fell to my knees and wrapped my arms around her, not saying a word, just listening to her breathe. Feeling her heart beat in her chest. Tears were streaming down my face as I hugged her close and felt her warmth against me— alive and unharmed.

We could hear sirens and squealing tires in the near distance as squad cars from the Briarwood Police Department arrived outside. Whether summoned by a silent alarm or Ben I didn't know, but I was glad to hear them nonetheless.

Somewhere inside the building a clock chimed out the hour with a series of twelve consecutive notes.

Ben folded himself to the floor next to me with a tired sigh, Beretta still in hand as he rested his arm on his knee. "Merry Christmas, Kemosabe. Merry fuckin' Christmas."

CHAPTER 30

"I am actually very proud of you, Rowan," Helen Storm told me as we stood at the railing of the outdoor smoking lounge in her office building.

She was working on a cigarette, but for a change, I was not. I hadn't had a craving for one since Christmas, go figure. I did, however, have a Maduro *Cruz Real #2* hooked under my index finger, and it was slowly growing a grey-white ash at its tip.

I took a puff, consciously placing the cigar in the left corner of my mouth to avoid the pair of stitches that were holding my lip together on the right. The bruises had worked their way into the reddish-purple and yellow haloed stages, and I still looked pretty frightening. My injuries had come from crashing the van into the building for the most part. Mainly just the bruises and split lip, although the jolt had fractured my left wrist and it was securely taped. My shoulder was sore and I'd ached all over for several days, but even that was now subsiding.

"What for?" I asked. "Waiting until you were out of the van before running it into the building?"

This was the first chance I'd had to talk with Helen since Christmas Eve; not that it had been all that long ago. New Year's Eve was tomorrow, so less than one week had passed. Still, it seemed like forever.

"For not killing Harold McCree," she answered. "You retained your strength. That is very important."

"I think it was more along the lines of luck," I offered as I stared out across the dull sky. "Because I can guarantee you that it wasn't for a lack of desire."

"The fact still remains that you did not kill him."

"Given another chance, the outcome could be different."

She ignored my comment and we stood in silence for a moment. I had grown accustomed to her periods of quiet thoughtfulness interspersed throughout our conversations, and realized they were as much a signal as an action. They were, in part, her way of triggering my own introspection.

"How is Felicity doing?" she finally asked.

"Good," I nodded. "As well as one can expect. The Rophynol was a bit of a blessing in a sense, because she doesn't really remember much of what occurred after Harold dropped by to deliver those photos.

"She's having a little trouble coming to terms with the fact that nine women were raped and two are dead, all because he was playing out a fantasy involving her."

"She should come visit me," Helen offered. "She needs to understand that what transpired is in no way her fault."

"She knows that, I think. But emotionally..." I allowed my voice to trail off.

"Yes?" she looked at me with a smile.

"Okay, so I forgot who I was talking to for a minute." I smiled back. "Like I've said before, you don't come off as your average shrink."

She laughed musically. "How are you both handling the change of scenery?"

We were living in an apartment in a secure building for the time being. It had been a clandestine move, made in the middle of the night, without warning or fanfare. It was comfortable enough, but it wasn't home. Until Eldon Porter was in custody, though, it was something we were living with— for a while, anyway.

"It's okay," I shrugged. "Not the same. And we miss having the animals around."

"Are you boarding them?"

"Couldn't do that to them." I shook my head. "Some friends took them in. That way they'll get some attention from people they are familiar with."

"Well," she announced with a sigh after glancing at her watch. "Unfortunately, I am afraid our time is up for today and I do have another appointment this time."

"It flies when you're having fun doesn't it?" I grinned.

"Funny," she replied. "Of course, you are the only patient I see who is willing to stand out here and watch me smoke."

"Therapists need love too," I joked.

She smiled at me. "I see that your sense of humor is returning. That is a very good sign, Rowan."

I gave an abbreviated chuckle as I knocked the ash from the end of my cigar, then carefully sealed it into a spring-loaded tube designed to tamp out the coal and keep the remainder somewhat fresh. "Maybe," I half agreed, "but I get the feeling I'm not out of the woods yet."

"But, Rowan, you can see the trail now, and that is important. As long as you can keep it in sight, you will not lose your way."

"Next week?" I asked.

"I will be here," she returned.

"If it was up to me, you wouldn't even be seein' this shit," Ben said as he massaged his neck. "But, Helen seems to think it will offer some closure. I dunno. I think it's just friggin' crazy myself."

We were standing in a conference room at City Police Headquarters, staring at a table full of tagged evidence that was still being sorted. Some of it had already appeared on the evening news when the story broke, though my friend had done his best to play down my connection.

Worn boxes of everything from five by seven, to sixteen by twenty photographic paper sat in ordered stacks. An entire rack of women's clothing— evening gowns to business suits to lingerie— occupied one corner of the room; of immediate prominence to me was the wedding gown Felicity had been wearing. Even though it was crammed together with the other apparel, it stood out to me like a beacon in the darkness.

Rectangular boxes were stacked next to the rack in a mound with several pairs of stiletto-heeled shoes on display. At the far end of the long table sat three head-shaped Styrofoam stands, all supporting long, spiral-curled, red wigs; each of which was carefully pinned into a different stylish coif. The man had a small fortune invested in his lurid obsession.

I rested my hand against a pile of black and white photographs and slowly shuffled through them. Each contained a woman who on first glance looked somewhat like my wife, but upon closer inspection obviously was not. The poses and modes of dress ranged from sophisticated fashion to tasteful nude, from cheesecake to downright pornographic.

Two things they all shared in common were the vacant stares and highly contrasted makeup jobs. In grey tones they looked ghostly. In color they looked plastic and even clown-like.

"He shot enough close ups of all of 'em to be able to positively identify each of the women, even with the hair and makeup," Ben was telling me. "Including Debbie Schaeffer."

"What happened there, do you think?" I spoke the question softly as I continued to peruse the visual diary of infatuated insanity.

"Nut job says she just quit breathin'," my friend harrumphed in a disgusted tone. "Doc over at the morgue says that could be consistent with a Rophynol OD, so that's what we're figurin'."

"So he admitted that he took her?"

"Hell, he admitted to all of them," Ben returned.

"Did he say why he dumped her out on Three Sixty-Seven?"

"Yeah, actually," he spat. "Get this— it was convenient for him because he was heading in that direction."

"What about Paige Lawson?"

"Just like we figured. When he saw the blood he just left. Asshole actually had the gall to look me in the eye and say that it was unfortunate, because both of them were 'almost perfect'."

"What did you expect?" I shrugged.

"I dunno. Maybe a little remorse."

"So, even without the confession you have enough evidence to charge him with murder, right?"

"Jeezus, Row, we've got enough evidence to charge the SOB with everything. Murder, rape, stalking... He'll even come up on Federal charges for kidnapping." He sighed heavily. "Unfortunately, he'll never see prison. He'll end up in a mental institution."

"Something inside me still wants him dead," I stated coldly.

"That stays between you, me and the fuckin' wall, okay?" he told me sternly. "I lied my ass off about what really happened that night and I don't need you screwin' it up with an uncensored attack of emotional honesty."

"Sorry. I just can't help feeling that way."

"I know, but he's a whack job, Row. Shrinks say he's delusional. He actually believes that he and Felicity are a couple. Hell, he's been accusing you of taking her from him."

My fingers brushed against another pile of photographs and I slid them into view. Images of my wife leapt out at me. There were pictures of her in front of our house working in the yard, getting into her Jeep, getting out of my truck, different times of day, different clothing, even different seasons of the year. He'd been watching her for a long time. Too long.

"By the way," Ben added. "You were right. I forgot to tell ya', but when we talked to Heather Burke I found out she does have Dyslexia. Very mild case, but she does have trouble with it if she's tired."

"Thought so," I answered.

"So, you answer one for me."

"What's that?"

"You and the Red Squaw are so tight that you can feel each others pain, right? I mean… I've seen you do it."

"Yeah," I acknowledged, "it's been known to happen."

"Well, with all that hocus pocus *Twilight Zone* shit you do, why didn't you feel it when she got zapped by this creep?"

"I was otherwise occupied by an angry cheerleader at the time. Then, after that, a combination of the Rophynol shutting her down and my own mental state kept me from feeling her presence at all. Wrong place, wrong time, and a lot of supernatural interference."

"So, Schaeffer really fucked with you didn't she?"

"Yeah," I nodded without looking back at him, "she is a very determined spirit."

"She gone?"

"I'm not entirely sure," I returned. "I haven't felt her around since that night, so I hope so."

"Too freakin' weird for me."

"Me too, Ben," I agreed as I looked back at him. "I'm a

Witch, not a Ouija board. I'm starting to wonder if the spirits on the other side understand that."

Silence filled the hollowness behind my words and we continued to stand there, Ben massaging his neck in deep thought. I turned back to the table and stared at a picture of Felicity as she was seen through the eyes of a lunatic. As I looked at the photograph, I had to admit to myself that the composition and tone held a message. In this particular instance at least, he seemed to view her with almost as much reverence as I did.

That fact did little for my current state of mind.

After a moment my friend cleared his throat and spoke quietly, "You done here?"

"Yeah. Yeah, I'm done," I finally answered. "For now."

"Oh yeah, I almost forgot," he said as he pulled open the door. "There's one other thing I need to tell ya'."

"What's that?"

"You owe me for a radiator, one tire, and a crapload of body work."

EPILOGUE

"You don't have to do this, then," the woman insisted, her words were thick with an Irish brogue that would always seem to beset her when she was emotionally distraught.

"Yes, I do," the man answered her with a calm note in his voice.

Her long, spiral curls of auburn hair were piled atop her head in a loose Gibson girl, and her green eyes flashed wetly with deep concern. She'd tried anger already and it hadn't worked. She'd even been willing to try guilt, but he still hadn't budged. He knew her too well.

Now, she was back to making demands.

"What did Ben say?" the woman contended, as if the answer to her question would somehow make a difference.

"The same thing you just said," the man replied.

She watched as he ran his hand across the lower half of his face, thoughtfully brushing his bearded chin. She noticed that he winced for a moment as his fingers caught the still healing wound on his upper lip.

She took on a pleading tone. "Then why are you doing it?"

"Because we can't keep living like this," he answered. "Because I want us to have our lives back."

"How can we have our lives back if you get yourself

killed?"

"I'm not going to get myself killed."

She was crying now. "Damn your eyes, Rowan Linden Gant, you'd better not, then. Aye, you'd better not."